MEASURES
OF
VENGEANCE

**BOOKS BY
KELLY L. MARSH**

THE AGENTS OF KARMA SERIES
Kill Karma

MEASURES
OF
VENGEANCE

BOOK TWO *in the* AGENTS OF KARMA SERIES

KELLY L. MARSH

Published by Jellyrum Press
www.jellyrumpress.com

MEASURES OF VENGEANCE
Copyright © 2023 by Kelly L. Marsh.

Cover design by MiblArt
Interior design and chapter art by Kelly L. Marsh

ISBN: 979-8-9850331-2-0 (Paperback)
ISBN: 979-8-9850331-3-7 (Ebook)

Printed in the United States of America.
First edition: February 2023

For my dad,
who loves all things fantasy and, to his surprise, Hell, or rather the
Hell dimension I created.

GLOSSARY

Agents of Karma: A sisterhood of assassins who work along-side Goddess Karma. Their primary duty is to permanently remove the evilest beings from society.

Awakening: The moment an Initiate channels vengeance and becomes an Agent of Karma.

Battle of Pandæmonia: An epic and bloody crusade in Hell that pitted Queen Lilith against the recently-ousted-from-Heaven Lucifer and his fellow mala'dayyas. After Lucifer and his army declared victory, he assumed Lilith's throne and crowned himself the King of Darkness.

Bonding Ritual: A spell that only a ruachti can conjure that ties the demigod to another being and allows them to communicate telepathically.

Chaosgate: A portal forged from raw magic, thought to have been created by Underlord Chaos.

Chaosnauting: The action of traveling through a chaosgate.

Chaospocket: A manufactured dimension that abides by its own laws and physics.

Chaosway: The tunnel inside a chaosgate leading from point A to point B. It only exists if the chaosgate leads to a location within the same dimension.

The Damned: Former soul-selling humans sentenced to eternal damnation in Hell.

Department of Inter-Dimensional Security and Intelligence: (Abbreviation DISI) The governmental body that acts as Hell's first line of defense. It enforces security, the use of magic, and protects Hell's borders by managing the flow of beings and enchanted objects into and out of the dimension.

Department of Possessions and Hauntings: (Abbreviation DPH) The governmental division responsible for policing demonic activity on Earth concerning lowlies and ensuring laws established in the peace treaty are adhered to.

Department of Soul Brokering: (Abbreviation DSB) The governmental division responsible for creating and storing signed soul contracts. The department is headed by Mephistopheles, the Deputy Director and First Underlord of Hell.

Department of Soul Sundering and Assignments: (Abbreviation DSSA) The governmental division responsible for cleaving souls from the newly damned and assigning work details to the damned freshly released from the Pits of Tartarus.

Drainer: A being gifted with the rare ability to deprive beings of their magical powers and fill a vessel with the taken magic.

Ever-active rukba: (See Rukba) An undocumented and highly illegal inter-dimensional transporter that enables chaosnauters to travel undetected in and out of other dimensions.

Fixer: A demon hired to fix problems no matter how big or small.

Fleshie: Short for flesh note. A lower denomination currency in Hell that is made from the skin of the damned.

Fluster dust: Fine blue-hued magic gem particles that render a target dazed and confused when the dust is blown in their face.

Fur'moria: (Fur-MORE-ee-ah) A mage skilled in the dark arts of stealing memories and mind manipulation.

Grissel's ale: A sweet-and-briny alcoholic beverage in Hell, with hints of pomegranate.

Hounds of Hell: A gang of vicious vampires who answer directly to Vlad Dracula. All have animated dragons and a firebird tattooed on their bodies.

Indys: Plural. Abbreviation. Short for indigo magic gem.

Initiate: A newly enrolled student in Karma Academy who's not yet fully trained as an Agent of Karma.

Inter-Dimensional Protection Agency: (Abbreviation IPA) As a division of DISI, this agency oversees security in all modes of transportation into and out of Hell, from soulcars to chaosgates to rukbas.

Karma: The goddess of vengeance and justice, who presides over Earth, wielding the Sword of Truth in one hand and balancing the cosmic Scales of Justice in the other.

Karma Academy: An institute headed by Goddess Karma that trains Initiates to become Agents of Karma.

Laramaic: The official language of Hell.

Limnocular: An enchanted object that serves as a memory visualizer. It resembles an old-fashioned projector cast in bronze.

Lingua Franca: An enchanted object resembling a mechanical spider that enables users to comprehend and speak Laramaic fluently.

Lolly'kas: Pint-sized Mobsters who run the underbelly of Hell. They are purported to be direct descendants of Lilith, the former queen of Hell.

Lowlie: A non-magical human.

Lu'kowsa: (Lu-KOW-sah) A dragon native to Hell.

Lum'bhra: (LUM-bra) A soul-powered lamp in Hell that resembles floating jellyfish.

Magic gem: A small ball of colored glass that acts like a conduit conveying magic from the spellcaster to their target. Resembling a glass marble clueless lowlies once collected, its outer casing is made up of fulgurite. Vaporous magic in either the color of red, orange, yellow, green, blue, indigo, or violet fills the inside. Different spells require certain color gems.

Mala'dayya: (Mala-DIE-ah) Fallen angels turned princes of Hell that serve in prominent positions within Lucifer's ranks. They are also referred to as archdemons.

Mala'kha: (MALA-kah) Hell's assassin and soul reapers who drag the damned to Hell. Some serve as wardens in the Pits of Tartarus situated within Oblivion's Fortress in Gehenna.

The Ministry of Mischief and Mayhem: (Abbreviation M-cubed) The central executive authority of Hell that has its headquarters on the outskirts of Pandæmonia. Hell's government is led by Lucifer and the princes of Hell. Most government departments are located within the menacing complex, while the rest are sprinkled around the dimension.

The Nine: A cabal that works alongside Goddess Karma. Little is known about their role save for assisting Karma in inviting Initiates to attend Karma Academy.

Nitherian: An alloy of unknown elements mined in a dimension thought to be inhabited by gods.

Oblivion's Fortress: A prison where the damned are held for however long the Ministry sees fit as punishment for selling their souls.

Order of Shi'rue: (See Shi'rue) A secret society of mages that worshipped Shi'rue and, through the goddess, learned the rare skill of speculuming. The Order was wiped out centuries ago.

Pandæmonia: The capital city of Hell.

Para doxea: A sentient, poisonous plant that confuses the mind and drains Agents of Karma of their magical defenses. So far, its origins are unknown.

The Pits of Tartarus: (Abbreviation the Pits) A maximum security prison nestled inside Oblivion's Fortress that houses the most wicked of the damned who had committed untold acts of savagery while on Earth and elsewhere.

Ruachti: (Rue-AK-ti with the "r" rolled) Descendants of an ancient line of animal warriors charged with protecting deities. Because of their storied acts of valor, they achieved demigod status.

Rukba: (RUHK-bah) An inter-dimensional transporter that resembles an elevator. Official rukbas are operated by Inter-Dimensional Protection Agents.

Rune-revealer: An enchanted object that detects runes and sigils naked to the invisible eye. A malleable orb in appearance, with a similar texture to a stress-relieving ball that humans squeeze.

The Sentries: Spectral entities specializing in soul verification and determining a target's true intentions. Unlike a lie detector test that can be manipulated, souls can't lie. Immediate death comes to those the Sentries find to have ill intentions.

Seren: The goddess of fortune and destiny. She is considered to be the patron saint of thieves and assassins.

Shadow-cloaker: A being who can summon the shadows to do their bidding.

Shadow-summoner: A quarterstaff forged from nitherian that only those with divine blood can wield.

Shi'rue: The goddess of misfortune and curses.

Soulcar: A wheelless, hovering vehicle in Hell powered by the souls of the damned.

Soul shard: A form of currency in Hell. To the human eye, a soul shard resembles a microscope slide with a vaporous soul of the damned trapped within.

Speculumist: A mage with the ability to travel through mirrors. A dead art shared only by those in the Order of Shi'rue.

Speculuming: The act of traveling through mirrors.

Sunburster: An enchanted object that resembles a grenade but with blindingly bright sunshine in place of shrapnel. It's a must-have for vampire slayers.

The Starless Souk: A black market thought to only be found on the dark web rife with supernatural goodies.

Tun-fendin'ga: (Tun-FEN-din-gah) The tongue of the mystical Ancient Ones and considered the darkest of dark sorcery. Little is known about this form of magic as it's not taught in a formal setting.

unCloaking: The process by which a human becomes a mage and taps into their magical powers. It usually occurs during adolescence, around the age of ten to thirteen.

Ven-ad'tsay: (Ven-AT-say) Laramaic for the Hunter.

Vs: Plural. Abbreviation. Short for violet magic gems.

Wanderer: A breed of extremely aggressive demons that covet human vessels. Up until recently, they had never tread Earthly soil.

Witherwhere: A terrifying dimension that ensnares the souls of the lost.

Xykree: (ZAI-kree) A creature native to Hell that is a cross between a feline and a human.

PREVIOUSLY IN KILL KARMA

Have you noticed that the world has descended into madness, and the guilty are getting away with murder? Pepper observed that, too. And just like you, she clung to the hope that the guilty would get theirs one day. But that day never came. So, a few years back, she started a covert karma-for-hire business. Where there were cheaters, embezzlers, or anyone dodging the long arm of the law, Pepper was ready to uncover their dirty little secrets—for a fee, of course. And business was booming in her small Gulfside town of Naples, Florida. *Ka-ching!*

Meet Pepper Li Bell, an eye-for-an-eye enthusiast, a soon-to-be seventeen-year-old, an only child to her beloved pops Larry, and a high school graduate. Except for a rap sheet a mile long and a judge sentencing her to house arrest, most of the world would deem her average, which is a fair assessment. Still, Pepper served her time and stayed out of trouble. Little did she know, trouble would find her on her birthday and turn her world upside down.

Unbeknownst to Pepper, Karma isn't a notion but the goddess of vengeance and justice who presides over Earth, watching all and sundry from her celestial perch in the aether. But Karma didn't always have a firm grasp on her domain. Eons ago, unruly demons wreaked havoc on Earth, like starting wars and possessing humans without their permission (the nerve!). Eventually, things went from bad to worse, so a fed-up Karma extended an olive branch to Mephistopheles, the demon leading the charge. Yes, *the* Mephistopheles of legend, preeminent soul collector, a prince of Hell, sex personified to those with a pulse, and best friend to the King of Darkness, Lucifer. After much warring back and forth, the two reached an amicable agreement and drafted a peace treaty between Earth and Hell.

As per the treaty, every soul contract that a demon peddles around Karma-ruled Earth must abide by a strict chain of custody that starts and ends with Mephistopheles. As for Karma's end of the bargain, neither she nor her Agents can lay a finger on the soul-selling human, regardless of the crimes they committed on Earth. However, when a soul contract expires and mala'khas drag the human to the Pits of Tartarus in Hell, the damned fall under Karma's jurisdiction. There, the goddess repays in kind each vile act her jailees committed Earthside. (Word on the street is that Karma is a genius regarding torture. Living artwork, some demons have called it.) Assisting the very busy Karma with keeping the cosmic Scales of Justice balanced are her Agents—a sisterhood of mages whose identities are shrouded in secrecy; they rid society of the most wicked.

For millennia, Mephistopheles and Goddess Karma maintained law and order over Hell and Earth until now. A criminal organization called the Syndicate—run by Vlad Dracula, Ember the Firebird, and Cazzian (currently imprisoned in the Pits for selling his soul)—set their sights on serving that meddling bitch Karma her just deserts and then world domination. But a few things need to be done before deicide, like resurrecting Cazzian from Hell, which is an impossible feat that involves exploiting a soul contract loophole. Cazzian must convince millions of humans to sign an official soul contract containing Mephistopheles' seal of approval at the stroke of midnight on All Hallows' Eve. If he's successful, then Lucifer will relinquish Cazzian's soul. Challenge accepted.

Mephistopheles was the first domino to fall, as the Syndicate needed to steal an ungodly amount of his soul contracts. Demons have no clue that the Mephistopheles they've been interacting with daily is a body-possessing wanderer aligned with the Syndicate.

Every god has a weakness, and to kill a god, you must exploit that weakness. Unfortunately for Karma, the Syndicate discovered hers. On Vlad's orders, the vampiric Hounds of Hell have been killing Karma's Agents around the globe. As a result, Goddess Karma is severely hurt and missing in action. But before Karma disappears, she sends out a missive to Earth's last hope—clueless, juvenile-delinquent Pepper, who does not know gods, magic, and otherworldly beings exist, let alone other dimensions. But she's about to find out.

The night before her seventeenth birthday, Pepper's former childhood best friend, neighbor, and supreme jackhole Kimball Garcia spies Pepper sneaking out of her house and violating probation. As an early birthday gift, he blackmails her. Either Pepper proves his father, Shelly, killed his mother, Bunny, and summoned a demon to possess her body, or Kimball will send the oodles of compromising evidence he's compiled against Pepper to her probation officer. Then to juvie, Pepper goes. Pepper reluctantly agrees to help prove Bunny's "murder." Still, she is convinced Kimball has lost his mind, is on a bender, or both.

Pepper and Kimball don't know that the Syndicate moved their headquarters to Naples and is recruiting members for their end game. Two such members are Kimball's father, Shelly, and Miles Leagan, a serial killer who terrorized the streets of Naples until the police apprehended him. A jury found Miles not guilty, regardless of the mountain of evidence against him. And he can thank the Syndicate for getting him off scot-free, but it came at a hefty price.

Like many others around the globe, Miles sold his soul to the Syndicate, Shelly Garcia included. In return, Miles could commit any crime with impunity while avoiding Karma's wrath and eternal damnation in Hell. To further sweeten the deal, Miles and all the others before him were granted the ability to wield magic, which, until now, was impossible for lowlies and vampires alike. But somehow, the Syndicate manifested the unfathomable, which involved draining mages of their blood. (It should come as no surprise that murder-enthusiast Miles volunteered to track down the mages.) To the shock of no one, the Syndicate's numbers have snowballed, with a vast regiment of soul-sellers around the globe at their disposal.

With their plans to resurrect Cazzian from Hell a foregone conclusion and Mephistopheles and Karma dealt with, all that remains to secure the Syndicate's stronghold over Earth is finding Cazzian's archenemy, Pepper Li, the last remaining Li sister, who fell off the face of the earth twelve years ago. Poor Pepper. If only she knew the hell barreling her way.

On her seventeenth birthday, Pepper receives a curious letter from an anonymous sender. But they sure know Pepper, for inside the envelope is an invitation mentioning how they've been observing Pepper for some time. And because of her innate ability to exact vengeance, Karma and the Nine cordially invite her to attend the prestigious Karma Academy to be trained to become an Agent of Karma. Should Pepper accept, explicit instructions follow, involving an incantation to open a chaosgate to the Academy. Demonic possessions,

Goddess Karma, and now magic—they didn't exist. But that didn't stop her from reciting the spell, which ended up not working.

While investigating a lead on the murder case at a marina, things take a turn for the worse when Pepper visits the last man to have seen Bunny Garcia alive. Unfortunately, he isn't much help with obtaining answers, what with a poisonous dart puncturing his jugular. His killer, Sawyer van Arsdale, a double-crossing Agent of Karma who works for the Syndicate, decides eyewitness Pepper is a loose end that needs cutting and begins tossing powerful magic her way. It was a miracle that Pepper made it out of the marina alive.

Pepper soon discovers that her life is a lie, all the mythical and supernatural legends truly exist, and magic is real. Pepper was once a mage herself and had an older sister to boot, Jaylyn. But she has no recollection of her past. And for good reason. Twelve years earlier, she and her sister struck an eleventh-hour deal with a demonic fixer named Bhi'gow and his capuchin, ruachti companion Loki. Pepper and her sister paid for the fixer's services by selling their magic. Unfortunately, Jaylyn died on Bhi'gow's watch. In a last-ditch attempt to save Pepper's life, Bhi'gow "stole" Pepper's memories to protect her. Since then, a spell has cloaked Pepper from the Syndicate's sight, but that spell expired on her seventeenth birthday.

Determined to find the demon and ruachti who stole her magic and memories, Pepper accepts the help of an enigmatic soul broker named Jhi, who conveniently "runs" into Pepper when she needs him the most. He vows to protect her from Sawyer and the Hounds of Hell—all hot on her heels—if Pepper helps him with a dire matter. Jhi's co-worker, JD, went missing while investigating a case of missing soul contracts taken from the Ministry of Mischief and Mayhem under Jhi's boss' nose—boss as in Mephistopheles—and his search for JD led Jhi directly to Pepper. Jhi believes Pepper is somehow connected to JD and needs Pepper's help to find his friend. With her life on the line, Pepper agrees to the quid pro quo.

Pepper and Jhi travel to Pandaemonia, a bustling metropolis in Hell populated by demons and other terrifying creatures. Once there, she gains new friends, Loki and Perrin. Along the way, they unravel the Syndicate's nefarious plans, including Cazzian's resurrection from the Pits and his intention to exact revenge on the last sister Li standing. This vendetta began in another life—a life erased from Pepper's memory. And after Cazzian assumes Karma's mantle of judge, jury, and executioner, he plans on destroying Pepper once and for all.

But Karma might have gotten her last laugh yet. Another sister Li lives—Jaylyn, aka JD. Though her life's in peril for the Ven-ad'tsay is hunting her—Jhi. He adopted the cover of a harmless soul broker looking for his dear friend JD. Unfortunately, he lost JD's scent at the Tenth Circle Tavern in Hell, an establishment linked to the same demon that stole Pepper's magic and memories. But now Jhi has a new lead—Pepper, and little does Pepper know she is leading Jhi right to her sister. Too bad Pepper's developing an incurable malady—an unrequited crush on Jhi, her feelings strengthening by the day, which is what Jhi was hoping for.

Back in Naples, all is revealed at the All Hallows' Eve masquerade ball, where Pepper spectacularly fails at stopping Cazzian's resurrection. Now that Cazzian is immortal, his army of the damned and corrupted humans legion, he should have no problem wiping out the Agents of Karma line forever. Then, in short order, he will assassinate Goddess Karma, which leaves the last remaining sister Li to contend with—all part of the prophecy to establish a New World Order where the damned call the shots from here on out.

Just when Pepper thought her night couldn't get any

worse, she suffered a soul-crushing betrayal at the hands of Jhi. In a shocking twist, Jhi turns on Pepper and her motley gang and joins the Syndicate's ranks. And since Jhi knows Jaylyn's alive but in hiding, it's only a matter of time until Cazzian does, too.

Pepper and her motley crew escape the masquerade ball bloodbath, where terrifying mala'kha slaughter most soul-sellers around the globe. Still, Cazzian reveals he has Pepper's father. And Pepper has Kimball to thank for that. Shelly blackmailed his son Kimball by threatening to destroy Bunny's soul if Kimball didn't help the Syndicate by turning over that which means the world to Pepper. So Kimball did just that to save his mother's life. That heart-squeezing, soul-crushing revelation that her father's life hangs in the balance destroys Pepper and sets her aflame. A mystical fire born of roiling rage consumes her, and when the flames extinguish, a new Pepper steps out of the chrysalis. With that, an Agent of Karma is born.

A dying Karma materializes and delivers a grim warning: Armageddon is all Pepper's doing, and it's up to her to end it. This is Pepper's final chance at redemption. Karma then issues marching orders to her new Agent. Pepper must find one of the last remaining Agents of Karma, who is unaware that Jhi and Miles Leagan are hunting her down to kill her. Find the Agent, and she'll lead Pepper to her long-lost sister.

Time's running out. Faced with an impossible decision, either Pepper rescues her dad, who's her everything, or saves Goddess Karma, her sister, Beatrice, and the world. Pepper chooses all the above. It's now a race against Jhi and Miles Leagan to find this Agent.

As for Jhi, Pepper is counting the days until she exacts sweet revenge on that no-good, lying, rotten bastard. Sleep with one eye open, Jhi, for Hell hath no fury than a Pepper scorned.

MEASURES
OF
VENGEANCE

1

Howling winds tore through the vast caves like laser missiles on their sole mission to destroy the man who dared to spoil the sanctity of the Caves of Altira'me-tum. And they were almost successful in their assignment; they nearly knocked Jhi off the miles-high stone pillar he artfully balanced upon.

Annoyed, Jhi stood back up in defiance of the wind, rooting the heels of his boots further into the summit's craggy terrain, and trumpeted, "That all you got?"

"C'mon, Jhi! I'm trying to get you outta there, and you're not exactly helping matters," Friday huffed through Jhi's earpiece.

Slender rock formations taller than the skyscrapers in Pandæmonia dotted the caves and traveled to infinity in every direction. Some were higher than others, a few dangerously low, but the crests of them all were barely big enough to house a body.

As Jhi surveyed the dank and dimly lit death trap to determine his next course of action, he made the mistake of looking down. His head spun, and his body swayed dangerously close to the pillar's edge. The silt and stones knocked off by his unsteady feet had yet to reach the bottom.

By the grace of Seren, Jhi regained his balance and crouched down. "That was too close," he said jokingly, his voice echoing about. "You still there, Friday?"

"Sure am," said Jhi's jinn partner. "And from the sound of it, you're screwed."

"Your concern is truly palpable."

Jhi was in the midst of trial number three out of who knew how many. He barely survived the last one when he went toe-to-toe with a furious lu'kowsa with no weapons or magic at his disposal, which amounted to him dodging the dragon's fireballs, swinging barbed-wire tail, and snapping snout. Good times! Oh, but the fun didn't end there. With no visible points of entry, just endless slime-coated walls, part of the trial was figuring out how to escape the lu'kowsa's underwater lair as it slowly filled with water.

This current trial tested Jhi's strength, dexterity, and, if he was being honest, his patience, which was about to flatline. "There's no way I can make the jump to the next pillar."

"Can you move in another direction?" Friday replied.

"Yeah, but—" A loud rumbling shook the caves. "Uh, Friday"—Jhi glanced over his shoulder—"we got a problem. I can't backtrack. The pillar behind me is a pile of crumbs on the non-existent ground." The same pillar he had been on moments before.

The rumblings intensified, and the upright pillars in the distance trembled in response until they, too, began collapsing like dominos. Beads of sweat sprouted on Jhi's forehead as the only way out of the gods-forsaken cave dismantled before his eyes.

"Feel free to chime in here, buddy. Anytime." Jhi's voice jumped an octave.

"It's not like I have a handy reference book on the Caves of Altira'me-tum at my disposal, jam-packed with tips and tricks. Just let me mull this over for a second." Panic set up shop within the usually unruffled jinn.

"Sure, by all means. Take a breather. It's not like I'm going anywhere." A loud burst of wind in the distance stormed through the caves like Goddess Karma's wrath, hellbent on destroying the intruder. "And Friday, hurry up! The wind's coming again."

Jhi didn't scare easily. He was a trained killer, the storied Ven-ad'tsay—the hunter of whatever his overlords desired. Only one thing set his teeth on edge, and that was falling into a pit of nothingness, trapped and lost and alone, with no way out. Walking through chaosgates unnerved him for that very reason. So, looking down and not seeing ground—a case of the willies broke out. Jhi never shared his greatest fear, and would never express it out loud, not to anyone, and for good reason. Never let others know your weakness or your enemies will exploit it.

Thankfully, Jhi set out on this expedition of sorts with Friday. Well, technically, Friday was back in Pandæmonia— the lucky bastard—but happily, the enchanted two-way com-device in Jhi's ear still worked, thanks to Goddess Seren. Right about now, Jhi could use all the goddess' good luck and fortune.

From this point, Jhi had made quite a few jumps and was now out of options, what with the pillars crumbling around him like a soul-seller's body after a mala'kha came a-reaping. He couldn't even see the finish line. To be fair, the finish line had never presented itself in the previous trials, so why stop now?

As the tornadic winds fast approached, Jhi dipped down again and held on for dear life. The stormy winds knocked off his well-worn beanie, blew back his chestnut hair, and pressed against his chest with all its might, his Henley ruffling behind his back. But Jhi held firm to the edge, his fingers white-knuckling the craggy sides. Then the wind stopped abruptly and retreated, most likely thinking up another plan of attack.

"So, you can't jump anywhere?" Friday asked.

"Affirmative. It's about ten soulcars in length between me and the pillar up ahead. You can forget left or right. They're dust. Same for the ones behind me. And before you ask, climbing down isn't an option."

"Why? What's down below?"

"Good question, Friday. I'm not sure. It's too far for me to make out. Also, there might not even be a bottom." Jhi could feel his face blanch from fright from just voicing that possibility.

"Magic still a no-go?"

"It sure is, buddy." This realm forbade magic—something Jhi had learned during trial number one.

"Caves of Altira'me-tum," Friday said, more like a thought. "Roughly translated to Caves of Nightmares—"

"Friday? Come in, Friday. You there?"

Nothing but static responded.

"Dammit!" Jhi removed the earpiece, then took a breather by sitting down cross-legged. "Wow, didn't think I'd go out like this." Until today, Jhi had been in his fair share of perilous situations, including encountering the lu'kowsa. But these caves offering no chance of escape took the cake.

Jhi had to reach the end of this quest; he had to retrieve the relic. Death wasn't an option. It wasn't an out. Not for Jhi.

Death, for Jhi, meant something far worse than beings could imagine.

"Goddess Seren," Jhi said to the empty air. "I could really use your help. I know I've done a few horrible things. Okay, fine. There's been more than a few. I've killed some beings, or *a lot* of beings, actually. But they deserved it. Sure, I've broken hearts, but the girls cursed me in return, so doesn't that even out? You can't force love, right?" He chuckled, thinking it ridiculous that he confessed his sins to a goddess who probably couldn't care less. "Anyways, I have a proposition for you. If you help me out, I'll pay it forward and give a helping hand to a poor bastard, one much like myself, who's nearing the end of their rope. Sound like a deal?"

Everlasting silence pervaded.

"Seren, you there?" Jhi's echo was all that kept him company. "I'm losing my mind."

Jhi knew his efforts at praying and offering his blood as a sacrifice to Goddess Seren might prove fruitless, but it was worth a shot. In a last-ditch effort, he sliced his palm on a jagged-edge rock and used his blood to trace an intricate pattern in the air, his index finger elegantly twisting and turning, a single dot here, three horizontal slashes there, a triangle and an interlocking whorl.

A few minutes passed, and Jhi sighed.

And then the air crackled. Before Jhi, Seren's sigil materialized, glowed fiercely, and mushroomed in size. Then it popped out of sight.

A feeling within Jhi gave rise to a clear-cut voice inside his mind that told him to do the most ludicrous thing imaginable, second to bargaining with a demon. *Jump!* the voice said.

"Nah. I'm good," Jhi replied.

Jump now!

"Still good."

Jump before the wind returns and knocks you off the pillar; otherwise, you are a dead *man!*

The wind snarled and shot his way.

Jhi, about ready to vomit, his heart pounding, his body quivering, let loose a few unsavory curse words, then leaped off the edge.

Free falling, his arms pinwheeling, eyes stinging from the frigid air piercing them, he landed with a soft thump on the silty ground.

Grunting, he pulled himself to his feet and immediately spotted what he had quested for—Yad Id'danos, roughly translated to the Hand of Destiny, thought to be a legend. But there it was. A mystical golden glow limned the sacred relic that rested on a dais in the middle of a temple. And it was all Jhi's.

Jhi laughed. He couldn't believe he had made it, that he had found it. That ten feet stood between him and his freedom—

A whirling noise served as a prelude to a chaosgate materializing and the door of a rukba gliding open.

"No! No-no-no-no!" Jhi bit his lip while considering his next course of action. What if it was another trial? The ultimate test? And he had to fight whoever or whatever stepped out?

He hid in a shadowy corner of the temple to size up his enemy before striking, then quickly traced a defense sigil on the floor to act as a trap, but it remained inert. The elements continued to ignore his commands, and magic gems proved useless. Perhaps there was something here he could use as a weapon. Still, they wouldn't see what was coming—Jhi!

A girl stepped out of the elevator—a human girl from the looks of it.

Oh, come on! Jhi thought, pissed off, bloodied, and bruised.

He had tried countless times to open chaosgates during his earlier trials, to no avail.

When the girl came into focus, Jhi immediately thought, *Hello, goddess,* her striking beauty taking him aback. It was hard not to appreciate all five-foot-whatever of her, that slight frame, her form-fitting jeans, tight sweater, and perky breasts.

When she made a beeline for the Hand of Destiny, Jhi snapped out of his trance. *Well played, gods!* Then he stormed to the relic, beating her—the ultimate test?—to the punch.

Jhi swiped the relic before the girl could. "Not so fast. I don't know how you did what you just did"—he waved his finger toward the waiting rukba—"but this is mine."

Her sultry, whiskey-hued eyes opened wide with shock. "I —I wasn't expecting you." She seemed thunderstruck. Then stammered more to herself, "This surprise wasn't foreseen."

"Same thing my mother said when she found out she was pregnant with me. Let's just say she was none too pleased, just like you, sweetheart. Listen—"

"Don't call me sweetheart," she said measuredly.

"No? What should I call you?" Jhi fished.

"The girl who killed you."

Quite the firecracker, she was—a quality that immensely appealed to Jhi. "Look, we obviously came for the same thing."

"Yes. But only one of us will chaosnaut out of here alive. And that would be me."

"Whoa, now. That sounds awfully murdery. Let's talk about this. Maybe we can strike a deal." Jhi's first deal with Seren worked, so perhaps he was on a role. "What can I offer you? Name it, and it's yours."

"Nothing. You don't understand. I need the Hand of Destiny."

She rushed toward Jhi, but he dodged her lunge. "Oh, I understand. I need it, too, or I'm a dead man."

That response seemed to resonate with her. But it was short-lived. "I don't want to kill you, but I will if I have to."

Dear Seren, the girl was serious.

She stepped back as if retreating, then hooked a loose tendril of her long, caramel hair behind her ear while biting her bottom lip, her long lashes fluttering.

Jhi asked, "Can I at least know the name of the most beautiful woman to have graced my presence?" He wasn't above using charm as a tactic.

"JD. And yours?"

"Jhi."

She let out a cute giggle. "Rhymes with die."

Jhi cocked his head and said, "I guess you could say that," then searched the area frantically for anything he could use for self-defense.

JD produced a fiery whip fashioned from the elements, cracked it, and knocked Jhi off his feet. When his head banged into the limestone and smarted something fierce, JD grabbed the Hand of Destiny from his grasp.

While hovering above Jhi, she said, "If it's any consolation, this is about something bigger than you or I—" Blood-curdling, soul-quaking wails sounded from nowhere and everywhere. JD's pupils dilated. She whipped her head about, then returned her focus to Jhi, intimate knowledge written all over her face, which bespoke danger. "I'm sorry." JD sprinted to the chaosgate.

"Sorry, for whaaa—" The stench of death and decay assaulted Jhi's nostrils, and he nearly vomited. He quickly recalled just what that stench heralded.

Banshee-like shrieks pierced the airwaves, and Jhi clasped his hands over his ears to halt any bleeding. Wraiths—they were everywhere. Crawling out of the crevices, corners, and ceiling, their trajectory split between Jhi and JD. Their skin, taken from their prey and shoddily stitched together, formed a mockery of a body. Melted faces and hollowed-out eyes filled with hellfire, they carried spectral swords used for piercing souls in their bony hands.

Wraiths were the zombies of Hell dimensions, the haunters of the Spirit Realm, one-track minds that smelled fear and fed on flesh. But they needed souls desperately to keep a firm footing on the ground, to remain somewhat whole, doomed to live their lives forever on the hunt. And if you were one of the unlucky ones to cross their path, your odds of survival were slim to none.

Hurriedly, JD uncorked a vial and tossed its bloody contents into the air. A wraith picked up the scent of her fear and zipped through the air, closing the distance between it and JD. Right as the ghoulish phantom extended its cold, undead talons, its flesh-tearing nails touching JD's arm, the chaosgate fired into existence.

The second the rukba doors glided open, JD hopped inside the waiting elevator. In her haste to escape, the vial must have slipped from her fingers. Jhi heard it ping to the ground and roll to a dark corner.

JD cursed her mistake, popped her head out of the rukba, and gave a cursory search for the vial. But a wraith thwarted her attempt to grab the glass container. Though visibly irked, she tossed a smile and a wave goodbye to Jhi right as a wraith pinned him down, and others piled on top of him in a feeding frenzy.

2

Present day: 12:49 p.m., October 31

"Woo-wee! Even Lucifer's sweatin' tonight," BB's mother, Eloise, shouted from inside the house, clanging pots and pans and the sizzling of oil in a frying pan accompanying her bellyaching. As Shi'rue would have it, the overtaxed AC had coughed out its last bits of chilled air on the hottest night on record. Though all the windows were open and ceiling fans spun their little hearts out, nothing could beat the stifling heat.

On the verge of dying from heatstroke, BB plucked up The Bellowers' glossy resting tableside, highlighting the latest news around the dimensions. After folding it over, she fanned herself, hoping to dry the sweat dripping down her back, neck, and deep brown chest, wetting her tank top. While trying to cool off, BB got lost contemplating her next plan of attack until a snapping and cracking sounded in the woods in the distance, like footsteps on broken twigs and pine needles.

BB shot to her feet and placed her hands in a defensive pose, prepared to summon the elements in what would shortly be the fight of her life, for the Hounds of Hell had tracked her down and most likely surrounded her house. She swept her eyes past the Jeep and vintage pickup truck parked on the gravel driveway to the woods surrounding her family's homestead, seeking out the vampires.

When a fluffle of rabbits exited the copse of trees and hopped toward the vegetables in the bountiful garden, her shoulders dropped, and her rolling heart slowed down as she fell into the rocking chair. Regardless of how many times this jump scare event had occurred today, she reacted the same way, mainly because the odds of the bloodsuckers finding her were not in her favor. She would have grabbed the spiked beverage on the tray by her feet to calm her rattled nerves, but she couldn't afford to go off script.

A few kits jumped into a pile of leaves and sent them scattering. That annoyance prompted the teenager to return to her chores. BB muttered under her breath in the elemental language of Air—that would sound like a whispered curse to a lowlie—then raised her pointer finger and wrote a string of glyphs. The once invisible intricate shapes and symbols sprung to life, pulsated a vibrant bluish-green for a few seconds, then dissipated.

Following BB's written commands, the rake tossed on the lawn levitated and dragged across the grass, gathering crinkly leaves, clay soil, and other detritus into piles. Zephyrs of summoned Air took the shape of giant hands and then scooped up the vegetation into trash bags—a task that would have taken hours if not for magic.

While the element continued with the lawn work, the rake floating to another area of the yard, the garbage bag trailing behind, the teenager drank up the transient amber hues of twilight before night took the reins. BB marveled at how everything stilled at dusk, like a captured photo, even more so in the wilds of Georgia. It was so deceptive, the feeling of comfort and safety this moment in time brought—a summer night spent with her family.

If only this were real and not the terrifying danger that awaited her outside. While most kids BB's age looked forward to dressing up and celebrating Halloween later at various costume parties around Dillard, BB was doing everything in her power to keep her and her sister Josie alive.

"Mama's gonna whoop your behind." Josie joined BB on the front porch, the screened door slamming behind her. Wafts of hickory smoke commingling with other barbecue deliciousness trailed after BB's older sister, taunting BB's grumbling belly.

"Busy Bee, what did I say about using magic? Put that rake down now, young lady, and pick up the leaves *with your hands!*"

"But Mama—"

"Don't 'but Mama' me. I want the yard work done before supper. You hear me?"

"Yes, ma'am." The words just spit out of BB's mouth of their own accord. Then she whispered to her sister, "I swear Mama magicked eyes in the back of her head. You can't convince me otherwise."

"Or she secreted an All-Seeing Eye on the porch somewhere." The girls giggled in unison, then stopped, giving the comment consideration, and darted their eyes around the verandah.

BB lifted a mirrored serving tray off the wood floor and passed the drugged alcoholic beverage to her sister. Then BB yelped in fright when she caught her reflection—the thirteen-year-old version of herself stared back, not her true nineteen-year-old self.

Josie grabbed the drink right before the tray slipped from BB's shaky hands and crashed to the ground.

Afraid she somehow had interrupted Josie's memory that had been playing on a loop all Halloween morning, BB remained as still as a frightened opossum. After a few seconds, she side-eyed her sister to check if she had noticed something was awry. But when Josie sipped her spiked lemonade, her other hand playing with the frayed edges of her jean shorts, and rested her head on the rocking chair, BB breathed a sigh of relief.

"The night seems to never end." Josie's spindly fingers dug into her black shoulder-length hair to satisfy an itch on her scalp. "I feel like there's something I'm supposed to do. That something isn't right."

BB's heart juddered, as Josie's comment was off script. BB had to check if the memory-trapping potion she'd slipped into the cocktail had run its course earlier than expected, which was what BB feared. And if her hunch was correct, BB had a short window of time before her sister realized the truth—that the events that played out weren't reality but a long-ago memory BB had stolen from Josie before imprisoning her sister in the memory locked within a chaospocket.

When BB attempted to grab the tumbler glass from Josie—the same action she had performed years ago—Josie swatted away her hands and said, "Not so fast. Try again in another two years. When you're legal."

She's supposed to say eight years, BB thought, her heart revving. *And all morning, I had stolen a sip of the spiked lemonade just as my thirteen-year-old self had done years ago until now.*

"Blessed Hekate! Is that my Josie, I hear?" Ketteline's reedy voice called out from inside the house.

"Yes, Gran. Your favorite granddaughter's back home."

Josie tossed a companionable wink at BB as she dashed inside the house, the slamming screen door further agitating BB's shot-to-hell nerves.

Ketteline shuffled carefully down the staircase, her hand gliding down the railing. "Oh, dear!" she exclaimed as she nearly lost her balance because of the shaky handrail.

"Be careful, Mother!" As Eloise raced out of the kitchen, a whoosh of wind in the form of a giant hand proceeded her and immediately stopped Ketteline from crashing onto her well-cushioned tush and helped her back to her feet. "I've been meanin' to tighten the screws. The newel post's too shaky for its own good," said Eloise, Helping Hand spell-caster, talented chef, widow, and single mother to two daughters.

Ketteline canted her head as she paused on the starter step, then slightly nodded as if conversing with the unseen. With her silver, wiry hair whipped up in a bun, BB's grandma donned her usual muumuu that did nothing in the way of hiding her plump belly. But Ketteline couldn't care less. "*At my age, who am I trying to impress?*" she'd tell her grandkids whenever they tried to update her wardrobe. The average lowlie wouldn't guess Ketteline was ancient years old. But like anything, the years had caught up to her, as evidenced by her achy joints and tender hips.

A ghost of a smile touched Ketteline's lips, and to her daughter, she said, "No need to go messin' with things, Eloise. One day somethin's a nuisance, the next a blessin' in disguise." The Budreaus knew to not ask follow-up questions to the matriarch's cryptic statements.

When Ketteline's slippered feet landed in the living room, her "favorite" granddaughter, Josie, fiercely hugged her. Ketteline's soft gray eyes, framed by the slightest crinkling of wrinkles, narrowed as she inspected her firstborn grandchild, whom she hadn't seen in quite a while.

"Nothin' but bones. We gotta fatten you up, like your gran." Ketteline patted her pudgy belly. "Now go back out with your sister. I'm gonna help your mama with supper."

Unlike Beatrice, Josie favored the maternal side of the family and was the spitting image of Ketteline when she was Josie's age—fine-boned and pole-thin, whereas Beatrice had more of an athletic build. Josie clocked in a few inches taller than Beatrice's five-foot-five frame and had piercing gray eyes to Beatrice's brown and amber skin to Beatrice's milk chocolate.

After Josie returned to the porch and fell into the rocking chair, BB said, "Joes—"

"Joes? Is that extra syllable in my *nickname* too exhaustin' for you to say?" Josie half-joshed.

"Yep. As is this conversation. Do you know how much time we've wasted already?"

"You're growin' up on me way too fast." Josie shook her head and smiled.

"Pshaw. What I was about to say before you interrupted is that right outta the blue, Gran started preparin' for your return yesterday. Told Mama and me to get your room ready."

"Explains why no one seemed surprised when I showed up. Yet Gran didn't return my amulet or other necromancy tools."

"Well, between you and me, I think Gran's butt-hurt she won't be crowning you as the archOmega."

Josie sighed. "I wouldn't want that burden. Besides, the last thing I wanted to do was to embark on the Trials of Hekate."

BB had undergone her own trials, ones far more deadly—knowledge that remained a secret to this day.

"Who's to say I would have won?" Josie smirked.

"Puh-lease. Don't even try to deny it. You had it in the

bag, just like Gran and her great-great-grandmother before that. So, you not assuming the role is kinda a big deal."

"Who's side are you on, little sis?"

"I'm just sayin'. I understand Gran's disappointment is all."

"You don't understand what it's like to have carried that heavy burden since you were born," said Josie. "You were the lucky one, always free to do whatever you wanted. Not me. Others planned my life out, dictating what I would do, when, where, with whom. What about what I wanted?"

"Normal's overrated. Besides, you left and abandoned magic."

"No other choice. It's not like you'd be my replacement, and trust me, I asked. But Gran nixed the idea of you being picked to undergo the Trials of Hekate. Said it didn't align with your destiny and left it at that." Josie noted BB's raised brow. "Didn't know that, did you?"

Tiny electrical impulses of shock coursed over BB's skin from that family-secret revelation, regardless of how many times she'd heard Josie speak about it today. Unfortunately, Ketteline died before BB could ask how her gran knew what Goddess Seren had in store for BB.

"You were allowed to be a kid, BB, and still are. Not me, though. Even before my unCloaking, Gran trained me in the ways of magic, and I had to spend countless hours reading boring books on the history of the gods, magecraft, magical laws in other dimensions, and take exams—Ugh. I just wanted to live according to my own rules. To not have responsibilities that others forced on me."

"Yeah, and how'd that turn out for you?" BB could feel her younger self, or rather the body she had slipped into as part of the memory-trapping spell, attempt to tap into Josie's energy, a skill younger BB would hone to perfection in a few short years.

"Hey, I felt that. Stop tryin' to sneak a peek inside my mind," Josie said.

"Not like I saw anything. You locked your memories up real tight."

"Now, what was I saying? Oh, yeah. What happened with Jagger will never happen again. You live, you learn. Bad boys are officially out of my system." Before BB could interject, Josie quickly added, "Things turned out how they were supposed to. I never wanted that responsibility of arch-Omega. But Ellie May did. She always dreamed of wearing the crown, so I'm happy for her. Besides, who the heck wants to live as long as Gran, anyway?" The girls shared a weak laugh.

But then Josie's laughing ceased, and her rocking stilled. No longer in a relaxed position, she sat up, her back ramrod straight, and swiveled her head slowly in BB's direction. Her eyes morphed from gray to emerald green and bored into BB's soul. So much so that a chill snaked down BB's spine. Then, in a voice not her own, Josie uttered, "On the third night, the dragon devours the moon, and all the planets watch from the sky, the gods secretly assemble on the mighty mountain of Bel, and time slowly dies."

Fright gripped BB's thumping heart and squeezed tightly. Through quivering lips, she managed to stay on track and choked out robotically, "You at least gonna join Gran at the Summer Solstice coronation ceremony in Miami? Ellie May will be the youngest archOmega ever to wear the crown. Supposedly, Goddess Hekate will be in attendance."

But Josie remained corpse-still, except for her eyes—those probed every inch of BB. At that moment, BB's heart sped into action, her chest rapidly rising and falling, wondering what version of BB Josie could see—memory BB or real BB.

While the tense moment lingered, BB tried to whip up an escape plan.

In a snap, Josie's eyes changed back to gray, and she returned to her usual self, as if whatever had possessed her body vacated, then said casually, "Nah. I'll skip going to Miami."

BB gave serious thought to fleeing the porch but couldn't. She had to stick to the memory script. "I'm still shocked that Goddess Hekate let Gran go just like that, her closest confidant for over a century. She still had a few good years left in her."

"That's where you're wrong. Gran told Hekate she wanted to retire from her position of archOmega," Josie said conspiratorially. "Admitted how tired she was. Wants to enjoy her golden years in peace."

"And helping Mama run the restaurant and giving readings to love-starved lowlies is peace?"

"Helping Mama with the restaurant is probably more relaxing than serving as Hekate's proxy and ruling over mages." Josie looked behind her and into the living room to ensure Ketteline wasn't nearby, then leaned closer to BB and whispered, "A few major contenders were competing in the Trials of Hekate, like Ellie May, all vying for the all-powerful position of archOmega. So, while Hekate made it clear she didn't like the idea of Gran retiring, not one bit, she agreed under one condition. That Gran would ensure you or I won the Trials to keep the title of archOmega in the Budreau bloodline."

"OMG, a god trying to cheat?" BB said deadpan.

"May wonders never cease," Josie snickered. "Gran told me all this in confidence, so don't go sayin' anything to her, you hear me?" When wide-eyed BB nodded her head, Josie continued, "But it's what Gran didn't say that I heard loud and clear: if I didn't leave, the Nine would force me into assuming the title, and that was something she refused to let happen."

"What? No way. That doesn't make any sense. It's what Gran always wanted for you and our family. Then what was the point of all the training she put you through?"

"My thoughts exactly. Somethin' must have changed her mind. Maybe a vision?" Josie paused as if carefully considering what she was about to say. "What I'm about to tell you, I never told a soul, not even Mama." Josie's face and eyes grew heavy from the sadness she carried. "The night I left, Gran came to my room, pinned my arms and legs down on my bed, then started draining the magic from my body. I couldn't scream for help because she silenced me with a spell. And when my body convulsed and I cried from the excruciating pain of losing a part of myself, Gran didn't flinch or show any remorse. Stone-faced, that's how she appeared. I'll never forget it, BB. Afterward, she said she had no other choice. I hated her with a passion. So, that night I ran as far away from Georgia as I could."

"That's horrible. And doesn't at all sound like Gran. You sure it wasn't a golem?" When Josie nodded affirmatively, BB added, "Then she had to have a good enough reason, right?" Older BB waited patiently while younger memory BB processed the damning information, which involved dramatic brow squinting and heavy sighing. "Y'think Gran will give you back your magic now that you're home? Like a peace offering?"

Josie shrugged. "No clue. Not sure I want it back, to be honest."

For reasons unknown, Gran refused to return Josie's magic when Josie had a change of heart. "*All in divine timing,*" their grandma had said, leaving it at that. Unfortunately, Gran took the whereabouts of Josie's magic to the grave.

"Well, you'll need your powers if you change your mind and go with Gran to Miami. Besides, you were once besties with Ellie May. Like, 'sewn at the hip,' as Mama always said.

So don't you want to be at her coronation as a show of support?"

Josie smiled. "I don't know. Things are so different between us now. There was a time when Ellie May and I did everything together. Talked on the phone for hours every day." Her smile weakened. "But I haven't seen hide nor hair of her since mage camp before our senior year in high school. That was like, what, four years ago?"

"You're old," BB teased.

"Twenty-one's not old." Seemingly out of nowhere, tears welled in Josie's eyes. "I miss those days, BB. Not having a care in the world. No responsibilities. Playing and laughing and trouble-making, wholly innocent, mind you."

"Mm-hmm," BB sounded.

"Those were fun summer and winter breaks. Speaking of which, now that you underwent your unCloaking, shouldn't you be at camp now, learning all manner of magecraft?"

"I don't have time for that. Besides, I have Gran. Who better than archOmega and one of the camp's founders to give me private lessons?"

As the girls rocked in their chairs in companionable silence, Josie said, resigned, "I forgot how far removed we are from everything out here in the country. Just never-ending woods. Not a neighbor around for miles. So. Damn. Quiet. Except for the crickets that never shut up or the hooting owls."

"You gonna up and leave us again, Joes?"

"No," Josie replied. "Maybe. I don't know. It depends on the day, I suppose. But I really missed this. Besides, I promised to help with the restaurant. Mama can't do it alone anymore. But she's too damn proud to admit that. And if I'm gonna help out, I have to up my culinary skills."

"I'd say. Because your cooking sucks!" The sisters snickered.

Sixties music lilted in the background. "Turn up the volume," Eloise instructed her mother. Giggling ensued from the kitchen when Ketteline razzed her only daughter and child, Eloise, along with more pots banging around.

BB turned away before Josie noticed her wiping away an escaped tear. This memory segment needed to end already so BB could regroup and give her heart a much-needed break.

Almost there, BB reminded herself, then said, "The AC's donezo and has to be replaced." *Come on, Josie, it's your turn to reply, and hurry up so I can leave!* Her rapidly tapping foot outpaced her heartbeat.

"I'm not sure I have enough cash to cover the cost," Josie admitted.

"Girls, you stop that worrying!" Eloise shouted. "Your Mama has a plan, and it's my chili. Gonna win us some money at the county fair and save the restaurant."

Mama always had a plan. Until the end, at least. She certainly didn't plan on dying and leaving her girls as orphans.

"I have some money saved up," BB said. She had developed fur'moria skills at such a young age and realized she could make a killing by putting that memory-stealing and mind-manipulating to work. Only her grandma knew of this acquired gift to keep the Budreaus safe from harm.

"I feel off … like we've had this conversation before?" Josie looked straight through BB.

BB swiped the beverage out of her sister's hand.

"Give that back! It's helping with the edge."

"Simma down. I'm gonna refill it for you, is all." Her eyes nearly bugging out of her skull, BB slinked through the squeaky screened door and walked past her gran on the couch, busy peeling potatoes. BB didn't want to look. Couldn't. It was too painful.

But all that changed when Ketteline's head jerked

upward, and she tossed a spell at BB, magically rooting her in place. BB fought against it, fought against whoever pulled the strings, but the magic overpowered her.

The same voice from before used her gran as its messenger. "On the third night, the dragon devours the moon, and all the planets watch from the sky, the gods secretly assemble on the mighty mountain of Bel, and time slowly dies."

BB broke free from the spell—or maybe the entity had released her—and she zipped past her mama in the kitchen, humming happily in front of the stove while the chicken sizzled in the frying pan.

A blink later, the humming stopped, and the hair on BB's neck raised. She pivoted around to see her mama standing in the hallway, racing toward Beatrice, her eyes wide with fright.

"What happens on the third night?" Eloise's voice cracked with panic. "You must find out before we're all doomed!" The entity closed the distance between them and reached out its arms to Beatrice.

Her hands quivering, BB removed the athame from the small of her back and stabbed the air, dragging the dagger downward. An opening formed, appearing as a rip in canvas. BB dove through the tear right as the entity's ice-cold hands grabbed her shoulders. As BB exited, her thirteen-year-old body morphed into her nineteen-year-old self; summer turned into fall, and night turned into day.

On the other side of the chaospocket, she pinched the tear with her slender fingers, watched it seal, and then exhaled a massive sigh of relief and wiped sweat from her brow. The stolen memory hidden within a chaospocket was gone from sight save for an easy-to-miss shine.

In the living room where her gran had once sat on the sofa peeling potatoes, BB paced back and forth to get her wits about her and not have a full-on panic attack. But seeing the sea of sheets layered in dust covering all the furniture was too depressing and not helping matters, so she headed to the kitchen.

The reading room where Ketteline had conducted her psychic sessions now served as a catch-all for neglected furniture and a scattershot of unpaid bills. The dining room that once held so many happy memories of the Budreau family was now devoid of life.

BB landed in the L-shaped kitchen, where her mama had been moments before, cooking Sunday dinner. Time was not on BB's side, and her options were on life support. It was one thing to steal a memory—which BB had done earlier to her sister—but to trap someone inside their memory and ensure they remained unaware of their prisoner status for hours on end was something else entirely.

Thank Seren for the potions. Even so, the effects of the Memories are Made of This elixir BB had been dosing her sister with had gone sideways. Luuksan swore this potion was well worth the hefty price tag. *"It'll keep your target in a hypnagogic state and trapped in their fondest memory for days,"* that sneaky lying demon had promised. Well, that certainly wasn't the case. Old Josie went to war with present Josie, and the latter got stronger by the minute. *Wait till I get my hands on that damn demon!*

Frigid air stole inside one of the cracked kitchen windows, the massive spider web holding dominion on the casing blowing back and forth. Desperate to warm her shaky hands, BB summoned Fire. The element replied and ignited the gas stove. Still, she cursed as she watched the yellow vapor escape from the every-color magic gem she held.

After warming her hands, she turned off the burner and conjured Water. A beat later, ice cubes filled Josie's cocktail glass, then more cursing ensued as orange vapor drained entirely from the every-color gem. Add more magic gems to the list of things to buy at the Starless Souk. (More money BB didn't have!) And maybe they had a money tree for sale there, too.

At this rate, BB nearly burned through her reserves. She'd have to take on more fur'moria gigs when she wasn't on the lam and hiding from a gang of vicious vampires and some creepy man on the hunt for her.

BB's shaky hand generously poured the bourbon and a dash of lemonade over the ice and topped it off with a dessertspoonful of Memories are Made of This that resembled a violet-indigo-hued syrup. She gave the drink a quick stir, then poured herself a shot of bourbon to calm her nerves. And poured another for good measure.

What confounded BB was why Josie cherished that remembrance. At the time of the memory, their gran's health was failing, the family restaurant had nearly closed, and Mama struggled to pay the bills. Then a short time later, everything went to pot. Still, this memory was at the forefront of Josie's mind, and the one BB had removed in a panic. No time to plan. And it was this memory BB had mixed into the Memories are Made of This concoction.

"Gran, I seriously need your help!" BB beseeched the empty kitchen as she desperately looked around. But not a soul responded. "Rats. I wouldn't haunt this depressing house either." BB then yelled to the prophecy-spewing being that had tried to contact her earlier, "You have my full attention. Now speak!"

Silence pervaded.

BB had no clue how to fix the problem other than returning to the Starless Souk and demanding Luksaan remedy the dud he'd sold her. She had to keep her sister imprisoned, for lack of a better word, in the memoryscape. It was that or death. Josie did not know the life BB had once lived or the danger she faced daily, and BB needed to keep it that way—protecting her sister was her primary concern. As it stood, Josie was the only family BB had left, and she wasn't about to lose her, which made the thought of leaving her sister alone and defenseless much more terrifying. But BB had no other choice.

Earlier, a waiter at her family restaurant had handed BB a note during the sunrise shift. The written message said: *Leave now!* When she asked who it was from, the waiter shrugged. Before BB could process the cryptic warning, a man named Miles, wearing a menacing smile and a form-fitting sharkskin suit, sauntered through the doors, asking around for Beatrice Budreau.

His beady eyes scoured the establishment as the hostess, Emily, donning a vampiress Halloween costume, expressed her sincerest apologies that Beatrice was out of town. Still, the stranger refused to leave and said he'd stay for a bite to eat, that it had been a while since he ate real Southern food. Emily sent an SOS text to Beatrice, warning her to stay in the back.

Terrified, BB snuck a peek at the man from where she stood in the kitchen and homed in on the animated dragon and Firebird tattoo on his neck. Instantly, she knew he worked for Vlad Dracula, as the dragon was the original vampire's insignia. It was daytime, so this man wasn't a Hound of Hell. Still, the fact remained that BB had been made.

At that point, she had to enact her escape plan, so she placed a vivid-green canima crystal inside a poppet, activated it with Josie's blood, and hid the doll. Then, she snuck up on Josie in the back office and knocked her out with a round kick to the side of her sister's neck. It wasn't like Josie would have gone willingly to their family's dilapidated farmhouse on the outskirts of Dillard. There was a lot about BB Josie didn't know, and now wasn't the time for reveals. BB dragged Josie into the adjacent walk-in fridge. After BB sliced her palm, she drew a chaosgate inside, then tossed more of her blood on the skeleton lock, her blood the key.

A few years back, Beatrice had had the wherewithal to change the name on the deed to the farmhouse to something fictitious.

Something she was forced to do because of her old line of work.

Making enemies a hazard of the job.

From the days when she was an Agent of Karma.

3

3:39 a.m., October 31

The comforting aroma of decadent chocolate greeted Pepper as she exited the chaosgate. Through the wan light, she padded through the backroom of a random store on Peachy-keen Lane in Dillard, Georgia, and stopped dead in her tracks, directly under a security camera. One more step and she would have triggered the alarm.

A sprinkling of old-timey iron tables and ceiling-high shelves stocked with candy populated the coffee shop slash ice cream parlor slash candy store. Pepper could have eaten everything in sight, from the every-flavor candy sticks to the nutty caramel turtles to the peanut butter fudge to the limitless choices of ice cream. And she would have devoured all the sugary delectables if not for the security camera and motion detectors.

"Way to go, dickwad!" Perrin whispered while smacking Kimball on his head.

"Ow!" Kimball whined, rubbing his skull, his other hand white-knuckling the vodka bottle to his chest, his mother's soul pinging off the glass walls of her cage.

"We're going for stealth mode, not bumbling idiot!" Perrin snapped.

"I only tripped over a box because you pushed me," Kimball clapped back, then automatically massaged the bottle and added gentle tappings—actions that quieted Bunny, her restlessness all but gone.

Loki scampered on all fours out of the chaosgate last and rolled his eyes at the spectacle before him.

Pepper pointed to the security camera above her head, and the duo quit bickering. Still, Perrin couldn't hide her disdain for Kimball and balled her hands into fists, then inched closer to him.

When Pepper stepped in between the two before Perrin chose physical violence, the Lolly'ka said, "Mother Lilith! Seriously? You tried to kill rattilocks not even an hour ago on the boat. And would have, if not for Loki. That fuh'karing …" Perrin vomited a stream of curse words while shaking her fists in disgust. "Has everyone here forgotten he's the reason why Larry was abducted?"

Just hearing her dad's name inflamed the abject dread Pepper tried her damndest to keep under control. As the bucketloads of tears threatened to spill over, a hitching sob gearing up, she snapped a rubber band on her wrist several times, the hairs on her arms yanked from their roots, then reminded herself, *The sooner we find Jaylyn's contact and then Beatrice, the sooner I can rescue my pops.* Once the salty betrayers dried up and she sucked the snot back into her nose, Pepper got her head back in the mission. Goddess

Karma had coldly delivered an edict to Pepper to find Beatrice before the Syndicate killed her.

So the hunt was on. Miles and Judas Jhi were searching for Beatrice, too.

After a few more snaps of the rubber band, her wrist smarting, Pepper whispered to Loki and Perrin, "I don't see a way to leave the store undetected that doesn't involve magic."

Pepper and the others had made a pact to use magic sparingly because it caused a disturbance in the aether, and the Hounds of Hell trying to pick up their scent could triangulate their location.

"We don't have any other choice, sweetling." Perrin returned her focus to Kimball, watching her "prisoner" like a goyle.

No stranger to playing the role of gumshoe detective, Pepper gave a cursory search to her surroundings, considering what she would do if on a karma-for-hire case. After tiptoeing to the inkjet printer in the backroom, she plucked a printer toner from the garbage bin and then delicately shook its contents on a piece of paper to avoid massive spillage. Much to Perrin's chagrin, Pepper used one of the Lolly'ka's pricey makeup brushes—its bristles plucked from the hair of the damned—as a makeshift fingerprint duster.

"I'll buy you a new one," said Pepper.

Deftly, Pepper swiped a small amount of black dust over the alarm pad keys to pick up the sweat and dirt on the employees' fingers. Ridges and whorls and arches on various numbers came into view. The next step was to determine the order of the numbers.

Pepper plucked out the requisite gems from her satchel. "An indigo gem for the code revealing and blue to vocalize the intention," Pepper said, not entirely confident. "Y'know, if I screw this up, then—"

"Then we're fuh'kared, and you'll never make the same mistake again." Perrin's response didn't instill confidence in Pepper. Quite the opposite. Noting Pepper's hesitation, Perrin added, "Right now, about all you can magic into existence is a flame. So when the Syndicate has you over a barrel, perhaps you can *be a dear* and light their celebratory cigars before they tear your soul from your body." When Pepper gasped, Perrin said, "School is in session. So get to it," and finished with two snaps of her fingers.

Loki seemed to take the pint-sized Lolly'ka's side, for he said nothing, just stared, his eyes communicating, "Hurry it up!"

Eyes closed, Pepper imagined the numbers appearing, then quietly verbalized an order to the gems, "Show me the correct sequence of the alarm code." Vaporous carbon copies of the numbers levitated and then rejiggered in the correct sequence before dissolving.

"I hope someone memorized those numbers because I sure as hell forgot the order already," Kimball said over his growling stomach.

Pepper's hand froze over the alarm pad. "The moment I disarm the alarm, it could alert the owners. So, we probably have five minutes at the most before the cops arrive."

In response, Loki quickly removed his quarterstaff and twirled it in a figure-eight pattern. The summoned shadows slithered along the ground and swallowed the group whole.

After the alarm disengaged, the gang scurried out the back door and ran about half a mile down the road until they reached a copse of trees directly behind an antique shop at the edge of town. Nighttime had a few more hours left on its shift, so Pepper and the gang hunkered down and discussed their next move.

Since Jaylyn's contact was most likely a mage, the gang

devised a way to trace their magical essence. But how to do that undetected?

"Potions are difficult to pinpoint. Technically, you're not casting magic, which is what causes the disturbance in the aether," Loki said to Pepper. To everyone else, his reply came across as a capuchin's chittering. But to Pepper, she heard words loud and clear.

After Pepper shared Loki's idea, Perrin beamed, "Brilliant, my little furball."

Loki hissed back, his yellowed needle-like teeth on display.

Pepper poured out the contents of her drawstring pouch, which amounted to one gem, red vaporous magic swirling inside the marble. Unfortunately, that was the wrong color.

When Perrin dumped a few items she'd procured from Bhi'gow's laboratory—dried medicinal mushrooms, unidentifiable herbs, and a pinch of magic gem dust in every shade—Pepper's lips curled into a smile of relief. "Use these sparingly. Like, this is it, sweetling."

Pepper placed a pinch of violet gem dust into a vial, knowing that Vs would enable her to see the unseen magic essence. Then she moved on to the next ingredient. "Looks like a reishi mushroom, which I always make my pops take." Her breath hitched in her throat, and Pepper told herself that the fact Larry was staring down the barrel of a shotgun was all her fault. Then a smaller voice within demanded that she focus on the task at hand. That it wasn't too late to rescue her pops. And to do that, she'd have to learn magic. So the pressure was on, and Perrin and Loki hovering over her shoulders weren't helping matters. Neither was her internal temperature, which kicked up a few degrees.

"Sweetling!" Perrin barked while pinching Pepper's arm. "Get back in the game. Now's not the time for tears and woe-is-me."

After a half-nod and more rubber band snapping, Pepper continued her magic studies while suppressing her freak-out. Now, what had Pepper remembered about reishi regarding psychic matters? The mushroom did wonders with cultivating the third eye and awakening the mind; she knew that much, among other miraculous healing benefits. So, she crumbled the dried mushroom and added it to the magic gem dust.

After adding a wad of her spit to liquefy the concoction, Pepper placed the cork on the vial and shook it, all while imagining the desired result. The contents within swirled, sparkled, and belched. A bubble formed on the surface, then popped before the potion stilled. Something about this process felt eerily familiar. Perhaps because it resembled Pepper's love of cheffing.

When Perrin nodded off for the tenth time in a row, Pepper said they should all catch some shut-eye in shifts until the sun clocked in for the day and stores opened to the public.

GRAVEL CRUNCHED as a car drove behind the antique store, followed by the door slamming shut.

Pepper smacked the others' arms to wake them up.

Rays of morning sunlight limned Pepper as she stood up, draped the messenger bag around her waist, and wiped the dirt from her jeans. "Everyone ready?"

"So, what's the plan again?" Kimball asked, running his fingers through his tousled mane.

"The plan, Kimball, is for you to be quiet—Actually, I think we should sew his mouth shut." Perrin wasn't joshing.

Before imbibing the crafted potion she coined To Catch a Mage, Pepper waited for the go-ahead from Perrin and Loki. But they said nothing. Tough audience, those two. The concoction went down like a slushy at 7-Eleven, only it didn't possess that quintessential sugary deliciousness. Pepper's eyes stung for a beat, like dry eye. An instant later, a faint multi-hued aura surrounded Perrin and Loki like a second skin, then vanished. While Kimball looked the same—a righteous mess, his curly sunflower and black-rooted locks in need of a hot oil treatment, bags under his dung-hued eyes, his skin bloodied and bruised. "Spell worked," Pepper said, relieved.

Once inside the antique shop, Pepper scoured the establishment for traces of magic while pretending to be oh-so interested in Victorian glass. The clothing, however, sparked her interest. Kimball's, too, because he purchased a wool-like cloak that matched Pepper's, along with a sweater and jeans, opting to ditch his blood-soaked, button-down white shirt and black trousers. And since the Georgia weather dipped into the forties, it was a wise decision on Kimball's part to purchase winter wear.

Even though it was Halloween, the store clerk wouldn't stop glaring at Perrin and Loki, so Pepper purchased a plastic Barbie costume and mask from the early 80s and handed it to Perrin. As for Loki, the eye mugging ceased after Pepper informed the clerk that the capuchin was her emotional support animal.

After coming up empty in their search for a mage, Pepper and the gang footed it to the next store along Peachy-keen Lane.

Almost two hours later and no mage sightings, an exhausted, discouraged, and hangry Pepper collapsed on the curb outside Javayum—a retro-themed cafe and kava bar—wondering if the To Catch a Mage spell was even working. Perrin said they couldn't afford to take a break, to quit whining, and forced Pepper to get back on her feet.

It wasn't until they visited the candy shop that they struck gold. (Go figure!) A faint golden line popped into Pepper's line of sight. It traveled inside the store and then down the street, where it ended.

A bell over the door chimed as Pepper crossed the threshold. She paid no mind to the familiar backroom or the barista stocking the shelves, her eyes riveted to the thin trail of magic that ended at an alcove to her right, in front of a PO Box.

"Cool costume," the teenaged barista said to Perrin. "Love the vintage vibe."

Perrin curtseyed in response.

The barista rocked a costume from years past: an obvious wig—shoulder-length and over-crimped—an elaborate mustache belonging to an evil cartoon villain, an ankle-length kaftan cinched by a wide belt that resembled a cummerbund, loose-fitting trousers that tapered around his ankles, and boots.

"Who are you dressed as?" the barista asked Perrin as he walked behind the counter.

"Demon Barbie." Perrin noted his name badge. "And you, Jacob?"

"I'm Vlad Dracula, Prince of Wallachia, disguised as an elite Janissary serving Ottoman Sultan Mehmed the second, aka Mehmed the Conqueror," Jacob beamed. "After tonight, on this seventeenth day of June"—his voice dropped an octave—"in the year of our Lord fourteen sixty-two, I will free my countrymen from paying the jizya and the constant Ottoman threat at Wallachia's borders." He giggled. "That was me, in character. I'm a cosplayer and treasurer of the South Regional Cosplayer's Guild." Jacob appeared to take great pride in holding that title. "I'm sure you've heard of us."

"Nope. Sure haven't. And you look nothing like Vlad." Leave it to Perrin to dole out the truth without a second thought. "Er, I meant what he is supposed to look like."

"Uh, nobody really knows what Vlad looks like," Jacob replied petulantly. "Seeing as how his enemies are the ones who commissioned paintings of him. Anyway"—he twirled around to showcase a janky-looking steel crossbow strapped to his back—"I made this from papier-mâché and aluminum foil. Betcha thought it was real."

"No, I knew it was fake." Perrin finished with a hundred-watt smile.

Jacob ignored Perrin. "Pretty proud of it. Vlad loved his crossbow. But not as much as this." He wore a sheepish grin as his eyes darted left and right to ensure the coast was clear, then produced a saber with a dramatically curved single-edged blade and hilt from under the counter. "Feast your eyes on Vlad's most prized possession. Mine, too, actually. It's a genuine replica of Vlad's kilij that he used in battle. Mostly close combat. My boss would totally fire me if he knew I was packing heat. Anyway, this baby cost me a king's ransom." Light glinted off the curved metal when he placed it on the counter for display. "But totally worth it."

Pepper ran into a display case housing solar and lunar eclipse viewers and glasses. As she attempted to re-stack everything that had crashed to the floor, she huffed quietly, "What an odd thing to sell in a coffee shop."

"Not really," discount Vlad replied. "We'll sell out way before the event of the century. Just you wait and see."

"The event of the century?" Pepper pressed for more information.

"What rock have you been living under? The eclipse, duh."

"Which one? There's going to be two in December, in case you were unaware," Kimball, the armchair astronomer, shared.

"The lunar eclipse," Jacob said. "Never in the history of ever have all eight planets been in perfect alignment.

Astronomers have stated that a supreme planetary alignment would never and could never happen. But it is, and it's occurring the same day as the lunar eclipse."

The gang exchanged looks of concern. Kimball had mentioned that Cazzian planned on killing Pepper's dad soon at some vampire ritual. What if it was related to the lunar eclipse a month and some change away? Her heart dropped.

"Anyway, our annual Winter Festival this year will be off the charts, and we sell the best way to view the celestial phenomenon right here in our shop. I'll let you in on a little secret. It's not the lunar eclipse that I'll be celebrating. Rather, the total solar eclipse that falls on Winter Solstice. We're throwing an underground party. Invite only. Gonna be so rad. And you're gonna totally die when you hear this. Guess what else took place during another total solar eclipse?"

"No idea," Perrin said, monotone, "and don't leave me hanging in suspense, or someone will die alright."

"The battle waged between Vlad Dracula and Mehmed the Conqueror on June seventeenth, fourteen sixty-two." Still no reaction. "Otherwise known as the Night Attack at Târgoviște." Exasperated, Jacob said, "I can't believe you guys don't know this. My costume, *hello*! Were you not listening to me earlier?" When nobody answered, he slipped into a tone prime for a campfire tale. "That event sealed Vlad's fate."

Disguised as Janissaries, Vlad and his advance guard snuck inside the Ottoman camp and split up. Using the sun's total eclipse to his advantage, Dracula made a beeline for the sultan's tent, visions of finally besting his greatest foe carrying him onward. Only Vlad failed.

Sighing, Jacob shook his head, then continued with the yarn spinning. "According to historians, Vlad made a terrible blunder, one where death tagged his heels when he snuck into the wrong tent and murdered a grand vizier and some other dude. Vlad and his men escaped into the forest. Mehmed's soldiers eventually caught up to the Wallachian prince and assassinated him, then sent his head to Mehmed as a trophy."

Perrin plucked the kilij from the counter and caressed the blade, most likely considering swiping it if her wicked grin was any indication.

Jacob snatched it back, then leaned across the counter and whispered as if sharing a state secret, "According to an anonymous guest on Chloe's Casefiles and Conspiracies podcast—"

Pepper huffed and chased that with an eye roll, as she was all too familiar with that podcast and its host but kept her biases to herself.

"Anyway," Jacob said. "As I was saying. Historians twisted the account of the Night Attack at Târgoviște, along with Vlad's purported beheading. First of all, it wasn't technically a night attack. It happened in the daylight hours during a total solar eclipse. And secondly, Vlad Dracula, a prince, ruling member of the secret Order of the Dragon, storied warlord, protector of his lands and countrymen, and one of the most important rulers in Romanian history, didn't make mistakes."

"That he doesn't," Perrin said. "Anything else you gleaned from this podcast about that event? About Vlad?"

"Oh yeah. Hellbent on doing whatever it would take to fight for his country and defeat Mehmed the Conqueror—the order of importance is debatable—Vlad became a vampire soon after the camp raid." Jacob pulled back and let out a chuckle. "And that's where the podcast guest jumped the shark. Obviously vampires don't exist, so I called into the show and challenged him. If Vlad's the original vampire, then how did he become a night-walker if he wasn't sired? I totally stumped the dude. So epic. You should have heard it."

Growing impatient and riddled with anxiety, Pepper said, "I was supposed to meet my friend here, and I'm late. Their phone's turned off. Probably pissed at me for my tardiness. They have a PO Box here. Most likely picked up their mail a little while ago. Ring any bells?"

"Nope. What's your friend's name?"

"Jacob," Perrin started, "the shop manages a handful of PO boxes. Surely, in a town as dinky as yours, you know every single person who has one."

"Actually, I don't. Even if I knew, I couldn't give out that information to solicitors. I'd get fired. Company policy."

Perrin's hands balled into fists. Before Pepper could calm the Lolly'ka, Loki chittered for her, and Pepper waltzed his way.

"Loki, I'm gonna strangle him." Something about that idea tickled her pink. Or she could knock an ice cream scooper over Jacob's head.

"What do you smell?" Loki asked in his capuchin tongue.

Pepper inhaled deeply. "Ugh. Smells like my pops after being out in the Florida sun all day. Wait. There's something sweet mixed in with the BO. Spicy. Earthy. Hearty. Mmm. Sautéed onions and garlic … Chili! That's what it smells like." Pepper made her dad that dish all the time.

Pepper flew to the counter. "Jacob, I smell chili. Please tell me it's your soup du jour. I mean, I don't see it on the menu."

"Sorry. We don't sell chili here. You should go visit The Budreau House. You just missed the owner, actually."

"This Budreau House. That a well-known family in this town or something," Perrin inquired.

"No," Jacob said. "It's a restaurant. Voted the best chili in the state of Georgia. It also serves all things barbecue if you're into dead carcasses. Though I wouldn't know because I'm a vegan."

"I wonder what vegans taste like," Perrin said out loud. "Probably horrible."

Jacob crinkled his nose and brow in confusion.

"Thanks, Jacob!" Pepper grabbed a clearly up-to-no-good Perrin and ran out the front door, Loki and Kimball trailing behind.

Finally, they reached their destination. The Budreau House resembled a sizable single-story home with a front porch and loads of rocking chairs filled with hungry guests waiting their turn to eat lunch. Kimball entered the restaurant first with shadow-cloaked Pepper, Perrin, and Loki hot on his heels. A chorus of incoherent chatter and silverware scraping on plates rang out. The smells of homemade food, sweet smoke, and freshly baked biscuits taunted Pepper's hungry belly, but eating was not on the agenda.

Kimball, his face and neck a riot of bruises and dried blood—thank Seren, it was Halloween—flirted with the costumed hostess named Emily, buttering her up like one of the piping hot biscuits feet away from Pepper. Between doling out compliments, Kimball asked if the owner was in today. Emily nodded and said she would go get Miss Josephine from her office.

"Oh no. Don't bother. I was curious, is all," Kimball said.

Time of the essence, Perrin unleashed Tavi from the chain fastened to the inside of her purse that he called home and gave him his orders: feed on Josephine Budreau's memories, see if you can find her home address, then report back. The charcoal-colored sprite—built like a blob the size of a hand, with noodle-like arms and a tail that seamlessly ran into his torso—nodded his humanoid head the size of a finger pad, his protruding horns dipping down and up.

While Pepper, Perrin, and Loki followed Tavi's trail,

Pepper plucked biscuit after biscuit from the plates of unsuspecting patrons and shoved one in her mouth while squirreling away the rest in her satchel. They squeezed through the cafe doors as they swung closed and then navigated through a hallway to the backroom of the eatery.

The open-concept space contained industrial shelves housing everything from canned tomatoes, bags of flour, and all the cooking staples to cleaning supplies and other whatnots. A walk-in commercial fridge resided at the far end of the room.

Josephine was bent over a desk, cocooned in a faint aura of magic. As was Tavi, who balanced on a zephyr of air, his head buried in Josephine's hair. The pocket-sized sprite jerked backward, his black brows knitted. From what Pepper had witnessed before, when Tavi would suck on his victim's brain matter, blood would coat his fangs and little pointed chin. Only this time, the sprite's face was bereft of gore. The little devil stroked the wiry hairs on his chin. It appeared as if his memory-sucking hadn't worked.

In response to her head being attacked, Josephine rose from her seat and tried to crush the life out of Tavi. Utterly terrified, the sprite pinwheeled away from Josephine's flailing hands and zipped back inside Perrin's purse.

"She has to be Jaylyn's contact. What do we—"

A furious Josephine interrupted Pepper's question and nearly steamrolled over the invisible trio.

But how could Josephine possibly see them? As Pepper attempted to escape Josephine's wrath while doing everything she could to not let go of the staff and break the shadow-cloaking spell, Miles Leagan interrupted Pepper's forward momentum.

The soul-selling serial killer entered the storage room and secured the door behind him.

4

Miles blocked the only exit in the backroom, a feral sneer forming on his cadaverous, pockmarked face. Then he magicked box after box to levitate to the door, trapping Pepper and the gang inside.

"Miss Josephine Budreau. Not exactly the Budreau I've been patiently waiting to see. But you'll do."

As he strode in Josephine's direction, his stubby nails grew, their ends tapering into dagger-like points, the metallic sheen of his suit's fabric shining under the fluorescent lights, the same for the scales of his alligator-skin loafers.

Josephine remained mum, her face not even radiating an ounce of fear. But her eyes told an entirely different story—one that involved bloodshed and carnage.

Pepper inched back, as did Loki and Perrin, and couldn't help but wonder how Miles could have known about Jaylyn's contact. One word: Jhi.

"Josephine, aren't you a beauty. I like pretty girls. Lithesome. Silky skin. Delicate. Their bones are easier to break. The way they cascade to the floor after being gutted, so graceful and swanlike." Miles slunk closer to her. "Because I'm feeling generous today, and I happened to sample your award-winning chili and cornbread, which were"—he curled his fingers and audibly kissed their tips—"delightful, I'm going to give you two options. You tell me where Beatrice is, and I kill you quickly. You can even choose how. If you don't tell me where your sister is, I can promise you a prolonged and painful death. What'll it be?" Judging from his tone, he seemed to want Josephine to choose the latter.

Josephine's eyes widened with anger, and with a brute strength that shocked even Miles, she went berserk and pummeled him in the jugular. Then she kicked him in the gut and sent the serial killing flying, his back slamming into the wall, and he crashed to the tiled floor.

A feral grin yanked the corners of Miles' lips ever high. "You surprise me." He levitated to his feet. "I like surprises. You want to play a game of chase?" But the lowlie fell again, most likely because he tapped out his source of magic. Which meant he'd need to feed on another mage, and soon. "Sources say you are the black sheep of your family. The only lowlie in the Budreau clan. It must have felt so inadequate growing up around such power. Taking a back seat to your baby sister. To make up for it, you juice up on borrowed magics, I see? So pathetic."

As Josephine's hands raised, cords of magic surged out of Miles, and she tugged them to her.

A wrathful Miles fought against whatever spell Josephine had cast, his arms punching through her defensive charms, and picked himself up. "The thing about borrowed magics is that the power is short-lived." He struggled as he walked toward her as if fighting category-four hurricane winds. "The hard way it is." He whipped out a vial and knocked back the brownish-red substance. With a supersonic speed much like a vampire's, he soared through the air and snapped Josephine's neck. Her body crumpled to the tiled floor.

He removed a handheld projector from his business suit pocket. As it whirred to life, a beam of light showcased nothing but dust particles. Until those dust particles collided and formed an impression, or rather a recreation, of an earlier event. Using the buttons on the device, Miles sped up the scene to double time. A teenage girl around Pepper's age snuck up on Josephine in the back office, knocked her out, and then dragged Josephine into the adjacent commercial fridge.

Whatever happened inside, Pepper could not witness. Not Miles, though. The serial killer opened the fridge door and disappeared within.

A moment later, Miles exited and spoke into an earpiece. "The girl escaped through a chaosgate. ... No. Gateway's gone. She got a head start. ... No, but I got the address. ... Let's just say Josephine's not going to be a problem. ... Curious indeed. You said she was a lowlie. ... Oh really? Then explain how she could cast magic? ... You watch your tone, Jhi. I don't care if we needed her alive. She left me no other choice but to kill her. ... So? Whether she had magic at one time but doesn't now, she's a lowlie in my book and is no use to us. ... That so? If you expose what happened, you're going down, not me. ... End of discussion. ... I *said* end of discussion. Tell Vlad I'll deliver Beatrice to him shortly. I'm heading out." Miles magicked the boxes away from the cafe doors, tossed them into the walls, and stormed out of the restaurant.

Upon hearing Jhi's name, Pepper's once-corralled heart escaped and went wild. So it took her mind a minute to process what had just happened. That Miles had mentioned another name—Beatrice. Perhaps Josephine wasn't the contact after all but her sister. And if that was the case, Beatrice, considered an Agent of Karma, could help Pepper track down Jaylyn. A jolt of adrenaline ignited within Pepper from that thought alone.

"Now they're using a surveillance device to detect magic casting here on Earth?" Perrin exchanged a look of concern with Pepper and Loki. "This dimension is looking more and more like Hell every day."

"Miles is gonna kill Beatrice if we don't stop him!" Pepper said.

Kimball slunk into the backroom, his usually sun-kissed face blanched with fright. "I had to quickly hide when Miles showed up. Didn't have enough time to warn you guys."

"Where'd Miles go?" Loki asked, which Pepper quickly translated.

"Drove off in a heavily tinted car. My guess is there are passengers inside who have an aversion to sunlight."

"We can take Josephine's car. It's not like she'll need it anymore." A tinge of guilt shone through Pepper when she voiced that harsh truth. "Also, we better get out of here before we're accused of murder."

Kimball spotted Josephine's dead body folded on the floor and gasped. Pepper was about to tell Kimball to be quiet when Josephine sat upright, her twisted neck crunching while it swiveled forty-five degrees.

Josephine then rose to her feet, as if Miles hadn't broken her neck minutes prior, and set her sights on Pepper. With the shadow-cloaking spell broken, Pepper grabbed Josephine's purse hanging on the chair and trailed after the others as they thundered out the back exit.

Kimball fired up Josephine's Jeep while Pepper and the others crouched in the backseat. They caught up to Miles on a two-lane road, keeping a few car lengths behind the heavily tinted Rolls-Royce Ghost.

"Any guesses how Josephine survived a broken neck?" a stunned Pepper inquired.

"That wasn't Josephine but a golem," Perrin replied. "Which means Josephine is still alive."

Tall trees bookended the two-lane road. Their leaves, dressed in vibrant shades of royal reds, oranges, and yellows, rustled as if waving to passersby, warning them to turn back around. A gust of wind pushed the Jeep dangerously close to the guardrail. Kimball regained control and swerved back into the right lane.

Up ahead, the Rolls-Royce Ghost crossed the double yellow line, inching into the left lane, then vanished, and the chorus of rustling leaves quieted.

"Uh, guys. What just happened?" Pepper cried out. "Where'd they go?"

"Quick. Give me Josephine's purse." Perrin grabbed the satchel from Loki's furry palms.

After rummaging through Josephine's belongings, most of the contents tossed about, Perrin found a well-loved picture of what she surmised was the Budreau Family standing in front of a two-story farmhouse with a wraparound verandah.

Perrin slashed her arm with her razor-sharp fingernail, then removed a lip gloss tube from her purse. She unscrewed the top and poured a dollop of violet power onto her palms, which combined with the blood to form a paste. "Aeolus, Keeper of the Winds, I summon thee—So get off your lazy ass already and come to me!"

A whirling vortex appeared, running parallel to the speeding car. A mystical hand fashioned from air punched out of the cyclone and formed a sizable disembodied face. "Mistress Perrin. Oh, how Seren has blessed me with your beauteous presence." The elemental god's voice boomed, dripping with sarcasm. "I don't have time for your antics. Not when I'm mired within a shitstorm back in my realm."

"Ooh, anything I can help you with?"

"Not unless you can find an irreplaceable relic that's gone missing on my watch. Or can lead me in the thief's direction, who I'm about ready to immolate."

"Oh, that bad, huh? Wouldn't want to be you," Perrin singsonged. "Listen, Lussy, we can iron out what was a colossal misunderstanding on *your* part later. Right now, I need your help. You owe me. And unless you've switched sides, one of your minions has broken rank, and they're helping the Syndicate."

Aeolus' sigh nearly knocked the Jeep off the road. "Oh, I've heard of the Syndicate. Recently. They're involved in this shitstorm—And what is this about one of my minions?"

Perrin described how the Rolls-Royce disappeared with the help of a mysterious burst of wind.

"Oh. That's not good," the elemental god breathed.

"Exactly. So, here's what I need you to do." Perrin showed the picture to the lesser god, jabbing her finger at the numbers on the house. "And keep to the roads." Perrin looked at the others and added, "Lussy can be sneaky."

"As you wish." Aeolus morphed into an airstream, complete with leaves and other visible detritus.

Kimball stepped on the gas, the odometer rising as he followed the winding trail. When the elemental god twisted in the opposite direction, then howled down the road and disappeared down a side street, Kimball made a fast U-ey, tires squealing.

"Told you," Perrin said smugly.

Eventually, the cyclonic wind navigated down Chicory Lane. It ended about three-quarters of a mile later, smack dab in front of a dirt road, then poofed out of existence, the leaves and orangey-red clay soil sifting to the ground.

From Pepper's vantage point, she could barely see a two-story, ramshackle farmhouse at the end of the dirt driveway, a twin to the one in the crinkled photo. Before she got out of the car, Kimball drove into the woods to hide the Jeep from sight.

Here's hoping they beat Miles to the punch.

5

"Here you go." BB tendered the last bits of the Memories are Made of This potion to Josie, hidden within her favorite cocktail. "I'll be right back. Gonna go give Mama a helping hand in the kitchen." BB hoped the tonic would tide her sister over until she returned from the Starless Souk.

After changing into warmer attire to prepare for chaosnauting—jeans, thick hoodie, and combat boots—BB inserted her nose ring stud back into place, secured her curly, medium-length, black locks into two space buns, then fastened her sling bag around her chest. *Time to pay that lying demon, Luksaan, a visit!*

Wind chimes faintly rang on the wraparound verandah at the back of the house. BB leaned over the kitchen sink and peered through the cracked window to the perimeter of her property, noting that not even a breeze tickled the leaves on the tree branches or blades of unchecked grass. The Budreau house was the sole residence on Chicory Lane and well-hidden at that. Trick-or-treaters wouldn't dare look for candy in this isolated area. Still, Halloween festivities weren't scheduled to begin for another few hours.

She closed her eyes and tuned into her surroundings like PK had taught her at Karma Academy. Creaking sounded near the mud room in the back, followed by the front door snicking to a close. The floor above BB grumbled. At least three hostiles were inside—could be more.

It looked like BB's plan of slipping out undetected wouldn't be happening. So, combat it was. The only problem: her nearly empty magic arsenal would have to be used sparingly. Unless …

BB grabbed hold of the tiny teardrop vial tied to a hemp cord secured around her elongated neck. Inside the vial resided a sliver of Goddess Karma's essence. She had swiped it from PK's secret stash of illicit and hard-to-come-by spell ingredients before she peaced-out of the Academy months ago, opting to take a break from serving as one of the goddess' Agents.

"GK, I swear my leave is only temporary," BB had promised Goddess Karma and meant it.

"It's all cosmic. Our BB'll be back better than ever," Sawyer had said in BB's defense to the enraged goddess. Alas, Sawyer's assurances had fallen on deaf ears.

If things were different, BB would have called upon her sisters, and they would have chaosnauted to her side in a heartbeat. But Karma had cut BB off from them and the Academy in retaliation for leaving. It had been months since she last saw or spoke to the other Agents.

BB removed the stopper, deeply inhaled Karma's power, and then quickly corked the vial. At once, the goddess' essence slithered up her nostrils and surged through her body, oxygenating every fiber of her being, purifying her blood, and energizing blood vessels, every organ rejuvenating and protected. Epithelial to endothelial cells fortified, their strength eclipsing the dragline silk of a Darwin's bark spider, which outranked Kevlar in toughness.

BB's brain electrified, and her entire being thrummed with vitality. Flames licked her pupils. A blink later, the fire stilled, and her eyes returned to their usual brown.

Depending on how many hostiles she had to fight, BB figured she had ten minutes max before the godlike powers would run out of steam, her body exhausted and needing recharging. So, she'd need a weapon as backup and knew precisely where to find one.

After hiding her bag, she wrapped a dishtowel around the bourbon bottle, then smashed it on the counter, its jagged teeth ready to tear into a jugular. Then she padded through the arched opening in the kitchen to the formal dining room, staying as quiet as a ghost. The chaospocket imprisoning her sister was in the next room over. A Hound of Hell stood a foot away from where BB needed to go—the chaospocket—making hand signals to his comrade. But where was the other vampire?

Placing magical defense wards around homes was a real money drainer; on top of that, they had to be recharged peri-odically—yet another cost. So BB had improvised by discreetly placing shards of mirrored surfaces near all points of entry and in various spots throughout the house.

While crouched down and out of sight, BB plucked out an enchanted makeup compact from her sling bag. Opening it ever so quietly, she rotated the mirror this way and that way, motions that allowed her to spy through the mirrored shards scattered about, seeking that which didn't belong—Gotcha! A Hound blocked the back exit. The mirror showed her the vamp she had spied in the living room near the chaospocket. Another on the stairs. One upstairs.

If BB cast heavy magics, they'd feel the shift in energy and isolate her location. But if she caused a ripple …

After fisting a grocery store receipt discarded on the dining table, she envisioned it changing matter in perfect clarity; green, red, violet, and blue vapor escaped the gem and swirled around the paper. The receipt vibrated, curled up into a ball, then a beat later, a newly formed stone that had some significant weight to it rested in her palm. She threw the rock into the kitchen. Through the compact, she watched the Hound in the living room run in that direction, down the main hallway.

BB bolted through the doorway connecting the dining area to the reading room and then slipped through the French doors to the living room. The shine coruscated, catching BB's attention, and she quickly hid the liquor bottle, then sliced the area with her athame.

As she dove into the chaospocket and sealed the opening, two vamps entered the living room, barking in Laramaic, their razor-sharp fangs on display. Though she could see them, the same wasn't true for them.

"BB, where'd you go?" Josie yelled from the covered porch.

"I'll be right there," thirteen-year-old memory BB said while skipping past current BB on her way to the front porch.

"Dinner's almost ready," Eloise shouted to the girls as if current BB weren't standing next to her mother in the kitchen.

BB jumped onto the counter and ran her fingers along the top of the cabinets, trying to locate the secreted revolver. *Found you!* She jumped back down.

Extracting something from a chaospocket to the waking world was a magic drainer and would use up the last of her gems. It came down to a life-or-death decision: side with caution or take a chance?

No risk, no reward, BB mentally repeated PK's words that he would drill into his students.

BB decided on the spot she'd take the risk. Before her eyes, the incorporeal gun transmogrified into physical form, the metal cold to the touch. She fed the revolver the last remaining silver-dipped bullets—three, to be exact—secured the handgun in the waistband of her jeans, then scrambled to the chaospocket exit.

One Hound stood on the stairs, preparing to climb to the second floor, his back to BB. Refusing to entertain the fear clenching her heart, she quietly sliced an opening into the chaospocket and snuck out. She swiped the bottle near the couch, crept up behind the vamp standing on the staircase, then stabbed the jagged glass into his neck, slashing his skin at the base of his skull.

BB jumped out of the way as the Hound crashed into the handrail. With no time to waste, she gripped his head and twisted it to the side until his neck broke—a temporary solution that incapacitated the bloodsucker. Eventually, she'd have to return and decapitate him, so he didn't rise again.

The noise alerted the others.

A Hound careened toward her in the living room, zipping through the air, feet out in front of him. BB folded her body backward. Just in time for the vamp to soar above and past her. When she righted her spine, another Hound kicked her in the abdomen, sending her soaring back first.

A sharp pain erupted as she landed smack dab in the glass window near the front door and fell onto the wood floor. The Hound that had punted her barreled her way, another joining his comrade.

In one fell swoop, BB kicked her legs directly into the air and landed in a squat.

She fired the revolver. *Boom!* The first bullet ran clear through his shoulder and slowed him down enough for Beatrice to land the second bullet right in the vamp's heart. He was down for the count.

As the other Hound charged down the hallway, BB pivoted, stared down the barrel, aiming right at his heart, then pulled the trigger. The vamp didn't see what was coming. Blackish blood spurted, and the Hound dropped to the floor.

Three down, one more to go.

As the last Hound bulleted in her direction, she legged it to the stairs and kicked the never-fixed rickety newel post with all her might. Then she grabbed a loosely hanging spindle from the handrail and broke it over her knee. Stake in hand, she was ready to take the vamp on.

When the Hound bypassed the stairs, she leapfrogged over the railing and landed on his back. BB shoved the wooden spindle into the vampire's chest with all her might.

"You little bitch!" growled the bloodsucker as an inky black substance surged through his veins and bled out his eyeballs. Beatrice helped him to the ground with a swift kick to his groin.

Feeling relieved that she took out all the Hounds of Hell before running out of Karma's powers, she tried to catch her breath. Unfortunately, Beatrice failed to notice a Hound sneak up on her from behind. Before she could act, he shoved her head into the wall, and she collapsed. Blood spurted out of her nose and trickled down her throat.

Blinking away stars occluding her vision, she got back on her feet and was ready to unleash her wrath on the vamp. But her arms betrayed her and wouldn't budge. An unseen force held her in place.

Fangs on display, the vamp yanked out the spindle from his fallen comrade's chest and went to stab BB in the heart. But his forward momentum stopped when the wood made contact with her skin, a rivulet of blood trickling down her chest.

"Now, now, Andre. You know the rules. Beatrice must live. For now," a disembodied male voice chided. "Doesn't mean we can't have some fun, though."

An invisible force thrust BB into the living room like a rag doll. Then it levitated her and thrust her arms out to the side, nailing her to the air. BB struggled to free herself but couldn't. And ended up in a nearly horizontal position, eyes facing the ground, as if belted inside a Multi-Axis Trainer. BB felt a force push her forehead, which righted her body to a vertical position.

A man entered her home through the front door. Thin in build, skin tanned, cheeks pockmarked, his ebony hair slicked back. The last time she had set sights on this man, he stood in her family restaurant, asking for Beatrice by name.

"Beatrice Budreau, you were a hard girl to locate." With his hands, he made a come-hither motion, and in response, BB's treacherous body dragged her toward him, stopping feet away. She hovered in place, her toes barely touching the ground.

At first, BB pegged the man as a human, but when his nails grew and narrowed into sharp points meant for slashing veins, she changed her mind and reassessed her attack strategy.

"My my, aren't you a pretty little thing." He placed his finger under her chin and raised her head, then inspected every inch of her, which skeeved her out. "Though not as pretty as your sister." This man's eyes were soulless, his energy a pool of utter darkness. "It's a pleasure to make your acquaintance. The name's Miles Leagan, and I'm the last person you'll see alive." He produced a silver dagger out of his coat pocket, the blade coated in a purple-blue, viscous matter that seemed to bubble like acid.

A yelp tore through Beatrice's throat as Andre bit her wrist and slurped down her blood.

"Ah-ha!" Miles scolded Andre. "Ease up on the bloodletting. We're to bring her back alive." Miles sliced BB's other wrist and drank as if BB were on tap.

High on Karma's powers, Miles' pupils dilated and rapidly quivered. "Whoa." Dizzy, he staggered but regained his balance just as quickly. "That was amazing." He looked downright euphoric, as if drugged-up to high Heaven. "Oh, the fun I'm gonna have with you."

BB could feel her life slipping through her fingers. She had to escape. But she couldn't move, let alone cast spells, so she pleaded to her ancestors, to her Mama and grandma.

A Helping Hand is always needed, she could hear her mama say.

Mama's Helping Hand spell. How could BB have forgotten? Her mama had discretely hidden the sigil for Air throughout the house.

Beatrice mumbled, a sound resembling the rustling of leaves. In response, sigils on the walls materialized and glowed a vibrant bluish-green. Not a moment later, Miles impaled BB, the knife coated in viscous matter slicing into her stomach. After a twist of the blade, he yanked out the dagger.

Her eyes agog, mouth agape, a vision of Beatrice's family flooded her mind and took away the agonizing pain for a brief moment.

Then the wind howled in the distance as it gained momentum, moth-eaten curtains billowing. Faster and faster, Air blew, sounding like a freight train. Shutters banged around the house; the front door slammed open, and then the back door.

Distracted, Miles lost control of the levitation spell, and BB collapsed to the floor right as the tornadic winds ripped down the hallway. Powering through the excruciating pain,

BB scrabbled to the staircase and held on for dear life, her body airborne. As Miles attempted to cast another incantation, his target BB, the cyclone whirled around the hostiles, snatched them up, and blew out of the farmhouse.

Her back to the wall near the stairs, BB applied pressure to her bloodied wrists and the gaping wound on her stomach, wondering how Miles broke through her godlike defenses. But then Karma's powers kicked in, and skin re-weaved over the jagged lacerations. Still, her energy felt off, siphoned, her legs heavy as if walking through water. How could this be?

Before escaping, BB tried to summon her sling bag to her location and anything else she needed, but nothing happened. Her magic was unresponsive. After she retrieved her backpack, BB staggered out the screened door and down the rotted wooden porch steps to the gravel driveway.

Her strength waning, she dragged her body to the abandoned garden overtaken with weeds, hitchhiker plants, and burrs. The rusted metal bench by the foul-smelling, algae-choked fountain swung lazily back and forth.

Her destination was close at hand: a windowless, tiny shed big enough for sundry garden equipment. Her bloodied palm on the knob, BB heard rustling in the woods to her right. She threw her eyes in the disturbance's direction, but it was a rabbit hopping about.

Something bit her ankle, and she jumped. But there was nothing there. Her hand shot to her heart. Her body nearly giving out, she leaned into the doorframe.

"You're almost to the Starless Souk," she whispered. "Luuksan will know what to do." The encouragement gave BB the boost of energy she needed, and she disappeared inside the shed.

"Did you seriously trip? Again?" Perrin snapped, then kicked Kimball in the shin. "You nearly ruined my plan!"

Moments ago, Perrin tossed an enchanted jump rope into the grass, its alternating yellow and white plastic tubes *click-click-clicking* as it crawled on the ground toward Beatrice before camouflaging itself from sight.

"The weeds are out of control. And I don't do woods," Kimball whined, "or whatever hicks do in the wilds of nature. And I have burrs all over my new vintage jeans. But hey, at least this chick isn't siding with Team Evil, so we have that in our favor. Amirite?"

"Wow, Sherlock. What gave that away?" Pepper snapped. "Beatrice's beat-up, bloodied body? Or did her fleeing the house clue you in?"

Kimball added, "After what happened with Sawyer and Jhi, you can't trust anyone—"

"Isn't that ironic? Snitch Kimball talking about trust." Perrin clenched her fists into balls, their normal position as of late.

Loki scampered back to the gang and chittered his findings with Pepper, which she shared with the others. "There's no sign of Miles or the Hounds. But a fight definitely went down inside."

"We don't even know if Beatrice is one of Karma's Agents," Perrin said. "And it's not like Karma referred to her as one. Need I remind you we are solely going on rat Kimball's word? What if the Agent of Karma list he said he saw isn't on the up and up?"

"I wasn't lying about seeing the list on my dad's desk!" Kimball spat.

Before chaosnauting to Georgia, Pepper tried to have Tavi suck out Kimball's brain matter to retrieve that memory so they could be one step ahead of Miles and Jhi, but it had failed to work. Perrin posited that a hex most likely interfered with Kimball's memory retrieval process.

Loki chittered his two cents and Pepper translated: "Loki just said that Miles isn't about to let Beatrice slip through his fingers, so chances are he's hot on her heels." Pepper spoke directly to Perrin. "I understand your hesitancy, but Miles is after Beatrice, right?" Perrin nodded. "So you agree that there's some credence to the Agent kill list?" Perrin sighed and nodded again. "Regardless of what Kimball thinks he saw or didn't, Goddess Karma handed me her marching orders to find Beatrice or else." Of its own accord, Pepper's hand sailed to the area on her cheek that still stung where Karma had slapped her when Pepper dared to defy the goddess' direct order and opted to rescue her pops instead.

"My jump rope tagged Beatrice's heels, but the tracking spell only works if we're in the general proximity of the target."

"There's obviously a gate inside that shed, and it's gonna disappear if we don't hurry," Pepper said and started walking toward the garden.

"Wait!" Perrin called out. "We need to think long and hard before blindly following Beatrice. Just because she might be an Agent of Karma doesn't mean she's on our side. Did everyone forget about Sawyer?"

"I agree, Perrin," Pepper said. "But listen, we have no other choice. I know we're all exhausted, but there's a good reason Karma demanded that I find Beatrice. She has to know something, like how to find Jaylyn and stop the Syndicate." Finding Beatrice meant Pepper could finally refocus her efforts on rescuing her dad.

Loki nodded assent and climbed onto Pepper's shoulders. "Two against one," Pepper said.

Perrin huffed, "Full disclosure. If we get stuck in Mother Lilith knows where, I'm gonna lose it and probably kill

Kimball. I'm hungry, tired, haven't bathed in a few days, my dress is dirty, the crinoline is ripped. And never will I ever eat a Shi'rue-awful, butter-slathered biscuit or convenience store pizza again."

"Hey, what about me? Don't I count? And what about my mom?"

"You are a rat, Kimball, and our prisoner, so no, you don't get a vote," Perrin barked while Pepper shot daggers at Kimball. "And your mother is a ball of vapor stuck in an empty vodka bottle. So no, she doesn't get a vote either." Perrin sighed. "Fine. Let's go. But rattilocks goes first."

They gingerly entered the shed and were greeted by a dirt floor, busted flower pots, and torn open bags of mulch. The archway of the ever-active chaosgate was feet away. Arcane sigils thrummed along its rectangular frame, a bloody hand-print on the wall.

"Lovely. Inter-dimensional travel it is." Perrin wiped the dirt off her Mary Janes and inhaled deeply, preparing for the worst. "This could lead us anywhere in the cosmos. Better not be Hell, or we're fuh'kared."

"The gate's still active. No directional, though," Kimball said.

"There's one, but it's hidden from our sight. So, shut up and push the button before the little demonic parasites devour all of Beatrice's sacrificial blood." Perrin kicked Kimball in the back, and he lurched forward.

Kimball smacked the nondescript round button that resembled one found in a standard elevator. In response, the doors glided open. Pepper and the gang thundered inside the stark white elevator as the doors snapped shut.

Weapons at the ready, off they went, tossed like a frisbee to their doom for all Pepper knew.

6

The instant the rukba abruptly stopped, Kimball hurled in the corner, spittle landing on Perrin's Mary Jane's stitched from the skin of the damned.

Her eyes reflecting murderous intent, Perrin stood stock still, took a measured breath, and readjusted the askew headband on her raven black locks. "Someone remind me again why we're keeping numb nuts alive."

"He's more valuable alive than dead," Loki responded matter-of-factly, his voice silky and deep, like a disc jockey.

"Well, look at that. Our little furball can talk," Perrin said, eyes wide with amazement.

Before "What the …?" flew off Pepper's lips, the ruachti scampered out of the rukba as the doors parted. Pepper and the others followed suit.

A tingling sensation surged within Pepper, causing the hairs on her arms and legs to stand at attention, and lasted all of a second. Perrin must have felt the same sensation because she stared at her hands, flipping them back and forth as if she had slipped into new skin.

Slack-jawed, Pepper spun around, taking in her surroundings. A bank of rukbas occupied an entire wall behind her with a revolving door of countless beings coming and going. Above, wet smears of deep purples, reds, and blues like a bruise painted the sky. Comets sailed across the heavens, ultraviolet colors left in their wake for a beat before exploding and fizzling out of sight like fireworks.

Below, a sprawling bazaar unfurled and splintered into various narrow passageways. Vivid-hued fabric served as roofs and partitions for storefronts and kiosks. A deafening chorus of barkers jockeyed for attention with passersby, their enchanted wares on full display.

"Welcome to Mythe Nummthyr." Loki sounded as if he had spoken with a mouthful of peanut butter, and his tongue was stuck to the roof of his mouth. He briefly explained that Mythe Nummthyr—roughly translated to the Starless Souk— was an area within Cal'lya-mír, an elven dimension. "Be careful! We're in my dimension. And things are not always as they seem. The fae are not to be trusted, and magic is free to wield." And by *the fae*, Loki referred to non-humans except for a few, like ghosts and jinn.

Then Loki described the Starless Souk as a black market of sorts where beings of all types and from all dimensions exchanged goods and services, some illicit, others rare. It was like the Wild West of the magical world. "Anything goes here. No rules. And magic is permitted."

There were so many beings milling about, most bipedal, some not, that Pepper had never even laid eyes on before, only in books, from elves to axe-carrying dwarves to pint-sized, caped goblins to—"Is that a ghost?" Pepper whispered to Loki. He nodded affirmatively, and she replied, "Huh."

Then there was an even mixture of what could pass as

Earthly humans, or perhaps some were elves as they appeared humanlike, save for their ears, but they could easily glamour away those tapered points.

At first, the multiple languages spoken were foreign to Pepper until they weren't. She could understand every word, reminiscent of when Jhi had implanted the Lingua Franca spider in her cerebral cortex, enabling her to understand Laramaic. Pepper's heart sunk anew with that remembrance. Whether or not she cared to admit it, she had fallen for Jhi, had trusted him fully, which made her cringe from shame. But that was old Pepper. New Pepper looked forward to the day she'd exact vengeance on that no-good, rotten, lying SOB.

Perrin "ugh"d and her eyes rolled to the back of her head when a half-naked female pranced by, while Kimball appreciated every ounce of the woman's body. "Fuh'karing succubi. They're gonna prey on rattilocks. Listen to the words I'm speaking"—Perrin spoke slowly, eyes focused on Kimball—"don't eat, don't drink a fuh'karing morsel, or drop of anything they attempt to give you. Don't even speak a word —You know what"—she tossed her hands in the air—"I'm not leaving anything to chance. Rattilocks needs to be muzzled." The moment Perrin spoke, a muzzle formed over Kimball's face.

Kimball squirmed and attempted to rip the device off and failed. When he tried to vocalize his anger, he couldn't.

"Oh my Goddess Seren, you bless me so!" Perrin rejoiced, her hand covering her heart. "I can use magic freely! Take that, gems." Perrin sashayed in place, the hem of her dress swishing around her bobby-socked legs, her smile eating up half of her face. "I think a collar and leash would totally complete the ensemble. What do you guys think?" Just like that, her wish was granted. "Now ties for rattilocks' hands so he can't steal food." Ties materialized and wrapped around

Kimball's wrists. "Best. Day. Ever!" Perrin finished with a twirl.

"How did you do that if we used all our gems?" Pepper held the drawstring pouch before her, the clear vaporless marbles clinking within.

Perrin's brows raised. "Don't know. Don't care."

Not having the bandwidth for another mystery to solve, Pepper dropped the oddity. "Speaking of gems, we need more. I wonder if they accept crypto." Pepper already knew the answer was a big fat no.

"We can worry about that later. Time to find Beatrice," said Loki.

"We accept crypto, fleshies, soul shards, gems, hammered locwas ..." a female singsonged. The heavenly sounding voice was a siren to Kimball's sailor, and rattilocks navigated toward the female as if walking the plank moments from being tossed overboard.

The female elf sat before a vanity, brushing her silver locks with an ornate brush, her pointed ears peeking out. Her perfectly symmetrical face, sharp cheeks, and angular nose were powdered to perfection. There was a regal air about her, and the circlet balanced atop her head bolstered that vibe.

"You were totally right, Perrin, said nobody!" Perrin yanked Kimball's leash, and he crashed into the Lolly'ka.

"Yoo-hoo," the shopkeeper sang, her eyes anchored on Kimball. "Let me run my brush through your unkempt locks. After a few swipes, your curls will glisten like spun gold." The elf then shifted her attention to Perrin. "And for you, my dolly, I have the perfect shade of rouge to make your azure eyes radiate their splendor even more. Or perhaps I can tempt you with an every-shade lip gloss or lipstick." That caught Perrin's attention, and the elven female demonstrated her product. "Speak the desired shade, and voila! It appears."

After swiping the wand across the elf's plump lips, the magenta color melted into an iridescent hue.

Perrin allowed the elf to rub what resembled rose petals on her cheeks and lips. Utterly mesmerized, Perrin enjoyed admiring her rosy cheeks in the vanity mirror affixed to a makeup table.

Loki stood on his hind legs and chastised the elf.

The elf blew a raspberry, then said, "You're no fun." Then she broke the spell she had cast with a wave of her hand. The net that ensnared Perrin and Kimball left, and the duo swayed and stumbled into each other. "My name is Lora'lie. Should you two change your mind, I'm here until I'm not."

A tongue-tied Kimball drunkenly giggled in response, then chuckled through his gag and mumbled, "Ha mmh ba pwaay." The gag dissolved, and Kimball gulped down the air. "Looks like you're the prey, too, Perrin." He then held out his manacled wrists.

Perrin told the girl she'd be back and then shifted her attention to Pepper, ignoring Kimball, "What? So she compelled me. I'm exhausted and fungry, and, quite frankly, Kimball is trying my patience."

"Okay, but we need to focus. Beatrice could be anywhere." Pepper scanned the environment.

In Laramaic, guttural in sound, Perrin whispered for her jump rope to reveal itself and to guide the gang to the target. A faint yellow-and-white line appearing like an afterglow materialized on the cobblestone ground.

Like a path of crumbs, Pepper and the gang followed the trail. They navigated through narrow alleyways, passing kiosk after kiosk, selling everything from weapons to bizarre magical ingredients. Pepper speedily bought in bulk a dangerously sharp dagger, vampire-destroying silver-dipped stakes, blades, and sunbursters.

Beatrice's trail ended at the next shop they passed—GAUL'S GALLIPOT, written in glistening gold—that offered a hodgepodge of herbs, sundry ingredients, artifacts, instruments, enchanted items, delicious-looking food, candy, ornate petits fours, and inviting libations housed in fanciful cups.

"Now what? Beatrice can be anywhere," Perrin said as her eyes swept through the crowd.

"Wait here. I'll be back," Loki said before scampering off.

Pepper's stomach growled. Unable to help herself, she went to stuff a sample into her mouth, but Perrin shouted, "Pepper, stop!" and grabbed her hand. "No touching or eating. The fae can't be trusted, remember?" The Lolly'ka was clearly a tad butt-hurt after falling prey to Lora'lie's spell.

"Now, now, Lolly'ka," the proprietor teased. "I guess I could say don't befriend your kind, or you'll get eaten or killed. The order matters not." The wizened old man floated from the far corner of his shop to where Pepper and Perrin were standing, his midnight-blue robe adorned by speckled owl feathers skirting the ground. "Though I must admit, you're not entirely wrong. Those libations are of the poisoned variety."

The hoary wizened fellow's long spindly hair and an equally long beard traveled down the robe's length. His wild brows were plaited at each end and curtained his beetle-black eyes free of scleras.

"Pepper." He said her name as if he were tasting the eponymous spice. "What an interesting name. It's an essential ingredient in alchemy. Poisoners add it to various concoctions to … ensure absorption."

Pepper nodded and mouthed, "Wow." But inside, she felt discomfited. It wasn't so much the items this man sold—actually, those were downright creepy—but how his eyes crackled with curiosity when he looked at Pepper. And he didn't just look at her but inspected and clearly deduced something when one side of his mouth quirked upward or when he nodded in agreement to no one in particular.

"I go by Gaul. If there's anything I can interest you in, please don't hesitate to ask." He only spoke to Pepper, his eyes glued to her. "I offer the rarest of poisonous ingredients. If killing or incapacitating isn't on the agenda, I have every herb imaginable for potions, hexes, and enchantments."

After giving his offerings a cursory search, Pepper filled baggies with the top items on her shopping list: magic gems. Then she moved on to the mundane that made up a mage's starter kit: dried medicinal mushrooms, belladonna, mugwort, lavender, chamomile, frankincense, myrrh, gotu kola, and dried blue lotus.

Next on her shopping list were spontaneous purchases. Quickly, she grabbed River Lethe water, lu'kowsa scales, dragon blood, ectoplasm measured in dollops, and bottled lightning. She wasn't sure why she chose those spell ingredients other than going on instinct alone.

A jinn's unspent wish commanded prime real estate on its own shelf, under a spotlight, with an ASK A CLERK FOR PRICING sign hanging underneath.

"How much for one of those?" Perrin asked, pointing at a smattering of mirrors of various shapes, sizes, and conditions, including vintage-looking handheld ones, in the back of the shop while the clerk rang up Pepper's items.

"They are not for sale," Gaul said sternly.

One mirror, in particular, caught Pepper's attention—full length and unassuming in appearance, yet undeniably old, the silver in the throes of tarnishing. But it wasn't just the mirror. Something beyond the glass darkly, beyond her reflection, summoned her.

A supernatural force tugged Pepper toward the speculum. She could feel her feet moving, but she wasn't the captain.

Standing before the mirror, she instinctively relaxed her eyes, and her reflection disappeared, allowing her to peer inside the mirror.

Gaul appeared to stand directly behind her, peering over her shoulder. But when Pepper turned her head, he was in the shop's front, assisting another patron.

"… eeelllo?" Pepper snapped to full alertness as Perrin waved her hand in front of her face. "Vain much? Fuh'kar's sake. Loki found Beatrice. C'mon." Perrin yanked a still-dazed Pepper onward.

Confused, Pepper didn't recall walking toward the mirror, let alone standing in front of it, apparently gaping.

"Do come see me again, Pepper," Gaul said, smirking.

Pepper crouched down behind a wall, joining Loki. He pointed down the major artery, about fifteen storefronts from their hiding spot. They watched Beatrice yank a demon by the collar and drag his pencil-thin body over a counter—

Kimball jabbed his elbow into Pepper's arm as his hands struggled to break free from their ties.

"Ow! What's your prob—" A sharp inhale cut off Pepper's words and knocked her heart out of rhythm when her eyes sailed to precisely what had grabbed Kimball's attention. Jhi!

The no-good, rotten liar stood not thirty feet away from Pepper. And he brought along company of the vampire variety. After Jhi delivered orders that amounted to hand signals pointing this way and that way, the Hounds dispersed. Once the fanged ones were out of eyeshot, a man materialized next to Jhi. He didn't stand on the ground but hovered in place, yet he wasn't a ghost; Pepper could tell that much. From a quick lip-reading, Jhi referred to this man as Friday.

While Jhi and his companion conspired, Pepper mentally noted the stranger's features before he vanished: early to mid-twenties; dark, smoldering eyes; black hair; copper skin with a smattering of tattoos and leather arm cuffs; wiry goatee; built like an MMA fighter; clothed in everyday attire, except for the tunic that seemed a bit dated and the scimitars holstered to each hip. He was dangerously attractive and the type to avoid at all costs to stave off heartache, like Jhi, a lesson Pepper had learned the hard way.

Loki twirled his quarterstaff like quicksilver in a figure-eight pattern, and in response, shadows left their dark corridors and slithered on the ground toward their summoner, looking like a knot of snakes. That caught Jhi's attention, and he stopped conversing with Friday and whipped out his staff, trying to one-up Loki and steal the shadows' attention.

Loki sped off like a fired bullet to Beatrice. Moments later, he and Beatrice vanished a second before a Hound of Hell grabbed her.

Jhi huffed and swore, his nostrils flaring, then looked away. And that's when he spotted Pepper, a sly grin pulling at the corners of his lips. He purred toward her, his motions fluid and agile, the jack-of-all-weapons strapped to his back, peeking over his shoulder. He slipped out of his beanie and tucked it into the back pocket of his jeans, freeing his brown hair threaded with a cinnamon hue.

Cassia cinnamon does wonders when trying to poison someone slowly, Pepper thought instinctively.

Though his build was athletic, five-foot-eleven of pure corded muscle, Jhi appeared to have lost a few pounds since Pepper last saw him, which was a day ago, his cheeks sunken in, bags under his eyes. *Good!* Pepper thought. Then again, she seemed to have gained what he had lost. *Damn you, stress-eating.*

He halted his forward momentum; the width of a sidewalk was all that separated them.

Hatred and sadness, disgust and the stirrings of love, guilt and shame for wanting to touch Jhi and feel his pillowy lips on hers, to feel the warmth of his hands on her body, exploring her curves, warred within her. Until hatred bested them all.

Tightly gripping her newly purchased dagger, Pepper charged toward Jhi, vengeance her fuel.

7

Time to pay, Jhi. Pepper squeezed the dagger to prepare to gut the backstabbing bastard. Then took one step forward and another—

A force propelled Pepper backward, her dagger clanging on the hard cobblestone.

Jhi plucked up what was moments from piercing his flesh, inspected the weapon thoughtfully, then waved it tauntingly at Pepper.

Pepper struggled to free herself from the lasso coiled around her torso.

"Soon, but not today, killer. Beatrice trumps your revenge," Perrin said sternly. "I'll release the yo-yo if you promise to de-feralize yourself." After Pepper nodded, Perrin went through with her end of the deal and shoved the yo-yo back into her patent leather purse. "Holy Mother Lilith, what were you thinking?"

Teary-eyed, frustrated, terrified, blazing with the anger of a thousand suns, Pepper couldn't formulate a response, at least not a logical one. A dark presence seemed to have taken over.

Grinning wickedly, Jhi saluted Pepper and Perrin before cloaking himself in the shadows and disappearing from sight.

Not a moment later, a rug burn-like pain assaulted Pepper's upper back, *jab-jab-jabbing* into her skin, then stopped. Before she could wrap her head around what caused that discomfort, a supernatural force flung her body into Gaul's Gallipot. Writhing and fighting against whatever held her in place, Pepper screamed for help as she flew toward the looking glass that had stolen her attention earlier.

In the mirror's reflection, Pepper eyed Gaul's powerful arms around her, acting like chains, but in reality, Gaul was nowhere near her. As for her shrieks, of course, nobody could hear Pepper, for skin stitched over her mouth, swallowing it from sight.

While trying to rip away the flesh from her lips, a burning sensation flared on her hand, drops of blood marring the stone floor. Before Pepper knew it, Gaul slammed her bloody palm on the mirror's surface. As the glass liquified, blood-red sigils adorned with intricate knots and animated whorls and slashes glowed fiercely on the surface. Then Gaul shoved Pepper into the looking glass.

Perrin and Kimball pounded on the mirror. Pepper struck the other side, but she couldn't tell if they could see her. She cried out for help, but her friends couldn't hear her either. Gaul tossed a rock at the mirror. The glass shattered, trapping Pepper inside the looking glass.

Blinding white brightness stung Pepper's eyes. She blinked uncontrollably to chase away the stinging pain and get her eyes accustomed to the light, but the afterimages occluded her sight.

She stumbled around the confined area, the walls feeling

like they were closing in on her. Her arms could not extend outward, and her breathing became shallower and constricted.

Tears welled down her cheeks, some from the pain, others from fear. Once the afterimages died down, Pepper opened her eyes. Shards of glass were everywhere: the floor, the ceiling, the walls. Light emanating from nowhere refracted off every sliver, bouncing here and there.

Then came the noise. The ear-piercing babel of voices felt like daggers stabbing her eardrums. Pepper cupped her hands over her ears, hoping to smother the cacophony. No such luck. So she crouched down, nearly succumbing to defeat.

So very cold.

All alone.

Forever trapped.

Then pin-drop silence. The light was still bright, but at least Pepper could make out her surroundings.

She wiped away the spilled tears with the heels of her palms and stood up, breathing in wads of snot. Before her, a hallway unfurled into infinity. If she thought about the cramped confines of the hallway, she'd succumb to a claustrophobic attack.

Breathe, just breathe, kiddo. Pepper could hear her dad's comforting words. So she listened.

Plumes of her breath were visible as Pepper clenched her cloak tighter, burying her hands in the coat pockets. And as her heartbeat regulated, mirrors appeared on the walls every few feet on either side.

Though Pepper wore sneakers, she wasn't sure if the soles were powerful enough to withstand pointy shards of glass. She had no other choice but to test the ground. One hesitant step later, no glass cracked or crunched under her feet. Curious, Pepper inspected the floor and the walls. The shards appeared as mountains with deadly peaks. But in actuality, the glass was smooth to the touch.

Pepper stood before a random mirror and couldn't see out. Nor could she see her reflection. "Okay, Mirror Realm. How do I get out of here?"

An image of the vanity mirror at Lora'lie's Enchantery flashed in her mind. Organically, Pepper recalled the shop in as much detail as she could muster. An instant later, humming echoed through the mirrored hallway. Pepper padded toward the singsonging until she reached a recognizable face. Lora'lie crooned while lovingly brushing her glistening silver tresses and admiring her reflection.

Pepper touched the chilled, glassy surface and continued to push through. Warmth cocooned her flesh as her finger appeared on the other side of the mirror.

Lora'lie jumped with fright and fell off the stool.

Then Pepper pulled back her hand to ensure it remained intact.

The softest lilting of off-key music hitchhiked on the molecules of frigid air. A gentle singing joined the discordant tune. Whoever the voice belonged to, they were far away.

But the moment Pepper directed her attention to the melody, it stopped.

Something felt off. Wrong.

Panic-stricken, Pepper dove through the mirror.

But midway through, a claw grabbed hold of her foot, its talons digging into her heel as it tried to yank her back inside the Mirror Realm.

Pepper glanced back but couldn't see who or what it was. She kicked and fought with all her might.

It wasn't until Lora'lie grabbed Pepper's hands and tugged that a battle of strength took place, Lora'lie vs. the creature. One final heave-ho and a grunt later, Lora'lie won the war.

"How'd you do that?" a gobsmacked Lora'lie asked Pepper. "I've never seen such sorcery." The elf investigated the vanity and poked her finger at it curiously, but it flicked off the hard surface.

As Pepper climbed off the desk, she sent stacked makeup palettes flying. They landed on the floor in an explosion of rainbow glitter. "I'm so sorry," Pepper said. Her knee then struck a glass perfume bottle, which knocked over its siblings in a domino effect, and they all crashed to their death, their cloying aromas assaulting the noses of pedestrians nearby. To make matters worse, a trail of shimmery blood marred the desk's surface, courtesy of the bloodied gash on Pepper's ankle. The wound would've gone bone deep if Pepper had stayed a second longer.

Perrin's yellow-and-white jump rope manacled around Pepper's ankles, the plastic tubing pinching her skin and further irritating her gaping wound.

Perrin caught up to Pepper after following the jump rope's trail. "Thank Seren!" Then noted Pepper's ankle. "What the fuh'kar happened?"

Pepper wasn't exactly sure herself, but she spat out everything that had occurred.

"When calling out her name, you must do so thrice, then look beyond what you see," Perrin singsonged. "If she believes you worthy, then passage awaits. If not, so long, farewell to thee. Bloody Mary, Bloody Mary, Bloody Mary." Perrin finished with a maniacal chuckle.

"Are you serious?" A chill reverberated through Pepper's whole body.

"No. You're so gullible. Bloody Mary's just an urban legend, sweetling. You most likely ran into a wraith. Terrible beasties, on par with wanderers as far as bloodlust goes—"

"We have to get out of here," a disembodied Loki interrupted, cloaked from sight. "We eliminated a few Hounds hot on Perrin's heels. But more will follow."

Right before Pepper's eyes, Beatrice materialized in the graveyard of glittery makeup, her body crumpled in a heap on the ground.

"What happened?" Pepper noted a rip in Beatrice's sweatshirt and dried blood around the area and on her hands.

"From what I can tell, there isn't a fresh wound. Not anywhere." Loki's eyes radiated worry.

"Help me up," Beatrice breathed with a slight Southern twang.

A handful of Hounds stood sentry before the bank of rukbas, blocking the only point of escape.

Pepper quickly hid behind a display table of sundry cosmetics and ushered for the others to do the same. And just in time, too, for Jhi showed up and pointed commands to his fanged underlings. Some Hounds stayed in place, while others broke up in duos. But Jhi's orders were clear: find Beatrice.

Out of nowhere, a Hound snuck up on the gang and grabbed Beatrice.

Perrin lassoed the air molecules around the vamp with her jump rope, creating a makeshift invisible box, trapping the vamp inside.

"We have a few minutes before the molecules wake up from their slumber and the jail crumbles," Perrin said.

"I know a way out," Beatrice cried out.

With Perrin's help, Pepper attempted to lift Beatrice's body upright. Though Beatrice was thin in build, she must have been all muscle, for getting her to her feet was a struggle. Pepper attempted to breathe through the agony and limp to safety, but her foot screamed in protest. So Kimball took over the reins.

Beatrice navigated them through the bazaar while artfully dodging Jhi and the Hounds.

Many twists and turns later, Pepper and the gang left the souk and landed under a canopy of trees with a nearby babbling stream cutting through the soft downy grass. Beatrice used one of the gargantuan red trunks as a brace, needing a moment to rest before—

Beatrice produced a gun. "Tell me who you are, or I'll shoot!"

"Oh, shit!" Kimball backed up, hands raised.

"Put the gun down. We're not your enemies," Pepper pleaded.

Beatrice cocked the gun in response.

With her hands up, Pepper replied softly, "Goddess Karma sent me to find you. My name is Pepper, and my sister Jaylyn is missing, and we need your help to find her."

Beatrice barked, "What do you know about the goddess?"

"I'm an Agent, like you, or technically an Initiate, I don't know. Listen, we don't have much time to explain. A demonic regime called the Syndicate has been unleashed from Hell and declared war on Earth. We think they've assassinated most of your fellow Agents, and you're the last on their list. Goddess Karma ordered me to find you before the Syndicate took you out. That's who's after you. And they won't stop looking for you, Beatrice. Not until you're dead. And after they're done with you, they plan on killing Karma and assuming her cosmic mantle of judge, jury, and executioner." Pepper finally took a breath.

Beatrice's arm almost lowered until Perrin said, "Y'know, we risked our lives to help you. So you could at least show some gratitude." Kimball seconded that with a head nod.

"You're not the only one who's in danger. None of us here are safe." Loki jumped in to remedy what Perrin might have ruined. "We have nowhere to run and nowhere to hide, just like you. We're united by a common goal—to stop the Syndicate dead in their tracks."

"But we can't do it alone, Beatrice." Pepper took back the reins. "The Syndicate's getting stronger by the day and building an unstoppable army of powerful and well-connected allies on Earth and in Hell. So we need to do the same. As it stands, Jaylyn is the only one who has answers. The only one who possibly holds the key to stopping the Syndicate. We believe you were the last person she reached out to. You're our last hope of finding her and saving the dimensions."

Beatrice blinked back the terror that held her eyes wide open and tucked the gun into the waistband of her jeans. Then she pulled down her sweatshirt's collar, revealing a golden-hued tattoo on her chest in the shape of the Karma Academy emblem—a broken infinity symbol. Only this tattoo appeared sentient and thrummed with vitality the closer Beatrice's fingers ventured to it.

When she pinched her skin along the area where the linear line ran underneath the broken infinity loops in a forward direction, the pressure forced a section of the tail to jut out, and Beatrice grabbed it. With an audible wince, she extracted a replica of the emblem from underneath her skin. The wispy, vaporous design dangled from her fingers, blood clouding the once-golden hue.

The Agent of Karma tossed the broken infinity insignia to the wind. Where it landed, a doorway materialized, its archway licked by flames. A blast of heat blew back Pepper's bangs and ebony locks. The emblem pulsated at the top of the archway, serving as a directional.

"Karma Academy doesn't take kindly to the uninvited. Neither does Karma." Beatrice's warning came through loud and clear.

"That shouldn't be a problem anymore because your

goddess is most likely dead," Kimball responded matter-of-factly.

8

Reverent silence filled the airwaves of a nonagon-shaped lobby where the rubka had disgorged Pepper and the others. An exit was nowhere to be found. And if the passengers had designs on turning tail, they were fat out of luck because the inter-dimensional transporter had zipped away.

The distinct aroma of aromatic oils encompassed the lofty lobby, the sweet and resinous scent belonging to none other than myrrh. In the dead center, an elephantine brazier, its metal bowl licked by hellfire flames, served as equal parts incense diffuser and platform for a life-size effigy of Goddess Karma. Myrrh resin was sprawled out at Karma's feet like an oblation, the amber-hued, rock-like crystals burning, their ambrosial-imbued smoke coiling upward and limning the goddess.

As for Karma's likeness, the artist had carved it out of an element not of Pepper's world as it was fleshy and appeared lifelike, at least from the brief, one and only time Pepper had met the goddess. Her oval-shaped visage bespoke unparalleled beauty, her features perfectly symmetrical—full lips, heaven-high cheekbones, slim nose, and almond-shaped eyes, her unblemished, buffed skin a darker shade of brown than Pepper. A stunning lehenga swathed her slender form and long graceful limbs. Iron-straightened locks of liquid blackness traveled down the goddess' back.

In one hand, the goddess held the Scales of Justice, and in the other, the golden Sword of Truth that shone brightly like the sun. But one item was missing from the goddess' ensemble: the blindfold. Freed from that constricting fabric, Karma could observe all and sundry.

There was a bite to Karma, a mercurial yin-yang vibe. Her splendor would lull you into submission, where she'd bestow upon the worthy a kiss. Then, in a snap, you could balance on the precipice of her double-edged Sword of Truth, where the cooly detached goddess would be hot on your heels, bent on retribution, homicidal rage reflecting in her coal-burning eyes. Hell hath no fury like Karma scorned.

A ubiquitous whisper emanated from the effigy, an "I saw that," like a promise of forthcoming vengeance. Pepper's lips quirked into a half-smile. If she wasn't mistaken, the goddess seemed to toss a cheeky wink at Pepper from her celestial perch.

"Whatcha gazing at, sweetling?" Perrin sidled up next to Pepper.

"Karma." Pepper wouldn't be removing her dopey grin anytime soon.

"Where?"

Oddly enough, nobody except Pepper and Beatrice could see the statue of Goddess Karma, something Beatrice noted but remained mum.

When a wall glided open, Beatrice insisted that she'd go

first and limped over the threshold. Once she was a good enough distance away, she stopped abruptly near a blossoming fruit tree, its pyramidal, fuzzy fruit sparkling in the sunlight, then ushered the rest to follow, her brow raised in anticipation.

Whatever Beatrice had up her sleeve, Pepper cared not. Instead, she allowed her soaring heart to propel her across the barrier and into the bowels of Karma Academy.

Finally, Pepper had arrived!

While standing in an open-air atrium, Pepper's eyes bounced around. Where to start? At first blush, the Academy wasn't what she had imagined. Where ancient met otherworldly, a modern temple sprawled out before her. Not a sharp edge could be found within the structure. Regarding aesthetics, elements of nature touched every inch of the institution, from stone to wood to glass to fire, and the furnishings and walls were awash in neutral shades of rich browns and creams.

A smattering of wooden moon bridges populated the atrium, and underneath, running streams cut through the stone paving and wended their way into various reflective pools. Lanterns containing flickering flames hung in the air by magic alone and bobbed about on an invisible current. A multi-story waterfall gently cascaded into a pond.

Pepper craned her head skyward. Continuous spiraling glass ramps began at the third floor and traveled upward like a stretched Slinky to the rooftop that spanned the length of the circular Academy in toto. Fern-type plants hung down from the edges of the floors like curtains, so long their fronds that Pepper could swing on them or climb them should the desire strike her. Now, if they could hold her weight, that was another topic altogether. Also, who was Pepper kidding? Climbing equated to exercise, and that sounded downright exhausting.

Vines with vibrant gem-colored flowers, some giving Perrin's engorged head a run for its money, and moss colonized many of the walls. Hedges seemed to serve as railings on various levels. That was a tad disconcerting. After a few Grissel's ales, students could easily fall to their death. The richly oxygenated air tasted and smelled divine. Pepper, grinning as if drunk on ale, deeply inhaled the rich, earthy scents and felt a euphoric high buzzing through her skull, her cells enlivening. No wonder the plants were massive.

A sizzling sound in the distance snagged Pepper's attention. A familiar sight stared back. A row of plants girding the edge of a pond bore an uncanny resemblance to the firebush in Hell but with some striking dissimilarities in appearance. About ankle-high, their long cat-tail-like leaves swatted the water's surface, then sizzled and drew back just as quickly. Unlike its relative, this species didn't have flames that danced on the plant's nearly translucent, paper-white leaves that were so sharp they'd slice your finger right off if you weren't careful. Nor did this shrub spit out fireballs. At least not yet. But the leaves sure were hot to the touch.

Pepper took her eyes off her surroundings long enough to notice that the gang had joined her in the atrium.

Beatrice groused with a slight Southern twang, "What the …? I don't understand."

"What were you expecting? That we'd explode?" Perrin asked.

Beatrice replied with a slow nod.

"Can't say I expected that response," Perrin said. "Sorry to disappoint."

"The Academy's heavily warded. If y'all had ill intentions, you would've been a pool of blood and guts the moment you entered the atrium," Beatrice said, more to herself as she rested her back against a wall. Her face pinched from pain, but she seemed to power through it. "And I haven't properly thanked y'all for saving my life. But in my defense, I've had a day. Was nearly killed by a homicidal maniac. So forgive me if I'm not fully trustin' of strangers."

"We know. Ran into Discount Dexter ourselves, when"—noting Beatrice's face screwing up into confusion, Kimball added, "er, Miles, when he killed your sister. But then she—"

"What? No! I locked her away." A mental war played out on Beatrice's face—doubt vs. certainty. Beatrice fainted and crashed to the floor.

"See, sweetling, and my little ball of fur." Perrin's baby blues chastised Pepper and Loki equally. "This was why I wanted to sew Kimball's mouth shut back at the souk. But no! Nobody listens to Perrin. Except for my sisters. You all should take notes from the Lolly'kas."

"She came back to life is what I was *this close* to saying," Kimball whined. "Jeez! How did I know she'd get all hysterical and collapse?"

Loki scampered to Beatrice and then vocalized, "Her heart rate is steady." Apparently, in this dimension, Loki could communicate with everyone, too.

A massive railless staircase unfurled feet away from where Pepper stood; a wood-slatted divider that ran from floor to ceiling separated the stairs in half and led to different corridors, one to the right and one left.

"Hello!" Pepper's echo in triplicate replied to her. She turned her attention back to the others. "Where is everybody?"

A swarm of dragonflies fluttered Pepper's way and landed on the ferns and hedge railings. One even landed on Pepper's finger. Their glistening gossamer wings mimicked the vibrant gem hues of the flowering vines and strange fruits hanging from the various trees sprinkled around.

"You've gotta be fuh'karing kidding me." Perrin stomped her patent leather shoes on the stone floor. "I just tried to magic that candy-looking fruit to my mouth, and it wouldn't budge. I hate it here!"

"I don't know if it's where we're at or a defense mechanism, but something's definitely preventing us from casting magic," Loki shared.

The day was getting better and better.

"You think we're in Hell?" Pepper asked the demons, her thumb jerking toward the firebush-esque plants.

"If only," Perrin responded while scooping water in her palms from a pond.

"No," Loki replied, absolute certainty coating his tone.

"Wakey-wakey," Perrin cooed to Beatrice as she poured water over the Agent's face, but Beatrice remained KO'd. "Dear Lilith, give me strength." Perrin deeply inhaled, dried her hands on the front of her frilly white-and-green dress, then screamed in Beatrice's face, "Wake the fuh'kar up!"

"Ack!" Beatrice coughed as she sprung upright. Woozy, her body swayed. Before she kissed the ground again, Pepper and Perrin grabbed her arms. "Somethin's very, very wrong. Somebody should have greeted us by now." Beatrice's face twisted into a rictus of agony.

"Why'd you bring us here?" Pepper asked.

"Because it's safe—" She yelped and put pressure on her stomach, a few tears leaking from her eyes. "Help me ... to the hospital." Her head tilted, pointing the way.

The hallways were wide open to the elements and could easily fit five people standing side by side. There weren't any doors, rooms, or classrooms of any kind. Pepper yearned to be taught at Karma Academy, to learn the ways of an assassin. But where exactly did Karma's Agents study? Granted, Pepper had yet to explore the Academy fully and had only been given a taste, but still.

"Stop here." Beatrice winced before a rough stone wall.

The faintest of incoherent whisperings traveled to

Pepper's ear, reminiscent of when she first opened her Karma Academy invitation. By instinct alone, Pepper lowered her body, allowing her ear to ferret out where the whisperings had originated, precisely where Beatrice placed her shaky index finger on the rough stone surface and traced a pattern.

A clicking sounded when Beatrice's finger traced the linear line running underneath the double loops of what Pepper guessed was the Karma Academy emblem. The illusion of a silty wall melted away to reveal glass doors that opened up to a central hallway of a hospital with private rooms on either side.

"How did you do that? Open the door, I mean?" Kimball asked, gobsmacked. "Can I do that? I'm hungry and need to use the john, like now. So help a brother out."

Didn't anybody see her tracing the Karma Academy emblem on the wall? Pepper wondered.

"The Academy's in lockdown mode. I just disarmed the alarm. No choice. Only way we could access the hospital." Beatrice's eyes reflected worry. "Which means someone's infiltrated the grounds."

Sawyer? Pepper thought. Then again, Blondie would undoubtedly know the alarm code. "Is Goddess Karma here?" Pepper asked, hope outweighing panic.

"I don't know." Beatrice seemed to reconsider her statement. "The hospital's never empty. It's as if everyone vanished." Another wave of pain brought Beatrice to her knees. When she got enough strength to lift her head, fire blazed in her eyes, and then she blinked away the flames.

"Help me lift her onto the bed," Pepper barked. With the help of Perrin and Kimball and many grunts later, they lifted Beatrice's body onto an ergonomic bed. The room was awash in glass, and shafts of sunlight poured down from the ceiling and cocooned the Agent in its restorative warmth.

Beatrice raised her shaky arm and tried to grab Pepper's

wrist. When Pepper stopped resisting, Beatrice traced a smattering of symbols on Pepper's hand, her finger moving way too fast for Pepper to discern what they were. Soon a sigil resembling a henna tattoo blazed on her palm, then quieted.

"Rooftop. Elevator is quicker. Find PK. He'll know what to —" Beatrice convulsed, and her body levitated.

Loki held her down, with the help of Perrin and Kimball's help.

"What do we do?" Kimball asked, his eyes bulging.

Pepper didn't have an answer, but she knew they had to act fast and go into triage mode.

When the convulsions stopped and Beatrice's body stayed put without weights holding her down, Pepper cut the Agent's sweatshirt open with Perrin's switchblade. Dried blood coated her gut, but no wounds presented themselves. Pepper placed her finger on Beatrice's neck. "Pulse is racing. Body's burning up, too." Noting sweat coating her skin, Pepper said, "Could be internal bleeding."

"If that's the case, we don't have much longer before she dies," said Perrin.

Pepper's heart rolled in her chest. She paced and chewed her nails. *What to do? What to do?* Visions of Jhi healing his festering wounds in Hell filled her mind. Same with Loki when he was riddled with bullet holes back on the getaway boat. Then it hit her.

"Everyone, search through every cabinet. We're looking for a firebush tincture. The label might contain the name *Papyrus mactabilis* or something similar. And hurry! Before she levitates again." Pepper tore through the cabinet in Beatrice's room. Loki, fully aware of what Pepper was referring to, ran on all fours to another area, like a capuchin on a mission.

"I believe this is what you saw growing in the atrium," Loki said as he scampered back into the room on his hind legs, waving a glass bottle. "A decoction of wild nokka-tail. There's a supply of it in the pharmacy, along with remnants of its leaves."

"Let's hope it carries the same curative properties as the firebush." Pepper knew from experience that the styptic fire-bush cauterized wounds, so in theory, it should do the same for internal bleeding. Only one way to find out. "Keep Beat-rice's mouth open," she directed Loki, "and I'll pour the tinc-ture down her throat. Kimball and Perrin, you two hold down her legs."

A sea of eyes hovered over the Agent, watching, waiting.

Pepper was on tenterhooks. She'd have Beatrice's death on her hands if she were wrong.

And then Beatrice's convulsing stopped. Thinking the worst, Loki checked her pulse. "She's alive … Heart rate's steady." Finally, some good news.

A short time after that, the sweat on the Agent's skin dried, and Loki said, "Her body heat is cooling down."

Though Beatrice was on the mend, she wasn't out of the woods yet. Still, tears of relief welled in Pepper's eyes as she slid her back down a wall until her bum hit the cold lime-stone floor. The fear-laced adrenaline still rushing through her system, Pepper needed to blow off some steam.

"Why don't you head to the rooftop," Loki suggested to Pepper, "and search for this PK and anything else we may need. I'll stay behind and monitor Beatrice."

"And scrounge up some food while you're at it," Perrin added as she headed down the hallway, no doubt picking out her room for the night.

Pepper went to exit the hospital wing when Kimball said, "Bell, wait! I'm coming with."

Kimball would not take no for an answer, so Pepper sighed in response.

"While searching for drugs, I came across the dopest

health club. It's down the hall. There's a Grecian bath and car-wash showers. Dude, I hope we stay here a while because I could use a spa-cation." Kimball raised his brow while inspecting Pepper's palm. "What are you supposed to do with that?"

Pepper said, "No clue," as they traversed the open-air hallway. "Something to do with the rooftop, I think." She then changed the subject. "Did you notice Beatrice tracing a symbol on the wall when she disarmed the security alarm? Right before the hospital door appeared?"

"What're you talking about, Bell?"

"What about back at the Starless Souk? How did Beatrice open a chaosgate, the one that brought us here?"

"She tossed blood in the air and then bada bing! Listen, I'd love nothing more than to make small talk with you. Actually, that was a lie. But since I probably have no choice, I'll lend you my ear as soon as I eat. Promise."

Kimball's response proved Pepper's working theory that nobody could see the Karma Academy emblem except Agents. That would be handy to use when needing to verify an Agent's identity.

Pepper halted before a grand library crafted from glass and decorated with flowering trees and streams running along the floor. Bibliophile Kimball couldn't resist entering the room. When Kimball turned his back to Pepper, she slunk away.

The creeping discomfort of walking around an abandoned Academy, with the lurking threat of the Hounds of Hell, Miles, and Jhi hot on her heels, nipped away at Pepper's resolve to find PK the further she ventured alone.

Standing in the dead center of the atrium, she shifted her eyes from her palm to the rooftop, trying to puzzle out her next move. Stairs only led to the second floor, while the Slinkified glass walkway connected the third floor and up.

There wasn't an elevator in sight, so what was Beatrice talking about? But then she noted that a section of the stone floor, where the atrium met the interior hallway, contained a barely discernible transition line in the shape of a semi-circle, like an edge. Pepper stepped directly onto that section of the floor, and it shifted.

"I see what you did back there, trying to ditch me!" When Kimball stood next to her, his extra weight caused the railless platform to dip down like the foundation was air. "What now?"

"Stop asking questions I don't know the answers to. God, you're so annoying—"

A jerking sensation nearly knocked Pepper off her feet.

The platform glided up and up and up. The duo held onto each other for dear life as they inched to the dead center of the circular disc.

"Oh no, what is happening?" Pepper cried out. The "elevator" went rogue, left the edge of the building it had hugged, and sliced through the center of the Academy, gilding higher and higher.

"This better stop at the top, Bell, or we're screwed."

The transporter gained speed, the wind whipping through Pepper's hair. For all Pepper knew, this was Beatrice's backup attempt to kill the invaders. And from the looks of it, Beatrice might claim victory in a matter of seconds.

9

The possessed "elevator" chilled out and glided to the rooftop's edge. Pepper didn't wait for it to stop and dove off. Kimball followed her lead.

The only thing that made sense about how they had traveled to the roof was the hennaed sigil on Pepper's hand. And when her attention focused on a greenhouse standing prominently ahead, her suspicions were confirmed. A replica of the sigil formed from vines hung prominently on the building's outer glass wall.

Inside, rows of tables fanned out, with bits of soil sprinkled on the wood surface. In the back of the classroom, a written question hovered midair inches off a whiteboard: *What are the ABCs of poison?*

"Atropa belladonna. Batrachotoxin. Curare." The answer flowed mechanically from Pepper's lips. "But there are poisons all around us. It's the dose that matters."

The letters within the written question slammed into one

another, their bits and pieces sifting down like confetti, then swirled together and rejiggered into: *You are correct!*

"What did you say?" Kimball sidled up next to Pepper.

Pepper remained mum, unsure how to answer, as she wasn't certain what overcame her, but it struck a cord of unease in her all the same.

"Any idea how to reach the ground floor that doesn't involve that elevator thing?" Kimball waved his hand in the direction from where they came. "And I'm not about to jump from the third floor and risk breaking my leg."

Pepper shook her head, then said, "Obviously, this sigil brought us to the rooftop, so I'm guessing it will bring us down. Hopefully."

"Y'know, not for nothing, but they really should have railings on their"—his fingers curled into air quotes—"elevators. But seriously, how did you get the elevator to move, and is this a classroom?"

"I don't know, Kimball." She seriously wanted to wring his neck. "And yes, this is a classroom. I thought it was herbology, but now I'm thinking poisoncraft."

"Why, that's not alarming. Not in the least." He turned on his heel and exited the greenhouse. Not wanting to linger alone in the classroom, Pepper joined him.

Without the trees and ferns below obstructing their view, the heavens were as clear as day and awash in tangerine and every shade of pink imaginable, from dark to light, with violet touches here and there. Not to be ignored, the deep orange sun shone brightly. Dwarfed by the sun, a metallic-hued quarter moon drooped in the heavens as if balanced on the Scales of Justice.

A dense forest occupied one side of the Academy. Curls of mist carpeted the soil, eerie sounds emanating within. But the other side of the Academy stole Pepper's attention, so much so that when Pepper bypassed an infinity-edge lap pool, she nearly fell in, the land beyond to blame. As far as the eye could see, floating mountain after mountain housing lush greenery, vibrant jewel-colored plants, and cascading waterfalls dotted the terrain. Pepper couldn't figure out how to cross one flat mountain peak to the next, as there wasn't a bridge in sight.

Greenhouses dotted the sprawling circular rooftop. The one closest to Pepper held a cornucopia of dried, potted, and hydroponic herbs and vegetables. From beyond the glass panes of another, Pepper eyed exotic plants blooming within. She stepped inside one greenhouse, and a whoosh of moist heat akin to Naples summers nearly zapped her energy; housed within were unidentifiable plants and what resembled orchids. Throughout the smattering of nurseries, not one maintained the same temperature; a few were as Arctic cold as the Isles of Obolus in Hell, where Bhi'gow called home; others were too hot or cold to even step foot inside without protective gear.

"Hey!" Kimball said, sneaking up on Pepper, and she yelped with fright. "I found the cafeteria slash kitchen. C'mon."

The Academy's cafeteria had front-row seats to the show-stopping scenery. Circular tables that could easily fit a large party were scattered about with floating teardrop lanterns draped across the dining area in toto.

A room resided off to the side, and Pepper gravitated toward it and waltzed through swinging doors into a kitchen. An island marred with red matter ran through the center of the space. A massive range with ten burners held court in the middle, with a walk-in pantry and freezer off to the side.

Kimball extended his arms to the side and sang as if mimicking a choir of angels, albeit off-key. "Bring me all the food. Starting with bread"—he inhaled sharply—"and ropa vieja. Bell, you outcooked even my mom when it came to that dish."

"But not her sweet plantains. I never perfected those."

"Ha! Look." Kimball held the vodka bottle before him and watched raptly as Bunny's soul pinged about within the glass vessel. "Mom agrees." He looked around, bit his lip in concentration, then said, "I'm gonna get in a few laps in the pool while you cook. Just holler when dinner's ready."

"You must be joking. I'm not cooking, and certainly not for you."

"Can't you just magic something into existence?"

"No. Magic isn't permitted here. Even if it was, I don't know how to magic food from nothing. Also, I'm not your personal chef."

"Yeah, yeah." Kimball entered a walk-in freezer and immediately thundered out, his eyes bulging with fright, and vomited in the trough sink.

When Pepper placed her hand on the ice-cold latch, Kimball said, "I wouldn't go in there if I were you," then dry heaved.

Curiosity got the better of her, and Pepper stepped inside and nearly ran into a human body hanging from a meathook. She pivoted on her heel and shut the door.

"Told you not to go inside." He swallowed back bile. "I don't like it here, Bell."

Pepper snuck a peek back inside; she couldn't help herself. Two humans were imprisoned within—one male, the other female—intact and clothed with icicles growing on their skin and hair.

An eye on one snapped open. "You. Get me off this hook," the male curtly demanded.

"A damned," Pepper explained to Kimball from over her shoulder.

"No. I'm not whatever that is, young lady. You must be mistaken. Now remove me from this hook this instant."

"Or what?" Pepper retorted.

He blustered in response.

"Yeah, that's what I thought. What are you used for? Food?"

"How insulting! I'm not telling you diddly-squat."

What a charmer, Pepper thought. "When was the last time you saw someone other than us?"

"I'd say a few weeks, but something tells me it's been longer," the female damned replied.

"Can't keep your mouth shut, can you?" the original damned growled at the female.

"Where is everybody?" Pepper inquired, her attention focused on the squealer.

"We don't know. One minute we were in the kitchen with Professor Kymeo, the next, everyone up and disappeared."

Could Professor Kymeo be PK? Pepper nearly burst at the seams. But she played it cool. "And Kymeo is who exactly ...?"

"Resident potion master and all-around plonker," said the male.

"Now, now, Wolfgang. Kymeo wasn't the only one fooled," said the female damned.

"Was it a few weeks ago, too, that you last saw the professor?"

The female damned nodded in response.

"How do you tell time from—"

"From our humble meat locker dwelling, you mean?" Wolfgang retorted, then added, "It's a guesstimate. The dracos come knocking at our door every night, like clock-work, right after sunset. For two fortnights, they've come, their snouts *peck-peck-pecking* to be let in, their dagger-sharp talons scraping along the metal door."

"They come for drinks and a good time?" Kimball tentatively joined Pepper inside the freezer.

"Hardy-har-har," Wolfgang voiced. "Who doesn't love a court jester? But, yes, and when they come tonight, you should greet them. I'm sure a good time can be had by all."

"Listen. I'll prop open the door for much-needed sunshine, or I can just leave it open permanently. Your choice." Pepper grew tired of this back and forth.

"Dracos are venomous raptors that fancy human offal," the female explained. "There's never just one but the entire rage."

"What's your name?" Pepper asked the only one complying.

"Lady Melisende, Marchioness de Canondí." Pepper thought the woman's affected French accent was a tad too much. "I ruled over —"

"Yes, we know, Melly," the male interjected. "You had hundreds of peasants at your beck and call. Lady's maids dying to do nothing but scrub the scum off your hairy feet. The Mad Marchioness feared far and wide."

"Cool story, bro. Uh, Bell, I found food. Like a massive pantry full."

"We'll continue this conversation in a bit." Pepper spun on her heel. She wanted to continue talking to them, but the need for food outweighed that idea. Perhaps when Pepper returned, they'd be ready to speak.

Inside the spacious pantry that didn't contain prepared food, Pepper contemplated how she could end Kimball's life. Death by drowning in the pool. Death by falling. By poisons. The choices were endless. "This isn't food, you silver-spooned halfwit. These are what us common folk call ingredients."

Exasperated, Pepper took in her surroundings. Bags, cans, and sacks were scattered and stacked everywhere; basically, all the items a chef would need to whip up gastronomic delights populated the space, including a curious object that resembled a stove. But one element, in particular, made it very clear that it wasn't your run-of-the-mill cooking apparatus—a turn knob and a magic gem-feeding mechanism found on gumball dispensers.

"Zho'zho used something similar back in Hell." When Kimball's brows raised, Pepper added, "She's the owner of the Tenth Circle Tavern. You know, the one where the Talking Heads alerted Perrin of my arrival in Hell. No thanks to you!" she snapped, then deeply inhaled and exhaled a centering breath that didn't at all work. "As I was saying. This oven is enchanted. We just need to feed it gems."

"And then what?"

"Why do you keep insisting I know what to do? I'm new to all of this." Pepper's hands flailed about. Honestly, what she needed more than sustenance was a nap. If she sat down, she'd pass out. So, she had no choice but to continue moving. "Trial and error, Kimby."

His lip curled into a grin.

"What're you smiling about?"

"You haven't called me Kimby in a while."

"A slip of the tongue. I'm tired. Don't get used to it. I still hate you." Pepper tossed all the ingredients one would need for pasta into the oven: tomato sauce and a few boxes of linguine. "I imagine Beatrice would eat spaghetti, but would Loki or Perrin for that matter, or is she strictly on a damned-only diet? We shall see."

"Okay, Chef Boyardee. There's a room full of food, even food clearly not from our world"—Kimball cast his eyes to a jar of pickled eight-legged serpent—"and you pick pasta?"

"I've never done this before, so I'm picking something easy. You'd have to be extra thick in the head to screw this dish up." Pepper let out a weak chuckle, then said,

"Remember that one year when you got an Easy-Bake Oven for Christmas, and your mom even bought you your own apron?" Pepper's laughter kicked up a notch. "I still can't believe you burned sugar cookies."

Kimball couldn't suppress a giggle. "Yes. But you still ate the burned cookies."

"I did. Only because I felt sorry for you, and they were cookies." Through chuckles, Pepper said, "And then remember when Bunny dunked the burnt-to-a-crisp cookies into milk and squeezed out *mmms* while choking them down?"

"Fondly. That's the day my mom taught us to bake actual cookies from scratch in the kitchen. And the devils we were got into a flour fight."

"Yep. And Bunny joined in. We were chasing each other around the kitchen island. White powder everywhere. It was like a cooking crime scene." A smile touched Pepper's lips.

Kimball's face grew serious. "Then Shelly came home and threw a colossal fit because his six-figure newly reno'd kitchen was a mess."

"I felt bad when—"

"When Shelly ridiculed me and stood by until I cleaned up the last of the mess?"

Pepper weakly nodded. "But later that night, you and your mom came to my house, and my dad ordered pizza."

"Oh yeah. From Sutton House. And we watched scary movies. Sometime later, didn't my mom buy you an Easy-Bake Oven? One of her 'just because' gifts."

"She did. I loved the heck outta that oven. I think that started my love of cheffing, to be honest."

"And your love for food."

"Why do you always end up going there?" Pepper snapped, disgusted.

"Go where?"

"Make a dig at my weight! That's what you were referring to, right?"

"Well, you grew into a porker, Bell."

Pepper had momentarily let her guard down with Kimball. But it wouldn't happen again.

While blinking back tears, Pepper turned her attention to the enchanted oven. Now, what color gems to use? As she searched through her pouch, gems clanked about. Red for grounding and basic necessities. Yellow for fire. Blue for— Wait! What if Pepper was going about this all wrong? This was an enchanted object, after all.

"Bell, don't waste your gems. There's an entire supply over here. It's like a pirate's treasure chest."

The chest didn't house gems of each color; instead, magical vapor made up of *every* color filled the inside of the fulgurite casings. Pepper had never encountered gems like that, not even at the Starless Souk. She took what was needed and then more for the road.

After feeding the dispenser a handful of the newly acquired gems, she rotated the lever, and the oven fired up. Vapor swirled inside the oven's window, enveloping the dry ingredients.

A *ding* later, Pepper opened the door and sighed. Glass shards and cardboard mixed with tomato and pasta were everywhere, on the walls, racks, and heating coils. "I should have put it all in a pot." Trial and error, Pepper's new reality.

"And removed the pasta from the box and the sauce from the jar."

After an angry scrubbing, Pepper tried again. Attempt number two worked like a charm.

Hellfire within the hanging lanterns flickered on as the sun began its descent, the invisible Scales of Justice lowering while the moon climbed up the heavenly rungs on its way to its nightly throne.

As they put the last of the licked-clean dishes in the sink, the fog in Pepper's head cleared, her belly stopped grumbling, and she felt fueled enough to continue the search. "There are no signs of Kymeo here, and the damned know jack squat."

"We've looked everywhere."

"That's not entirely true." One area remained.

Back at the School of Poisoncraft, Pepper ventured to a door at the rear. Inside, a decoction machine lording over one corner of the room remained intact, but the same couldn't be said for everything else. Tables were overturned, chairs on their side. A sophisticated chemistry apparatus out of a mad scientist's lab occupied the length of a rather large table, its equipment knocked over, spilled solutions eating through the work surface. A crackling sounded as her sneakers stepped on a straggle of broken flasks.

An oily substance swooshed and bubbled in one of the collection bottles as if in a state of agitation. Gloves and masks were resting next to the flasks. "Seems as if someone was in the middle of creating a potion before they disappeared," Pepper said.

"Ambushed by the Hounds, you think?" Kimball asked.

"That's what's confusing me. Beatrice said that the Academy kills those who have ill intentions on the spot. So that eliminates the Hounds. Then I immediately thought of Sawyer. But she isn't exactly Pollyanna, so how could she have bypassed security?"

"Who better than Sawyer? She probably knows this place better than anybody. Or maybe she was already on campus when the lockdown happened?" Kimball shook off a chill. "But you're forgetting something. Beatrice turned the security defenses off. So what if that means anyone can enter? I don't know, Bell. Something's off. Where's Karma? This is her

Academy, her realm, is it not? And you're telling me all the professors just vanished? Not adding up."

"I agree. If this has Sawyer's fingerprints all over it, why, though?"

"I don't know. Ice Queen works for the Syndicate, so obviously, it's on their orders."

"What could they possibly be after?" Pepper said more to herself. "Maybe it's not a what but a *who*."

"Remember when I told you all that Vlad is preparing for a ceremony? Something big?"

"Yes. The one where Vlad, Cazzian, take your pick, intends on killing my pops, you sack of shit." A burst of fiery rage overcame Pepper.

Extract of dialonaleaf. One drop will kill a man dead. Tastes divine, like ripe raspberries and whipping cream. Flashes of herself walking out of a chaosgate filled Pepper's mind, holding the harvested unassuming weed-like plant in her gloved hands.

"… descending into a carb coma? Bell, did you hear what I just said? The sun is setting, and I don't want to run into these dracos—whatever the hell they are. And if you haven't noticed, this whole Academy is basically open air and therefore *easy to penetrate*."

Pepper snapped out of whatever fugue state had stolen her attention. "Grab the food, and I'll gather some ingredients for Beatrice, and then we'll leave." Pepper wasn't sure where those disturbing thoughts had originated from, nor what had unlocked them from her mental vault, but she decided not to give them any more attention and continued on the medicinal herb hunt.

A few minutes later, she found precisely what she had wanted: oil of oregano, along with feverfew, chamomile, elderberry, and yarrow—along with a handful tinctures that were labeled and filed according to ailment. Pepper went with panacea and fever.

A few elevators were scattered about the rooftop. Pepper and Kimball boarded the one closest to them. The henna-like tattoo was fading fast, so Pepper didn't have a lot of wiggle room to figure out how this sigil worked.

When the elevator refused to budge, Kimball said with a snort, "Where's a down arrow when you need one?"

"Cállate la boca! I need to concentrate," Pepper said while inspecting the faint tattoo that looked like mountain peaks with interconnecting swishes and an open triangle.

"Give me your hand." When Pepper wouldn't budge, Kimball grabbed it. "Just placate me, okay?" He drew a down arrow. Immediately, the elevator glided downward all the way to the ground floor. "You've always overcomplicated things. Bet you're glad I didn't calla mi boca!" he said in a perfect Cuban accent. "You're welcome!" His greedy hand dove inside Pepper's satchel.

"What are you doing?"

"Looking for your phone. Ah, found it." Kimball asked her to stop talking with her hands and to stay still so he could snap a photo. "In case the marking fades."

Back at the infirmary, Pepper handed Loki and Perrin bowls of pasta.

"What am I supposed to do with this?" Perrin looked visibly disgusted. "While I prefer red sauce, this is not exactly what I had in mind. As in, *this is not blood!* I need actual sustenance, people."

"We found a few damned hanging out on the rooftop," Kimball chortled at his corny pun.

Perrin's eyes popped open. "Direct me to them."

"No! We need them in one piece. They know things. Just need some extra coaxing, is all. Trust me. I have a plan," Pepper lied.

"Fine. But you should know Beatrice hasn't woken up. Loki thinks she might have slipped into a coma." Noting panic seizing Pepper, Perrin added, "Her vitals are stable, though. But we can't determine what the fuh'kar's wrong with her."

"No! This can't be happening. We need to get out of here!" Her father's life depended on it. Pepper chewed on her thumb while pacing, then stopped and asked, "What about Tavi? Can he take us back to the moment of injury? Help us figure out what's wrong with her?"

Perrin had already thought that one through but said that two problems presented themselves. One, Beatrice was too weak. And while the byproduct of blood hemorrhaging from Tavi eating her brain wasn't that big of a deal like others made it out to be—bunch of drama queens—the risk of her body going into shock and then the inevitable death far outweighed the reward. And two, Tavi's skill set worked best when the target thought about the precise memory needed.

"In this case, the moment of attack. And since Peaches is Sleeping Beauty at the moment …" Perrin said.

"Well, that sucks," Pepper replied, her eyes growing heavier by the minute.

"You know what else sucks?" Kimball added. "Dracos." He then shared the news about killer birds of prey roaming the skies.

Perrin huffed, rolled her eyes, and stomped off.

While Pepper administered a few drops of each newly acquired tincture down Beatrice's throat, hoping for the best, Loki suggested they should sleep in shifts, then volunteered to stay up first.

The last thing Pepper remembered was smacking into the glass door of her room for the night, thinking it was open, then barely making it onto the bed right as blood-curdling screeches boomed from outside. Instinctively, she knew the dracos had arrived and were hunting for food and seeking out their prey on the Academy grounds.

A part of Pepper entertained fear, her heart pounding like an alarm clock commanding her to get up NOW and hide. But the sandman came and carried her away.

10

"Here you go, kiddo." Larry handed a cup to Pepper, filled with her favorite theme park treat.

"Pops, where's yours?" she asked in between licks of the frozen whipped pineapple and maraschino cherry concoction. "If you think I'm sharing …"

Larry let out a weak chuckle. "I'm not hungry."

"Since when?"

Under a blanket of stars, the father and daughter sat in companionable silence on a bench near the flying carpets. Not a single soul was on the ride that flew around and up and down. In fact, nobody milled about. It was as if the park, nearly always crowded, belonged to just the two of them.

"Better put on your shades." Larry slipped into rectangular cardboard glasses as a bucket of blood poured over the sun. "Otherwise, we'll die."

"Pops, you can take the glasses off. It's safe."

"No. It's not. We're not alone." Larry's eyes darted about.

"There's a tour group. We're all waiting—" He grabbed his stomach as if in pain and grimaced.

"'Waiting?' Because you think the line will be long?" Screaming in the distance punctuated Pepper's question. "Ain't nothin' scary about that water ride. The fall isn't even *that* big of a deal."

"Park is closing soon"—a cough flew out of her dad's mouth—"and we don't have much time left before the eclipse." A grim expression cemented on Larry's face. "Kiddo, I don't know if I can last much longer. Know that I love you to the stars and to infinite galaxies and back."

"Ditto, and then some, Pops." The ice cream cup disappeared in Pepper's hand.

"Where are we?" a familiar voice asked.

Pepper looked around, and her heart nearly skipped a beat when Jhi appeared.

"I keep wanting to ride something but can't seem to," Pepper said.

"Let's go on the flying pirate ship." Jhi took Pepper's hand in his and escorted her to the ride.

Pepper halted and unclasped her hand from Jhi's. "Did you see my dad?"

"Yes. He went to the bathroom."

Pepper's raised shoulders dropped as she searched the area. "Where did you come from?"

"I've been here all along." Jhi stood before Pepper and drank in her eyes, interlacing his fingers with hers. "I've missed you."

Though she snatched back her hand, a small part of her flirted with the idea of kissing Jhi. An even smaller part wanted him to hold her.

A blink later, Pepper plonked herself down on a bench in the middle of Main Street. Faceless people ambled about, incoherently chattering.

"Pepper, over here," Jhi called out. He slipped into a character hat and looked rather ridiculous. A laugh escaped from Pepper's mouth.

In a flash, Pepper matched Jhi's stride as they meandered into another area of the park. "Here. Put yours on." Jhi handed her a hat all her own.

"How many guests are in your party?" a park employee asked Pepper. Cardboard eclipse glasses rested on the top of her wild mane of red hair.

"Four," Jhi replied.

"Who's the fourth?" Pepper asked Jhi.

"Your sister, silly."

"Jaylyn's here?" Pepper whipped her head around.

"You tell me? If she's not here, then where is she?"

"You can't board the ride without your entire party present," the redhead said to Pepper only as if Jhi wasn't there.

Jhi held Pepper's hand. "We need to find your sister to board the ride. Think Pepper. Do you remember where she's at?"

"Where's my pops?" A sense of terror thundered through Pepper's body.

"At the castle," the red-headed employee replied to Pepper, her green eyes flicking back and forth as if looking for someone. "We need you to bring Larry back before you get on the ride." Urgency coated her tone.

"I—"

***

PEPPER'S EYES SNAPPED OPEN.

"For Lilith's sake! Your snoring is louder than a fire-breathing lu'kowsa before the dragon goes in for the kill." Perrin's engorged head loomed over Pepper.

"What time is it?" Pepper could easily fall back asleep.

"It's late afternoon. You've been down for the count for at least half a day. Anyway, Peaches got a nasty fever during the night." When Pepper gasped, Perrin said, "Her temperature broke, and she's mumbling now. But she's still not awake."

"So, what's the plan?" All Pepper cared about was grabbing another hour or two of sleep.

"While you were getting your thirteenth hour of beauty rest, Loki and I decided it was best to leave, what with Peaches deactivating the defense wards—"

"And go where?" Pepper wiped away the sleep crust from her eyes. "This is the only place we can be free and not constantly worry about the Hounds or I-must-kill-all-the-things Miles or Jhi catching up to us!"

"If you would have let me finish, I was about to say that that was the fuh'karing plan, but guess what, sweetling? We can't leave, even if we wanted to." Perrin's face empurpled with fury. "The lobby doors are sealed shut."

"Beatrice said the Academy is on lockdown, remember?" Pepper didn't mean to appear snippy.

"Yes, and she disarmed the alarms," Perrin snapped back. "It wouldn't matter, anyway. Sawyer obviously knows the code. Besides, just yesterday, you were desperate to leave."

"I still am, but where would we go?"

"No clue, but something's not right with this place. It's creepy here, and that's coming from a demon."

"I agree. And a part of me wants to figure out why that is."

"We need to get Peaches back on her feet like yesterday so we can unleash Tavi on her. In the meantime, I say we forage for supplies and more supplies and food that's not that Shi'rue-awful concoction you brought me last night. Speaking of last night, you probably were already asleep, nearly choking on your drool, and didn't hear the dracos. So, yeah, I don't want to chance an encounter with whatever the fuh'kar they are, so let's keep our foraging to daylight hours, kay? We have some time, though, before sunset. Also, your breath smells like hot garbage, so please fix that; otherwise, I'm gonna hurl. Bye!" Perrin spun on her heel and waltzed out of Pepper's room.

Pepper discreetly cupped her hands over her mouth and blew. *My breath isn't that bad,* she thought, then let her head fall back on the pillow.

Pepper couldn't recall her dreams, save for her pops playing a starring role and where they were. The location made sense; after all, that amusement park was the Bells' happy place, filled with nothing but fond memories. It also inspired the father-daughter tattoos they got on a whim last year on Pepper's sixteenth birthday—wholly Pepper's idea that Larry was all about. His bicep proudly displayed a silhouette of a father and his little girl holding hands with a log flume cascading down a mountain in the background. The same tattoo graced Pepper's back shoulder.

Since Perrin had jerked her out of the dreamscape, Pepper felt off. Punchy. Concerned. Dreaming of her dad left her with a sense of dread. All she could hear was Larry telling her he loved her. Something about it felt final. What made it worse was her inability to contact him. To check in with him. Pepper had to rescue her dad, but she had no clue where to find him. That only inflamed the hatred she felt for Kimball.

Busy work was what would take the edge off. That and a piping hot shower. Kimball had mentioned something about stumbling upon a Grecian bath, so Pepper set out to find it. With freshly brushed teeth (take that, Perrin!), Pepper grabbed her go-bag and exited her room.

The caduceus symbol lorded above the hospital exit, something Pepper hadn't noticed earlier. More notably, a triangle rested on the crown of the staff with a spiral pattern inside as intricate in design as the strange sigil Beatrice had hennaed on Pepper's hand—the same sigil that had transported Pepper and Kimball to the rooftop.

Pepper padded down the hospital's main hallway, which seemed to defy physics now that she had a clearer head. On the outside, the hospital appeared to occupy a handful of rooms. In actuality, the inside mimicked that of a university-sized institution. The air emanating from a few rooms rivaled that of dry heat. And in others, the temperature was hot and humid, like Naples, ten months out of the year.

Eventually, she came across a wing devoted to an infinity-edge bath the size of a pool, wall-less and open to the outdoors, with a view of the cascading waterfalls and an endless sea of mountains. This had to be the Grecian bath Kimball had referenced. The eucalyptus-impregnated air energized Pepper as a balmy breeze blew back her unbrushed locks. The air was heavenly, the temperature Goldilocks perfect. She considered dipping her feet into the warm bath water, then said, *Screw it.* It's not a shower, but it would do.

While drying off with a towel in a locker room, Pepper thought about the sigil Beatrice had scribbled on her palm. What if that sigil on the rooftop was Earth? And the one above the caduceus denoted the element of Air? After all, various climates *were* present in the hospital: desert, tropical, temperate, and polar. Then a plan hatched, one that involved dorm rooms. This was an Academy, after all—guaranteed Pepper would find study material there. Hopefully, magic spell cheat sheets, too. And she knew just who she could ask. But first, she'd test out her theory.

As Pepper entered the atrium, Kimball popped out from nowhere and joined her on the elevator. "I don't need company, Kimball, so—"

"So nothing. I was already heading to the sky lounge."

Pepper rolled her eyes as she penned the Earth sigil on her

palm, using the picture on her phone Kimball had snapped as a reference. The moment Pepper finished tracing the last swoosh, the platform shimmied and began its ascent.

On the rooftop, outside the doors to the School of Poisoncraft, Kimball raced to the pool and cannonballed into the salty water while Pepper remained on the platform. On the other hand, she sketched the Air sigil hoping the elevator would transport her to the hospital and avoid the long walk they usually had to take from the atrium there. But nothing happened, except her frustration that escalated. And Kimball's splashing around in the pool further agitated her.

While everyone was trying to figure out how to leave the Academy and fretting over Beatrice, this fool was swimming, lounging on the sky deck, and getting his daily vitamin D intake—in other words, engaging in his day-to-day rich-kid activities back in Naples and living his best life.

"The water is amazing, Bell. You should jump in."

Annoyed at his mere presence, Pepper ignored Kimball's summoning and returned to her investigation. She stared at the two sigils on her hands, concentrating, and then the solution hit her. *You can't go to two places at once,* she reminded herself.

After scrubbing away Earth, the elevator descended diagonally toward the hospital. In fact, it delivered her right outside the glass doors. She might have celebrated her victory midair before it landed, then nearly fell off and immediately halted the sashaying. Still, what did the sigils mean other than directionals for the elevator? Between that mystery and discovering where the dorm rooms were located, Pepper decided it was time to pay the damned another visit. Hopefully, they were ready to play ball.

"To what do we owe the pleasure?" A corpse had more life than Wolfgang's tone.

"I hope you've had enough time to consider my earlier proposition," Pepper said.

"And what was that again?" Melisende inquired.

"I will spare your lives for information."

"Then I will share what I know in exchange for fresh air. I don't even care if I'm carrion for the dracos. I can't hang in this frigid hovel surrounded by a peasant any longer." She tossed Wolfgang a smile.

"Get off your high horse, Melly. You are marchioness of nothing," he joked.

"Deal!" Pepper grabbed a chair and freed the damned. "If you try anything funny, I'll—"

"Save your breath," Melisende said. "The Department of Soul Sundering and Assignments placed me in Goddess Karma's care for a reason. I'm not a flight risk."

"What is your assignment here?" Pepper asked as they exited the kitchen.

"Wolfy prepares all the meals while I serve as the groundskeeper." Noting Pepper's squinting eyes, Melisende added from over her shoulder, "What were you imagining, hm? That the goddess uses us for target practice? Experimentation, perhaps?" That's precisely what Pepper had thought. "Karma isn't all wrath and fury. She has a soft spot. Don't you dare tell her that, or she'll have me killed. Besides, there are other damned who fill those roles."

"What kind of experimenting?" Pepper's brow creased at the mere thought.

"Poisons mainly—how long they take to enter the bloodstream and the side effects." Noticing Pepper grimacing, Melisende said, "It's the nature of the beast for the damned. Our eternal torment." She tilted her head to the crisp seventy-five-degree breeze, tasting it, letting it cascade over her. "To taste the air and feel free, even for a moment."

With yellow teeth, sunken cheeks, and a pointy chin,

Melisende certainly wasn't a looker. And the century or two of the torture she had endured in Hell didn't help. But as she soaked up the shafts of sunlight, her sallow skin poking out through her potato sack ensemble brightened, and her green eyes enlivened, a spark apparent within. There was a glow about her, a glimmer of her former self that awakened in the sun's rays, hinting that she was once a beauty before she had kicked the bucket and the mala'khas dragged her to Hell. And Pepper wondered what had caused the marchioness to sign a soul contract. All the damned had a story to tell.

"I'll tell you whatever you want to know. Just don't put me back in there," Melisende said.

Pepper had no intention of keeping Melisende and Wolfgang locked up. But she wasn't about to share that news until after she culled whatever intel she could from the marchioness. "How long have you been at the Academy?"

"What is time when you're dead?"

"But if you had to guess?"

"I didn't start out here. Served my handed-down sentence in the Pits, like all the damned. Thank Seren, I wasn't beheaded and hung on a wall in a tavern somewhere. For a time, I was a runner assigned to a coachman who operated a damned-drawn carriage business. Then the DSSA sent me to" —she air quoted—"*work* as a coat hanger in this upscale boutique on Main Street in Pandæmonia. But it beat being whipped daily. I spent half a century stuck on a rack, wearing the latest sartorial trends in Hell. Oh, how far the mighty fall. Before death, I wore the most exquisite silk dresses. It took seamstresses months to create my wardrobe. Sewing in the thousands of pearls and crystals by hand." Melisende's lips bowed into a wistful smile. "*Tsk-tsk*, ask away before the moon rises and my time draws to a nigh."

"Where has everyone gone?"

"We don't know. We heard a ruckus the day everyone

disappeared. It made me harken back to when assassins breached my castle and killed my soldiers one by one. It was my head they were after. I fear that's what's happened here." When Pepper's brow raised in a question, Melisende added, "Wolfy and I were in the kitchen with Professor Kymeo, preparing dinner when we all heard the crash-boom, then a scream from who I think was Vesta. She's the resident poison master. She has such an unfortunate high-pitched voice, so it was definitely her squealing. Professor Kymeo darted off, and that was the last time I saw him and the others."

"How many professors are here? And what about students?"

"There are a handful of professors. As for students, none. Which is very odd. It's usually a revolving door of Initiates."

That reply chilled Pepper to the bone. "If the Initiates were here, where would their dorm rooms be?" When Melisende pointed to the fifth and sixth floors, Pepper said, "Is there a code I need to know to enter?"

Melisende shrugged, her lips sealed.

"Let me guess. You're prohibited from speaking anything about the goings-on with students." After Melisende nodded, Pepper asked, "Okay. What about Goddess Karma? Do you ever see her? I desperately need to talk to her."

"Does her eminence ever grace me with her presence? Certainly. But not recently. We've tried to contact Karma with no success. It's as if she's blocked from us."

"Great. We're stuck here at the Academy, and Beatrice's health isn't improving." Pepper sighed heavily and noted the waning quarter moon rise to its nightly throne, as did the dracos from their daytime slumber. Their bloodcurdling screeches boomed from the forest on the outskirts of the Academy. This interrogation would have to end shortly, so she asked one last question: "What do you think happened? Like, where did everyone disappear to?"

"You mean *who* happened? Why, Sawyer van Arsdale. She's who magicked Wolfgang and me on the meathooks inside the freezer and locked us inside. She said she wasn't done looking and delivered a stern warning to all. If we wanted to live, we better give her the object. Then said she'd be back soon."

11

"I'm starving," Pepper said as she exited her bedroom. "Pops, we dining in, picking up, delivery?"

"Pepper, he's coming!" Larry called out in a panic.

While standing in the center of her living room, Pepper instinctively knew that she had looked everywhere within her modest-sized ranch home for her father, even though she didn't recall searching.

"I can't move … He's—"

"Who's he? Pops, where are you?" Pepper dashed out the front door, stood in the porte cochère next to her dad's wood-paneled station wagon, and searched beyond the circular drive for her dad.

"Don't know," Larry said. "It's cold. Wet. The group … Jolene's with me. She needs you to contact—"

A waitress with a mane of fiery red hair knocked into Pepper with a tray she carried filled with entrees. The redhead grabbed Pepper by the shoulder and uttered, "We need help before the dragon devours the moon. Can you hear—"

Sutton House pizzeria was hopping, nameless faces chattering away, the din drowning out the woman's question. A blink later, the woman disappeared.

"I'm looking for Larry Bell. He should be here?" Pepper asked a stranger behind the counter while she cast her eyes about the jam-packed restaurant. "He's with the tour group." She wasn't sure why she mentioned that, but something about it felt familiar.

"Pepper, over here. I got us a table." Jhi escorted her to the back of the restaurant, where silence permeated the space. "You come here often?"

"I—um, yes. Every Friday with my dad. Pizza and movie night." Pepper swiveled around in her chair. "Did you see my dad? I was supposed to meet him here?"

"No. I'm sure he's fine. It's good to see you."

"I don't know why, but I hate you." Pepper wasn't sure what Jhi had done to have provoked her ire; that knowledge lived at the edge of her mind, obscured by a curl of fog.

"I know you do," Jhi replied softly. "Y'know, I never got the chance to take you on a date, so I figured now would be a good enough time. You brought me here when I asked where you wanted to go."

"I did? Oh, well, it's my second favorite restaurant." A thin-crust pizza appeared on the red-and-white checkerboard tablecloth. "Do you even eat pizza? You are a demon, right?"

"I do eat pizza, and no, I'm not a demon."

"You sure act like one," Pepper said under her breath. The mind fog started lifting, and memories surfaced in all manner of Jhi. "Do you at all feel bad about what you did?"

"No. I did what I had to, and I don't expect you to understand."

"I'm sure you and Sawyer got a good laugh at my expense

over how stupid I am for believing your lies. She's probably your girlfriend. Or maybe that's Ember. Or someone else."

"There's no someone else. And no, there's nothing funny about what happened. I understand I hurt you."

"But you're not sorry?"

"I'm sorry I hurt—"

"Don't you dare finish that sentence! What you did to me goes beyond hurt feelings. I trusted you. I was falling for— You betrayed me. Shattered my trust in you. Made a mockery of me." The words slipped out of Pepper's mouth like water.

"I never lied. Not really. I omitted the truth. Still, I told you I was looking for JD, did I not?"

The warm Gulf waters pooled around Pepper's feet, and her toes sunk into the squishy sand. Her favorite beach down the street from her home sprawled out in either direction and was deserted, save for Pepper and Jhi.

"I've never swum in the Gulf of Mexico or any body of water just for fun, now that I think about it," Jhi shared.

Pepper started trudging through the sand toward the pier, and Jhi caught up to her and asked, "Why did you bring us here?"

"I don't know."

Jhi stopped, removed his t-shirt, kicked off his boots, and unzipped his jeans.

"What're you doing?" Pepper asked.

"What does it look like? Wanna join me?"

A part of Pepper feared going in the water, not just because she could have sworn she spied a fin circling close to the shore.

"C'mon in. Water's warm. I promise I won't bite."

I'm dreaming. Which means I can't die. And I can do whatever I want without repercussions or anyone finding out, Pepper thought, then threw all inhibitions to the wind, stripped off her jeans and top, and ran into the surf wearing her bra and granny panties.

She swam over to Jhi, his wavy hair soaking wet, drops of salt water dotting his handsome face, the greenish-blue of his eyes as vibrant as ever, and locked her lips to his. His arms wrapped around her and pulled her ever closer, snuffing out all the space between them, skin touching skin, and she wrapped her legs around his waist. Their kissing was achingly tender and left her feeling dizzy.

Pepper's heart was at odds, the guilt front and center. Jhi was her sworn enemy. Then again, she told herself this was a dream. It would only ever be that. It wasn't like the real Jhi would ever find out, or anyone else. Perhaps she could get everything out of her system here. And she meant *everything*. She wanted to go further. Tried to—

"Better stop you there." Jhi pulled back, out of breath. "As much as I want to, Pepper, and you have no idea how strong that desire is on my end, we can't."

"Why?" she panted. "You're rejecting me? In my own dream?"

"I need your help with something."

Pepper kissed his earlobe. Then lightly sucked on his peach-toned neck. Her not-quite-satisfied lips adventured back to his, and she lightly bit his bottom lip. He fiercely kissed her, his hands exploring every inch of her back, and squeezed her tush.

Jhi cleaved his body from hers. Gently, he tucked a strand of hair behind her ear, then warned, "Your sister is in danger."

Pepper repeated what he said, nodding her head while going in for another kiss.

Jhi pulled back and asked, "Do you understand what I'm saying? Nod yes if so." Pepper did as asked, which prompted

Jhi to continue. "Only you can reach JD. Do you know where she's at?"

"She's with someone who is keeping her hidden. Don't ask me who because I don't know. Neither does Karma." She instantly regretted divulging that, but the truth had a mind all its own. Then she figured it didn't matter. What happens in a dream, stays in a dream. All she wanted was to taste more of Jhi's lips.

"Witherwhere?"

Damn, was Jhi relentless. Pepper sighed, then said, "No. Not there." There was something very sobering about this conversation. "I know this is a dream—a lucid one. And I can do and say whatever I want without consequence. I know you know where my father is. The least you could do is tell me where Cazzian is holding him prisoner."

A blink later, Pepper found herself on the beach, her legs coated with salt and sand. Jhi, fully dressed, his hair wet and slicked back, leaned in. His lips inches from her ear, his stubble tickling her lobe, he whispered, "He's at Vlad's castle."

PEPPER JOLTED AWAKE, her back ramrod straight, sweat coating her chest, neck, and brow. While trying to catch her breath, she rested her head on the unforgiving headboard and ruminated on how the past two nights she had dreamed about her dad—unsettling fleeting dreams wrapped in dread that chilled her to her core.

What if Larry was trying to communicate with Pepper? Or what if it all amounted to just a dream, where her mind tried to process all the stress? Still, who was Jolene?

After Pepper tore herself out of bed and got dressed, every motion feeling like she walked through mud, tears at the ready to spill forth, her heart racing, she ran into Loki. He notified her that Beatrice had mumbled in her sleep during the night, as if carrying on a conversation. However, Loki couldn't make heads or tails out of her words. That set Pepper's teeth on edge, and one frustrated-laced tear slipped.

Unfortunately, Loki and Perrin couldn't cast magic; they couldn't even use the elevator without help. And the capuchin could forget about jumping to the second floor to climb on a palm frond—he tried and failed, his strength rivaling that of a lowlie. Oddly enough, Kimball had no problem traveling to the rooftop and back.

Pepper assuaged Loki that today she would make up for yesterday—which was a wash as she slept most of it away— and planned on exploring the Academy for answers that would help Beatrice and enable them to leave.

Perrin sauntered into the atrium to join Pepper on her hunt. "Whoa! You look like crap."

"I'm exhausted. Not sleeping well." *And I think my pops is dead*, Pepper dared not to utter.

"That's too bad. I, on the other hand, haven't slept better. Those beds are everything." Perrin inspected their surroundings. "So, what's the plan?"

"According to Melisende, Sawyer is on the prowl for some object at the Academy. And seeing how we're trapped here and living on borrowed time until Blondie returns, which could be any day now, we have to find this object before she does."

"Use it as a bargaining chip?"

"Yep. At the very least, it could help us thwart whatever the Syndicate has planned. And maybe we'll discover some answers, starting with where everyone disappeared to," Pepper said.

"Sweetling, I'm not down with needle hunting in this massive haystack. What about torturing the damned? Once

I'm through with them, they'll tell us everything we need to know." Perrin's baby blues glinted with excitement.

"Sorry to burst your bubble, but Melisende basically confirmed in so many words that the damned were hexed from divulging anything about the Academy's inner workings or the Agents themselves."

"I can't do magic. Now I can't torture. I hate it here," Perrin huffed, then whined some more and kicked stones into a pond.

Pepper then went over her findings regarding sigils. "There has to be more here."

"And finding more sigils will help us how?"

"The Academy prohibits spell casting here, right? What if they use a different kind of magic than gems? Air, Earth ..."

The living dolly nodded her head slowly in a gesture of finally understanding. "You think we're going to find Fire, Water, and Aether?"

"Yes. Now, how to use the elements, magically speaking, I have no idea."

"So, where do we start this needle hunting?"

"The dorms. I found out where they're located." Pepper pointed to five floors above. "And the entrances may or may not be locked, so we have that to look forward to."

Perrin's pout bowed into a grin—a look that never failed to strike the fear of God in Pepper. It was terrifying, as in the Lolly'ka was moments from devouring prey. She rubbed her dainty hands together, the tips of her ruby-red nails stake-sharp, and said, "Finally, we're having some fun! But why are we starting at the Agents' digs?"

"If I were a student here"—Pepper swallowed a throat-constricting lump of jealousy—"I'd keep a cheat sheet of all the sigils on hand. If we're lucky, we'll find coursework or something containing a list of all the Schools or at least some mention of them. Ultimately, we need to find Karma. The goddess has to have an office here. So, maybe we'll find an indicator of that, too."

Noting the splinter of delight in Perrin's eyes, Pepper asked, "What?"

"I can't wait to introduce you to my sisters. Especially Kirby. The creator to my suggester. How you think reminds me of … well, me and her." Perrin tee-heed. "Let's do this."

Pepper felt sluggish, like she had just eaten two Thanksgiving dinners. The Academy was enormous, to begin with, and traipsing down four levels on the continuous glass ramp was the equivalent of a mile. "I'm too lazy to walk, so I say we take this elevator to the fifth floor and jump off in time." Luckily, Perrin didn't object.

Pepper's palms still had some remnants of ink, and while giving her hands a thorough search of areas to write on, Perrin said, "Don't make me take back my compliment."

"What?"

"Try drawing the Earth sigil in the air."

Pepper did just that; the minute she lowered her hand, the elevator rose, then sped up.

When the correct floor was in sight, Pepper yelled, "Jump!"

The girls rolled to a stop in a tangle of bougainvillea, not a door in sight. Before Pepper could say, "Now what?" a glass wall glided open as if sensing visitors, revealing a large common area filled with sparse and utilitarian furnishings: a couch, some chairs, and tables. A sprawling hallway was off to the side and housed about twenty-odd windowless rooms with beds, dressers, and drawerless nightstands. Nothing in the way of intel had presented itself, so the girls ended their search and moved on.

They walked up the Slinkified ramp to the next floor and came across a locked door. Pepper used the whisperings only she could hear as a guide to where to draw the Karma

Academy emblem. With a snick, the door yawned open and revealed a new set of quarters. Only these were more stately in appearance and design. Lanterns blazed to life and chased away the gloom with their buttery light. A modest library with bean bags for chairs occupied a corner area, its shelves well-fed and organized.

"Are these quarters for the best in class?" Perrin twirled around, drinking up the grandeur of her surroundings.

Soaring ceilings, classically modern decor, and all the creature comforts at one's fingertips. A gigantic sectional commanded the center of the room. There wasn't a TV or game console to be found, so what did the Agents do for entertainment? Unless gazing at the majestic mountainscape and endless waterfalls through the wall of pocketing glass sliders served as amusement. Or the open-air balcony with a fire pit hugged by sofas.

"I'm already bored," Perrin said.

Pepper turned her attention to a smattering of doors. While entering the first dorm room, Pepper said, "We're looking for a notebook, a slip of paper, something that contains all the sigils."

While Perrin took the area downstairs, which contained a cozy living area with a desk and floor-to-ceiling windows serving as front-row seats to the spectacular scenery, Pepper headed up the circular stairs to a loft. A made bed and a nightstand stared back at her. She rifled through the two drawers, but they were empty. Same for the walk-in closet.

"Unlived-in," Pepper said loud enough for Perrin to hear. "Someone wiped the entire area clean, too."

"Same down here."

The upstairs bedroom seamlessly bled into the doorless ensuite bath, which was essentially a glass cube, offering no privacy. Hopefully, the mountainscape beyond was uninhabited. An in-ground spa occupied the same space as a rainfall shower with views of the mountainscape beyond. Pepper searched the vanity and came up empty. Unable to help herself, she even searched the toilet tank; in the days of working karma-for-hire gigs, Pepper had resorted to hiding evidence in that very spot for her clients to retrieve.

"I don't think anyone has been here for quite a long time," Perrin called out from the first level.

"I agree," Pepper said, descending the stairs. "This room's militaristic. Not even a hole in the wall."

"Then again, this is a school for assassins, so—"

"All work and no play?" Pepper added more to herself. "But this place feels more like a studio apartment, except for the lack of a kitchen. But who needs one when you have the damned cooking all your meals?"

They continued to the next room and had to rethink their theory. Black pants, socks, and shirts were strewn about and tossed on the lounge chairs, the couch, and the floor. "I guess assassins don't enjoy hanging up their clothes."

"I don't know, Perrin. Someone has definitely lived here. I'm talking recently."

The vibe went from safe to uneasy in a snap. Like the owner would return any minute. That alone sent Pepper's arm hairs to stand at attention.

"There's moldy remnants of food on the plates. And maggots. Lots of them." Perrin bunched her nose at the miasma of rotten food wafting about. "Judging from the amount of fur the plates are wearing like an accessory, I'd say it's been at least a few months since someone's been here."

Pepper couldn't judge the dorm's messiness. Larry often commented that her room looked like a bomb had gone off. And Pepper would tell him that cleaning wasn't her jam.

"The Agent left nothing behind," Pepper shouted from the second floor, then swiveled around to give the room one last glance and noted that all the nightstand drawers were left open. "Drawers are empty. I think someone was searching for something up here. Besides the nightstand, the mattress isn't level with the frame. Like it had been removed and hastily thrown back in place."

"Same down here. The couch cushions are wonky."

After thoroughly searching the room, they entered the third dorm and stopped dead in their tracks. Someone had either punched or kicked the walls in a fit of rage, hole after gaping hole. A trail of Tiger's Milk snack bar wrappers littered the stone floor. The drawers to the study desk were ripped out of their home. Chair cushions with stab wounds bled out their feathers all over the throw rug in the living area. However, the bed upstairs was untouched, but the drawers weren't closed.

"I'm taking a wild stab in the dark here, but this has to be Sawyer's handiwork," Perrin said.

The remaining rooms—a handful in number—were untouched, like the first one, so Pepper and Perrin gravitated back to the torn-apart dorm room and surveyed the mess.

"We must have missed something. Sawyer went hog-wild in this room for a reason," Perrin said.

"Agreed. I'll take the upstairs." After giving the space an exhaustive search, Pepper dropped her elbows on the glass railing and leaned over the living room below, watching Perrin toss cushions off the couch and search every nook and cranny.

While pacing back and forth, it wasn't until Pepper had switched her position and gotten farther away from the study area—mainly the desk—that she noticed a shimmer in the air. Reminiscent of hot summers in Naples, where water mirages sprung up on nearly every road. That same effect took place feet away from where Perrin stood below.

"Don't move!" Pepper raced down the winding stairs and then poked the area. But nothing happened. Though the air went a tad slack. If only Pepper hadn't chewed her nails to the quick, she could have used them as a sharp implement.

But Perrin took pride in her nails and filed them nightly with her switchblade. "Give me your finger." Pepper dragged Perrin's sharp-as-her-tongue nails in a downward motion, slicing the air molecules in half. Together, the girls pushed open the air like curtains, revealing a truncated space like a pocket, and then walked through.

Everything was a mirror to the outside reality, save for the walls. A detective's evidence board held prime real estate with a picture of Cazzian commanding the top.

"This picture was taken at Seafarers on the Gulf," Pepper choked out. "It's a super pricey beachside restaurant back in Naples." She glued her terror-stricken eyes to her archenemy, the same man bent on killing her, the man responsible for abducting her father.

Donning a tux, Cazzian stood in front of a bevy of dressed-to-the-nines guests dining alfresco, with the sandy beach in the background, the sun melting into the horizon, and the Naples Pier in the distance. Ember and Vlad, flanking Cazzian, remained seated, with Sawyer in a chair next to the OG vampire. Someone had circled Sawyer's mug in red with the date. And the question: *Who is the Firebird?* hovered over the picture of the elusive Ember with ruby eyes, resplendent in a ballgown dripping in gold and limned by fire.

Another picture showcased Vlad's castle, clearly taken with a telephoto lens. The fortress would befit the Romanian countryside, only it wasn't perched atop a snowcapped mountain but surrounded by boggy, sawgrass marshes.

"Syndicate headquarters is in the Everglades. This pretty much confirms it," Pepper shared.

Both girls noted the newspaper clippings from The Bellowers, Pandæmonia's premier news source, high-lighting the upcoming lunar eclipse and supreme planetary parade. One article detailed how Earthbound mages would celebrate those holy celestial events by attending festivals and honoring their goddess, Hekate. The Agent underlined the following passage: *The last time all eight planets aligned in the heavens was nearly one thousand years ago, thought to be around the time Underlord Chaos discovered the reservoir of magic that forever changed our lives for the better.*

"Back at the Ministry of Mischief and Mayhem," Pepper started, "I listened to this demonstration put together by the Demons for a Better Tomorrow—"

"Oh, sweetling," Perrin said in her patent condescending tone reserved for clueless lowlies. "DBT's an arm of King Lucifer and his regime. They're propagandists and nothing more."

"Okay. But DBT spoke about Chaos, mainly regarding the peace treaty between Hell and Earth. Then do you know anything about Underlord Chaos regarding magic?"

"I know about as much as most demons. Supposedly, Chaos stumbled across a reservoir of magic in its rawest form, the where in the cosmos a mystery. Rumor has it that it belonged to the gods. But that made no difference to Chaos because he kept it all for himself, the glutton he was. Finders keepers. According to hellfire-side tales, with this magic, Chaos created the first ever chaosgate using his blood and the stolen magic. Before, gods could travel to whatever dimensions and realms their hearts desired, but not other beings. Chaos changed that. Made chaosnauting possible for everyone."

Chaos went on to conquer realms and dimensions far removed from our own, and even that wasn't enough to satisfy his hunger. It didn't take long until absolute power corrupted Chaos to the core. He needed more. More power. More magic. He swore other reservoirs existed and set out to find each one. The Universal Elects had no choice but to assassinate him.

"'Magic is a part of me and always will be. The two can never be sundered.' Supposedly, those were the last words Chaos uttered before he died," Perrin said.

"Since Chaos is dead, I wonder why the Agent considered that clipping important enough to tack it to the evidence board. And what do the lunar eclipse and the supreme planetary parade have to do with him?" Pepper asked.

"I imagine the article's more about what Chaos found than the Underlord. What we know is that Sawyer tore this room apart. The question is why? This evidence"—Perrin waved her hand with a flourish—"would not be breaking news to Sawyer."

Perrin then pointed to a wallet-sized picture, its corner peeking out from behind The Bellowers' clipping, of a bob-haired girl that hovered midair and off to the side of the evidence board, more in the miscellaneous section than part of Cazzian's known associates. A girl Pepper knew all too well, who also happened to be Pepper's former classmate at Naples High and a righteous bitch to boot. Chloe Dhawan of Chloe's Casefiles and Conspiracies—a podcast that got its humble beginnings on the Naples Teen Scene website before it gained popularity. A snippet of Chloe's podcast magically plucked from the internet accompanied her picture.

"That's the podcast that nerd Jacob mentioned. Can't be a coincidence Chloe lives in Naples." Perrin added, from one look at Pepper's pinched face, "I take it we don't like her?"

Pepper explained how Chloe was part of the in-crowd, aka Kimball's clique, pageant-participator turned the reigning Swamp Buggy Queen. A head cheerleader who cared more about partying and gathering likes on social media than basic human kindness. It didn't help that she had poked fun at Pepper a time or two, along with Kimball.

"Ugh. What a bitch," Perrin added, arms akimbo.

Deftly, Pepper touched the photo, which felt like Silly Putty. A recording of Chloe's podcast began playing in 3D and showcased the podcaster inside her colorful bedroom slash filming studio.

"Hey, fellow Truthers. Chloes here." The podcaster sat at her desk, dressed in jammies, and talked into a mic. "I know we're all rattled and shocked at what transpired yesterday at Naples High, and some of you are terrified of going back until things return to normal. But I have news. Normalcy is gone. And nobody is coming to rescue our precious be-hinds. Hashtag sorry, not sorry. Our once-safe city has descended into mayhem. Lawlessness is rampant, and demons no longer hide in the shadows. Word to the wise: if you want to stay alive, don't go out after dark. Crosses don't work. Learned that the hard way last night. Same with hail Marys. A roided-out vamp laughed in my face. True story. As for most of the residents of Naples, they're Misted and can't be trusted. So, we must band together if we have any hope of surviving. Don't believe me. Watch this."

An unsteady video clip discretely captured on a cell phone played out right outside the retro-themed Javayum on Third Street South, a short walk from Pepper's front door. The sky was awash in a swirl of reds and pinks, so the sun must have just set. A vampire marched up to a patron idling at one of the bar's outdoor tables and ripped out the man's jugular while his date and other customers watched; then, they all shook off the horrific happenings and continued sipping their kratom-infused cocktails as if a vampire hadn't attacked in plain sight. As if the bloodless corpse hadn't just dropped to the sidewalk. Another clip showcased a car mowing down a civilian walking in a heavily populated place outside Coastland Center Mall and their companion continuing on their merry way as if nothing had happened.

"My inbox is flooded with y'all's firsthand accounts and gruesome pics. I've seen the terror on the streets. You've seen it. We witnessed it in Mister Stevenson's biology class, where our teacher nearly dissected Jeremy instead of the frog. And would have, if not for Tony kung-fuing the crap out of him."

Chloe took a swig from her thermos, then said, "So, Truthers, grab a snack and drink—make sure it's not tap water because I'm pretty sure it's poisoned—and lock your doors. Disable the doorbell cameras"—she faux-coughed—"listening devices"—then faux-coughed again. "And don't turn on the TV. Otherwise, you run the risk of being Misted. Okay, brace yourselves.

"Magic is real, folks. I know. I just got a case of the chills, too. We've discussed it ad nauseam on the podcast for funsies, interviewed alleged mages, and even those who swear they come from other dimensions like Hell. Well, it's safe to say that the proverbial wool has officially been pulled off our eyes. We all know at least one person who went to the All Hallows' Eve masquerade ball and disappeared or returned all bloodthirsty and *grr* evil. Our Gulfside town— once made up of sand, swaying palms, and salt-laced air—is now covered in thick mist and the stench of death, hot garbage, and fish guts. And with the mist came the demons and vampires and Vlad.

"Yes, our favorite bodice-ripping, hotter-than-a-September-afternoon-in-Naples, murder-enthused original vampire. After five minutes of watching that man on live TV, my auntie changed and turned on me and my mom. Waste Management hauled off her TV the next day. You're welcome, Auntie. Vlad's everywhere, though, Misting people. Don't even dare question his motives to anyone unless you trust them fully; otherwise, you risk being painted an enemy and put on a watchlist. You can forget about high-tailing it out of town. Some supernatural force is preventing anyone from leaving Naples.

"Now, onto the truly horrible news. I know. I warned you tonight was gonna be a doozy. Many of you may remember our neighborhood mage, David, who frequently appeared as a guest on our podcast to discuss all things: vampires, magic, mayhem, and mystery. Well, he's gone missing. When he was last on the podcast, he mentioned off-air that his archOmega called in the big guns for help, whoever they are. Looks like the big guns were no-shows. They Misted, too? Wouldn't be surprised. An aside, if not for David casting spooky, mystical magic crap before he disappeared, Chloe's Casefiles wouldn't be airing.

"Vlad's even Misted our local news outfits, and they've stopped televising the missing person cases. Instead, they're reporting on dumb crap like the vampire high king, giving him constant airtime so he can continue Misting the locals. Or sending their correspondents to film behind-the-scenes footage of his weekly reality TV show *Romancing Vlad.* I still can't wrap my head around the fact that bars host viewing parties for this show. Or that every Friday at five p.m. sharp, people all over town drop everything to watch Vlad go about his day-to-day life as he prepares for the upcoming lunar eclipse gala at his castle.

"And don't even get me started on the opening credits of *Romancing Vlad* with the sweeping violin music as he slowly walks out of the Gulf ... I can't with the thirst-trap nonsense. And it's not like we can change the channel. Gone are the days of choices. Streaming TV is dead. Team Vlad's blocked the internet except for their crap. No working satellites either. Just Vlad and more Vlad spread across all 4 local channels. The reality show's enough to send a non-Misted person over the edge."

Pepper and Perrin exchanged looks of pure terror.

"Still, between Vlad's publicist Sarah and her upspeaking voice-overs on the *Romancing Vlad* clips she posts five times a day on every social media platform, her 'get-ready with me's, 'what I eat in a day's, and makeup tutorials while talking incessantly about the upcoming lunar eclipse gala at Vlad's castle … Ugh!" Chloe placed her finger in her throat. "Gag me. Enough already! Ads for the celebration are plastered all over town. We're bombarded with them on social media. Gotta ask yourself why? It can't be good if they need every single person in Naples to tune into the televised event. Listen, I'm not gonna pretend I'm not terrified. Because, Truthers, I am. And I'm sure you are, too. But we have to band together. We have to be the voice of the missing and the imperiled. We must be vigilant and work together to take back Naples from the forces of darkness—"

The clip ended, and Perrin snapped Pepper's jaw shut. "Some drool was about to escape."

"I didn't think that Naples would be affected. I—"

"Me either, sweetling. And we all know how the Syndicate's galas turn out. Let's just say a good time is not had by all. But did you notice something else that was off?"

"You mean how it seems as if more time has passed?" When Perrin nodded, her eyes emoting concern, Pepper added, "The All Hallows' Eve ball was a few days ago. Yet Chloe's acting like it was weeks. Perrin, we're screwed." Feeling sick to her stomach, Pepper collapsed on the sofa and buried her head in the palms of her hands. "Oh God. What if time moves differently here? I hadn't thought of that. And we're trapped. What if the gala is when the Syndicate plans on killing my father? You heard what Kimball said about the vampire ceremony —"

Perrin sat down next to Pepper and placed her arm around her shoulder. "If you don't holster that defeatist attitude, I will revoke your status as an honorary member of the

Lolly'kas." Pepper sighed in response. "All joking aside, sweetling. You're stressing me out. And I don't do stress. Karma rules over Earth, right? So, wouldn't time in her realm run parallel to Earth? I get there are other time zones in your world, but you get the hint."

Pepper nodded and calmed down a tad, as that explanation made sense.

"Look, I'm homesick, too. I miss my sisters. My life of queenpinning. As it stands, you are the closest thing we have to get the fuh'kar out of the Academy because Peaches is pretty much useless, and Loki and I can't cast magic. For Lilith's sake, we're prevented from using the elevator without help. But you can. Somewhat. So until we get answers, freaking out isn't going to do you any good."

Perrin was right. Pepper needed to get her butt in gear. Her dad's life depended on it. She shot to her feet and began pacing and chewing on her barely there nails. "The lunar eclipse is fast approaching … What if the Syndicate needs this object Sawyer's desperate to find for the gala at Vlad's castle?"

"Would explain why Sawyer's still alive. C'mon. We better find that needle!"

Since time was of the essence, Pepper and Perrin decided to divide and conquer. Pepper continued walking up the circuitous path that wound its way to the rooftop while Perrin navigated downward.

After bypassing an endless wall of moss, Pepper finally came across the entrance to what was assuredly another School. As if expecting its newest student, the wooden door pivoted on its axis, granting Pepper passage. A circular foyer was inside, with several archways leading to separate rooms.

Mosaic tile art in the center of the hallway depicted a sigil, intricate in its design, with curlicues of flames inside a triangle. "Hello, Fire."

Pepper walked through door number one. Inside, a riot of wood made up the classroom's interior—on the walls, the sloped aisles, and the stacked levels housing long banquet tables that served as desks. Shelves of fat reference books ate the space on the other side of the room. She heaved one from off the shelf and thumbed through it. The law book contained theories on vengeance and historical case studies.

Pepper's eyes alighted on what appeared to be the U.S. Constitution framed on the wall. Only it wasn't the Constitution she had studied in American History this past year. This one transcended the supreme law of the United States and encapsulated all of Earth, and included does and don't evers as far as cosmic laws were concerned: *Agents of Karma adhere to retributive justice. Never strike first. The punishments must befit the crimes, and the means are in the eyes of the Agent. Not every offender ought to be assassinated. Perpetrators not sentenced to death must be brought to their knees by taking away what means the most to them.*

But the rules for Agents of Karma didn't stop on Earth. Every dimension had different laws regarding magic. In some, casting spells came at a cost, as every being could wield its chaotic powers. Only governing bodies could wield magic, like in Hell. On Earth, gem conduits were a must. *Strange, that,* Pepper thought, and made a mental note to discover why.

Another thing Pepper found odd was the number of Agents helping Karma maintain law and order across multiple dimensions, or rather, a handful if the dorm rooms were any indication. Unless she was sorely mistaken and there were far more Agents in existence than just a few. No, there couldn't be; otherwise, Karma wouldn't be knocking at death's door. Still, how could a few Agents police the entire cosmos?

Even Hell had a constitution, which included the treaty

between Hell and Earth, overseen by Goddess Karma and Mephistopheles that Pepper had learned about briefly at the Ministry of Mischief and Mayhem, courtesy of Demons for a Better Tomorrow presentation. There was another treaty between Earth and Cal'lya-mír, the Elven dimension. Unfortunately, Pepper couldn't read the Elven tongue.

Mentionings of Goddess Hekate were sprinkled here and there, but only regarding magic use for Agents visiting other dimensions. Just like the impartial Universal Elects had selected Karma to preserve cosmic law and order, they picked Hekate to oversee magic throughout the cosmos.

Though Pepper could only read in full the Earthly Dimension Constitution as the others were written in foreign tongues, the law was simple: using magic freely without a conduit was strictly forbidden and impossible. What Pepper couldn't comprehend was the need for magic gems. Why? Perrin had cast spells without using them at the Starless Souk, so why couldn't the same be done on Earth?

Furthermore, how was the Syndicate defying the rules of Earthly magic? Because they were, according to the Constitution. Nowhere in that official document did it state that magic could be derived from draining the blood of mages.

Pepper thumbed through one of the reference books nearby in the Earth section—*Marvelous Magic* by Joe Snelling—and shamelessly picked that one in particular because, unlike the other doorstoppers, it was a quick read that weighed next to nothing. In the opening chapter, the author brought up the fundamental difference between a mage and a lowlie, which came down to DNA.

Then an entire chapter sang the praises of magic gems and how truly marvelous they were in their use and design. *It is a widely known fact that cosmic matter exists in a non-local state in the fifth dimension, or what alchemists refer to as non-reality, and is, therefore, transformable. Because of that, a mage can transmo-*

grify matter into whatever they desire, within reason, of course. And though tiny, the gems play a decisive role by serving as a vibrational match to non-reality and as an extension of a mage in dimensions where conduits are required.

As for the gem's composition and role in spell-casting, fulgurite is nothing short of godly, as it is born of lightning and Aether. And when filled with vaporous magic, it is a physical representation of all five elements. In action, the mage envisions what they want to bring about and then determines what colors are vibrational matches to the end result. As for the magic gem's role, it would then entangle with the mage's desire in non-reality and materialize it in reality, and voila! A spell is successfully cast. Marvelous indeed.

One of the final chapters discussed how chaotic magic was, which made sense as it was nature itself and, therefore, unpredictable. But the envisioning, verbalizing, and writing of spells and commands were what organized the disorder. Enraptured, Pepper kept reading and even considered picking up a thicker book.

"There you are, sweetling." Perrin sashayed into the room, her frilly dress swooshing with each step. "You look confused."

Pepper unburied her nose from the book. "Perrin, remember at the Starless Souk when you cast a spell on Kimball without gems, and we were confused about how that could be possible?" Perrin nodded. "Well, you're not going to believe what I just read in the Q and A section with the author." Pepper read aloud: "I am one of the many mages who agree with Goddess Hekate's decision to suppress the magic in every mage's DNA. Humans have quite the appetite for conquering and enslaving the weaker-minded—and that's without magic added into the mix, which is quite the aphrodisiac. So, our beloved Hekate had no choice but to step in and level the playing field."

"Mother Lilith! The gods are so sneaky."

"Agreed." Pepper then went over what she had uncovered about the rules for magic varying in different dimensions. "The little knowledge I have of magic came from Jhi, for the most part. Still, you and I were both under the assumption that you need gems to cast spells in every dimension. But that's not entirely true."

"The fact I could cast spells at the souk without gems disproved our assumptions." Perrin wasn't exactly an encyclopedia of knowledge regarding magic use anywhere other than Hell and Earth, so she didn't offer any insight. Perrin noticed Pepper's raised brows and asked, "What's got you worried, other than the obvious?"

"Casting magic on Earth without magic gems is impossible. Says so right here on this official document." Pepper pointed at the Earth Realm Constitution hanging on the wall. "And selling your soul to obtain powers doesn't change that fact."

Perrin jumped onto Pepper's page pretty damn quick. "And we're certain the Syndicate isn't using gems?" Doubt peeked through Perrin's tone.

"Not one hundred percent, but—Actually, I am." Pepper thought back to the masquerade ball when Cazzian tossed around magic and didn't run out of juice like Loki had and shared that memory with Perrin.

"Yes, but he also was amped up on mage blood." Perrin considered what she had said, then added, "So was Miles at the Budreau restaurant, now that I think about it. Regardless, what difference would it make if Cazzian, Miles, and all the other soul-sellers the Syndicate recruited drank blood? According to the rules, they would still need gems to wield magic."

"I know, but Vlad and other vampires *shouldn't* have mage-like magic to begin with, but they do."

"Yeah. Not good. Wait till I tell my sisters that the Hounds found a workaround and didn't share it with us. Those fanged douchelords are gonna pay."

"I have a bad feeling, Perrin. That what we discovered is just the tip of the iceberg. If anything, the playing field is no longer level. So what does that mean for other mages?"

Rotten apples always ruin it for others. And as history had shown, those rotten apples would eventually figure out a way to abuse the system like the Syndicate. One thing was certain: Pepper might not have been any closer to figuring out how the Syndicate beat the system, but she wouldn't stop investigating until she discovered the truth.

"Well, I found something that will de-bitchify you, hopefully," Perrin said.

Pepper scrunched her face and frowned. Here she thought her edge from earlier had dulled. Apparently not.

"I found the School of Magic and another element—Aether. But the door's locked."

"Then how do you know it's the School of Magic?"

"The Wheel of Hekate cemented on the door is a fairly good sign." Perrin couldn't contain her glee. "Let's see, we have Earth on the rooftop"—she clapped her hands as she recited each element—"Air at the infirmary. Fire is clearly this School." Her eyes flicked to the side, and she bit her over-glossed lips as if deep in thought. "What element am I missing?" Perrin sang the alphabet in Laramaic. "Mem—that's it. Water."

Perrin followed Pepper to the other rooms that were separate entrances to one big sparring area. The wall showcased knives and other weapons. The damned—their eyes removed and mouths sewn shut—were used as macabre wooden man posts and boxing mannequins.

"What other disciplines did you say were taught here?" Perrin asked as they returned to the glass walkway.

"Vengeance, assassination, martial arts, spells, magic

gems, and poisoncraft," Pepper recited all the skills mentioned in the Karma Academy invite. "Necromancy, deception, dark sorcery, and memory manipulation."

"I'm guessing the last ones you mentioned must be associated with Water. I didn't come across any other sigil besides Aether, though. And I walked all the way to the roof before joining you, too."

"Neither have I. So, what are we missing?" A gunmetal gray hue spilled over the orange sherbet sky, obliterating its vibrancy as the sun nearly finished its descent.

A blood-curdling screech boomed in the distance.

"Well, that's our cue to get the fuh'kar back to the hospital and call it a night."

12

As the sun peeked through scalloped clouds and the temperature held steady at ninety degrees, salt-laced air and the carefree aroma of coconut suntan lotion swathed Pepper in their comforting embrace.

"Afternoon showers are coming like clockwork," Larry said softly, as he and Pepper strolled down the creaky wooden planks of the Naples Pier.

The father and daughter bypassed a gaggle of giggling girls twirling the hair on the ends of their ponytails while batting their eyelashes at a group of board-shorts-wearing boys fishing at the end of the pier. Only these teens weren't dressed like Pepper's peers. Their sartorial choices were more vintage in design.

Larry paused, not so much to take in the sparsely populated beach where his eyes trawled along but to catch his breath. "I never thought I'd return to Naples. Not in a million years. Watching my small hometown disappear in the rearview mirror of my GTO on the way to boot camp was my teenage dream fulfilled. Still, the best decision I made was to return home to Naples to raise you," he beamed, then grew serious. "I wish my parents had met you, Pepper." Larry pulled her in for a hug.

"I wish I would have met them, too," Pepper shared.

"Looking back on my life, I've realized how growing up in small-town Naples was nothing short of magical before it became overdeveloped," Larry said. "When you could be a kid and play outside after dark and feel safe. And I hope I gave you that life, too, kiddo." His lungs rattled, and his voice was scratchy like sandpaper. Tears welling in his eyes nearly spilled out, but the coughing fit that tore out from his throat interrupted their forward momentum.

Once the coughing attack subsided, Larry settled onto a bench, and Pepper joined him. "Carefree and wearing nothing but swim trunks and a smile ..." He continued fondly reminiscing, spinning golden tales of his childhood, and Pepper soaked up every word.

Every weekend and every day during summer, Larry spent his mornings and afternoons sprawled on a beach blanket, hands clasped behind his head, watching clouds scud by and thinking of all the pranking and harmless trouble-making he and his friends could get into. Nightly parties. Sleeping in late. Scrounging around sofas for loose change so he could enjoy a root beer float with his buddies at the soda shop nestled within the beach store on Third Street. "That was before your time, Pepper," Larry said.

And on the days Lady Luck took a shining to Pepper's pops, he had excavated enough money left behind in the sides of his grandpa's recliner—thanks to Uncle Rob's stretched pockets—and could order his crush a grilled cheese and fries.

"Jumping off the pier and diving feet first in the warm

Gulf waters. Ain't nothing like that feeling of freedom. Salt stinging your eyes. Swimming to shore and doing it all over again. Fishing and boating and swimming and partying and first kisses and first heartbreaks. If only every day could be like the endless summers from my youth."

"Who's that, Pops?" Pepper pointed to a girl in a modest bikini and jelly sandals that Larry couldn't peel his eyes away from.

"Patty. And the boy she's flirting with is me."

"Pops, you were so handsome." Pepper lovingly stared at her dad. "Still are. And so … gangly. What happened?" She poked his chunky belly, which wasn't as chunky anymore.

"Your cooking is what happened. And beer." Larry struggled to raise his lips into a weak smile. "Patty was the first girl I ever loved. Sapphire blue eyes, long blonde hair, and legs to match."

"Ew. Don't need to hear the specifics."

"Every boy at school crushed hard on Patty. But she only had eyes for your pops, and I her. Didn't think I could ever love anybody like Patty. Not even close. Would have done anything for her. She was *the one*."

Larry's coughing returned anew. Once done, he inspected the tissue, and his eyes grew heavy from the results. Though he tossed it before Pepper could see for herself, she caught shades of red.

"They say there's only one soulmate in your lifetime, and you're lucky if you find them. And for the longest time, I thought that role belonged to Patty. But they couldn't have been more wrong. You are my greatest love, Pepper. You are my soul—"

"Pops—"

"Let me finish, Pepper."

She choked down a panicked breath and reluctantly obliged.

"I never knew unconditional, soul-fulfilling love until I became a parent. And I never realized how incomplete my life was until you came into it. I thought I'd always be a bachelor, childless, the world my home. But you changed all that. You grounded me. Gave me a sense of purpose. Brought meaning to my life. And I don't regret for a single minute raising you solo. Honestly, I wouldn't change anything for the world, kiddo. I know you didn't have a mom, but I tried my damndest to be both. I might not have been the best parent, maybe too lax—"

"Pops, please, stop! I never wanted for anything. Not once did I ever feel incomplete. Why are you talking about all this? Just stop!" Pepper didn't understand why she felt so utterly terrified or why there was such a note of finality to his tone and demeanor. And it wasn't until this moment that she noticed her dad's dirty blond hair grayer than usual. His once reddish-tanned skin was now sallow, his ordinarily bright hazel eyes cloudy and weighed down by heavy bags. Or that he had lost a chunk of pounds.

"Pepper, I would spend eternity in deep regret if I didn't express how I truly feel, how you are my greatest joy, the love of my life, and how I am honored to have been picked to be your dad. My love for you is eternal, kiddo. Regardless of what happens, please always know that."

Pepper wanted to grab tight to her dad and never let him go, but he vanished like sea foam. Just barely could she see him. Pepper fought her way through the crush of faceless teens, desperate to reach her pops before he left her.

She caught up to Larry as he sat on the edge of the pier, about to jump off. The gunmetal gray water below fiercely crashed against the wooden piles, crests of waves climbing their way up as if to pull her dad under and drag him to his watery grave.

Blood trickling out of his mouth, Larry said, "Pepper,

listen to me very clearly. I don't know how much time I have left. But she said you could hear me. And that maybe you can help them—us."

"The tour group?"

"Yes. The woman with red hair and green eyes. Contact someone who can help her and her conclave. But I told her I don't want you helping me, not anymore, because I don't want you *anywhere near* that man. You hear me?" Larry's face grew thunderous, eyes squinting, brow creasing, jaw set. "Stay away, Pepper, or Miles'll kill you, too!"

"Here lies Larry Bell, marine veteran, recipient of the Purple Heart, only son to William and Elsie Bell, and proud father to Pepper Li," the officiant said. Pepper tossed lilies onto her pop's coffin six feet below.

"I'm sorry for your loss." Jhi joined Pepper, just the two of them standing alone in the middle of a cemetery.

One moment Pepper held it together, putting on a proud face, but all it took was hearing two words: "I'm sorry," and she succumbed to body-convulsing, mounds-of-snot, river-of-tears crying. Grief was funny like that. Then came the lamenting, a mournful melodic sobbing, with notes of fear, anger, and sadness crashing together.

Jhi pulled a wailing Pepper into his arms and then placed a comforting hand on her back and another on her head, gently caressing her with his warmth while her snot wet his Henley.

When Pepper's tears took five, Jhi handed her a tissue from his coat pocket, genuine concern reflecting in his sea-glass eyes.

Pepper asked, "Did you have to bury your parents?" She blew a honking wad of phlegm into the tissue, then continued, "I remember you mentioning that they had passed."

"No. And I wasn't exactly truthful when I mentioned my parents," Jhi said sheepishly.

"Wow. Real shocker. Jhi lied." The silver lining? Annoyance extended the break time for Pepper's tears.

"Go ahead. Give me all you got." Jhi waved his hand in a come hither motion. "I deserve it. The truth is that my mother gave me up. And I never met my father."

That surprising response chipped away at Pepper's annoyance, and she adopted a softer tone. "Do you remember your mom?"

"I see flashes of this woman, in a white dress and barefoot, who I think was my mom. And I'm young, like three, maybe four years old. I'm sitting under a tree on the softest grass I've ever felt. Not a cloud in the sky. And I'm just watching her. Noting the way the wind breezes through her long hair, the color of moraberries. While smiling at me and picking fruit from the tree, she's humming this tune that is so familiar but I can't place it and haven't heard it since. Afterward, she picks me up and swings me around in her arms. I love it. Want to go faster. And her laugh is comforting, like the knelling of bells on the Temple of Seren. Later in the evening, she makes us moraberry jam and smears the light red preserve on toast and a dollop on my nose, and I giggle. Can still taste its sweetness. Even now. But I always go back to that memory." Surprise cemented on Jhi's face. "I've never shared that with anyone."

"Why *that* memory?"

"Because," he paused, perhaps contemplating whether or not to share, "it was the last time I ever felt safe."

"My pops ... he's my safety net. The thought of living without him"—tears welled, and Pepper's vision tripled—"I can't fathom it. I don't want to live a life without him." Perrin's flask materialized, and she took a whopping sip. When she attempted to screw the lid back on, Jhi grabbed it out of her hand.

He took a pull of Grissel's ale, then asked, "Is that your greatest fear?" as he handed her back the flask.

"What? My pops dying and leaving me behind?"

Jhi nodded.

"Unequivocally, yes." Pepper sniffled, then wiped the snot from her nose before gulping another finger of ale. "I needed to protect my father at all costs. It's … I don't know. I can't explain why. It's always been that way. Whether it be his health, my pops is—was—kinda chunky and has blood sugar issues, or dammit—" Pepper cried and couldn't get the words out. *Past tense*—everything regarding her dad henceforth would be relegated there.

"I get it," Jhi said, looking deep into Pepper's eyes, "the overwhelming need to keep someone safe."

"What's your greatest fear, Jhi? What keeps you up at night?"

"You're gonna laugh."

Pepper pointed to her face, the swollen eyes, the tears streaming unabated down her face, her runny nose. "Even if I wanted to, I can't."

"Fair enough." He let out a weak chuckle. "Being trapped and lost and alone, a prisoner of nothingness."

A chill snaked up Pepper's spine. "No self-sovereignty. Death would be most welcome then."

"Not always."

In a flash, the cemetery disappeared, and they stood in a cement jungle of strip malls close to her home in Olde Naples. Most shops were closed, some going out of business with final clearance sale banners tacked to the windows.

"My pops loved this place or what was once here— Tropics Drive-In. But it's long gone. Torn down like many other places in Naples and replaced with parking lots and luxury condos."

"But memories don't leave."

"They aren't crystal clear either. And with time, they fade."

The strip mall crumbled out of sight, and Tropics Drive-In appeared, looking disheveled and lackluster.

"Why did you bring us here, Pepper?"

"I told you why. This was one of my pop's favorite haunts when he was younger and where he would take me for ice cream whenever I had a bad day at school until developers razed the drive-in to the ground. We'd come here, eat all the ice cream and junk food, and forget all about my shitty day. And he would always say there's more to life than school and those kids who were cruel to me. That I'd move on and forget all about them. But there would come a time in my adult life when I'd long for those days of my youth."

Jhi held her hand, and Pepper let him.

"I'm by no means an adult, but I think he was right, Jhi. I'd give anything to go back to when I didn't have a care in the world. The days walking along the shore, swimming in my pool, but not the Gulf because I don't like salt water and sand on me. Gross and sticky, and who wants to swim with a bunch of fish? I miss living in my clammy bathing suit and getting stuffed on delivery pizza and fizzy fruit punch in a can. Or after sunset playing Ghosts in the Graveyard with all the neighborhood kids and hearing my pops scream for me to come inside 'because it was bath time,' and me shouting 'five more minutes.'" Tears welled in Pepper eyes.

Jhi said, "Sounds nice," and meant it.

They had wound up in a car, Pepper in the driver's seat. A woman with hair like fire and green eyes appeared as if taking Pepper's order. Her lips moved, but nothing came out.

Pepper peered at the waitress and said, "Red-haired beauty with emerald eyes."

"She's been trying to get in touch with you. But you're not listening," Jhi said ominously.

"I don't—She sounds familiar. Can she see you?"

"I don't believe so."

Memories from a previous dream were coming to light. "I think my pops mentioned someone like that right after he took me for a stroll down memory lane and showed me his first love. Patty was her name. They were kids when they met. He thought the world of her. No other female could compare."

"What happened to Patty?"

"She died," Pepper replied coolly.

"Oh." Jhi seemed taken aback by that response. "That's horrible."

"I don't know why I said that. Maybe you're rubbing off on me, the king of lies you are." Pepper playfully poked Jhi in the side. "Patty didn't actually die. She married some super-rich guy, had a crapton of kids, and got really dumpy."

Jhi's laughter was contagious, and Pepper joined in. Until the pangs of grief returned, and she grew somber. "I think my dad's dead." It pained her to admit that truth.

"What makes you think that?"

"I don't know." Pepper looked him dead in the eyes. "Jhi, something's wrong. This all feels off. Like a dream, but not."

"It's because you're remembering."

"I wasn't born in Naples, y'know. I think I was born in Manila, but I don't know for certain. My sister would know."

Jhi perked up and inhaled as if moments from speaking, but he sighed and opted not to.

"But Jaylyn's missing like everyone else I love. It's like I died, and I'm stuck in Hell, and maybe I'm one of the damned and just don't know it. Hell, that's where you were born, right? Maybe you can get me out of this nightmare." Pepper recalled Perrin mentioning that Jhi wasn't a demon, nor was he fully human, so she went on a fishing expedition.

"I wasn't born in Hell. At least, I don't think so. I could

never get a straight answer from Mephy, so I quit asking. Didn't matter anyways, not really. Mephy raised me. He took me in when nobody else wanted me. So why would I care about those who abandoned me?"

"I didn't know that about Mephistopheles. How old were you when you got adopted?"

"Well, he didn't officially adopt me. That's not a thing in Hell, but I was little. I don't know how old. Four, five, six? I don't even know my birth date."

"Wow. So, Mephy's your dad? But you never referred to him like that. Just said he was your dominus."

"It's best if I keep my private life under wraps."

"Because then nobody can harm your loved ones in retaliation."

"Precisely. Let's just say my upbringing was anything but conventional. Still, Mephy raised me as his own. And I think he did the best he could for a mala'dayya." Jhi winked.

"That's right. He's a prince of Hell and missing, too." Realization paid Pepper a visit. "Like my dad."

"Yes, only I'm no closer to finding him. I'm not giving up, though. And the other princes are unaware of Mephy's absence. They're hoodwinked by that wanderer that stole Mephy's skinsuit, but I'm not about to spill the beans to them. Not yet."

"I'm so sorry, Jhi. I didn't realize."

"I know you are, Pepper. But unlike me, your dad is within reach. You can rescue him." Jhi's voice changed, and another entity spoke through him. "But you have to tap into your past to do so. Do you remember when you cast powerful magic?"

"This lifetime?" slipped out of Pepper's mouth. She gasped from the shock.

Jhi's lips quirked into a devilish grin, and then he replied in a voice not his own, "Not this one. Your first life. When it all began."

PEPPER WOKE WITH A START. All she could see was her dad jumping off the pier. *It was a nightmare. It wasn't real,* she reminded herself. So why did she not fully believe it?

"Sweetling, get dressed and come to Peaches' room." Concern was stitched all over Perrin's features. "It's better if you see for yourself."

Pepper put herself together the best she could and schooled her features to appear placid and not *I'm moments away from a nervous breakdown.* Then headed to Beatrice's room.

"She started moaning and mumbling 'yes, I understand' during the night," Loki explained. "Then woke up a few times after that and acted somewhat normal. She ate and drank and let me check her vitals, but she wouldn't take her eyes off me. Then she snapped and nearly clawed my eyes out. I had to sedate her." His eyes sailed to the valeritonin tranquilizer they had found in the pharmacy that rested on the nightstand.

Perrin ambled into the room and held what looked like an essential oil bottle. "Ashwagamint. Melisende hand-delivered it. Said it's an herb so powerful it could wake up a corpse. Probably because it smells like ass." Perrin waved the bottle under Beatrice's nose.

Pepper concurred and plugged her nose.

Beatrice shot up in bed and gasped, "Who are you people?"

Pepper watched intently as Beatrice slid her arm under the sheets. "She's getting a weapon." Quickly, Pepper restrained one of Beatrice's hands, then cried out, "Loki, get her other hand!"

Perrin jumped on the bed and tied her kicking legs.

Beatrice fought with all her might. "Let me go!"

"Not until you calm down. We are not your enemy!" Pepper stressed.

Her thrashing halted. But it was just a ruse. So, Loki had no choice but to administer another dosage of valeritonin and shove it into Beatrice's arm. "This should hold for a few hours."

"Then what?" Perrin asked the loaded question. "Apparently, your brains have atrophied again from lack of exercise. So, listen to the words coming out of my mouth: we need to get the fuh'kar out of here! And Overripe Peaches is the only one who knows how to leave. Only she's gone all crazed. There has to be something in the herbary that can make the crazy go away."

"Hard to do when we don't know what happened when Miles ambushed her." A plethora of remedies was at Pepper's disposal, but not knowing what afflicted Beatrice made things difficult.

"What about a truth potion?" Perrin suggested. "There has to be some weed on the rooftop that will interrupt the brain's power of reasoning, just long enough to ask Peaches the right questions."

"Perrin, you're brilliant."

"Yes. I know. It's my burden to bear. While you're at it, find something up there that'll cure idiocy, m'kay?"

Pepper pushed past a whining Kimball, who had been tasked by Mistress Perrin to fill up buckets of water for unknown reasons. She might have elbowed him, causing him to fall into the lagoon. Watching him get sopping wet awarded Pepper momentary relief from the dread and anxiety.

When Kimball stepped out of the lagoon, he slipped and dropped the bucket of water, its contents spilling all over the stone floor. "Thanks, Bell. Now I have to fill it again."

"It's a good thing you have nothing else to do today."

Whatever Kimball snarked back, the wind ate as Pepper rose higher and higher on the elevator. She snuck a peek at him, floors below. For some odd reason, he was on his knees, his ear to the pavement. Irritated, Pepper shook her head and rolled her eyes.

On the rooftop, Pepper searched for Melisende. The damned made herself busy in the School of Poisoncraft laboratory, cleaning up the aftermath of Sawyer's ambush—sweeping broken glass and mopping up the spilled potions.

"Hi, Melisende. I need to craft a potion for Beatrice, only I don't know how or where to start. Can you help?" Pepper described Beatrice's symptoms.

After the damned rested the broom next to the table, she asked a series of questions, to which Pepper answered: "Yes, to the fever. No, to the rash. Blind as a bat, nope. Mouth bone dry? I think she's imbibed more water than what would be expected. Hatter mad? Debatable. You think she's poisoned, don't you?" The gravity of the situation hit Pepper hard.

"Sure sounds like it to me. Beatrice's body will go into shock if you don't administer an antidote."

"Are there reference books here?" Just what Pepper needed, more panic and the possibility of angering an already vengeful Karma for failing to follow orders and rescue one of her Agents.

"More so in the School of Magic."

Pepper hadn't visited that School yet because they ran out of time last night, and the locked door didn't help. "I need to craft a truth potion before I do anything else. It's the only way we can get Beatrice to trust us enough to give us an account of what happened to her. Then, hopefully, we'll know the identity of the poison we're dealing with."

Melisende guided Pepper to a library of sorts, plucked out a hefty tome, and flipped to a specific page. "I've watched Professor Kymeo pen his discoveries right onto the pages of this grimoire."

"Hm. Not sure where I'm supposed to get the final breath uttered from a deathbed confession, devilbee honey, or the captured vibration of rumbles of thunder."

Feeling thwarted, Pepper's temper flared, and she snapped the book shut in a huff and considered tossing it at the wall. With no warning, tears started welling of their own accord and worsened as she thought of the time ticking by, and she wasn't any closer to saving her dad. And on top of it all, she had a sinking feeling she couldn't shake that he was trying to contact her and crying out for help.

Immediately, breathing became a struggle, and she couldn't think of anything other than she was in the throes of a heart attack.

So when Melisende dabbed some concoction under her nose, Pepper's heart slowed its galloping. Once her panic subsided, she continued inhaling what she recognized as lavender.

Melisende said softly, "When our minds refuse to listen, our bodies have to resort to other ways to flag our attention."

Refuse to listen ... That sounded so familiar, as if said in a dream. But Pepper drew a blank. Perhaps she could find a spell or potion to help her remember her dreamscapes.

"Before you succumbed to your attack, I was about to tell you that most of the ingredients you require for the spell can be found on campus. As for the devilbee honey, their hives are in the forest. I can take you there, but we must hurry before the dracos awake from their slumber."

13

An ancient sandstone archway delineated the entrance to the dense forest. The marchioness stopped before it and said, "I'm not authorized to leave Academy grounds, so I'm afraid you're on your own. Listen for the sound of water, and you'll find the hives close to the stream. Good luck."

"Why do I need luck?" Melisende vanished in the fog before she could answer Pepper.

Trees were everywhere, smushed together, their deep green foliage canopying the daytime sky. The fog-obscured soil proved difficult to navigate as Pepper trudged deeper into the forest while desperately trying to listen for the sound of water.

I'll find the honey and then get the heck outta here, Pepper repeated every time twigs crunched or foliage rustled around her.

"*Hoot-hoot!*" an owl warned, its wings audibly flapping as

it took flight. Other critters scampered through the detritus as if fleeing.

Soon Pepper could not see two feet in front of her nose. On alert, she placed her arms in front of her and took tentative steps, unsure of where she was stepping, the ground slick with detritus.

"Ow!" A stick smacked her right in the noggin. Her hand flew to her smarting nose. Luckily, blood wasn't gushing out. The culprit looked like a long, fat bamboo stick a few inches taller than Pepper's five-foot-seven frame.

She plucked it up from the fog-laden earth and held it between her hands. In size, it rivaled Jhi's quarterstaff, the one used for summoning shadows. "Looks like I found myself a walking stick."

The further into the forest she ventured, the more viscous the fog became like blood.

Since when did fog curl around ankles? Freaked out, Pepper kicked out her legs in a cancan and was thankful no one was around to witness the spectacle. *Not a snake, phew!*

"Listen for water, Melisende said," Pepper snarked as she trekked onward, climbing over felled mushroom-crusted logs. "Well, I don't hear it!" Her meandering delivered her to a small clearing in the forest, the sky obscured by thick foliage.

"It's because you lack focus," a disembodied voice replied. If the male had a body, Pepper couldn't see it because of the blanket of fog.

"Who's there?" Pepper halted and swiveled around, seeking out the interloper.

If only Pepper had a weapon. Perhaps the bamboo stick could be helpful. She twisted it in the air like a reject baton twirler in a high school marching band and then held it out in a horizontal position.

"Unless you plan on using the quarterstaff as a limbo

stick, I suggest you readjust your hand placement. Otherwise, I fear the dracos will outmaneuver you. Then we're all screwed."

A booming symphony of flapping wings stormed out of the bowels of the forest toward Pepper. All the critters nearby fled, their tiny feet scritching on the soil.

"I'd get ready if I were you. They're coming," the stranger said.

After tossing her satchel to the ground and holding tight to the quarterstaff, Pepper assumed a fighting stance. To date, the only martial arts training Pepper had under her belt amounted to … well, zilch, if you didn't count her kickboxing for weight loss DVDs. Or the time she spent obsessively watching episode after episode of Meiling Wu defending her hidden city from the forces of darkness and trying to emulate the kung fu master's movements in her living room. Larry watched from the couch at his daughter's request as nine-year-old Pepper kicked the air and yelled *hi-ya*, only to crash into the furniture. Pepper had to hand it to her pops for doing his best to nod his head while most likely suppressing laughter.

A thunderous noise quaked through the forest. Piercing screams and menacing howls came from every which way. The sound of hefty wings beating, bodies swooshing and slicing through the air, from one direction to the next, it, or they, charged. In front of Pepper. To her left. Her right. Behind. Penning her in.

The fog displaced as if it had never been there.

"No, no. Never meet your hands in the middle. Imagine the quarterstaff is a pool stick," the stranger said gruffly.

Though her hands were a shaky mess and her entire body trembled from fright, Pepper glided one hand down the shaft as if it had been oiled and ended at the rear quarter of the weapon; her other hand landed in the middle—eight-ball corner pocket.

"There you go," he said.

The invisible beasties sniffed her, and she nearly choked from the smell of death and decay emanating from their mouths. A beat later, they moved in for the kill, taunting her, their prey. Though attached to the ground, they grew in size and climbed up the length of the tree.

"They're shadows," Pepper uttered.

"Indeed, they are. Well, look at that. You're not the dolt I had pegged you to be."

Unsure of what to do, Pepper watched in horror as the creatures born from the shadows bounced from one trunk to the next. Then slithered on the ground like the fog toward her feet, getting closer. And closer. Nearly upon her.

Pepper slammed the quarterstaff into the earth, and they jumped back.

In a snap, the shadows cleaved from their home on the ground and stretched upward, joining together as they broke out of their 2D prison and morphed into a three-dimensional being.

"If shadows, how is that possible?" she cried out.

"The only question you should ask yourself is how to stay alive."

The ginormous rhino-sized silhouette stampeded toward her. Pepper batted it away with the pool stick, and it fizzled apart. Only to appear again as wisps of 2D shadowy figures. In perfect sync, they descended upon Pepper and snaked around the circle of trees, as if roping her in the truncated clearing. So fast they moved, twisting and twirling, threading around and between the trunks, becoming a blur of one continuous ribbon of darkened mist like light graffiti.

Pepper couldn't pick out one from the swarm to defend

herself against. There were so many, or maybe it was just one. "Help! They have me cornered."

"Are my suggestions not considered help?"

That wasn't the help she had in mind.

"Unless you're imitating a duck, put your feet in a fighting stance. And if I have to remind you what that is, then the cosmos is doomed!"

Without warning, the beasties stopped. Legions of them encircled Pepper, their ensnared prey.

Fear pinned her in place.

The shadows coalesced and formed a face of a ferocious beast and zoomed toward Pepper only to stop an arm's length from her nose. Ribbons of mist coughed out from its distended jaw that snapped open, showcasing smoky barbed-wire-like teeth that rivaled a megalodon. Where eyes would be, there were holes. Then the shadow dissipated.

"They're provoking me."

"Sizing you up before they go in for the kill, but yes. You're too focused on the threat, not on what can help you. Attune your senses to your surroundings or die."

The rage of draco-shadows halted their frenetic movement, their smoky wings pumping up and down, appearing like sheets blowing in the wind.

All at once, they pummeled Pepper and soared around her ankles. Then they knocked her to the ground. Others manacled her hands in place.

As if she had fallen in a pit of vipers, the dracos swarmed around her, over her, under her. She swatted at the air, wildly kicked her legs, then broke free and bounced up to a standing position.

"You're really horrible at fighting," the voice taunted. "Like the worst fighter I've ever had the misfortune of witnessing. Do you have any skills?"

When a draco knocked her feet out from under her—again

—Pepper snarled in response as she sprung back to her feet. "Do you ever shut up?"

"Your six o'clock," he warned.

Pepper squirmed and fought and tried to kick free of their shadows. But they were too powerful, too strong. Her body lifted upward, several feet off the ground. "Help! I can't move," she choked out as they carried her away.

"Weakness of the mind and insubordination are grounds for expulsion at Karma Academy," the male chastised coldly. "I told you earlier you weren't listening, and even now, you still choose to disregard my tutelage."

"And you're not listening to me! I. Don't. Have. Magic. Gems!"

"Gems wouldn't help you, anyway. Next excuse?"

Suddenly, or perhaps because of death calling, Pepper's ears attuned to the susurration of the wind. In fact, she could have sworn it spoke to her, told her to call upon it. For the first time, she listened. And abided. And talked back.

"Sshhhrrraaarrrsssshharrssss," Pepper uttered, barely audible but impactful all the same.

The sigil she had first seen above the hospital ward materialized. Limned in ultraviolet bluish-green, it pulsed, then exploded into a flurry of wind and funneled her way. The tornadic force ripped her from the dracos' talons and tossed her up and up. Then a blustering gale tossed the rage backward.

By some supernatural force, Pepper crash-landed on her feet and assumed a fighting stance with the quarterstaff held out before her.

Furious, the shadow-dracos darted and swooped around her, screeching in anger, but she fended them off. Hitting and swatting and batting them away. One after the other.

She caught one in her sights, the one that seemed in charge, the Alpha of the rage of dracos. Born of smoke, and shadow-black, the beast rose from the ground. With its body large enough for riding and wings with pointed tips formidable enough to impale, it rushed toward Pepper and then feinted. Every time she thrust the staff, it twisted away until she noticed a pattern.

"I think it's reading my mind."

"Then stop telegraphing your intentions before you strike your opponent. Remember, in combat, you must think quickly. It could make all the difference whether you live or die."

The draco torpedoed her way.

Pepper went to lunge with one hand, then switched positions at the last moment and thrust the stick with all her might as if performing a break shot. The quarterstaff knifed through the foul creature's chest, and then she vaulted into the air, using the weapon as leverage. With the snarling beast on the other end of the staff, she skewered it into the ground.

Flailing, it tried to free itself from its confines. A blood-curdling screech ripped from its throat before it stopped twitching.

"Well done!"

"Who's awesome? Me!" Though exhausted, sweat coating her brow and dripping down her back, Pepper celebrated all by her lonesome. Still, if she was *that* out of breath from capturing one shadow-draco, what would happen if there were more?

"If you think slaying a draco is that easy, I have a damned's soul to sell you."

"Wait. So I didn't kill it?" Her heart plummeted.

"No. You incapacitated it. A temporary solution. Long enough for you to escape."

"But the rest of the dracos just up and disappeared."

"Not disappeared. They retreated when you caught the Alpha."

"Will they come back?"

"Yes. Need I remind you, you just barely fought off their shadows." His tone suggested a child could have done the same thing. "Come nightfall, the dracos are whole, fully fleshed, and far more deadly opponents."

"Shadow creatures by day," Pepper said, more to herself. "These creatures are used for combat training, aren't they? That's why the stick was just lying around."

"Can't get anything past you."

"Why don't you come out and face me instead of snarking in the shadows?"

"If only I could. I'm afraid I'm stuck and could use your help."

"Oh, so you need my help, do you? Well, how about you tell me who you are first?"

"Fair enough. Professor Kymeo Khatri at your service."

14

"Thank Seren!" Pepper said with an exhale. "Something horrible's happened to Beatrice. She needs help, and actually, that's why I'm here in the forest, to find ingredients for a spell. Oh, and we're trapped inside the Academy—that's abandoned, by the way—and did Sawyer do something to you?"

"Aren't you a chatterbox. How delightful," Professor Kymeo grumbled, then chased the latter remark with a sigh. "No, I'm afraid my predicament can't wholly be pinned on Miss van Arsdale. The flask meant for her exploded on the wrong person—me. But sadly and daresay pathetically, I've been a prisoner of the forest ever since, and I require rescuing myself. I'm sure there's a karmic lesson I'm meant to learn from all of this. Or punishment. Depending on who you ask."

"Aren't you at all concerned about the missing professors."

"My dear, one problem at a time."

"Well, you should know Sawyer told Melisende that she'll be back."

"Yes, only this time I reckon she'll bring along company. Trust me when I say you are far from ready to go toe-to-toe with Sawyer. I've fought her. Hands down, Sawyer is a beautifully chaotic force of nature and one of the finest pupils I have ever had the pleasure of training. And when she's on her game and not off with the faeries, she's unstoppable."

Pepper scrunched her button nose with utter disgust at his waxing avuncular in all manner of Homicidal Ice Queen.

Kymeo added, "Full disclosure. I was never sure about you, Miss Bell. Many of us had reservations. But never Goddess Karma."

"Reservations about what?"

"About inducting you into the Academy, training you to become an Agent of Karma."

"What gave you pause?" Pepper asked, her heart rolling in her chest.

"I have my reasons." Intimate knowledge seemed to coat the professor's tone. "But Goddess Karma took a chance on you against—Well, let's just say not everyone was on board."

"Enough of the cryptic speak. If you know something about me, just come out and say it."

"Look, I will admit that you surprised me. I thought for a second there you were a goner," Professor Kymeo added with as little compassion as he could muster. "It's clear to even a dullard that you've had zero training in magic. And yet you spoke to Air without using gems. You bypassed the gem conduit and became the conduit yourself."

"Is that like a big deal or something?"

"Indeed, it is. You tapped into Aetheric magic—the magic of nature and the gods. And that, little fledgling, is what we train Agents of Karma in."

"Then why does my outsmarting the draco surprise you?"

"For the simple reason that nature has always talked to us, but most have never listened, especially chatterboxes like yourself. The rustling of Air, the pitter-patter of Water, Fire crackling, leaves crunching on the Earth, and Aether is a combination of all the elements. Each has its own language and vibration, and the magic in our veins, combined with our commands, attunes to the element's specific frequency."

Finally, Pepper had a captive audience, so she plied Professor Kymeo with her most pressing question: "If the use of magic without a conduit is impossible on Earth, which I recently learned is the case, then how come others have figured out a loophole—and by loophole, I mean drinking mage blood."

Kymeo might have remained quiet, but not the air around Pepper. Leaves eddied feet above the ground.

Kymeo piped up, "My dear, who's engaging in cryptic speak now? Care to elaborate on who you are referring to regarding this loophole?"

With more and more questions piling up, Pepper desperately needed answers. If Kymeo worked for Team Evil, then what she was about to spill wouldn't be breaking news. So, she brought the professor up to speed on everything she had uncovered regarding the Syndicate, starting with their soul contract heist from the Ministry of Mischief and Mayhem and ending with the upcoming lunar eclipse gala—where her investigation had stalled. After waiting for what felt like forever for him to say anything, Pepper blurted out, "Do you at least agree that the Syndicate defying the rules of magic on Earth isn't good? Since Hekate is the supreme ruler over magic, *how* are they doing it—and on *whose* authority, if not Hekate's?"

"Looks like I need your help sooner rather than later." Equal parts urgency and annoyance coated his words. "Unfortunately, the defense potion meant for Sawyer separated my consciousness and soul from my body and expelled me from campus. If I know Sawyer, who tends to be quite lazy at times, she didn't take my body with her but locked me away somewhere on the grounds. Find my body, and then return to me."

"We've searched the entire Academy and didn't stumble across your body. Where *are* the other professors? Wouldn't they be able to help us if we can reach them?"

"My dear, do you think I'd be asking for your help if I didn't already know they were missing and unreachable?"

Pepper had a mind to walk away after that curt reply but tamped down her annoyance and asked, "Who's to say they aren't in the same predicament as you?"

The professor sighed. "And you're certain you've searched the entire Academy?"

"Yes, except for the School of Magic, because the door's locked. And Water. We can't locate that School."

"So you haven't, in fact, searched the entire campus." He sighed again, only this time deeper, then said brusquely, "Spin Goddess Hekate's wheel to unlock the door. After sunset, revisit the atrium. There, you will find what you are seeking."

"But the dracos will be hunting then."

"Indeed, they will." Kymeo interrupted Pepper before she could reply and directed her to the devilbee hives. "I'd hurry if I were you."

THE WHEEL of Hekate was affixed to the double doors leading to the School of Magic. Positioned around the wheel were the four elements—Earth, Air, Fire, and Water—like directionals on a compass, with Aether in the middle.

One spin catalyzed blood-like liquid to pour forth from

each element and course through the labyrinthian wheel, twisting and turning through the maze, left and right, up and down, until all five elements combined in the center. The point of convergence glowed a fierce neon white. With that, the wheel unlocked, and the door ghosted open.

A laboratory greeted Pepper with impossibly long tables spattered about. In place of cauldrons were lab apparatuses with all the trimmings—flat-bottomed and rounded bottom flasks (Pepper could never remember their proper names), graduated cylinders, beakers, pipettes, and was it burettes, the one with the spigot? Even a glove box occupied a corner, which always reminded Pepper of a claw machine with prizes inside.

Reference books stacked haphazardly on bowed shelves took up most of the real estate in the back of the classroom. Another wall and a supply room behind it housed ingredients like a proper apothecary. A bank of windows showcasing cascading waterfalls and the endless floating mountainscape beyond broke up the sterility of the cold and spacious room.

Like raided pirate's booty, barrels were stuffed with empty fulgurite gems. Above, framed photos spelling out the how-tos of draining decorated the walls: *If you need a magical recharge, knowing how to siphon magic discretely from the unsuspecting and transfer the unstable powers into fulgurite gems on the fly could make the difference between life and death.*

Done dawdling, Pepper started creating her first-ever truth potion using Kymeo's grimoire. While flipping through the spell book, her finger landed unconsciously on a section devoted to dreams. Pepper desperately needed to remember her dreams, especially with her dad. But first, she'd help Beatrice.

Took quite a few page flips, but Pepper found the perfect truth potion named Tell Me No Lies. After gathering all the required ingredients, she placed them inside the glove box.

Before Pepper added the first ingredient, she read over Professor Kymeo's scribbled marginalia: *While Final breath uttered from a deathbed confession will coax the truth out from hiding, it is a slippery shit and a real bitch to catch. Threatening it works ninety-eight percent of the time.*

Pepper slipped her hands through the long black gloves and carefully picked up the glass tube, then looked sternly at the vaporous final breath bouncing off the flask and said, "If you try to escape, I have it on good authority that the mala'khas will lock you up in the Pits of Tartarus for all eternity." She felt stupid, but the threat must have worked, for the breath stilled. After quickly uncorking the rubber stopper, she poured the final breath into a beaker. Then she added a dragon scale to guide the truth to the surface. Instantly, the flask quivered as the breath bounced around.

The recipe called for two teaspoons of devilbee honey to trick the stubborn mind by binding to the prefrontal cortex of the brain and disrupting decision-making. Pepper's eyes coasted to the adjacent marginalia. *Experimental trials have shown that 1 tbsp produces pure candor; however, the subject turns into a drooling mess for a lengthy time. They're never quite the same after that. Best to use 2 tsps to stay in Karma's good graces.* She took measured breaths and repeatedly recited "steady hand" as she held the pipette over the flask and lightly pressed on the bulb. Once the drop of honey plopped into the mixture, Pepper immediately lifted her hand out of the flask.

The penultimate ingredient was one jar of captured vibration of rumbles of thunder that relaxed the mind and aided in memory recollection.

The last step suggested mixing the brew with an intoxicant. The marginalia suggested a sweet liqueur, like moraberry, then added: *Do not add more than 30 ml to avoid erratic behavior in test subjects.* Moraberry sounded familiar, but Pepper couldn't recall why. Still, the pyramidal fruit in the atrium was finally identified.

Once Pepper concocted Tell Me No Lies, she joined the others in Beatrice's hospital room. Loki held the Agent's mouth open while Pepper poured the cloud-like substance down her gullet. They didn't have to wait long for the potent brew to take effect.

"I'm going to ask you a few questions. Are you ready?" Pepper asked. When Beatrice nodded, Pepper began the interrogation. "Do you know your name?"

Beatrice nodded, recited her name, and then took a hearty sip of water.

"Where did the dried blood on your stomach come from?" Beatrice flicked her eyes closed and began panting in fear. "You're safe. Nobody can harm you. Now tell us what you see." Pepper placed a hand on her arm.

"He wants to kill me."

"Who?" Pepper asked while exchanging looks of concern with Loki and Perrin.

Beatrice replied, "Miles Leagan. I'll never forget his name. He nailed me to the air and stabbed me, and it burned and burned." A tear escaped from her eye.

"Can you remember anything else?"

A dreamy look washed over Beatrice's face. "A flashback. Of a family road trip. We were driving through Florida, and my sister and I were goofing off during the most boring tour of a paper mill. But Mama really enjoyed it for whatever reason." She smiled. "Then Josie and I were running through an orange grove. My gran was watchin' us while chillin' in a lawn chair and sippin' pulpy juice like a cocktail. As ushe, Mama was on cup number ten of black coffee—He's here," Beatrice gasped, and her whole body tensed.

"Who's he?"

Beatrice's head canted down, as if listening to his voice.

"Yes." Her voice softened. "A hospital room." She flicked her eyes to Pepper, then darted them away when Pepper noticed. "Yes—"

Beatrice's head snapped upward, then down. In a voice not her own, she spewed, "On the third night, the dragon devours the moon, and all the planets watch from the sky, the gods secretly assemble on the mighty mountain of Bel, and time slowly dies." The voice, now booming, proclaimed, "On the third night ..."

A sense of eeriness washed over Pepper. Something about the dragon devouring the moon felt so familiar. After blinking away the déjà vu, Pepper got her thoughts back on track and immediately catapulted over the hospital bed, grabbed the valeritonin off the sink, then stabbed it in Beatrice's arm.

When Beatrice returned to a coma-like state, Pepper jerked her head to the others to follow her to the hallway.

"What the fuh'kar ...?"

Out of Beatrice's earshot, Pepper whispered to Perrin, "Which part? Miles, most likely, or Vlad asking where she was and if I was with her? The fact she's poisoned by para doxea? Or what sounded like a prophecy?"

A concerned Loki said, "All three. Do you think Miles or Vlad already knows where we're at and was just confirming if Beatrice was still here before ambushing?"

"Oh, God! I hope not." Pepper chewed the skin around her thumb.

"No more wondering. Something's definitely going down during the lunar eclipse. Too bad we don't know what!" Perrin huffed. "You had *one job*, sweetling, to help us get out of here and epically failed."

"I didn't fail, Perrin, at least not with the truth potion. Unless you've passed through Perry, Florida, you wouldn't know that the smell of sulfur is rife throughout that town.

Why? Because of the paper mills. And then Beatrice mentioned oranges and coffee. Evidence that points to her being poisoned. The essence of para doxea was on that knife's blade. But I don't know how to cure that."

"I do." Melisende entered the hospital. "Oft-times, I serve as Professor Vesta's apprentice, and truth be told, I was quite fond of poison in my pre-damned life."

Pepper hesitated and stepped in front of Beatrice's room.

In response, Melisende held out her hand to show what looked like a bouillabaisse cube. "It's frankincense mixed with an activated charcoal paste. When you visited me earlier, Pepper, I recognized the telltales of poisoning but still had my doubts. It wasn't until I heard Beatrice mention the voice that I was certain." Melisende explained that when she had overheard the ordeal, she immediately ran back to the rooftop to grab the medicine.

Pepper stepped aside from the threshold and allowed Melisende to perform her ministrations.

Standing bedside, Melisende inspected Beatrice and checked her eyes and vitals. "The poison, which you identified as para doxea, has unfortunately already passed through her blood-brain barrier. So, I fear whoever is trying to control her mind has already sunk their talons into her. First, we give her this." Melisende put the cube under Beatrice's tongue. "Her saliva will melt it."

"Then what?" Perrin asked Melisende.

"Then we figure out if there is, in fact, someone trying to compel Beatrice. Still, the possibility exists that she could be hallucinating. I used many mind-altering poisons in my previous life, and she possesses a few indicators which give me pause. Now, I have a curative elixir for the poisoning, but heed my warning: there is no room for doubt. Once the devil's fang enters Beatrice's bloodstream, and it turns out she was just hallucinating, she will be dead within minutes."

"Let me get this straight. Peaches, aka our only way out of this spa-cation-nightmare, is most likely poisoned, under compulsion, and is dying." Perrin ticked off her statements with her fingers. "We're trapped, magically castrated. Professor Kymeo is bodyless and haunting the forest. Sawyer and the Syndicate could be headed to the Academy to murder us, and the grounds outside the Academy offer death. And now there's a prophecy we have to decipher. Did I leave anything out because I'm almost running out of fingers?"

"Nope. I think you covered it all," Pepper said deadpan.

In a fit of pique, Perrin stomped about, her arms swinging. "Fuh'karing fantastic. I swear Goddess Shi'rue didn't know I existed until I hooked up with the likes of you people. Now the bony bitch god can't stop showering me with her misfortune." She stopped her grousing. "Any suggestions for our continuing survival because I'm all ears?" Perrin didn't scare easily, but being cornered with no means of defense at her disposal terrified even the Mafioso Lolly'ka.

Pepper was at a loss. Compulsion or death—the outcome for both was the same. One could argue death would be a better option than being under the control of another for however long, if not eternity. "I can't make the call. Not until I talk to the professor."

Loki pulled Pepper aside and whispered, "I don't want to further set Perrin off, but I'm afraid we don't have much time. Have you noticed the moon?" His tiny grayish-white face scrunched up with worry, his piercing orange eyes conveying the same message.

"Yeah, but what about it?" Pepper had a bad feeling, her heartbeat gaining speed.

"Its phases are speeding up."

"We've only been here a few days, though," she replied.

"I know. But back on Earth, it's been weeks."

Pepper thought back to Chloe's podcast and mentioned the time discrepancies again.

"And that's precisely when I started paying attention to the moon. If we don't figure out how to leave the Academy, Pepper, then …" With his tail, Loki grabbed Perrin's flask from Pepper's hands and then gulped a shot's worth.

"Then who knows what the lunar eclipse will usher in?" Knowing the Syndicate, it was bound to be apocalyptic for humanity.

That heart-stopping warning catalyzed Pepper into action. She had to go back in. Back inside her nightmares to uncover what her pops was trying to warn her about. No other choice. Larry and Beatrice's life depended on it. Only this time, she'd be driving the train. At least, that was the plan.

15

id Pepper want to return to her terrifying nightscape? Absolutely not. Facing her worst fears of losing her father wasn't something she wanted to relive. But she couldn't shake the ominous feeling her pops had tried to contact her. Not only that, but Larry and Beatrice, complete strangers, were intricately tied to the prophecy. Now add in time on warp speed. And *all that* combined was the driving force to go back into her dreams to garner intel.

The goal of dream navigation was to not only remember the happenings after waking but to remain in complete control of her faculties and not get lost and caught up in the trippy hallucinatory dreamscape. Kymeo's Epic Dream Remembrances: *A potion to remember what the mind forgets* recipe seemed to fit the bill perfectly.

Pepper perused the brew's ingredients—thank Seren, all items were on hand—and added them to the flask in the order mentioned:

- 1 bottle of captured lightning (*The best trap for fleeting memories. Always use a glove box when working with this component.*)

- 1 tsp. of devilbee honey (*Binds to captured lightning and doesn't let go. The electric shock the subject experiences is inevitable, but the honey dulls it somewhat. *Steady hand. Half a drop more will bind to YOUR brain, not the captured lightning, and then you're wraith bait.*)

- 2 dollops of ectoplasm (*In test trials, 3 dollops trapped subjects in Witherwhere. 2 dollops acted as a round-trip ticket to their dreamscape and back to the present day. Of note: time at Karma Academy runs parallel to wherever you are astraling.*)

- 3 oz River Lethe water (*Wear gloves when bottling.*)

- 1 pipette of holy basil

- ½ sprig of horehound (*Steady hand. 1 sprig caused "revealing" side effects during experiments, and test subjects turned combatant and had to immediately be quieted.*)

- Lunabell oil (*Rare. Night-blooming.*) The author included a rough sketch of this odd-looking flower and placed an arrow next to where the petal was most vulnerable when harvesting, along with another note: (*Only collect during the day.*) But he failed to add measurements.

Oops! In a rush and erring on the side of caution, Pepper added half a teaspoon of the ingredient before reading further: (*Need to test on subjects before adding.*) Hopefully, the lunabell only enhanced the potion. Fingers-crossed.

- Dust from every-color gem (*1 V will work but lessens the spell's duration.*)

- 1 drop of valeritonin (*Induces a hypnagogic state. Steady hand. ½ a drop more than the recipe calls for renders the test subject comatose.*)

Blue lotus wasn't suggested, but Pepper felt compelled to add it. Five drops, to be exact, as it enhanced lucid dreaming and awareness, even allowing advanced astralers to change the script.

- Right after imbibing the potion, recite thrice: *I remember perfectly. I remember clearly. I remember all.*

Pepper had crafted the remembrance potion rather quickly with only one hiccup. Hopefully, that served as a harbinger of a successful fact-finding mission.

Perrin stood guard outside Pepper's room and had one order: do not allow anyone to enter or wake her up. Wearing a look of utter boredom, the Lolly'ka leaned against the wall, chewing blood-filled gum and filing her nails with a switch-blade, then blew a massive bubble while nodding her head in understanding.

In bed, Pepper swallowed the syrupy concoction and immediately felt weightless. "I remember perfectly." Her head collapsed on the soft pillow, eyes fluttering closed. "I remember clearly. I remember all."

<hr>

"ONE O'CLOCK, TWO O'CLOCK …" voices of unseen children called out in the distance. "Eleven o'clock … Midnight, midnight. We hope to catch a ghost tonight!" The neighbor-hood kids scattered about as they hunted "the graveyard" for ghost Pepper.

The moonless sky, with wisps of clouds scudding across, cast a blanket of endless darkness over Pepper from her hiding spot in the gnarled branches of a pongam tree rooted in the side of her yard and Kimball's property.

A kid stepped on the Bells' horseshoe driveway, his head turning left and right as he hunted for "the ghost."

Ba-bum-ba-bum-ba-bum! Pepper's heart thumped wildly as she crawled backward, not wanting to be found and tagged, seeking refuge in the rustling foliage.

The ghost hunter's attention riveted on the shade tree, and he walked toward it—toward Pepper. Ever so quietly, she scurried up a branch until her hand touched the cold concrete slab of Kimball's balcony. Pepper could just barely see into his bedroom and considered jumping up, but then—

The crunching of leaves and twigs sounded underneath her. The high pitch of the kid's voice when he said, "Come out, come out wherever you are," lowered and intensified into a distinctly male voice, morphing from harmless fun to a demand, an "or else" left unsaid.

A howl of abject pain boomed inside Kimball's room—a voice she could have sworn sounded like her father's. Pepper had to get to him. But she couldn't move from her position on the branch. Or else the hunter would spot her.

The faceless kid had vanished. And in his place was Miles, standing at the trunk. He caught sight of Pepper, and his lips curled back as he let loose a feral snarl. The serial killer climbed up the tree as if swimming through the water and was right behind Pepper. He reached out his hand to grab her. Terror-struck, Pepper grabbed the balcony railing and struggled to pull herself up. But Miles grabbed her ankle and pulled her down.

Kicking and squirming, Pepper broke free from his grasp and barreled into Kimball's room. Only it wasn't his bedroom, but a hallway, arched and mantled in stone. Behind her was a door bolted shut. The hall branched off to the left, and a circular stone stairwell was dead ahead. *Brr!* Pepper rubbed her bare arms, her breath feathering in the frigid air. A tapestry depicting Vlad Dracula on horseback glared back at her.

Her father's screams pierced the airwaves. Guttural shouts that bespoke pain beyond measure. Pepper padded in his direction along a threadbare runner rug, all the while risking glances over her shoulder for Miles. What if the serial killer caught her? Pepper was unarmed. Defenseless. Not even a magic gem on her person. But she had to get to her dad. Had to find him. Then a feeling within told her to remain quiet. *Or else.*

As Pepper reached a wooden door with hand-forged hardware and a wrought-iron speakeasy portal, she was instantly shocked. When nothing else happened, she disregarded the oddity.

On her tiptoes, she pushed open the peephole, and her heart tightened. Miles had chained Larry to a table housed within what could only be described as a torture chamber and silenced her father's wails with a ball gag. Barbaric devices like the iron maiden and weapons lined the walls and were sprawled out on tables. All had had their go at Pepper's father, judging from the fresh smears of blood.

Soaked in her father's gore, Miles sauntered around the table, a serrated, double-bladed knife stained red in one hand. "Lingchi. Death by a thousand cuts. I believe this is from cut number two hundred." Miles dangled pieces of Larry's skin between his bloodied fingers. "Only eight hundred more to go, Mister Bell." He took such delight in inflicting pain—it was written all over his face, and how his lips quirked up into a grin.

Larry's legs, arms, hands, and feet were all a battlefield of slashes and gore. Layers of skin sliced away. Tendons were visible. Bone, too, in some places.

Miles tortured her father because of Pepper. And then Pepper snapped. She remembered. This was a dream. She could walk up to Miles and gut him, over and over and over again. And bathe in his blood. Watching with glee as the life drained from his body.

Pepper placed her hand on the cold metal latch—

"Stop!" a female voice demanded. "If you walk through that door, you're as good as dead. As will be Larry."

Pepper feared to ask out loud who the voice belonged to. But the female heard her thoughts and said, "I am a prisoner inside the castle, just like your father."

A war raged within Pepper: to trust the stranger's voice or not to trust. What if the female engaged in reverse psychology and didn't want Pepper to rescue her father?

But the pull, having her father feet away, was too great.

I can have and do whatever I want. It's my dream, Pepper told herself as she went to take a step inside the torture chamber. But then stopped, her gut asking, *What if this isn't a dream?* Pepper stayed put, her heart and mind at odds, her hands balling into fists.

"You like the torture, don't you, Mister Bell?" Miles stared directly into Larry's eyes. But Larry spat at him, a mist of blood pooling in the pockmarks on Miles' face.

Miles sprung on Larry, the double-bladed dagger he wielded front and center, but he stopped mid-slice and couldn't move. The blade *clanged* to the stone floor.

"That's enough, Miles!" Though the female's voice hit the treble clef areas on the musical scale, there was an air of gravitas about her delivery that clearly stated, "Do as I say, or else."

When the woman exited the veil of darkness and stepped into the light, Pepper immediately thought that her childhood idol and martial arts actress, Meiling Wu, played a starring role in her dream.

But Pepper couldn't have been more wrong. This female wasn't Meiling, but Ember, the Firebird.

"Taking out your aggressions on Mister Bell after yet another demoralizing briefing, I see," Ember *tsk-tsk*ed. "You've brought Mister Bell to the brink of death more times than I can count. The man simply can't take anymore. Look at him. He's nearly dead as it is. Mister Bell is to be kept alive.

And I will not tell you that again." Her voice dripped in elegance, as did her ensemble.

Decked out in form-fitting trousers spun from the finest silk and a body-hugging satin blouse with a bow tie fastened around her elongated neck, Ember cut a striking figure as she sauntered to Miles. Her posture was exemplary, her back ramrod straight, as if balancing a book on her head.

Pepper had originally pegged Ember to be no older than twenty-one, twenty-two, and seeing her up close, Pepper had been right. *So young, yet so old*, Pepper thought.

Ember picked up a weapon from a table and traced her finger along its gleaming edge. "I'll never understand why Vlad wastes his efforts on the likes of you. The way you torture is pedestrian." She dropped the weapon, then turned on her heel to face Miles. "Your compelling is *pathetic* at best. Your behavior is puerile and erratic. You can't even spearhead a mission without needing backup. All qualities in direct opposition to our core."

"You dare insult and bark orders at me? You, a common lackey. Go back to Cazzian's chambers." Miles waved his hand at Ember in a dismissive gesture. "I'm sure he requires servicing."

What sounded like a whip cracked through the air at the same time Miles' head snapped to the side, and he nearly lost his balance. Blood poured forth from his split-open cheek—a vampire's snack worth.

"You bitch!" Miles said, a look of shock tugging at his features as he wiped the blood from his face. "You strut around this castle day in and day out, making demands and bossing others around, but you are nothing, Ember. You might have helped with Cazzian's resurrection, but you no longer bring value to the operation. I could snuff you out, and nothing would change. Nobody would even care you were gone but Cazzian. And even then, a five-dollar whore on a nearby corner could satisfy his needs. One of the many trollops begging to get into Vlad's bed would service Cazzian for free, no less. We save a few bucks—it's a win-win."

"I could turn you inside out without ever soiling my fingers with your blood." Ember stepped closer to Miles, her hands clasped behind her back. "I could use you as chum and watch the gators outside the castle gates swallow you whole." And closer. "Or sic one of the many pythons slithering about on you. Surely they're starving, as they've wiped out most of the food chain." She stood feet away from the serial killer and picked up his dagger from the gore-soaked floor. "So many choices. Haven't decided on one yet." The calm manner in which Ember spoke, the restrained disgust and homicidal rage, chilled Pepper to the bone.

The need to get closer to Ember consumed Pepper. That, and killing Miles with her bare hands.

Wholly confident that this was all just a dream, right as Pepper went to push the door open further, Ember's head whipped in Pepper's direction. Her blood-red eyes pinned the door in place. Her small nose bunched as if sniffing the air. The delicate features of her moon-kissed face and high cheekbones, framed by tendrils of auburn hair threaded with glistening gold, belied the evil monster that was the Firebird. The one who gleefully watched as her comrades horrifically murdered innocents at the masquerade ball, their blood spillage rivaling a charnel house.

Ember shrugged off whatever had caught her attention and turned it back on Miles. But that reaction convinced Pepper to not enter the torture chamber.

"Your threats are meaningless, just like yourself. You know damn well you can't harm me."

"That so, Mister Leagan?"

"Yes, that's so, *Miss Cazzian*. That soul contract I signed in *my* blood protects me from harm."

In a show of strength, Ember punched her arms out, grabbed a fistful of air, and squeezed and squeezed, her eyes all the while hooked on Miles.

Miles violently choked while trying desperately to breathe, his face tomato-red, his beetle-black eyes bloodshot and bulging.

Ember released her hands, and air whooshed back into Miles' lungs. "Care to amend your statement?"

Miles, struggling to get his breathing back on track, twisted his mouth into a wry grin. "Sure. I can't be *killed.*"

"That may be so *for now.* Heed my warning: don't anger me, Mister Leagan. Don't dare demean me in any way and keep my name out of your filthy mouth. Or come Winter Solstice, the minute you reap your promised rewards might very well be your last."

That confused Miles, his face crinkling.

If Miles can't be killed, which made sense because he sold his soul to Lucifer, what would change that fact on Winter Solstice? Pepper considered.

"Mind your manners, Mister Leagan, and you'll have nothing to worry about. One more thing. If you dare disobey me and torture Mister Bell again after next week's briefing, you will not like the consequences." Ember handed Miles the dagger, hilt first. "I believe this is yours. While you're at it, *lowlie,* bring Mister Bell back to the dungeon." Ember snapped her fingers twice, voiced, "That's an order," and then turned on her heel.

"Ain't nothing but lies spewing from your well-used mouth."

Ember halted, keeping her back to Miles. The air was tense with murderous possibilities. Without turning around, she said, "If you learned anything from Cazzian's resurrection, always read the fine print." Her chuckling, albeit dainty in tone, would have terrified even a maniacal clown.

Still, was Ember antagonizing Miles? Or was there an element of truth buried in her threat?

Miles, full of wrath, stabbed the dagger deep into Larry's side, and Larry cried out.

A soul-devouring shriek ripped through Pepper's throat, her hands thirsting to end Miles' life.

Miles snapped his head Pepper's way.

Before Pepper could lunge over the threshold, a supernatural force kicked her backward and sent her soaring through the air, down the hallway, and through a room where she crash-banged into a wall. With the wind knocked out of her, it took a minute for Pepper to shake away the stars to take in her surroundings. Her back abutted the bars of a jail cell, one of many housed within the dank dungeon, its jagged metal rods digging into her skin.

The same female voice as before that had warned Pepper to stay put stepped into the flickering firelight and uttered, "You foolish girl." Her ire matched the locks of her flaming red hair. Her eyes of emerald green weren't filled with rage, as Pepper thought they'd be judging from her tone but radiated urgency.

Locked bars separated the redhead from Pepper. Filth covered the twenty-something's barely clothed body. Inside the cell, moss clung to the damp walls. Piles of excrement in the corner. Pepper nearly gagged from the stench.

"Larry's still alive." The woman looked away, then returned her focus to Pepper. "I can feel his heartbeat. But it's weakened. He most likely won't survive the next time Miles comes around. And I'm afraid I won't be able to help him. I've used up most of my borrowed magic." Her freckled, peaches-and-cream face was inches from Pepper, her wavy hair brushing against Pepper's skin. The female pleaded, "They're going to kill me. Kill us all if you don't get us out of here."

"I'm working on it." Pepper needed to sneak into the briefing next week; everyone's life depended on it. "'Next time Miles comes around.' Is there a pattern to when he arrives? Please tell me anything you can." Tension and panic cracked through Pepper's voice.

"Every few days or so, he blows through the doors and drags Larry away." The redhead closed her eyes to summon up more memories. "Always around the same time, when the vamps bring us our one meal of the day. During a shift change, when Hounds replace wanderers."

That didn't exactly narrow the window of time, so Pepper pressed for more info, anything that cued the redhead into the time of day. Still, there weren't any windows on the dungeon floor, so telling time wouldn't be easy.

"I don't know," the redhead replied. "I'm sorry. The door's always closed, and the days bleed into one another. But if I had to guess, I'd say it was early evening."

Pepper observed uneaten bowls of sour-smelling stew and picked apart moldy bread. "What about when they bring you food? Any sights, or sounds, or—"

The redhead's eyes brightened, and she blurted, "I hear the WBBS channel-five jingle, followed by a dreamy violin concerto. I don't know who was playing the instrument in the castle, but they do so on the hour."

"Exactly. But what news hour?" This was promising, though. "And when Miles comes, it's always around that time?" Pepper asked.

The redhead nodded—

The door to the dungeon flew open and slammed into the stone wall. Ember stood at the threshold, anger blazing in her fiery red eyes.

Immediately, the red-headed mage cast out her hands in Pepper's direction, mumbling under her breath.

Frozen in place like a panicked rabbit in the crosshairs of a snake, Pepper couldn't possibly fight her way out and expect to survive.

"Who did you summon?" Ember growled at the redhead as her ruby eyes raked over the dungeon, bypassing Pepper completely. But how? "Stupid, stupid girl. Borrowed magics, I see. Not for much longer."

Ember's hands raised out in front of her, and something grabbed ahold of Pepper's arm and tore into her skin —

16

Pepper awoke, gasping for breath. Puncture wounds marred her forearm and blood beaded around the contact site.

While the reconnaissance mission had failed, the goal of remembering her dreams hadn't. Kymeo's dream potion had worked. Begged the question: was Pepper dreaming? Before Perrin could ask what had happened, Pepper flew out of bed and then bolted to the only person who could help her return to her dreamscape. To Vlad's castle.

As the metallic crescent moon rose higher in the tangerine-smeared, cloud-filled sky, darkening like the bruised spoilt fruit, Pepper raced through the fog-obscured forest, stumbling over countless moss-covered logs, her mind going a mile a minute.

On Chloe's podcast, Pepper recalled her former classmate mentioning the *Romancing Vlad* reality TV show and how it aired every Friday at five p.m., and then briefly mentioned a violin playing during the opening credits. The red-haired mage said a wrathful Miles would grab Larry in the early evening, and she mentioned hearing violin music. Miles most likely took her pops to use as a punching bag after one of the "demoralizing briefings" Ember had mentioned. And almost in the same breath, the Firebird alluded to a meeting next week.

Roiling rage overcame Pepper with the mere thought of Miles torturing her pops, and her speed picked up a notch. Putting together all her culled information, Pepper deduced that the briefing would occur next Friday around four in the afternoon, Earth time, if not earlier. So by Pepper's calculations, where one week on Earth equaled a day in Karma's realm—at least that was the running theory—she'd have until tomorrow to prepare to sneak into Vlad's castle.

"Did you find my body?" Kymeo asked as Pepper entered the clearing in the forest—also known as the draco-fighting ring.

Hunched down, hands on her knees and gasping for breath, Pepper replied, "Not yet." Truth be told, she hadn't even started looking. That fun project would take place later, but she'd keep that on the QT.

"You're courting danger by being here so close to dusk."

Standing up straight, Pepper took a few steps and nearly tripped over the fog-covered quarterstaff (yet again!) that no longer pierced the draco's shadow. She picked it up, just in case. "No choice. I need your help. We're running out of time." Pepper told Kymeo everything that had transpired. And how the remembrance potion didn't have the exact effects she had hoped for.

"Let me start by saying that I commend you for trying." Kymeo spoke woodenly, as if he had never voiced complementary words before and was trying to develop a taste for them. "Were you dropped on your head as a child?" Noting the disgust written all over Pepper's face, Kymeo added, "I suppose that remark was rather untoward. Look, I'm trying to gain back karmic credit points here, and it's not exactly easy, so give me some grace. Now, where was I? Oh yes. My dear, you should never have astraled without proper training or, in the least, protection. Frankly, I'm surprised you're still alive, hence my compliment earlier. With that said, you were definitely immersed in a dream from the onset. But somehow you left the dream world and astraled to the Spirit Realm. Curious."

At Kymeo's command, Pepper showed him the deep scratch marks on her arm. "Did you actually see this Ember cut you?"

"No. I can't say for certain." But Pepper felt it in her gut all the same.

"Could be a wraith, then. They do haunt the Spirit Realm. And this red-haired mage, you say she spoke to you? Or rather, warned you?"

Pepper nodded emphatically. "Are you thinking she brought me there?"

"No. Capitalized on it, absolutely. How the redhead knew you were there—now that's a mystery to be solved at another time. But back to the problem at hand. The potion you need to craft is Conscious Astraling, which constitutes essentially the same ingredients as Epic Dream Remembrances, with two exceptions: mugwort and angelica."

"'Night-cloak saves a bloke,'" Pepper spit out mechanically. There was a hint of familiarity about that rhyme, but she couldn't put her finger on why.

"It does indeed," Kymeo said, curiosity coating his words.

Snapping out of her reverie, Pepper asked, "What does that mean, 'night-cloak saves a bloke?'"

"'Don't dare go anywhere in the Spirit Realm without night-cloak.' I mention that exact warning in my grimoire."

"Mugwort. Isn't that associated with dreamwork?"

"That's a misnomer propagated by novices. When dreaming, your subconscious is at the helm. But when mugwort is introduced, the conscious mind wakes up, and that, my dear, transports you from a dreamscape to the Spirit Realm, surreality to reality. That realm is not to be trifled with and is feeding grounds for wraiths. And when armed with Angelica, your chances of death are significantly reduced, as this unassuming plant cloaks one from harm if you're careful."

Terror struck Pepper down as she remembered what turned out to be not a dream. How she stood feet away from Miles and occupied the *same space* as Ember. She was inside the enemy's stronghold—Vlad's castle. How, like a fool, she walked around feeling safe and protected because, after all, it was just a dream. Yet the words *or else* kept popping into her head. And now she understood why.

After a few deep breaths, Pepper continued, "So night-cloak will cloak me from sight? Like, legit make me invisible?" When Kymeo said yes, she continued, "And protect me from harm?" She needed ironclad reassurances before she tempted fate again.

"Not exactly. Cloaking and protecting one from harm are two different beasts. Even ghosts can be discerned by those attuned to their sixth sense. Here's a piece of advice I've doled out to my Agents regarding astraling: never entertain fear or any highly charged emotion that might cause an energy disturbance in the aetheric atmosphere. And you should be fine."

"What about bringing along a weapon?" Was that even possible?

"Unfortunately, you can't bring a weapon or pick up one along the way. Ghost, remember? Night-cloak will disguise your scent and keep you unseen and unheard. Just make sure to keep it that way."

"Then how can I protect myself if I get ambushed, or Ember tries to kill me again? I can't go back in defenseless." Pepper's voice quantum leaped to the top of the musical scale.

"What about you being a ghost did you not understand?"

"Well, I'm going to need defenses of some kind. Can I at least summon elements in the Spirit Realm without magic gems like I can at the Academy?" Perhaps a silver lining existed after all.

"Slow down the rambling," Professor Kymeo snapped. "Magic is not permitted in the Spirit Realm. End of story."

"That's bullshit!"

"Watch that temper, young lady, and holster that tongue when speaking to me. If you don't like the rules of magic, take it up with Hekate."

"Makes no sense." Pepper kicked the dirt.

"It makes all the sense. We train our Agents in the ways of astraling, so they can sneak into enemy strongholds and eavesdrop. Strictly reconnaissance, in and out. Still, Agents are technically infiltrating territories and breaking cosmic laws in the process. To even the playing field, Hekate strictly prohibited magic in the Spirit Realm. You wouldn't want a ghost tossing magic at you on any given day, now would you?"

"There should be special rules for Agents." Pepper couldn't explain why exactly, but how he had said *strictly prohibited* left the door open for a workaround. She was barking up the wrong tree today if she thought he'd spill. *For another day*, she told herself.

"You'd do best to learn that everything in the cosmos is about balance, just like the Scales of Justice Agents are trained to defend and ensure remain level."

Pepper wasn't satisfied and was about to share her

thoughts, but Kymeo interjected, "I don't need another goddess up my ass, Pepper. Need I remind you …"

Convinced Pepper was about to commit an act of harakiri, he tried to drill into Pepper's head the ABCs of magical law enforcement. Rules and more rules and laws in various dimensions and realms to abide by.

Right as her eyes glazed over, Kymeo finished with, "Can't harm another without facing the consequences—"

"That's a load of BS." Pepper didn't curse, so he couldn't get his panties in a wad. "You're still free to murder someone unprovoked, just for giggles. Happens every day. There are plenty of criminals who get off scot-free. I started a karma-for-hire business because of just that."

"Those lowlies you speak of might not meet Karma in Hell. But retribution doesn't have a shelf life. You can't outrun the goddess of vengeance and justice. Mark my words: Karma will come for them one day, whether in this life or another. And when she does … oof, I wouldn't want to be them."

"What about the corrupted mages who didn't sell their souls? They get a free pass?"

He chuckled. "That is where you come in, my dear. Your kind handles *mostly* cases of a magical nature involving ridding the dimensions of wicked mages who exploit magic for their own selfish desires."

"Or that was the case until the Syndicate discovered Karma's weakness and nearly killed the goddess by picking her Agents off one by one," Pepper blurted out and cringed from regret.

Kymeo said nothing, but the air felt thick with anger until he released it. "You'd be best to corral that flapping tongue. I could be a trickster for all you know, and you just sealed Karma's fate."

"I'm sorry. It won't happen again." A ten-ton blanket of regret blanketed Pepper.

"You're right. It won't. Because the next time, you'll be dead."

Pepper gulped, her heart pounding in her ears. Still, that precise point reminded Pepper of something that niggled away at her ever since finding two wildly different dorm rooms. She had a captive audience in Kymeo, so she figured she'd ask. No harm, no foul. "How can a small number of girls single-handedly help Goddess Karma rid the dimensions of bad actors? And because Agents are few in number already, explain to me how Karma is severely weakened when there are still three—that I know of—alive, counting me?"

The professor remained silent, most likely stewing from Pepper's earlier blunder.

But that didn't stop Pepper. It spurred her on. "How many girls serve as Agents at any given time? If I were to guess based on dorm rooms, I'd say a handful. But how is that possible, even if they are mages?"

"My dear, nothing's impossible if you put your whole heart into it."

"How many Agents? I'm gonna keep asking until you tell me." When the professor ignored her, Pepper added, "Don't I have a right to know?"

"Let's get one thing straight. That entitled attitude is poison to the mind and will lead you down a path of destruction if not rectified. In the least, it's grounds for suspension from the Academy." Kymeo let out an audible sigh, causing the fog to eddy around Pepper's feet. "Still, you would have found out eventually," he proclaimed, as if stating his case to an unseen entity to prevent any future punishment. "Agents aren't the only ones to rid the dimensions of 'bad actors,' as you call them.

They have help. Everyone invited to attend Karma Academy does so as an Initiate, but not everyone becomes an Agent. Most become Karma's Vigilantes. While some are mages, and most are not, what they all have in common is that they believe in justice. And they use that tenet to carry out their karmic duties of handling the day-to-day protection of civilians."

"Oh, like a Karma delivery service. Like I had."

"Sure," Kymeo said coolly.

And just like that, the mystery of how lowlie Kimball could draw sigils to move about the Academy was solved. "You train the Initiates here?" Pepper asked.

"Yes. Initiates receive training in combat, spells and poisons, the art of vengeance, and the like, but on graduation day, we scrub all memories of Karma Academy from their minds. As for those who aren't mages, Goddess Hekate gifts them with the ability to use borrowed magics—granted the titles of honorary mages, if you will."

"I was told borrowing magic was impossible for lowlies."

"It is impossible unless Hekate overrules it."

Pepper then shared what she and Perrin had uncovered on the evidence board in one of the Agent's dorm rooms. And she didn't hold back when she pegged Sawyer as the one who ransacked the furniture and kicked holes in the walls.

"Whatever Sawyer's on the hunt for, she obviously thought one of her fellow Agents had it," Pepper said. "We believe the Syndicate most likely needs this object for whatever they have planned on the night of the lunar eclipse. If we can find it first, we have leverage. Do you have any idea what it could be?"

The wind eddied, sand and silt spinning in a whirling dervish. "It's getting dark, and I imagine the moon's almost finished its ascent. By now, the dracos have smelled your blood and will know where to find you unless you get to safety first."

He imagined … Pepper looked up. Dense foliage covered the clearing. "You can't see the moon from here." After dropping the bomb on Kymeo about the time difference between Karma's realm and Naples, she said, "I need to sneak into the briefing, but I'm not sure when to go. I think it's tomorrow, but what if I'm wrong. I have one shot at getting this right before the lunar eclipse."

"That could only mean one thing. The Syndicate's killed more Initiates, and Karma's life force is nearing the end." Kymeo's somber tone chilled Pepper to the bone. "The goddess and this realm, by default, are intricately tied to Earth, time running parallel. But since she's MIA, that bond has shattered. So we are literally hurtling through time and space. And the Academy is vulnerable to outside forces."

"So you agree then that next Friday on Earth is tomorrow for us?"

"Yes. And, Pepper, I need you to *immediately* report everything you uncovered at the briefing. And I mean *everything*, regardless of how inconsequential it might have appeared." Kymeo then told her where to look for his secret stash of the night-cloak mixture. "One more thing before you leave: find my damn body and fast!"

Pepper wasn't sure what terrified her more: the fact she would sneak inside enemy territory come tomorrow, filled with countless vampires, savage wanderers, and her greatest foes, or that Kymeo tried his damndest to hide his fear but couldn't.

As darkness descended, Pepper scurried back to campus and even summoned Air to push her forward and faster through the forest. The Academy entrance was within sight, but it was too late. The dracos had already found her. And the Alpha was ready to settle the score.

17

A frightening dragon patrolled the bronze-tinted sky. Only this dragon didn't resemble the giant lu'kowsas in Hell. And unlike its descendants that could crush buildings with their tails and devastate villages with their mouth-breathing fire, this beast was the size of a ferocious rhino, the better to squeeze through doorways and maul you alive. The draco's reddish wings, coated in a scaly hide, were interspersed with strips of phalange-like bones that ended in talons, aching to gut prey—to gut Pepper.

Its eyes like burning embers, its body all muscle and red scales, caught Pepper in its sights, and it shrieked, a booming sound that caused the earth to quake under Pepper's feet. More of its rage joined their Alpha on the hunt.

The Alpha banked its wings and then dipped down as it changed direction and tore through the air. As it swooped down, its snout pointed toward Pepper, its jaw unhinged, its teeth bared. The draco flew dangerously close to Pepper

—so close she could smell the death and decay on its breath.

When she let loose a shriek, the summoned Air picked up its pace, scooped Pepper up, whooshed to the Academy, and then tossed her into the atrium. She rolled to a stop, her knees scraped and bloodied.

Perrin stood arms akimbo, her frilly white and coral dress swishing at her knees from the breeze wending through the atrium. "About fuh'karing time. I was going to send in the search party but couldn't." She craned her head upward at the rage of dracos that swarmed the sky above.

The dracos don't know the Academy's defenses are down, Pepper thought. *Otherwise, they'd attack.*

"While you were dating death, I discovered something very interesting." Perrin snapped her head to the side and shouted, "Get out here!"

Kimball appeared, looking rather prideful. "A little kindness goes a long way."

"Don't test my patience." Perrin sighed.

Pepper needed to get what she gleaned off her chest. "I have news to—"

Perrin interrupted, "You're going to want to hear this first. Trust me. Apparently, while we've all been running around like crazed idiots, dickwad here has been living his best life. Side note: I was unaware we were on a fuh'karing holiday."

"Hey, don't hate," said Kimball.

Pepper picked herself up and winced from the pain. "Can someone tell me what's going on?"

"Well, go on!" Perrin instructed Kimball.

"Bell, I tried to tell you what I had discovered earlier, but you ignored me."

"Forgive me for not wanting to be around you," Pepper snapped.

"When you bumped into me, and I dropped the bucket I

was carrying, I heard the water falling through cracks in the ground. That's when I realized something was underneath, but I couldn't figure out how to get below. Not until a little while ago after sunset. Look down." Kimball pointed at the bottom of a reflection pond to a Water sigil that glistened in the moonlight. "It leads to caverns. I explored a little but then got creeped out. I think it's haunted."

Pepper joined Kimball and Perrin on the elevator, and once Kimball finished drawing the trio of waves inside a triangle, they descended to the last school they had yet to visit.

The moment the elevator delivered them to a cavern, a waft of sulfur ambushed Pepper's nostrils, and with it came a biting chill in the air. Sconces flickered to life, their flames casting twisted shadows on the craggy walls of a hallway that ran to infinity. Rivulets of water streamed down giant stalactites as sharp as tacks that colonized the cavern's ceiling and splashed on Pepper's bangs, matting them to her forehead. Pepper hugged her arms around her chest and wished she were bundled in her cloak.

The first chamber they entered contained long autopsy-like tables with a sprinkling of indigo gem dust coating the silty stone floors. The only thing that screamed classroom was a chalkboard and a professor's desk in the back of the room.

"Lemon balm and holy basil." Pepper read the labels on quite a few vials resting on shelves. "If I'm not mistaken, they're for calming the mind and relaxation."

Burlap figures sat clumsily on more shelves. "Are these voodoo dolls?" Kimball asked with a note of terror in his voice.

"Poppets," Perrin corrected as she sauntered to Kimball's side and plucked a dolly from the shelf. "Pepper, didn't you say the Academy taught dark sorcery, memory manipulation, and mind control?"

"Yep. Necromancy, too." Pepper continued perusing the curious supply of herbs and ingredients that seemed to get stranger by the minute: powdered vampire fangs, poltergeist essence, the essence of unreachable dreamscape destination, shed blood of an innocent, captured screams inside a nightmare, and devil's claw, which was an actual claw suspended in a fluid to preserve it.

"Look at this one. Stolen breath of a vampire," Kimball said. He held a glass container, and the murky gray vaporous substance inside swirled angrily, bouncing off the walls. "I don't feel so hot."

"Put it down, you idiot!" Perrin demanded. "It's feeding off your emotions."

They exited that chamber and wound their way into another one darker in vibe and creepier than the last. The spacious room had floor-to-ceiling shelves deep enough to fit coffins; many were stacked with bones, skulls, other skeletal body parts, and scrolls stacked atop scrolls. Tables like those found in surgical rooms were situated around the room. Sigils marred the floor—all intricate in design, with interconnecting lines and every geometric shape imaginable—with blood-drawn runes written within.

A darkened corner contained a bank of jail cells. Rustling sounded, followed by howls. A ghost shot out of a cage, the metal door clanging open, and whirled past them, nearly knocking Pepper off her feet.

"Come here." At Perrin's request, Pepper joined her at a table in the front of the room, most likely belonging to the professor. A notebook was flipped open to a page discussing shadow work and questioning how long a soul could survive if sundered from its shadow.

Perrin pushed Pepper off a sigil she had accidentally stepped on. "They're glyphs, sweetling. Whatever they signify, it can't be good."

From what Pepper could glean, runes were the letters, and the glyphs were the set of runes that made up a complete sentence, or rather a command, and the sigil, with its various interconnected shapes, was the combination of all three.

"They're traps," Kimball called out from across the room. "Says so in this book. Meant to imprison whatever entity the Agents summoned."

"Conjurings of spirits or demons and summoning the dead. That's the subject taught here," Perrin said.

A case of the chills ricocheted through Pepper's body.

"Guys, there's something inside," Kimball said, pointing to a body tucked away in the far corner of the jail cell, swathed in darkness.

Pepper toed the body, and it rolled over, revealing an ageless man with long ashen hair and a mustache adorning an oval face with a pointed chin. "I wonder if that's Professor Kymeo."

"Melisende would know," Kimball replied.

That prompted Pepper to regurgitate all the transpired events to Perrin and Kimball since she had returned from astraling.

"Whoa, Bell. So you were legit inside Vlad's castle? Inside the Syndicate's center of operations?"

Pepper nodded slowly to Kimball's questions.

"And from the sounds of it, you would have been killed if you had stayed one minute longer," Perrin offered. "Explains the cuts on your arm."

Pepper's heart raced to new record-breaking speeds. "If not for the red-haired lady, I would have been." Pepper's hands were frozen to the bone, and she sought warmth in her jeans pocket.

"And you're sure this meeting is taking place next Friday?" Perrin asked.

"On Earth time, yes. But the professor and I think it's

tomorrow as far as this realm is concerned. A day here equals a week there. Something like that."

"Not going to lie. You're risking your life by returning, but you already know that. I wish I could join you. It just concerns me you're going in defenseless."

"Trust me, I know. But I have no other choice. I have to attend this briefing." Pepper's bowels gurgled from uttering those words.

"I agree. First thing tomorrow, you tell Kymeo the news about finding his body. Then we wait until evening for you to go back into Vlad's castle."

This time tomorrow Pepper could either have intel to report, or she'd be dead.

18

"If you've been able to cast magic all this time, why didn't you say anything?" Pepper grilled Loki as they walked under the enchanted archway that marked the entrance to the forest. The canopy of towering trees and carpet of fog occluded the sun's warmth and allowed the foreboding chill to prosper. At least it blocked the moon from Pepper's sight because staring at what amounted to a lunar eclipse countdown clock wasn't helping her anxiety flare-ups.

"Didn't know until now. This is the first time I've stepped outside the perimeters of the Academy," Loki explained, his tenor deep and powerful.

After Melisende had ID'd Kymeo's body first thing this morning, Pepper found a Soul Reunification spell in Kymeo's grimoire. Slight problem: the recipe was incomplete and required Kymeo's advanced skills to craft. Luckily, Loki had figured out a solution to the professor's unfortunate incarceration, so Pepper immediately hightailed it to the forest. Only this time, she had company—Loki.

The goal of returning Kymeo's soul to his body and making the professor whole again was afoot.

When the duo reached the clearing in the woods, Pepper unlatched her tongue and spilled all the happenings to the professor.

Kymeo still wouldn't verbalize his concerns, but they were felt and growing stronger. He certainly didn't hide his exasperation when he cut Pepper's babbling off at the pass and demanded that Loki get on with the magic casting.

The ruachti stood on his hind legs, put his lips together as if preparing to whistle, and blew through his mouth softly. The sound mimicked the howling wind, only much quieter and more subtle, the s's sharp, the r's guttural, the h's and a's nearly silent. Loki asked Air to carry Kymeo's voice to the Academy, like two tin cans separated by a cord. The plan was rather rudimentary, and of course, Pepper hadn't thought of it herself, what with her overcomplicating everything.

A tornadic gust of wind blew toward Pepper and Loki, her ebony locks billowing crazily around her head in a crown. The wind compressed and tightened until it formed a coiled string. Its end, pointing heavenward, shook like a hand wave, prompting Loki that it was time to begin.

The duo started the trek back to the Academy, and Air, in the shape of a barely discernible string, joined them, its other end staying behind with Kymeo.

As they got closer and closer to campus, Pepper's nerves kicked up a notch. Within a few hours, she'd willingly return to the enemy's hands. And if things went south, she'd be on her own, defenseless and without backup. But to be honest, that wasn't any different from reality. To combat that, she needed to learn as much about magic in as little time as possible.

Until now, Pepper had already figured out the difference between drawing sigils and envisioning them—it all came down to muscle memory. You do something long enough, and it becomes engrained in your mind. Elemental sigils were intricate in design, with their symbols, swirls, curves, dots, and slashes. But having to draw them repeatedly to get anywhere in the Academy, students eventually committed the sigils to memory. And that was just one sigil that summoned a single element. So how could she call upon two elements simultaneously? That was what happened whenever Loki channeled the ancient dark magics of Tun-fendin'ga, his powers increasing tenfold, all the elements at his beck and call, even the shadows.

Then, at Jaylyn's house in Carmel-by-the-Sea, Pepper had encountered the mystical dynamic language when it was scrawled all over the attic walls. She'd never forget how the glyphs took on a life all their own, shifting, changing, and rearranging as if being drawn by an imaginary hand.

Pepper hesitantly asked, "What's the difference between elemental magic and Tun-fendin'ga?"

"Ahh, the tongue of the Ancient Ones," Kymeo said, his tone coated in intrigue. "Tun-fendin'ga is a form of Aetheric magic. With everyday magic, mages can manipulate that which already exists. But with Tun-fendin'ga, they can create something from nothing."

"Is speaking Nature's language not part and parcel to Tun-fendin'ga?" Pepper asked Kymeo as she stepped into the atrium and bypassed the stories-high waterfall, cool water spraying her arms.

"My dear, that's like comparing basic math to quantum mechanics. What you have been learning is merely toe-wetting when it comes to Tun-fendin'ga," Kymeo said mysteriously. He then added, "I'm afraid that is not a skill that can be taught in a formal setting, on top of the fact that it takes a few lifetimes to master," and left it at that, leaving Pepper back at square one.

How could Pepper defeat the Syndicate if she couldn't match their skill level? At this point, she'd have to have years of training under her belt, along with an unlimited supply of magic gems at her disposal.

Pepper might not fight like the best of them or weave powerful magic or summon shadows, but she did have something to bring to the table—potions. There had to be a spell she could craft that could give her a leg up. Besides, her anxiety was reaching an all-time high, her heart refusing to do anything other than race as she played the waiting game, so busywork seemed most appealing.

Decision made. After helping Kymeo craft the Soul Reunification potion, she'd start perusing the professor's grimoire and whatever else resided in the caverns.

Loki left Pepper to her own devices as she boarded an elevator. Below the rising platform, Kimball ran around the atrium blindfolded, smacking into various things while holding the vodka bottle housing his mom tight to his chest. He hopped on an elevator and headed to the rooftop. As their elevators bypassed, Pepper was about to call out his name and ask, "What the heck?" But she didn't because ... well, it was Kimball.

As the elevator soared higher, she felt a tinge of disappointment, like a swift kick to her gut, that she hadn't experienced life as a student at the Academy and hadn't received proper training from Kymeo or the other professors. The Academy would never be fully functioning again unless immortal Cazzian, Vlad, and the rest of the Syndicate were destroyed. And Karma couldn't aid Pepper in this endeavor as she was MIA. But what about Hekate?

When they reached the School of Magic, Pepper asked

Kymeo, "What can you tell me about Hekate?" She gave the wheel on the door a spin.

"She can be a real pain in the ass, depending on the phase of the moon."

"Okay. What about her role in the cosmos?"

"Oh. She's the goddess of magic and chaosgates. Only she can giveth and taketh away magical powers."

The professor's response wasn't in the least bit helpful, so Pepper inched closer to that bush she was beating around. "Have you had any dealings with Hekate?"

"I have met the goddess, yes." The professor closed the door on that topic.

Pepper considered another tactic, a warm-up to her key question. "Tell me, Kymeo, are the elements tied directly to Hekate?"

The wind eddied again before Kymeo spoke. "Nature is unbiased and sovereign unto itself."

Seriously, Pepper thought, *that's his answer?* And her face wore her annoyance beautifully. Even her arms got into the action and went akimbo. Pepper really needed to work on suppressing her tells. Add that to the mile-long to-do list.

Enough with the kid gloves. "For God's sake, Kymeo, you have to have some pull with Hekate! Her labyrinth wheel thingy is smacked on the door to your classroom." Pepper was getting worked up, her head throbbing. She would if she could choke the stiff breeze that currently represented the professor. "You teach the ways of magic. You work right under Goddess Karma. Need I go on?"

Kymeo paused for a beat, the eddying wind dying down and disgorging dust and sheaths of paper to the stone floor. "Let's say I did. What are you asking of the goddess?"

"To take magic away from the Syndicate."

"Hekate doesn't decide who can and can't cast magic," Kymeo said measuredly. "Just like Karma can't stop people from harming others. Hekate controls the *use* of magic. Not magic itself. I will not lead you astray and tell you that proficiency in gems and elemental magic will save the day because that would make me a liar. If I pride myself on being anything, it's that I am unabashedly honest." Kymeo could say *that* again. "We've wasted enough time. Time to craft the potion."

As the professor went over the steps, he spoke slowly, as if Pepper were addle-brained. "Aged ectoplasm is inside the center barrel." A bank of barrels lined the walls in one of the backrooms. "While holding down the spigot, count to five."

Pepper did as instructed, and a gooey, electrified glob of ectoplasm slid out and plopped into the waiting flask. "Cork it. Quickly. Otherwise, we'll have a fright of ghosts to contend with." Kymeo explained that the ectoplasm donated by Goddess Brigitte served as a guide to shepherd the soul from the ghostly Spirit Realm of Necropolis to the Physical Realm.

"Now add three drops of Seren-blessed water from the Lake of Destiny. Place the flask on the burner, and heat it for exactly seven minutes. Also, please jot down those notes in the margins if you would."

Pepper noted the time on the wall clock. T-minus six hours until go-time. She tried to take in calming breaths, but that didn't soothe her frayed nerves.

"Within each of our Agents, there's a strength, something unique they bring to the table, and it's my job to identify what that is," Kymeo shared. "To defeat Cazzian, you will have to be smarter than him. Quicker. Cleverer. And it's not to say you can't, Pepper. But time is not on your side. Still, you have an affinity for potion making, and if you were my student, I'd tell you that is your strength." Kymeo shifted his attention back to the spell-crafting. "I suggest wearing gloves for this next part."

Smiling like an idiot from Kymeo's words and getting a

confidence boost as well, Pepper slipped into a pair of gloves, then cautiously extracted half a pipette of moon-weaving spider venom. According to the notes, its purpose was to get blood in the conscious-free and soulless body pumping.

"Stop! Don't add the venom yet. This part is tricky. Take the tweezers and pluck out one flickering ember from a human immolated by Karma."

In her shaky hands, Pepper double-fisted a speck of ash and venom.

"When the last drop of venom touches the mixture, immediately drop in the flickering ember. Timing is everything. On the count of three. One …" Kymeo started.

About ten beats of Pepper's pounding heart filled the spaces between the counted numbers.

"Three. Go." The mixture ignited into a fireball that quickly froze in time. "Well done," Kymeo said. "Now add the phoenix feather." Once the ingredient for Air joined the concoction, the fireball silently exploded in slow time, and then the mixture sifted down.

The final spell ingredient remained. Pepper added a single strand of Hekate's hair coated in orangey-red hellfire. As it floated to the bottom of the flask, a river of fire covered the surface of the potion.

"Hekate doesn't know I swiped a lock of her hair, so let's keep that knowledge to ourselves, shall we?"

Kymeo flippantly stated that the last remaining step could make or break the spell. "So, please don't screw it up. Listen closely. I want you to mimic my movements to the letter. Do not deviate, not even in the slightest. You must use my blood as the ink. I have a spare vial in the chest, under the glove box." Kymeo then directed Pepper to toss a jar of soot on his desk so it would coat the air molecules, allowing her to see his precise movements.

With her fingers coated in Kymeo's blood, Pepper artfully

recreated his airy movements. The drawn sigils fenced her in —glyphs written on top of glyphs, over them, layers of intricate symbols. The bottom layer morphed into something else entirely and began moving, adjusting, and making space.

Once done, the golden-red glyphs connected to one another, forming one sigil that resembled a complex organic compound. Incoherent whisperings emanated from within, then, after a beat, the sigil shot into the Aether and vanished.

"If you're curious, it's looking for my untethered soul cord."

Pepper was indeed curious and smiled. "Will it work?"

"My dear, I certainly hope so. For optimum results, charge the potion by moonlight."

"Oh, like fermenting."

"Sure." Not even the Crooked Dunes could match the dryness in Kymeo's voice. "The duration is determined by how long the conscious mind and soul have been away from the body. In my case, it's been weeks—"

"Was that before or after time went wonky?"

"Oh my. I'm not sure. Well, I tossed an SOS to Seren into the glyphs, hoping the goddess would give us a break, so let's hope she listens. In any event, go ahead and place the flask in the atrium. It requires at least forty-eight hours of brewing. You'll know it's done when it's stopped bubbling. I wish you luck tonight, Pepper. And remember, mind your emotions, and all shall be well." Then Kymeo's voice dissipated in the still air.

19

T-minus four hours until go-time.

Nail-biting fear brewing within, Pepper decided to distract her overthinking mind by crafting a Shadow Trapper potion. But where to begin?

Back inside the caverns, Pepper came prepared. This time, she donned a wool cloak to ward off the biting chill in the air. Her footsteps echoed throughout the vast cavern as her sneakers slapped into puddles of shallow water.

No doubt about it, the caverns were unsettling, but traipsing through them alone seemed to up the creep factor exponentially. The feeble light and random smatters of blood. Air rushing from nowhere. Moans and howls in the distance. Incoherent whisperings from myriad ingredients stored in various classrooms, their glass bottle prisons and locked boxes quaking on the shelves.

Kymeo's warning regarding Cazzian and the Syndicate

stuck in Pepper's mind: *To defeat Cazzian, you will have to be smarter than him. Quicker. Cleverer.*

Pepper had pinned—just barely and by the skin of her teeth—a draco's shadow with a quarterstaff. What if she could do that with magic? With a potion? Though Kymeo and the other professors didn't have an index of various ingredients and their practical purposes on hand, Pepper could formulate what ingredients did from reading other spells.

Inside the shadow-cleaving and necromancy classroom, she focused her attention on the sigils staining the stone floor that, if activated, could trap demons. *But what about trapping a shadow?* she thought, adrenaline rushing through her veins.

Pepper eagerly flipped through Kymeo's grimoire and various other spell books she'd plucked off the shelves until she located Shadow to the Rescue—a close-enough spell to what she had in mind. As her finger traveled under every word, she read over the description: *Sometimes, the only person you can rely on is yourself. If you are ever outmanned and outgunned, summon your shadow as backup. Best of all, your enemies will never see it—YOU—coming!*

This spell wasn't precisely what she had in mind, but perhaps she could use bits and pieces to create a new recipe. Upon further inspection, the incantation wasn't in Kymeo's handwriting but belonged to another. Hopefully, this curly cue script didn't belong to Sawyer. But without other options on the table, Pepper moved forward with the spell-crafting.

Before beginning, Pepper gave every single incantation a once-over to pick up tips and tricks. The Shadow to the Rescue spell called for potion crafting and sigil magic, the latter wholly new to her. So, she'd start with what she already knew rather than focusing on what she didn't.

Once she perused the books from front to back, she had jotted down a bevy of ingredients and their purposes. The first ingredient called for five tablespoons of every-color gem dust. Why the heck not? Into a flask, it went.

Ectoplasm enabled shadows to occupy the Physical Realm. Pepper scrawled down that ingredient.

The shed tear of a soul-seller had popped up in various other spells. In Pepper's own concoction, she'd use it to trick the shadow into trusting her. Her thought process was simple: a soul broker had once duped soul-sellers. Case in point, Pepper might as well have used one of her tears after having fallen for Jhi's bullshit.

Metal filings scraped from bloodied manacles found in the Pits of Tartarus to trap the shadow—Pepper's own creation. This might be a stretch, as the item wasn't listed anywhere Pepper had searched, but more of a collector's item found in Kymeo's office.

The spellcrafter had written *captured breath of a mala'kha + hellfire* but didn't provide amounts. Pepper huffed, then said, "A flame or flames? Measurements matter!" In fact, someone had written the two ingredients as more of a mental note for further consideration than as actual ingredients. Pepper would never know until she tested it. Kimball could be her first victim. She just had to convince him.

Now that Pepper had created the recipe, she averted her attention back to the sigil magic involved in the Shadow to the Rescue spell. The unknown spellcrafter had drawn various sigils that looked like first cousins to elemental sigils, then erased them and amended them repeatedly, the end result unreadable. *Sigils + flask=* was written underneath.

"Equals what?" Pepper muttered. Incensed at the mage's lick and a promise way of spell-crafting, she kicked the reading stand, tossed her knotty hair into a bun, and paced, trying to untangle all the thoughts in her head. She would have bitten her nails, but they were still smarting from her earlier ravishing. "What if I'm overcomplicating this?"

"Occam's Razor," Kimball said, bending down to retrieve the grimoire from off the floor before returning it to the stand. "Always go with the easiest solution. A foreign concept to you, Bell."

"What do you want?" Pepper grumbled.

"I'm bored. Entertain me."

Oh, she'd entertain him, alright.

After tamping down her temper to that of not murderous, she asked Kimball to help her retrieve all the ingredients for the newly written spell. When he asked what it was for, she lied and said it would summon a wish-granting jinn. In her defense, her plan worked, and Kimball eagerly volunteered to be the ginny pig. Pepper suppressed the shit-eating grin threatening to split her face in half.

Pepper and Kimball returned to the necromancy laboratory after rummaging through every cabinet, shelf, barrel, and darkened corner for every element needed for the spell.

After adding all the items to a flask, one last step remained. Pepper drew the sigil from the Shadow Rescue spell on the air, using a piece of multi-hued chalk fashioned from magic gem dust. But nothing happened other than it hovering before her.

"Do you think it's waiting for a command?" Kimball asked.

"Go to the flask?" Pepper commanded the sigil with a clap of her hands, then felt like an idiot.

Kimball laughed when the sigil stayed put. Pepper did, too. "You've got skills, Bell. Watch out, world."

"You have a better idea?"

"Sigil plus flask," Kimball said, then bit the inside of his cheek. "Try tracing the same sigil on the flask. Better than your clap-on-clap-off approach."

After Pepper traced the final stroke of the sigil directly on the flask, the other sigil floating in the air whooshed to its vibrational match and whorled into the mixture in a tornadic fashion, the contents within amalgamating.

Pepper hated that Kimball was right, and he would never let her forget it.

"I began practicing gratitude," he said smugly. "So I thank the Academy for allowing me to recharge and gifting me with much-needed *me* time. It's really cleared my mind and—"

"Got it!"

"Do you? Well, you should be thankful for that, too. Otherwise, you'd still be clapping like one of those toy monkeys with cymbals."

"Did you hear that?" Pepper said, swiveling her head in the hallway's direction.

"No. What?" Kimball's dung-hued eyes widened with fright as they went on alert.

Discretely, Pepper fisted the flask and tossed it at rattilocks' shadow on the wall, limned in the firelight. The contents coated the silhouette. Kimball failed to notice his shadow stretching on the floor and moving independently of its host.

Pepper waited with bated breath for something to happen. When she thought her potion was a big fat failure, Kimball's shadow squirmed and fought against its 2D prison. It didn't take long until the smug shadow sprouted upward, joining Pepper and Kimball, matching their heights and appearing somewhat fleshy. With the magicked smoky chains meant for it dangling from its hands, the shadow then hurled them like a net at Kimball. As the metal links winged through the air, they morphed from 2D to 3D and then coiled around Kimball's torso.

Pepper needed to test out the Shadow Trapper potion to see if Kimball could escape, so she said theatrically, "We're not alone. Hurry up! We better get outta here!"

Kimball tried to run and fell forward on his knees. "Bell,

something's wrong. I can't move. I—" Shock ate his words as he slowly turned his head to see his shadow holding the other end of the chain like a leash.

The concoction worked … sort of. Perhaps more metal filings and less breath of a mala'kha would do the trick. As for how long the incantation would last or the possibility of Kimball's shadow up and leaving—Pepper would worry about that later. First, she'd check on the Soul Reunification elixir, currently brewing in the atrium. Afterward, she'd make a batch or two of the Shadow Trapper.

"See you later, Kimball."

"Wait! Don't leave me!" Kimball's shadow creeped Pepper out with its mischievous wink, devilish smile, and a buh-bye wave.

"Bell, what about the jinn and my wishes?"

Pepper could still hear Kimball prattling on as she ventured down the cavern's dank hallway.

20

C onscious Astraling 101: *As you slip into a hypnagogic state, hold tightly in your mind's eye a picture of your destination; otherwise, you risk getting lost in the Spirit Realm. Or worse—becoming food for wraiths.*

Pepper followed Kymeo's instructions to the letter. She had one chance to get this right. One opportunity to gain much-needed intel that could tip the Scales of Justice in her faction's favor.

"This is solely reconnaissance, Pepper. Anything else is a suicide mission," Loki said sternly, as if reading Pepper's mind.

As far as Pepper was concerned, this mission was more than gleaning information. The lunar eclipse was fast approaching, judging from the metallic half moon. And it wasn't just a celestial body but a doomsday clock. Tonight, she planned on rescuing her father, somehow, someway.

"And when the Syndicate's done with you, they'll kill

your father, me, and our little furball demigod here," Perrin piled on.

Pepper deflated. How could she venture back inside Vlad's castle and not help her father?

Kimball entered the room. "By the way, Bell, your nifty little shadow spell sure doesn't have staying power."

"Shut up, Kimball!" Perrin shifted her attention back to Pepper. "You have one hour, and then we're yanking your ass back out." Perrin wasn't messing around.

With all eyes on Pepper, she sipped the spicy elixir topped with night-cloak while picturing the castle dungeon, then recited: "I remember perfectly. I remember clearly. I remember all."

A BLAST of icy cold air greeted Pepper right as she landed inside a dank room, mantled in stone above, to the side, and below, with bits of moss and water growing in place of grout. The stench of death churned her stomach. Pain-imbued whimpers hitchhiked on the air.

They can't see me, Pepper told herself. *I'm a ghost.* Her heartbeat quickened. The last time she had ventured within the walls of Vlad's castle, she thought it was a dream and that nothing could hurt her. Oh, how naive she had been.

Once Pepper got her bearings, her eyes winged to the redheaded mage manacled to the wall, her wrists bloodied and abrasions marring her flesh, bone visible. And she wasn't alone. There were others in their own jail cells, some awake and rocking in place, some not and prone on the floor. It was hard to tell if the ones prone were sleeping or dead. But all the prisoners were scantily clad, most likely a humiliation tactic.

And then she saw her dad slumped against a moldy wall,

lying in a pool of blood and excrement. "Pops!" His eyes remained closed, and he didn't respond. Seemed lifeless even. "Pops, wake up!" Pepper whispered. But he couldn't hear her. Of course not, because Pepper was a ghost.

"Your father's alive. But just barely," the red-haired woman breathed. "Wanderers are patrolling the castle. If I can feel your fear, then so can they. If you don't banish it, you won't make it out of here alive."

"You can hear me?" Pepper asked. If she could, did that mean the others could? "Can you see me, too?"

"I can't see you, but I can hear you."

"How is that possible?" Pepper said, more to herself.

"Not sure. Your father and I have tried to contact you through your dreams on several occasions, and perhaps a link was formed between us as a result."

When Larry coughed, Pepper whipped her head in his direction only to see blood-tinged spittle on his lips. Heat ignited along her body, her internal temperature soaring. The roiling rage incinerated the fear. All Pepper could imagine was the pain she would inflict on Miles. The amount of his blood she would shed.

"Miles is fiercely protected by forces far more powerful than you can imagine. Whatever you have planned, table it."

"Who are you?" Pepper snapped, her jaw clenched.

"My name's Ellie May." The redhead tried to get closer to Pepper, but the wall-mounted shackles locked around her legs and hands extended as far as they could. "Pepper, put aside your hatred for Miles for the time being and listen to me. Vlad has something in the works. Something big that revolves around the lunar eclipse. I overheard the Hounds discussing some upcoming gala and how it's the most talked about event in Naples. But they need us alive for whatever they have planned. Otherwise, we'd be dead. Your father included."

Pepper nodded understanding.

"You've gotta help us escape before then."

"That's why I'm here." Pepper didn't have the heart to tell her she didn't actually have a plan.

"Time's running out." Desperation seeped through the cracks in her voice.

The door flung open. Thirty-something, bleach-blonde, and tanorexic Bunny Garcia, or rather the wanderer that stole her body, stood at the threshold, trading in the pedal pushers and oversized sparkling tee-shirt for trousers and a blouse that hinted at another time and place. The wanderer scampered inside the dungeon, its nose scrunching as it sniffed the air.

Ellie May hollered at the wanderer to bring them food. The distraction helped Pepper skirt around the bloodthirsty demon and get as far from it as possible. Pepper could still hear Ellie May screaming in the background, but her cries faded the farther away she ventured.

Pepper couldn't touch anything, which put a damper on her rescuing her father. Oddly, she couldn't flit through walls either because she tried, and her nose smacked into the cold stone. So much for her being ghostlike.

A circular staircase was at the end of the vast hallway and only led upward, so she climbed until she reached another floor. Another hallway sprawled out before Pepper, lined with doors on either side. Inside one room, wan light peeked through a narrow opening in the buttoned-up curtains. Between the fireplace and the canopied four-poster bed, the room would fit perfectly inside a castle. But not the damned skin rug, complete with a head attached, ears removed, eyes sewn shut, its mouth fixed open as if frozen in an eternal scream of regret.

Pepper walked gingerly past the damned to peer through a tiny opening in the heavy drapes. Beyond the windowpanes, endless rivers of sawgrass made up the terrain, a few alligator sightings, and even a snake's head poked out through the surface of the soupy water. Unfortunately, not a single recognizable landmark presented itself to aid Pepper in pinpointing the precise location of the castle in the middle of the Everglades, which clocked in around 7800 square miles.

Staircase after staircase carried Pepper further into the bowels of Castle Dracula. A smattering of voices caught her attention, and she followed the chatter and wound up in a populated kitchen with cleaver-wielding demons cutting up human meat—a severed hand was tossed to the side—and rolling chunks of the filleted flesh in flour. Serrated knives were fanned out on the island. If only Pepper had tactile abilities, then she'd have a weapon to use for defense and wouldn't feel so vulnerable.

When the butcher swung the cleaver and then severed an arm, Pepper dashed out of the kitchen and through the dining chamber that opened up to the great hall big enough to host hundreds of demons and froze in the dead center of the hall, her head slowly craning upward as if sensing something watching her. A stone gargoyle stood sentry atop a ceiling-high platform in one of the four corners of the vast great hall, its eyes firmly focused on Pepper. And it wasn't alone. Three others joined in the observing from their respective corner perches. Her heart rattling in her chest, Pepper took a tentative step and silently rejoiced when the goyle's eyes didn't move.

A door at the far end of the hall creaked open. Pepper's breath quickened, her palms sweaty, her thoughts playing the devil with her resolve. Was she truly invisible? What if the Conscious Astraling potion expired? *Get it together!* Still, she didn't dare move a muscle.

Sawyer sauntered out of a room in skintight jeans and a halter top, then slowly slipped her aviators to the top of her head. Her heels *click-clacking* on the stone floor echoed about the vast space. Soon Jhi met her stride.

"Oof, that's a nasty cut ye got there. How'd that happen?" Sawyer said in between bites of a Tiger's Milk bar. She crumpled up the wrapper and casually discarded it in a nearby planter.

"Occupational hazard," and Jhi left it at that.

The duo paused next to Pepper and before an archway that led to a long skywalk flanked by a bank of windows and lined with the reddest of red carpets. A few beefy vampires stood guard before double doors at the far end.

Pepper was so close to Jhi that she could touch him, her nose getting stuffy from the aroma of Sawyer's rose-vanilla perfume.

"Yer energy and chakras"—Sawyer waved her hand about —"they're all over the place and messing with mine. Rude!"

"I think you have more things to worry about than my chakras," Jhi replied.

"It's not part of my journey today to deal with the likes of you. But because I'm in a generous mood, just a heads up. Vlad's knickers are in a twist," Blondie said. "Cazzian is none too happy with ye as well."

"What are you going on about, Sawyer?"

"Ye missed last week's briefing, so where have ye been? Not a difficult question. Unless —"

"That's classified and above your pay grade."

"Ye are an absolute wanker!" Sawyer swept escaped strands of her iron-straight, ashen locks behind her ear. "Vlad is bloody pissed ye haven't attended a briefing in weeks. It's a real energy drainer, having to be around all that negativity and venom. Of course, Cazzian defended ye. Still, the whole episode dampened my vibe. Now they're questioning yer loyalties." She made a moue of concern. "As am I."

But Jhi didn't flinch. Didn't give away a tell that he was

concerned. Until Pepper noted his index finger imperceptibly tattooing the tip of his thumb. Jhi was worried. But why?

Jhi took a centering breath, and Pepper could have sworn he looked right at her. Whatever she thought Jhi had felt—perhaps he sensed Pepper's presence after all—he shrugged off and said, "Looks like your chakras could do with some cleansing."

Sawyer smirked, adjusted her ponytail, and said, "As much as I'd love to continue this wee little chinwag, the meeting is getting started, so we better crack on."

Blondie led the way down the skywalk, her blowgun strapped to her thigh. But her shadow didn't follow suit. Instead, the black silhouette—occupying its 2D home—slowly swiveled its head toward Pepper.

Pepper didn't dare move a muscle for fear she'd been spotted.

A few panic-laced seconds later, the shadow slithered away, appearing like a heat haze, and caught up to Sawyer's stride.

Pepper got her wits about her and strode purposefully down the skywalk to uncertain death with fear but a memory and vengeance at the helm.

21

"And you let that little beetch slip through your fingers?" Vlad growled at Jhi from behind an executive desk in the back of the turret. Behind the vampire high king and around the curved castle walls, velvet drapes shut out rays of the impossible sunlight struggling to lance through the mullioned windows. "I—"

"It's not—" Jhi attempted to say.

"Don't you ever interrupt me again!" Vlad spat, loosening his tie as if considering strangling Jhi with it. "I made it very clear that we needed the Budreau girl. Not that I *wanted* her, but *needed*." His fangs glinted in the artificial light—fangs so sharp the vampire didn't have to apply much pressure to puncture his victim's skin. Ever so slightly, a wicked, puckered scar on the high king's neck peeked out from underneath the pressed collar of his ironed shirt.

"And where are you at with the extraction?" Cazzian asked Jhi pointedly, a slight Scottish burr shining through.

"We've been waiting for an update for weeks, but our patience is wearing thin." Cazzian stood with his back touching the turret's wall, his strawberry-blonde hair purposefully messy and muted freckles speckled on his fair complexion. Adorned in business casual wear—an untucked shirt, jeans, and oxfords—one would never guess from his appearance that he had resurrected from Hell. Or that he was immortal, as he didn't look a day over twenty-six. And by his side stood Ember, dressed to the nines as if expecting to attend a board meeting of a Fortune 500 company and an unlikely match to whatever Cazzian was to her.

"There are a few kinks that need ironing out—"

Vlad slowly raised his head from the document he was signing to bore holes into the Ven-ad'tsay. "'Beatrice escaped,' you said. You're still ironing out a few kinks. Tell me, Jhi. What have you been doing other than *not* showing up for briefings?"

Sawyer smirked at Jhi, wearing an "I told you so" look.

Jhi's mask of unflappability slipped for a brief second before stoniness assumed its rightful position on his gaunt face. But Pepper had seen enough. Jhi's piercing stare that lasted a beat. The way his muscles tensed under his Henley. His hands balling into fists. Make no bones about it—Jhi craved ripping Vlad to shreds, verbally and physically.

If not for the unquenchable thirst for revenge coursing through Pepper's veins—her list of targets all in attendance— Vlad's unbridled anger aimed at Jhi would have coaxed the fear Pepper tamped down to come out and play. And then the wanderer Bunny, standing next to its husband-in-name-only Shelly, would have sensed fear and attacked the unseen Pepper on the spot. So, Pepper had no choice but to monitor her emotions and keep anything that could give away her presence on a tight leash.

"Sir, with all due respect, if you aren't happy with my

work, then find someone else," Jhi said measuredly. "For what it's worth, I wasn't tasked with hunting Beatrice down. That mission falls under Miles' purview. But Miles needed help, so I was called in and had to step away from my other mission. Isn't that right, Miles?" Jhi channeled suave perfectly. "As for the extraction, need I remind you, if I make one wrong move, let's just say living out eternal life as one of the damned would look like nirvana compared to my fate."

"Understood. Starting today, you are to focus all your efforts on the mission at hand," Vlad commanded. "Now, appease me by reviewing the plan one last time."

"On the afternoon of the lunar eclipse, I'll make my way to the Lake of Fire in Gehenna," Jhi said by rote, his nerves steely. "I have exactly fifty-nine seconds to break inside. Once I'm in, I'll extract the package, escape Hell, then deliver the package to the castle and lie low until things cool down."

"Once the minute is up, DISI'll sense the package is gone and shut down all chaosports. So, how do you intend on escaping Hell?" Cazzian asked.

"I'm working on it," Jhi said curtly.

"Miles, any light you can shed on Josephine Budreau?" Cazzian inquired, urgency coating his words. "We could use her to smoke Beatrice out."

Miles turned his attention away from Vlad and looked Cazzian dead in the eyes, then said, "She's dead."

Other than exchanging a glance with Vlad, Cazzian took the response in stride, and if the answer displeased him, he didn't express a telltale. The same, however, couldn't be said for Vlad. Muscles visibly shifted under the vampire high king's silk shirt, and his jaw clenched. Calmly, Vlad asked for a follow-up, a reasonable explanation of the events that led to that fate.

Miles defended himself, outright lies his shield, and

described Josephine as a lowlie—intel supplied to him by Jhi, who had vetted the Budreau sister beforehand.

Jhi's index finger subtly tattooed the tip of his thumb. Clearly, Jhi hadn't revealed that damning truth to Vlad and, consequently, had been pinned into a corner by Miles.

"Blood is blood!" Vlad growled, his animus aimed at Jhi. Jhi might as well have killed Josephine himself for all Vlad cared.

"Not when it's free of magic." Jhi remained the picture of calmness, but when Vlad wasn't looking, he tossed Miles a feral look Pepper knew all too well, one that communicated, "You're going to pay." Then turned his attention back to Vlad. "Miles killed Josephine on the spot. Broke her neck. I disagreed with his actions and made that abundantly clear to him at the time of the incident. But it wasn't my call to make. You tapped Miles to lead the operation to retrieve the Budreau girl, so who was I to question his motives? I'm just here to assist when need be."

"The elder Budreau sister attacked me, and—Shit happens," Miles admitted and left out the details. "But when the storied Ven-ad'tsay tells me Josephine's a lowlie, who am I to argue? No harm, no foul. The girl was of no use to us. End of story. Besides"—Miles locked his sights on Jhi—"I'm close to pinpointing Beatrice's location, no thanks to Jhi."

Vlad's shoulders dropped. "Very well." He strolled behind his desk to one of the heavily tinted glass windows in the turret. With his back to his audience, he pushed back the velvet drapes and took in the scenery, the toes of his loafers stopping before the pool of sunlight drenched on the stone floor. One identifying feature separated vampires from humans: they were shadowless—something Pepper had never noticed until now. A beat later, the vampire high king pivoted on his heel and said to Miles, "We can still smoke Beatrice out. I suggest using Josephine's death to your advantage if you haven't already. Then report back to me." A Hound handed more papers to Vlad to sign, so Vlad took a seat back at his desk.

Miles nodded in response.

Vlad spoke to Miles like a mentor to his apprentice, grooming the next in line. Until this point, Pepper had painted Miles as a hanger-on-er like Kimball's father, Shelly. Not someone moving quickly up the Syndicate's ranks. Especially a homicidal psychopath like Miles. Now add in him wielding magic and whatever else the Syndicate had planned, making him an even more dangerous opponent.

"What about Pepper?" Cazzian asked Jhi. "Ember tasked you with keeping track of her, did she not? I shouldn't have to tell you, Jhi, that it's *unacceptable* you haven't updated us since you last spotted her at the Starless Souk with Beatrice."

"There hasn't been any news to report." Jhi remained the picture of calm.

Ember leaned gracefully into Cazzian, her lips barely brushing against his peach-hued lobe, and whispered into his ear. He then asked, "How is it that Pepper joined forces with the Budreau girl? What is their connection?"

Pepper's heart went arrhythmic. *Did Jhi know Beatrice was an Agent of Karma like Pepper?* It was hard to think through the sheer panic. If Jhi knew, he hadn't learned from their time together. She only learned about Beatrice after Jhi's betrayal once the two had parted ways.

The moment of truth had come: would Jhi spill or not? The former had dire consequences for Pepper and the Agents of Karma.

Doing everything in her power to calm her wildly beating heart, Pepper raptly watched the rise and fall of Jhi's chest; at first, it seemed to escalate, but he got it under control relatively quickly.

"Kimball. He's responsible for Pepper making Beatrice's acquaintance," Jhi replied.

Pepper's knees buckled. Jhi was going to spill; she just knew it. This was the end.

"I was present when Kimball shared a conversation he had overheard between Miles and Shelly regarding Beatrice," Jhi lied. "Pepper is wicked smart, so if Miles was after Beatrice, then the girl must be of great importance, so Pepper had to beat Miles at his own game. And Pepper did just that." Jhi relished adding that last part. "Quite honestly, we wouldn't be having this conversation had Miles kept his mouth shut."

Relief washed through Pepper, so much so she could cry.

Ember canted her head in Pepper's direction. Her ruby-red eyes fixated on the very spot Pepper stood. Had Pepper's uncontrolled emotions given her away?

"And you haven't heard hide nor hair of Pepper Li since?" Cazzian grilled Jhi.

"Not since she disappeared at the Starless Souk, no. Her use of magic is increasing and rather impressive—"

"'Impressive,' hm … Interesting choice of adjectives. Personally, I would have used *alarming*." Cazzian seemed to question Jhi's loyalties.

"I give credit where credit is due. Nothing more, nothing less," Jhi said.

Pepper might have wanted to kill Jhi with her bare hands, but she appreciated him not mentioning her speculuming skill. After all, Jhi had borne witness to her disappearing inside a mirror. In this briefing alone, Jhi could have exposed Pepper on two separate occasions, yet he didn't. Why? What did he have up his sleeve?

Shelly stepped forward. "To answer your question, Mister Cazzian. Pepper is with my son."

"And that helps us how, exactly?" Vlad barked, annoyed.

"Kimball is vulnerable," Miles added, stepping in. "Malleable. I believe what Shelly's inferring is that we can coax him back to our side."

"And why would we need a lowlie?" Jhi pressed. "What could Kimball possibly offer us? Better yet, what could *you* possibly offer him?"

Miles grew visibly angry. "Because the Hounds last saw Kimball with Pepper and Beatrice at the Starless Souk. Kimball will lead us to both girls if we play our cards right."

"Ahh, yes, Miles. The one job you had that you screwed up." Jhi was not a fan of Miles; his tone screamed as much. "So instead of you doing *your* job, it's become my responsibility, and apparently Kimball's now, too?" Jhi shook his head, exasperated. Mainly for show.

Miles charged at Jhi, tightly gripping his double-bladed dagger in his hands. Jhi remained in place, his feet firm, fists at the ready. Close enough to Jhi, Miles leaped through the air and swung a punch, Jhi's throat the target, but Jhi calmly stepped out of the way, and Miles crashed into the stone wall. Jhi let loose a weak chuckle.

Fuming, Miles magicked his dagger to carve Jhi into ribbons. Jhi didn't predict that his enemy would take their beef that far and failed to swat the weapon away before it pierced his stomach. Not enough to cause great bodily harm, but enough to rip through Jhi's Henley, right into his flesh, blood welling.

In one fluid motion, Jhi charged at Miles, grabbed the dagger out of Miles' hand, knocked him to the ground, then held the blade to Miles' throat.

"Enough!" Vlad growled as he willed the dagger out of Jhi's grip and into the high king's hands, beads of Jhi's blood splashing the air. "Get off of Miles, now!" Jhi obeyed. "And get up off the floor, Miles. You better mind that temper. I will not remind you again. Whatever issues you have with Jhi, table them. I tasked you as lead, so lead. We need the

Budreau girl before the ceremony. That is non-negotiable. Find her and bring her to me. And I don't need to remind you what will happen if you fail."

Vlad seemed to be the head honcho of this upcoming gala, with Cazzian willingly taking a back seat. But why?

Jhi got to work staunching his wound with a poultice he'd fished out of his backpack, his face pinched with untold fury.

"My stunning Sawyer," Vlad started. Regarding the double-crossing Agent of Karma, Vlad's manner hovered between avuncular to no-nonsense, order-barking king. "What news do you have to report?" Vlad tore his eyes away from the sheath of papers on his executive desk. "Friendly reminder: I am in no mood for anything other than glad tidings."

Utterly unfazed that she was being interrogated by the original vampire, Sawyer oozed boredom as if Vlad had taken her away from more pressing matters like sound bathing and napping. Hands clasped behind her back, Sawyer resolutely explained how she was getting closer in her search for the object, and Vlad should worry not, that everything was cosmic, only good vibes ahead, and to chill. She finished with a brazen wink meant for Vlad. But what the others didn't see were Sawyer's fidgeting fingers.

When Vlad's fangs extended ever further, as if saying he didn't appreciate her insolence, Sawyer didn't even flinch. She might even have suppressed a smirk.

Sawyer's lying, Pepper thought. *So the ice queen isn't so ... well, icy.* Still, Pepper noted how the Agent remained tight-lipped regarding *where* she had searched for the object.

Miles looked Sawyer up and down, as if noting her measurements. His lips spread open with a lascivious grin, his tongue wet his lips, and pride reflected in his beetle-black eyes. It was the same expression he had worn during his tele-vised murder trial when the prosecution had shared gruesome crime scene photos of the various-sized cages the acquitted serial killer had locked the "pretty, pretty girls" in. And then the grisly aftermath when Miles had grown bored with his victims.

"We need that relic, Sawyer," Cazzian added.

"Right-o," Blondie replied, her voice silky smooth, then followed it up with a sigh. "But just to verify, it's not exactly essential for the ritual, correct?" That question betrayed Sawyer's certainty that she'd obtain the mysterious object.

Ember, too, picked up on that telltale and addressed Sawyer. "Whether or not the relic is required to ensure a successful outcome for the Winter Solstice ritual is neither here nor there."

Cazzian interjected, "This bears repeating. Moving onto the next stage of our operation hinges on two events: Jhi's upcoming mission and the successful completion of the Winter Solstice ceremony thereafter. We retrieve the relic, and we control both outcomes." Cazzian bit the inside of his lip; Pepper took that as a sign that this operation wasn't as foolproof as she had thought.

Miles cleared his throat, then said, "Since Sawyer is having the dickens of a time tracking it down, I'd like to give her a hand. Two heads *are* better than one."

"That's unnecessary," Sawyer said firmly, her red-painted lips pursed.

"That so?" Miles pressed. "Mind apprising the group then of *where exactly* you've been conducting your search?" His eyes swept over everyone in attendance. "Because from what I've gathered, nobody knows where you disappear to on your *investigations*." He used air quotes for the latter.

"It's none of your *bloody* business where I go and what I do," Sawyer spat with as much disgust as she could muster.

Hopefully, Sawyer's sage supply was bountiful because

she'd have to do a boatload of smudging later to remove the mushrooming anger she directed at Miles.

Vlad and Miles glanced in each other's direction out of Sawyer's eyeshot. Vlad subtlety nodded his head, as did Miles, in return.

"Everyone"—Cazzian held his hands up—"let's take a deep breath." By everyone, Cazzian meant Miles and Sawyer. "Trust me when I say that I understand you're all feeling the stresses of the time crunch. Gentle reminder: the mala'kha dragged me to Hell, and I'll tell you this much. I didn't spend countless years tortured by that *bitch* Karma for nothing. I did it with the end goal in mind. A mindset I ask all of you to adopt if you haven't already."

Sawyer zoned out during Cazzian's speech, her Arctic blue eyes practically glazed over.

With cool precision, Vlad finished signing whatever had commanded his attention, placed the top on the pen, then rose from his desk. The famed warlord commanded the room, from his predatory gait to his business attire—slacks, tight-fitting, button-down shirt, and loafers—to his lean muscled frame wrapped in bronzed skin, piercing dark eyes, and shoulder-length hair. This man looked nothing like the historical depictions of the famed Vlad the Impaler. His height alone dwarfed his legendary counterpart. His features were finely sculpted yet prominent, his jaw as square as could be and stubble-free. All eyes were on the vampire high king as he strolled to the center of the turret to join his congregation.

"This has been an incredibly disappointing briefing," Vlad started, "and dare say pointless. I'm going to say this once. If anyone, and I don't care who you are, doesn't pull through with their end of the bargain, if anyone makes a mistake, even the slightest of missteps that to you were unavoidable, I will make your life a living hell. Incarceration in the Pits would feel like paradise compared to what I have in store for you." The undead warlord took a measured breath, then continued. "Need I remind everyone here today what is at stake for this ceremony?"

"When dealing with a prophecy, you don't get a re-do, so it's best not to muck about," Sawyer said deadpan, as if answering a question in class.

Pepper wavered on whether Sawyer's feelings for Vlad were romantic or platonic.

Vlad tossed a smirk at Sawyer. "This ceremony doesn't just benefit me." He lavished his attention on everyone in attendance. "It benefits us all. Though unlike you, I have waited *centuries* for this moment that was"—he paused, as if editing his words before speaking—"prophesied to my brother and me by a rather angry Roma when we were children." He let loose a weak chuckle as intimate knowledge radiated in his eyes.

"Before getting chased out of our village, the Roma spat, 'One blood brother would betray the other, and one of us would die.' I couldn't fathom my brother becoming a traitor. On the other hand, Radu opted to wave it away as crazy mutterings of a pauper. But what she said that day came to pass. My brother, blood of my blood, betrayed me, Wallachia, and our countrymen for power when he joined forces with our enemies, the Ottomans. Radu made a mockery of our family name and that gilded crown he'd stop at nothing to obtain. So I tracked down the Roma and … convinced her it was in her best interest to share the rest of the prophecy. And the old bag of bones did. 'On the first night, the dragon devours the sun, the devil tags his heels.'"

Vlad then described the moment when the first part of the prophecy came to pass: June 17, 1462, during the infamous Attack at Târgovişte. On the same day, a solar eclipse had painted the sky an impenetrable black.

The Ottomans and their leader Sultan Mehmed II, childhood best friend to Radu and Vlad's greatest foe, were a constant threat at Wallachia's borders. To end the threat and save his country, Vlad and his vanguard carefully plotted an assassination attempt on Mehmed and infiltrated the sultan's camp in the middle of the afternoon during a total solar eclipse while his enemies slept. After Vlad snuck inside Mehmed's tent, who was sleeping soundly, he slit the sultan's throat, but his neck rewove until it was buffed to perfection. When Mehmed's eyes snapped to attention, Vlad's kilij somehow wiggled out of his bloodied hands. Still, Mehmed had Vlad dead to rights, and Vlad and his men had no choice but to flee into the surrounding woods.

What Vlad bore witness to that night forever changed the trajectory of his life and his country's fate. Vlad learned of a secret kept hidden from the masses. A secret explaining how Sultan Mehmed II had thwarted Vlad and his vanguard's advances repeatedly, how the Ottomans broke through Vlad's mountain strongholds, and how the sultan couldn't be killed. Magic existed. It was real, and unless and until Vlad had magic coursing through his veins, he'd never be able to save his country from the Ottoman threat. He'd never be able to defeat the Ottomans.

Vlad cut his story short. "A monk once told me: 'Be the wise man who learns from the mistakes of others, not the fool who learns from his own.' I was once the fool and followed Mehmed's path. But unlike Mehmed, I still tread the earth. I am the victor." The warlord set his sights on Cazzian, who then nodded in response.

Vlad continued, "I bring this up because I notice you enjoy the fruits of my labor. But you're mint-rubbing and, in so doing, taking me and the gifts I've bestowed upon you for granted. So, let me remind you, if not for me, you wouldn't be able to drain a mage of their blood and wield powerful magics. Your lowlie bodies wouldn't even be able to absorb magic in the first place. *If not for me,* you'd all be chained in the Pits of Tartarus, tortured to your last dying breath by the mala'kha, only to be regenerated time and time again, your soul the rightful property of Lucifer, like the rest of the soul-selling damned."

Vlad paused and deeply inhaled, as if tamping down the desire for wholesale maiming. "Right now, the magic you all wield and relish so very much is temporary. And I can take it away just as easily as I had gifted it. The choice is yours. Do your part to prepare or suffer the consequences. If the Winter Solstice ceremony is not a smashing success, and you all failed to deliver what I asked for, then everything we've accomplished until now, the centuries of planning, will have been for naught."

"Team, everything that was prophesied to Vlad centuries ago has come to pass," Cazzian offered, serving as the good cop in this scenario, trying to soften the blow of bad-cop Vlad's gruff delivery, punctuated by threats of torture and death. "We're so close. Just keep all your eyes on the prize."

"I think I speak for everyone who sold their souls and joined the Syndicate when I extend my heartfelt gratitude to Vlad," Shelly said.

"What a bum licker," Sawyer said under her breath, quiet enough to not be heard by the others save for Pepper.

"Vlad didn't have to share his knowledge with us," Shelly said. "Or share his secrets to becoming mages. To eternal life. To cheating the king of darkness. Thanks to Vlad, those of us born as lowlies can wield magic like mages. What was thought to be impossible is now a reality."

A male and female, joined by a few Hounds, entered the room, showcasing their glee from having caught the tail-end of Shelly's speech.

Vlad acknowledged the newly arrived with a nod, then asked, "Shelly, any updates on your end?"

"We have some insurgents, but they're a fringe minority and not a threat to our plan." Vlad was about to object, but Shelly cut him off at the pass. "Even so, we're keeping our eyes and ears out for anyone speaking outside the narrative."

"And who are these eyes and ears?" Vlad asked.

"All the citizens of Naples and Collier County as a whole. They've taken it upon themselves to snitch on their fellow neighbors—without even being asked. Imagine that?" He snickered. "The fringe minority is surrounded by an army of people they once called friends and family. An army more than willing to do our bidding."

"What about para doxea? During the last meeting, someone mentioned a supply issue?" Vlad pressed.

"All handled and nothing you have to worry about," Shelly said confidently. "We've poisoned all public community water systems with para doxea. The same with all bottles of water in every store within the greater Collier County area, from Naples to Isles of Capri to Marco Island to Chokoloskee to Everglades City to Golden Gate to Immokalee. Every jug, bottle, brewed tea, kava, kratom, coffee, and even ice poisoned with para doxea."

"What about those who get their water supply elsewhere, like a well? And what are we doing about the fringe minority who aren't drinking the water?"

"That's precisely why I think it's beneficial for you to make another televised appearance aside from *Romancing Vlad* or morning talk shows," Shelly advised Vlad, "and do your vampire high king hypnosis thing and convince those who might be holed up in their home to take an outing. As for the fringe minority, they are not impervious to compulsion. They're just not so easily swayed as the majority. Still, I don't consider them a threat."

"What makes you say that?" Controlled savagery coated Ember's tone, and her face fostered a look of lethal curiosity.

"I, uh," Shelly stammered.

"'I, uh'—that's not the response I was looking for, Mister Garcia." Her back ramrod straight, thin arms at her side, elongated neck reaching ever high, thin lips forming a dash—Ember couldn't be more intimidating. As if further emphasizing that point, her eyes bored into Shelly as if saying, "One wrong answer, and I'll eat you alive."

"I misspoke. If there are mages or non-practicing ones in the fringe minority, then that's all the more reason Vlad needs to keep up with his radio, internet, and television appearances. Neapolitans are rabid, eating our high king up. He's the 'it' guy here. Naples' most eligible bachelor. We've created an army that will attack on command should the fringe say anything disparagingly against Vlad, let alone try to attack us, his coterie. But that enthusiasm can wane, which is why a steady stream of appearances keeps the energy going before the televised lunar eclipse gala." Shelly couldn't possibly clench his buttocks any tighter.

"Very well," Ember said.

Shelly discretely wiped beads of sweat from his brow with his monogrammed handkerchief.

"Enzo. Sarah. I hope you two have a good reason for your flagrant disregard of decorum," Vlad barked at the newly arrived.

"We're late, and for good reason," replied Enzo, wholly unfazed by the vampire warlord's apparent anger at being casually addressed.

Pepper last laid eyes on this man at the All Hallows' Eve masquerade ball. A man whose face had graced Southwest Florida newspapers. A man who had foiled one law enforcement operation after the other, his exploits unprovable and his hands forever clean. Enzo Bonovese was well-known and equally feared. The youngest scion of and only male heir to the Bonovese crime family. The youngest godfather in recent history—a ripe twenty-two—took over the family business when his father choked on his own blood, his tongue dangling through his slit throat in a mockery of a smile as he lay naked in bed with his mistress by his side.

The hired assassin's fate turned out to be much worse than his target's, Enzo Senior; his body was so mutilated that the nightly news couldn't even blur the footage or show the crime scene zoomed out because the hitman's body parts were tossed everywhere, as was his blood. According to the news, an unnamed source suggested Enzo had his own father killed. After what Pepper had witnessed at the masquerade ball, she didn't doubt the anonymous source's claim. After all, Enzo had savagely killed his plus-one in front of a roomful of witnesses without batting an eye, a kept promise for selling his soul for unlimited magic and power. And like all the other soul-sellers who had helped Cazzian resurrect from Hell, Enzo's crimes went unpunished.

"Sarah and I have been working in tandem." Enzo exchanged a glance with his female companion. "On my end, it's been a few months since I laid the groundwork. This involved calling in a few favors with contacts on my payroll in the federal government. They've been working in conjunction with our contacts inside DISI. And I just received word that everything's a go. And Jhi, you'll want to pay attention to this. On the day of the lunar eclipse, the wildly popular *Ultimate Death Match* will stream for the first time on every holo-gab throughout Hell, not just aired on the major networks. It'll be bigger, bloodier, and more carnage than ever before, and Pandæmonians are pumped!"

Vlad sensually bit his lower lip as if that news was a virgin he was moments from undressing, bedding, then draining their blood to the last drop before the enraptured virgin was any the wiser.

Enzo told Jhi, "I also suspect a few chaosports will be lax

in their otherwise draconian security measures because their eyes will be focused on the blood sports like every other being in Hell. Especially one in the Shores of Lethe."

Jhi nodded thanks.

"You got the floor, Sarah," Enzo said.

Sarah, another familiar face from the All Hallows' Eve massacre and one who carved out quite a name for herself in Silicon Valley, stepped forward. A phenom in the tech industry, Sarah had moved on from her many social-media-centric startups, selling them just as quickly as they had begun. At the ripe old age of twenty, she had accumulated enough wealth to make the list of the world's richest.

But why would Sarah, who had enough money to live out her days without having to work or lift a finger again, sign her John Hancock on an ever-binding devil's contract, forever forfeiting her soul to Lucifer? One word: magic—the one thing Sarah didn't have and the only thing money couldn't buy for a lowlie like her.

Pepper remembered clearly when the strawberry blonde Sarah, south of mid-twenties, had removed a diamond-studded stiletto from her name-brand clutch and stabbed her date at the masquerade ball right in his eye. After two swipes of the blade with a discarded cocktail napkin, the tech phenom wrapped the cleaned stiletto in a designer handkerchief and stowed it away in her clutch—all movements that lasted less than a minute and without her batting an eyelash.

As Sarah purred her way across the room and over to Jhi, she lobbed a coquettish smile his way. When Jhi smiled back, pangs of jealousy rippled through Pepper, followed by a wave of heat mushrooming all over her chest, neck, and face.

"Piggybacking on Enzo's task," Sarah started, "I've devoted my time and energy to the local Naples scene. After poring over analytics, we've realized that not everyone is susceptible to vampiric compelling, as Shelly corroborated. So

I refocused my efforts on building up your persona, Vlad, with the help of *Romancing Vlad*. And it's catching on. *Everyone* tunes into your reality show. It's the hottest thing, and it paints you as a modern-day hero who helps those struggling financially. FYI, we're holding a fundraiser during the lunar eclipse gala, and all the proceeds will go to the hottest celebrity charity: Stop Being Poor. I spearheaded a social media blitz on Naples Teen Scene dot com and all the hottest socials—HearAboutMe, ChitterMe, InstaMe—and wrangled in a few influencers besides myself to help me get the word out about the fundraiser."

Vlad nodded, his pleasure radiating across his heart-stopping features.

Emboldened, Sarah continued, "We've already raised hundreds of thousands of dollars and used all the funds to buy one poor person in Naples a solar-powered convertible," she proudly proclaimed. "It's all working as planned. Those who aren't yet compelled are falling in love with our favorite high king. As for those who can't attend the lunar eclipse celebration at the castle—as in everybody—we're televising it." Her lips slowly spread into a wolfish grin.

Still smiling, Vlad lavished his attention on Ember. "Are you ready for the event?"

Ember nodded. "Once I drain lowlies of enough energy to fill our reservoirs set aside for Winter Solstice, they will be primed and ready for your compulsion. In a fortnight, their energy will have recharged." Ember locked her eyes on the tech phenom. "Need I remind you, Sarah, we're counting on you to get every citizen in Naples to tune into the lunar eclipse gala? Trust me when I say we'll know if you slacked in your duties."

If Sarah felt the pressure, she didn't show it. A fine line existed between confidence and cockiness, and Sarah most definitely identified as the latter. "Never underestimate the power of social media, Ember," Sarah purred as she placed a manicured hand on Jhi's shoulder. "Hear something often enough, and you start to believe it yourself."

Pepper waited for Jhi to swipe away Sarah's greedy hands. Pepper continued to wait for Jhi to let Sarah know he wasn't interested in her overt sexual advances with that lethal stare of his. Then waited some more. *Any day now, Jhi!*

"The human brain is like a computer. And repetition is the software needed to reprogram the subconscious mind." Sarah's sharp fingernail trailed slowly down Jhi's toned arm. "Twenty-one days," she cooed. "That's how long it takes to recondition the human brain to accept something as fact. Case in point, between us flooding the airwaves with all manner of Vlad, his TV show, and the various press junkets he's attended, Neapolitans are either head over heels for or highly respect Vlad, the most eligible bachelor and hero among men. Word has since gotten out that not only is our high king throwing a huge charity celebration and donating all the funds to Stop Being Poor, but he was kind enough to invite everyone to attend the VIP event virtually. Trust me when I say *every single citizen* will attend virtually."

"Well done, Sarah!" Vlad proclaimed.

That compliment tickled Sarah pink, and she discretely tried to grab Jhi's hand, but he thwarted her attempts by stuffing them in his jeans pockets. Unfazed, Sarah wrapped her arm around his and leaned into him.

Pepper might have wanted to exact vengeance on Jhi, but until then, he was to remain single. Very single. And celibate, like a monk. So, this turn of events, this Sarah homing in on Jhi, sent Pepper into a fit of rage.

Pepper stood dangerously close to Jhi and Sarah, so close she could smell Jhi's musky cinnamon scent and the eau de desperation wafting from tech girl. Too close for comfort. So, Pepper took a step backward, giving a wide berth to the duo.

Ember's head snapped in Pepper's direction and seemed to follow Pepper's movements as Pepper artfully avoided the throng—back two steps, then quickly to the side before Pepper ran into a Hound that had just entered the turret.

Not breaking eye contact with ghostly Pepper, Ember discreetly touched wanderer Bunny on the arm, leaned in, and whispered into the wanderer's ear. After nodding its head, the wanderer left Shelly's side and subtly sniffed the airwaves.

Pepper was about to turn tail, but another Hound blocked the one and only exit.

Panicking, her heart picking up its pace, Pepper knew that the change in her body chemistry, the coursing cortisol, could give her away, so she did everything in her power to calm down. Until visions of Jhi kissing Sarah and Jhi lavishing attention upon Sarah flittered through her mind, and she wanted to vomit.

Jealousy had reared its head, and it would end up getting Pepper killed. So she thought of her dad and Beatrice. Then reminded herself why she had ventured into Castle Dracula. Pepper couldn't rescue her dad if she were dead. She then thought of killing Miles. She couldn't torture the serial killer to death if she were six feet under. Pepper's heart and mind got back in sync.

Still, the wanderer slithered toward Pepper and was getting closer by the second.

The Hound at the doorway readjusted his position, giving Pepper enough wiggle room to squeeze her five-foot-seven body through the space between him and the door frame.

When Pepper was smack dab under the Hound's smelly armpit, he lowered his arm and whacked Pepper on the head.

Pepper halted, unsure if the Hound had felt her.

Confused, the Hound shook off whatever had crossed his mind, and Pepper slipped through the doorway undetected.

Pepper looked back and noted concern written on Jhi's face as he looked right through her, seeking whatever had seized Ember's attention.

The wanderer bolted across the threshold and pounced on Pepper, nailing her to the ground.

Pepper kneed Bunny in the gut, jumped to her feet, and wheeled around, barely escaping the wanderer's clutches. Then she ran like the blazes for her life down the red-carpeted hallway.

"The castle's been breached," Vlad's deep voice boomed across the airwaves. "Put the castle on lockdown. I want everyone on patrol. Bring the intruder to me!"

Pepper risked a glance over her shoulder to see the wanderer Bunny hot on her heels. Ember, too.

What happened to me being a ghost? I shouldn't have been able to touch the wanderer and vice versa. Kymeo expressly stated just that. What if the night-cloak is wearing off? What if I'm visible? Those were some of the thoughts screaming in Pepper's head as her legs pumped and pumped.

Pepper tried her damnedest to retrace her footsteps, which proved tricky when running for her life. She zipped through the kitchen, but her movements were thwarted by a duo of Hounds, and she came to a screeching halt, moments from running smack dab into them, the runner rug bunching under her feet. A string of shocks assaulted her body like static electricity, knocking her for a loop for a split second, causing enough of a distraction for a Hound to come within a hair's breadth of her position.

Lighting quick, she crawled atop the butcher block island as each Hound navigated around it. When she readjusted her position, her sneaker stepped on the blood-stained cleaver. The vampires' heads snapped in her direction, and she paused. *Don't breathe. Don't breathe. Don't breathe.*

They continued moving around her and away.

Pepper plucked the serrated blade from the table. *Something's not right. I shouldn't be able to pick up anything, let alone hold it.*

Once the Hounds of Hell ventured out of the kitchen, Pepper jumped from the table, barreled over the threshold, and down the door-lined hallway to the first flight of stairs.

A wanderer in the track-suited body of the former mayor of Naples stood below, at the stair landing. With no other choice, Pepper climbed on top of the stone banister and slid down the staircase. Round and round she went. Her speed mushrooming. Faster and faster.

Twisting her neck to see behind her, she had to time the landing just right.

Closer. Pepper continued sliding.

Almost to the end, the wanderer was feet away.

Now! She kicked the wanderer in the back of the head and sent the demon flying to the floor. Then she jumped off the railing and ran away before the wanderer knew what had happened.

Flying down one staircase after staircase, through one hall after the other, Pepper was so close. One more flight of stairs, one more passageway. She had to make it to the dungeon. To her pops. To Ellie May.

When Pepper heard a cavalcade of bloodthirsty demons entering the corridor, blocking her from escaping at the other end, she slipped into an open room. Hiding behind the ajar door, she did everything she could to slow her pounding heart and quickened breath.

Ten minutes left until Perrin woke her from her slumber.

Ten minutes to remain alive.

A Hound of Hell stalled in front of where Pepper hid, conversing in Laramaic with an out-of-sight comrade.

Just Pepper and the vampire now.

Pepper death-gripped the cleaver and stayed put,

watching him through the crack in the door. Her heart raced anew, and sweat dripped down her back.

As the Hound entered the room and bypassed the door, his back to her, Pepper lunged for him and sunk the blade into his neck. But it didn't stop the bloodsucker. Pepper tore the knife out, jumped on his back, then sliced his throat straight across. Blackish blood spurted out and went everywhere, soaking Pepper's hands.

The vampire fell and nearly crushed Pepper, but she leaped off in time. His arms tried to staunch the surging blood, to no avail. Pepper kicked his legs out with a sweep of her own, and he crashed to the rug with a thud.

Pepper didn't have time for decapitation, so she fled. And soared through the door at the end of the hallway, thundered down the last stairwell, jumped half a story to avoid another Hound, her calves and ankles screaming in protest, and then rocketed into the dungeon.

"Help me get out of here!" she pleaded to Ellie May.

"I can't. I have no more borrowed magics. Ember found our stash."

"Then how did you summon me here before? In my dreams?" Pepper demanded, her tone barely restrained. "You brought me to the castle."

"I didn't. *You* opened a portal. Or somebody did. Otherwise, I wouldn't have been able to send your dad into your dreams."

"I didn't open a portal, though."

Concern coated Ellie May's delicate features. "Look for a mark on your body that doesn't belong."

"Listen," Pepper's voice cracked with pure fright. We were wrong. It's not the lunar eclipse but Winter Solstice. So we still have time—"

"Pepper?" Larry croaked as he sat up. He reached for the

bars of the jail cell. The wan light shone on him, tears welling in his eyes. "Kiddo, that you?"

"Pops!" Pepper grabbed his hands and held on tight. "I'm here. I'm so sorry. It's all my fault. I was trying to protect you —it's all I've ever wanted to do."

Larry couldn't see her, but he heard her loud and clear.

Voices boomed from outside.

"They're coming," Ellie May warned. "Get out of here. Go! Now!"

"I wanted to save you," Pepper cried to her pops and shook the cell bars, desperately trying to open the door, but it wouldn't budge; it just kept clanging to the beat of her racing heart.

The door swung open. Wanderer Bunny growled, licking its chops, and stalked toward Pepper, its movements jerky.

Pepper took one step back. Then another, until her back hit the damp stone wall.

"Hey, you. Shit for brains!" Larry taunted, exhaustion strangling his vocal cords. "I got somethin' for ya!" But the wanderer wouldn't budge.

"I smell you," the wanderer taunted Pepper. Its voice sounded just like Bunny's, only different. Darker. Demented. Evil.

It ventured closer, smirking, like a predator finally catching its prey.

Pepper considered taking her blood-soaked knife and stabbing the wanderer, but then she'd destroy Bunny's body along with any chance Kimball's mom had of returning to it.

If Pepper could pick up objects in the Spirit Realm, perhaps she could summon elements. Pepper imagined the sigil for Air and whispered to it. But nothing happened. *Freaking fantastic!*

Pepper grabbed her pop's hand for extra courage, but Bunny pounced on her. Its cold, calloused hands wrapped around Pepper's trachea and squeezed and squeezed. Pepper fought with all her might, her hands pushing and fingers clawing. But the wanderer seemed to derive pleasure from the felt pain. A galaxy of stars flashed and spun around, occluding Pepper's vision, and her hands flopped to the stone floor, her energy waning.

22

"**G**et off me!" Pepper screamed as she thrashed around in bed.

"Sweetling, you're safe."

Pepper bolted upright in bed, panting.

"Mother Lilith." Perrin pointed to the finger indentations marring Pepper's neck. "What the fuh'kar?"

As Pepper caught her breath and gathered her wits, the surging adrenaline to thank, she vomited all the details of what had happened.

Then Loki asked if Pepper had discovered any potential entry points to infiltrate Vlad's castle undetected.

Deflated, Pepper shook her head no. "It's in the middle of the Everglades. Even if we could airboat there, the Syndicate has a three-hundred-sixty bird's-eye view of the comings and goings. Let's say we somehow got past the security detail on the castle's perimeter—it doesn't mean a fat lot of good. Wanderers and Hounds guard the castle."

"And you can guaran-fuh'karing-tee that they've heavily warded the castle against chaosnauting inside and out."

"Oh, and about that prophecy …" Pepper saved the best for last.

"So, Jhi is stealing some package in Hell that the Syndicate needs for the mysterious Winter Solstice ritual," Perrin uttered, "but nothing about the prophecy itself?"

"No. They were tight-lipped as a whole. Oh, but Jhi's stealing the package during some huge televised sporting event."

"*The Ultimate Death Match*?" Perrin asked, and Pepper nodded. "Every Pandæmonian tunes into that event. It's like a dimension-wide holiday. Hate to be the bearer of bad news, but the lunar eclipse is right around the corner, and we don't know what Jhi is stealing or where in Hell. Not that we could do anything to stop him, as we're *stuck at the Academy*!"

"Still, something's not adding up. Not once did anyone in the briefing mention Beatrice being an Agent of Karma. They kept referring to her as 'the Budreau girl.' Stressing her last name. Isn't that weird?"

"What are you suggesting, sweetling? Why else would they want Beatrice? They're all about murdering Agents—"

Screaming erupted from down the corridor, and Melisende hollered for help.

Immediately, the gang bolted to Beatrice's room.

Inside, a snarling Beatrice had kicked Melisende away from the bed. "Where's Pepper?" Beatrice whipped her head around. Luckily, her eyes were blindfolded, and her hands were tied to the bed.

Pepper exchanged worried looks with the gang, then asked what had happened while she was gone. Loki explained that Beatrice began mumbling to an invisible entity and had tried to escape. Not a second later, Loki secured her wrists with Zip-ties, then chased that with a heavy dose of valeritonin. It had been lights out for Beatrice ever since. Until now.

Pepper had to play this delicately, knowing damn well Miles had come a-calling and was most likely firing a barrage of questions at Beatrice, starting with her current whereabouts.

From the threshold, Pepper mouthed to Melisende to retrieve something that would repel vampiric-type compulsion.

Melisende nodded understanding, then picked herself up and quietly skirted past Pepper as Pepper tiptoed inside Beatrice's room.

"I'm here, Beatrice." Pepper neared the sink to the bottle of valeritonin, but Beatrice ripped off a Zip-tie, yanked off her blindfold with her free hand, and donkey-kicked Pepper in the chest.

Pepper struggled to grab the lip of the counter to pull herself back up.

"You killed my sister," Beatrice growled, "and for that, you will pay dearly!" Beside herself with fury, the Agent cast her eyes around the room.

A sea of orbs stared back in utter shock from the doorway —Loki, Perrin, and Kimball. So it was anyone's guess who Beatrice had threatened, as she lavished her attention on everyone.

"Yes," Beatrice said to the voice in her head. "Pepper is here. She's in the hospital room with—"

Loki soared through the air, and Perrin leaped toward Beatrice. Loki didn't have time to fill a syringe with valeritonin, so he soaked a cloth with the sweet-smelling liquid.

While Perrin lassoed her yo-yo around Beatrice's body, her enchanted jump rope coiled around the Agent's feet. Loki jumped on Beatrice's chest, smothered her face with the damp cloth, and held it down as tightly as he could while

Beatrice thrashed with one arm, her other Zip-tied to the bed's railing. Less than twenty seconds later, Beatrice was KO'd.

Pepper didn't dare speak up. Nobody did, for fear Miles could hear all.

Melisende, out of breath, raced into the room with a tincture bottle. The syrupy substance, a black and neon purple hue, bubbled inside like acid. The glass pipette clanged against the vial as she vacuumed the medicine.

Before performing her ministrations, Melisende explained that once devil's fang entered the bloodstream, it would torpedo directly to Beatrice's brain and attack the invader trying to compel Beatrice. Then she delivered a stern warning: if Pepper had been wrong, and an entity hadn't infiltrated Beatrice's mind, devil's fang would turn on the host and attack Beatrice's cerebral cortex and wouldn't stop until Beatrice was essentially brain dead. For devil's fang required something other than the host body to attack.

"Are you absolutely certain?" Melisende asked one final time before administering the tincture.

When Pepper hesitated, not wanting to risk an Agent dying on her watch, Perrin jumped in. "Either Peaches is going to die or turn to the dark side. It's not exactly good when her death seems to be the better option."

Decision made. Pepper gave Melisende the A-OK. Besides, Pepper felt almost one hundred percent certain only because of what she had overheard at the briefing when Vlad suggested Miles use Josephine's death to his advantage.

Melisende advised, "Devil's fang works fast but is brutal going down." When Pepper asked what it would do exactly, Melisende replied, "It puts up a wall and boxes out the assailant. Before you ask me how long it will last, there's no simple answer. I suppose it depends on how badly this Miles wants Beatrice. But I'll tell you this much. If she vomits up blood, that's a clear indication that the devil's fang is waning in strength, and the enemy is breaking down the barrier. Should that happen, you have little time before the Change occurs." When Pepper asked how long, the damned added, "An instant. A few days. It all depends on the strength of Beatrice's will."

A FEW HOURS LATER, Pepper awoke with a bang, her fight-or-flight response in overdrive. After the lovely interlude of Beatrice possibly outing the gang's location and trying to kill Pepper before they knocked the Agent out—all this happening right after Pepper had escaped death's clutches while astraling—Pepper had needed Grissel's ale, food, more ale, and a nap, preferably in that order. But had ended up sitting down for what was supposed to be a few minutes, and that was all she wrote.

To calm her rattled nerves, Pepper opted for a piping hot shower.

While drying off in front of the mirror in her room, Pepper recalled what Ellie May had said about looking for something on her body that didn't belong. But she couldn't see anything out of the ordinary—

"I've gained some weight, too, sweetling, and I blame this place." The door to Pepper's room creaked open as Perrin entered. "It's exactly what I imagine Heaven to be. Boring. Eating food all day that doesn't have a pulse."

"God, Perrin. Ever hear of privacy?" Pepper wrapped the towel around her privates. Sure, Pepper had packed on a few pounds. She could feel the tightness in her jeans, but she didn't need a reminder. Also, Pepper had been under tremendous stress, so there was that.

"Someone's cranky."

"I sure am. Why did you let me sleep? That's the last thing I should be doing." Pepper reiterated the dire state of affairs, in case Perrin forgot.

"First, you were snoring and a drooling mess. I tried to wake you, but you wouldn't have it. Second, we're well aware of the shitstorm coming our way. Loki asked me to wake you up if you weren't already. He's been checking on the Soul Reunification potion, but isn't sure what he's supposed to look for. Said you would know when it's done. I'm just the messenger, sweetling." Perrin put her hands up in defense. "Kymeo's our only hope of getting out of this Heaven-hole, so we need to get the move-on and speed the process up. Whatever it takes at this point."

Before Pepper did anything else, she shared with Perrin Ellie May's warning about someone opening a portal into Pepper's dreams. "I can't be certain, but I think Jhi appeared in some of them. I just can't remember." She instantly regretted sharing that part, sleep grogginess to blame. Then mentioned that there could be a mark on her body that didn't belong.

Perrin yanked the security towel off of Pepper, and Pepper covered her privates with her hands. "Oh, sweetling, I have nubs, too, so it's not something I haven't seen already." Then finished with a sweeping roll of her eyes. Perrin ran her fingers through Pepper's hair as if looking for lice. "Fuh'karing gross! Ever heard of shampoo? Works wonders. Anywho, I see nothing out of the ordinary." Then she asked Pepper to turn around to inspect her thoroughly. "I've never seen your tattoo before. It's … cute." Pepper caught Perrin faux-gagging in the mirror. "Why is the poppy flower the only thing colored and the rest gray-and-black tones?"

"A poppy?" Pepper spun around to inspect the tattoo on her back shoulder in the mirror. The silhouette of a young Pepper clasped hands with her father as they stood before their favorite ride—the log flume splashing down the face of a mountain. In her free hand, she gripped a stem of a red-petaled flower that was barely discernible to the naked eye and easy to miss. "That poppy shouldn't be there!" Panic tore through Pepper's voice.

"I think you found your hitchhiker." Perrin then asked for details regarding Pepper's dreams, her piercing baby blues warning not to edit the dreamscapes whatsoever.

"I told you. I don't remember specifics, just that I think I've dreamed of Jhi a few times. But why can I remember bits and pieces of dreams with my pops but not ones with Jhi?" Granted, that was before Pepper had crafted the Remembrance potion. Jhi hadn't visited her dreams since then.

"Oh jeez, I wonder," Perrin snarked. Noticing the heat creeping up Pepper's neck and her face crinkling with anger and disgust, Perrin added, "I sure hope you said nothing damning to Jhi, like where we're at."

That thought hadn't crossed Pepper's mind and chilled her to the bone. No matter what, she'd be continuously drinking the remembrance potion, just in case.

After Perrin made her leave, Pepper grabbed her satchel, shoved Kymeo's grimoire inside, and then headed out of the hospital.

With the waxing gibbous moon standing sentry in the gunmetal gray sky and the lanterns suspended above her providing the only other source of illumination, firelight flicking within, Pepper searched the atrium for the flask but couldn't find it. In her fit of pique, she had failed to ask Perrin precisely where Loki had placed it for safekeeping.

"Poppet looks lost," a familiar voice taunted.

Pepper's heart nearly stopped working, a prelude to what would happen to her if she didn't get out of the atrium and away from Sawyer van Arsdale.

23

Sawyer sauntered out of the welcome lobby and into the atrium, donning her signature wartime slick catsuit and killer expression. Blondie's body mimicked a mobile armory: a katana was strapped to her back, her hand tightly gripped the blowpipe of death, a gun secured in a tactical thigh holster. Her red-stained lips split as they curled up in a wicked grin, her icy blue eyes fastened to her prey—to Pepper. At that moment, her hair magicked itself into a utilitarian bun, not a single strand or wisp available to grab.

Pepper attempted to dash away, but an unseen force rooted her in place. While squirming and desperately trying to lift her legs off the pavement, Pepper searched for what had captured her. Sawyer's shadow, half on the pavement, half blanketing Pepper's sneakers, its wispy, smoke-like hands coiled tightly around her ankles.

"Round two, poppet. Only this time will be your last." That notion tickled Sawyer so.

Pepper sized up the threat. Sawyer's black catsuit was impervious, something Pepper had learned the hard way during their first deadly encounter in the marina. So Pepper would have to stick to Sawyer's extremities to inflict any damage.

"Poppet want to play a game?" Sawyer rubbed her hands together. "It's called hand over Beatrice, or I kill you. And it starts now!" She finished with a clap of her hands.

Did she know Beatrice was here, or was she fishing for information, hoping Pepper would spill?

"Who's Beatrice?" Pepper's cool reply belied the corralled terror that was moments from escaping.

Sawyer sauntered in Pepper's direction, each of her steps like the slow ticking of a metronome. "Ye think me a prat?" Sawyer didn't take kindly to that, and her bunched aquiline nose, clenched jaw, and raised brows painted the picture of restrained anger.

"I know my sister is here. She told us as much and that you're keeping her prisoner. *Blindfolding* her. *Tying* her to a bed," Blondie *tsk-tsked*, disgust front and center. "You'll pay for that. Tell me where Beatrice is, and I'll let you go."

"You must think I'm the prat now?" When Sawyer nodded in response, Pepper clapped back, "She's not here."

"If there's one thing I hate more than disloyalty, it's liars. Ye were last seen at the Starless Souk with Beatrice. Try again."

Pepper couldn't pull out a response or anything that would stop Sawyer if her life depended on it. And it had. So, she let loose a scream that rivaled the ear-piercing screeches of the dracos patrolling the night sky in the hopes her friends would hear her.

Bullet-fast, Sawyer careened her way, fire blazing in her eyes. With the soles of her boots, Blondie kicked Pepper in the groin with such tremendous force that she was tossed across the atrium and crashed into the wood railing of the moon bridge, splintering it on impact.

Pepper tried to stand but couldn't. Her back muscles spasmed violently, and she tumbled off the bridge and splashed into the pond below. The quarterstaff she had taken from the forest dangled off the edge of a rock nearby, half in the water. If she could just reach—

Sawyer's boot thrust down like an axe, Pepper's head its target. Pepper rolled to the side and plucked the quarterstaff up before rabbiting away.

Smirking, Sawyer whipped out her katana. With a feral cry, Sawyer raised the sword over her head and charged in Pepper's direction.

Pepper held the quarterstaff out before her in a defensive stance, but Sawyer chopped it in half. The fractured, useless staff thudded to the ground, leaving Pepper defenseless. Or maybe not. Pepper kicked Sawyer in the chest, then landed a punch in Blondie's mouth.

"That all ye got?" Sawyer taunted, spitting out a wad of blood.

Though Pepper's hand smarted, she thrust her arm out again. But Sawyer dodged the blow, feinted a punch with her right hand, connected her left fist to Pepper's lip, and followed up with a right uppercut to Pepper's cheek, her knuckles damn near fracturing Pepper's bone.

The blade of the katana hungered for Pepper's neck. As Sawyer swung it down in an arc, Pepper dove out of the way and somersaulted to a stand, then scampered as far away from Sawyer as she could.

From a safe enough distance away, Pepper yelled, "They're gonna kill you! Cazzian, Vlad, Ember."

But Sawyer was on the chase and started closing the distance between them.

Pepper hightailed it to an elevator. "You're living on borrowed time, Sawyer. You know that, right?"

Sawyer shook her head as if something inside resonated with Pepper's statement.

Her stomach throbbing angrily, Pepper powered through the abject pain and continued talking to Sawyer, hoping to distract her long enough so she could discreetly scrawl the sigil to take her to the rooftop on her palm. "They're killing Agents of Karma. Your sisters, as you call them. What do you think they're gonna do with Beatrice should you catch her and deliver her to them with a bow wrapped around her? Think, Sawyer, *think!* To kill Karma, *all Agents must die!*" Pepper bellowed.

"No! Ye are bloody wrong. Karma betrayed us all."

"You think they're gonna leave you alive?"

"They, Vlad, wouldn't do me like that." Doubt reflected in Sawyer's eyes.

Sawyer's shadow slithered on the ground, then skittered over the surface of the reflection pond before leaping through time and space—through dimensions—and ended at Pepper's feet. Pepper hopped around as if hot coals were under her, avoiding the shadow's clutches, then somehow punted it off the elevator and sent the shadow soaring through the atrium.

After Pepper quickly scribbled the Earth sigil, the elevator took off. But Sawyer grabbed the platform's edge by the tip of her hands and hung on for dear life. She smashed Sawyers' fingers with her sneakers.

Blondie yelped in return. "Ye arsemonger, maggot-eating bloody bint. Ye will pay for that." More expletives sallied forth out of Sawyer's mouth as her finger slipped off the edge, and she fell.

Pepper looked down only to see Sawyer's body levitating,

a whoosh of Air raising Blondie up and up and delicately placing her on the rising elevator.

Pepper bolted away from the edge. But Sawyer closelined her. As Pepper struggled to catch her breath, her throat throbbing, Sawyer swiped her legs out from under her. Pepper crashed to her tailbone and fell back, slamming her head and almost falling off the soaring platform.

Sawyer held Pepper down with her boot, the kitten heel digging into Pepper's chest. Towering above Pepper, Sawyer pressed down harder, and the heel punctured Pepper's skin.

When Pepper cried out in agony, Sawyer lowered her body to a crouching stance, mimicked Pepper's yelps, then connected her fist to Pepper's nose. Blood squirted out and dripped down Pepper's throat, and she choked on the metallic tang.

A rock whacked Sawyer on the back of her head, and she collapsed on her back.

Pepper rolled to the side and got back on her feet.

Melisende stood proudly on the rooftop above, catapulting rocks at the enemy like a knight defending her castle.

Unfortunately for Pepper, the fighting interlude didn't last long. Sawyer kipped up to her feet and jumped at Pepper. The souls of her boots landed squarely in Pepper's midsection.

With nothing to grab onto, Pepper fell off the elevator. Free-falling, Pepper's windmilling hands grabbed a dangling gargantuan fern frond. As she speedily descended the makeshift rope, she caught a wink from the corner of her eye. The Soul Reunification potion, hidden near the waterfall, sparkled in the moonlight. But that damn betraying Air delivered Sawyer to the atrium before Pepper's feet crashed into the ground.

Pepper dashed to the potion, but Sawyer beat her to the punch.

"Little science project?" Sawyer's boot smashed the glass flask into smithereens, and the Kymeo-saving potion dissipated in the breeze.

"No!" Pepper cried out. With that, any hope she had of leaving this place vanished. Any hope of rescuing her father was gone. Rage overcame Pepper.

Sawyer whipped out her blow dart.

You're too focused on the threat, not on what can help you. Attune your senses to your surroundings or die, Pepper recalled Kymeo's warning.

Pepper could hear the elements, could feel them even. The crackling, snapping, and sizzling of fire in the lanterns suspended in midair above her—so crisp and loud … the howling wind wending its way through the atrium.

"Cre-cru-cre-shu-shshu-crr-uuhac-rraa," Pepper incanted while envisioning the sigil for fire in her mind. The strange guttural language flew off her lips, and it had no intention of stopping. To Pepper, it sounded like a language spoken backward, staccato, broken, a string of consonants spliced together. Fire roared angrily. Air rustled, its speed swelling. A beat later, fire burst out of the lanterns. One after the other, a string of explosions flashed in the air, the flames mushrooming in size and intensity. Dollops of sweat beaded on Pepper's face from the massive amount of heat generated.

Sawyer wrapped her lips around the blowpipe and blew. Poisoned darts soared out of their temporary home and ripped through the air toward Pepper.

As Pepper continued uttering the strange dialect, some unknown force at the helm, she mechanically switched and communicated with Air. Then Fire. Then Air again, changing tongues at a lightning pace.

At first, in her mind's eye, she could see their respective sigils as they took form before her. Yellowish flames encapsulated within a fiery circle sizzled. At the same time, bluish-green Air oscillated and branded the gaseous substances in the atmosphere with its intricate design.

On the wings of Air, fire shot across the atrium full-throttle, knocked the poison darts off their Pepper-killing trajectory, then traveled straight for Sawyer.

Sawyer dodged all the fiery blasts. But not her shadow; it took the brunt of the scorching flames and fizzled to the ground, appearing hurt. Sawyer wasn't as full of vim and vigor as before and retreated. The elements had wounded her indirectly.

Pepper had to act fast; she couldn't risk Sawyer gaining the upper hand again, so she commanded in the language of Air for it to bring her to her bag. The Air sigil materialized, and the string of glyphs within changed, rearranged, and then scooped up Pepper and winged her to her satchel. She fished out the Shadow Trapper vial in her bag and then searched the grounds for Sawyer.

A loud *crash-bang* sounded in the distance.

Pepper's head whipped toward the hospital ward to see two Hounds shoving Perrin and Kimball forward while pointing guns at their captive's heads. Then gruffly warned Pepper to halt whatever she had planned, or they'd kill the hostages.

Where was Loki? Or Beatrice?

Discretely, Perrin flashed five fingers, then three, and closed her fist. One for each Hound. Two were holding Perrin and Kimball hostage. So where were the other—

Pepper caught a glimpse of Sawyer, and the shock plastered all over Blondie's face. She was just as surprised to see the Hounds as everyone else.

One Hound screamed as it flew off the rooftop and splattered on the ground. Wolfgang grinned from his rooftop perch.

Though the vamp remained corpse still, the bloodsucker's

head would have to be chopped off; otherwise, it would resurrect.

That left five Hounds unaccounted for.

It was nighttime, and anywhere outside the Academy was hunting grounds for the dracos. The vast caverns, with areas still uncharted, were the only viable escape route. But to get to any of the elevators in the atrium, Pepper would have to sneak past Blondie and her injured shadow—easier said than done.

A bruised and bloodied Sawyer must have gotten a second wind. On her feet and ready to annihilate Pepper, her chest slowly rising and falling, she placed her lips around the blowgun and let loose a stream of life-ending darts. A dozen or so of the instruments of death tore through the atrium.

On Pepper's command, the molecules of air merged, forming an impenetrable wall. Sigils flashed, then dissipated quickly, creating a barrier.

An engorged head rolled and slammed into Pepper's foot; a vamp's bulging eyes stared at Pepper. Melisende took out the other Hound the same way. Using a gardening rake, the Mad Marchioness stabbed it right through its chest from behind before axing off its head. With that, Perrin and Kimball were freed, and the Lolly'ka plucked the firearm out of the other Hound's stiff hands.

Pepper tried to move but couldn't; Sawyer's shadow had slyly anchored her in place with its wispy hands that resembled puffs of smoke. In a flash, Pepper tossed the Shadow Trapper potion onto the misty blob. The glass vial cracked, its contents seeped out, and it immediately got to work. Pepper prayed that the adjustments she made to the potion worked; if not, she was a dead girl walking.

Pepper hopscotched away and raptly watched as the silhouette struggled to unpin itself from the ground, its grasp on Pepper releasing as it fought against the Shadow Trapper, morphing from 3D to 2D, its legs half-submerged in the stream under the moon bridge, its upper half on the mossy grass.

An irate Sawyer went to charge at Pepper but couldn't. The gooey potion bolted her feet to the ground, just like it had done to her shadow.

As if stuck in quicksand, Sawyer fought tooth and nail to extricate her feet from the stone floor. When she couldn't, she growled, "Mark my words, poppet. When I get out of whatever in the bloody hell you did to me, ye will pay."

"Get in line," Pepper said.

Sawyer then lobbed a barrage of vicious threats and other unsavory comments at Pepper, all preceded by the word "bloody."

Pepper summoned what little strength she had left and then kicked Sawyer in the head, knocking her out and happily quieting the sassy Agent's flapping lips.

Pepper wasn't entirely sure of the Shadow Trapper's duration but knew the effects wouldn't last long, judging from Kimball's experience. Moreover, she didn't want to face an epically pissed-off Sawyer, so she powered through the throbbing pain, grabbed her backpack from the bushes, and limped to where the others stood.

"There's a way out in the caverns. Head due north. Wolfy and I will man the Academy." Melisende didn't have to deliver that warning to Pepper twice. She scrambled to the elevator with Perrin and Kimball right behind her.

Pepper began drawing the intricate whorls and interconnecting geometric symbols and lines that made up the Water sigil—

"Impressive match!" Miles golf-clapped as he exited the lobby, a few Hounds of Hell flanking him.

"Pepper, hurry!" Perrin said under her breath.

Hounds cocked a chorus of guns, their business ends

pointing at Pepper and her allies, so she froze mid-summoning.

Melisende took a defensive stance, rake in hand, and Miles said, "Ah-ha. Put the weapon down, and everyone lives." When Melisende begrudgingly did as asked, Miles replied, "Good girl."

"That means you, too, Lolly'ka. Place the gun on the ground." Perrin followed his orders. "Now, put your hands on your head. All three of you!" Having no other choice, the trio followed his orders.

"Now get on your knees—both of you." Miles gestured to the damned with his gun. "And face the wall." Miles snapped his fingers, and a Hound joined him, then shoved the muzzles of the guns at the backs of Melisende and Wolfgang's heads. Another Hound retrieved Perrin's weapon.

The damned could feel pain as part of their souls were left intact, and they could die only to be reborn again, something Miles must have known, or maybe not. But Pepper wasn't entirely sure of the timespan between the moment of death and regeneration. What if their souls returned to the Pits? She had heard a rumor about that happening. She certainly hoped that wasn't the case, as she'd grown fond of Melisende and cantankerous Wolfy.

"I said to get on your knees," Miles barked.

Pepper and the gang slowly lowered their bodies.

"I must thank you for handling Sawyer for me," Miles said directly to Pepper. "She's a bit of a live wire and would be none too pleased if she found out I followed her. Though you better not have killed her." His tone made it clear that he wanted to be the one to do it.

Then Miles barked an order at another vamp to check on Sawyer.

The Hound marched to the rogue Agent, crouched down, and replied over his shoulder, "She's still got a pulse." Luckily, the vamp didn't notice Sawyer's shadow under the moon bridge, struggling to break free from its confines.

"Now, where was I?" Miles said from across the atrium. "Oh, yes. Pepper Bell, I don't think we've been formally introduced. I'll have you know I've been spending a lot of—how shall I say?—*quality* time with your father. Though he doesn't have much to say, what with the ball gag in his mouth."

Heat blooming on her face, her heart pounding wildly, Pepper took a step off the elevator, but Perrin grabbed the strap of her backpack, yanked her backward, and whispered, "Don't do it."

"And hello, Kimball. Long time no see." It did not surprise Miles whatsoever to find Pepper and Kimball together. "Perrin." He nodded his head in a gesture of acknowledgment. "Now that formal introductions are out of the way, let's talk business. Sawyer hasn't exactly been forthright, which is cause for concern. Case in point"—he waved his hand with a flourish—"what is this place? And why would she be under the impression that a certain object is hidden here?" When nobody uttered a word, he said, "Doesn't matter. But imagine my surprise to discover that the Budreau girl has been holed up in the same mysterious location. Curious how long Sawyer has known. But that's an internal matter that doesn't concern you all."

He sauntered toward Pepper, Kimball, and Perrin, his hands clasped behind his back. "I'm only going to ask this once. Where's the Budreau girl? We know you helped her escape from the Starless Souk. And it took some ... perseverance on my end to figure out where she took you all. I know she's here, and it's only a matter of time until we find her—"

"Go now!" Melisende yelled when she grabbed the rake and impaled the Hound holding a gun to her head.

Miles fired his gun in no time flat, and a bullet traveled

right through Melisende's forehead. The damned collapsed to the pavement.

Wolfy screamed, "You're gonna pay for that." Miles laughed and shot him right between the eyes.

Kimball capitalized on the distraction and traced the sigil for Water.

Hounds raced toward the trio, and Miles fired off a gun, the bullets tearing through the atrium, past the moraberry tree, on their collision course with the trio.

The gang ducked right before the bullets whizzed over their heads. At the same time, the elevator began its descent into the bowels of the cavern. The aperture above immediately closed, and utter darkness reigned.

All three tried to catch their fear-stolen breaths as they descended, the temperature plummeting quicker than the elevator.

"That was way too close," Kimball squeaked. "My heart can't take much more."

"Well, prepare yourself, Kimball, because there are still a few Hounds unaccounted for." Pepper didn't mean to come off as harsh, most likely coursing adrenaline to blame. "If the vamps found their way down here, what makes us think Miles won't?"

"Unpopular opinion. Peaches ratted us out. How else did Miles know where she was or where we were?"

"Miles said he followed Sawyer without her knowledge," Kimball interjected.

"Yes, but then he admitted he knew Peaches was here."

Pepper's heart skipped a beat when a terrifying thought crossed her mind. "What if Beatrice told him my sister's alive? Oh God, what if she told him I'm an Agent Initiate?"

"Let's hope not. But if Beatrice Changed, and she's working with the Syndicate, Loki could be in more danger than he realizes," Perrin said.

They didn't even wait for the platform to land before Pepper and the gang jumped off. She knew they weren't out of the clear just yet. It was only a matter of time before Miles figured out how to reach the caverns. And at least two Hounds were already on the prowl, following Loki and Beatrice's trail. And if Beatrice was the snitch, they had more to worry about than a few Hounds whose strength paled in comparison to an Agent of Karma.

24

"Shut up," Pepper whispered. She couldn't take the bickering between Perrin and Kimball anymore as they all traversed the main artery of the caverns. At this point in their journey, they passed the already explored areas and entered uncharted territory, all on edge, all jumping at the slightest of sounds.

"There's a cone of light up ahead." Standing stock-still, Pepper attuned to her surroundings, an action becoming more organic by the day. All the familiar sounds were present: the *drip-drip-dripping* of crying stalactites. Incoherent murmurings of ghosts. A footstep, then a *clanging*, accompanied by a stern reprimand in some Slavic language—not familiar! Another voice joined in and got closer by the second.

"In here!" Pepper, Perrin, and Kimball darted inside a darkened room, then snicked the door to a close. A galaxy of stars blanketed the ceiling. If they were artificial, it was one impressive glamor.

"Pepper," Loki whispered as his furry hand touched her arm. The ruachti wasn't alone. Beatrice hobbled into the wan light. Unsteady on her feet, she used the craggy walls for support.

"Oh, thank Seren," Pepper said. "We've been looking all over for you guys. Melisende said there's a way out."

"Did she happen to mention what we would find?" Beatrice asked, confusion stitched on her features.

Pepper felt squirrelly around the Agent and couldn't help questioning her loyalty.

"You're acting like this is the first you heard about this?" Perrin asked Beatrice, but it came off more like an interrogation.

"Because it is. I know these caverns like the back of my hand. If there's a way out, it's news to me."

"Okay, Peaches, listen up. The man who tried to murder you. The same man who's been squatting in your head. Well, he found you. So, before we leave this room, we need to know if you ratted us out. And don't try to pin this on Sawyer."

Beatrice's eyes couldn't have possibly opened up any wider. "I said nothing to him. I swear."

"Beatrice could have given me up at any time," Loki chimed in. "But she didn't. So, drop it, Perrin."

Respectfully, Perrin backed down, but her face screamed that she wasn't entirely sold.

"We counted at least three Hounds, all armed with guns and other unidentified weapons," Loki shared.

"Yeah, we heard the blood-suckers right before we ran inside," Perrin said.

"We're surrounded, and Beatrice is in no shape to fight." Loki didn't pull any punches. "As for Kimball, well, we can't rely on him. That leaves the three of us versus at least three Hounds."

"I say we charge at them," Perrin said, hungering for battle.

"Uh, Sawyer kicked Bell's ass," Kimball blurted out. "She's practically a gimp. Most likely has a broken rib. Will definitely have a shiner and a fat lip tomorrow. And my mom and I would really like to not die. That actually leaves two able-bodied fighters. So, what's the plan other than charging?"

If the Hounds wanted a sacrifice, Pepper wouldn't hesitate to give them one in the form of Kimball. Still, as much as it rankled her, Kimball wasn't wrong. Adrenaline was her saving grace at the moment, but when that subsided … She dreaded the thought.

Loki inspected Pepper, then asked, "You up for a fight?"

Pepper nodded, then asked Beatrice point-blank, "What about you, Beatrice? You able to defend yourself if it came down to it?"

When Beatrice nodded, Loki held his quarterstaff and stated that he was ready, prompting Perrin to dangle her trusty yo-yo and jump rope.

Pepper stuck her head out the door to ensure the coast was clear. Then shimmied into the hallway, sticking to the walls, listening for anything and everything out of the ordinary. Beatrice and Kimball trailed behind Pepper. Loki and Perrin served as the caboose.

A dead-end appeared up ahead with two caverns branching out on either side. Echoing footsteps proceeded two Hounds as they rounded the corner.

Before Pepper could summon the elements, a Hound lunged and placed her in a chokehold. Two other Hounds came up on her rear.

Perrin unleashed her rope and then strangled one of the vamp's hands with it. The Hound's gun crashed to the floor and skittered toward Perrin. She then swiftly kicked it to Loki.

Another Hound in the distance yelled for backup. A storm of footsteps boomed as a swarm of bloodsuckers raced to Pepper's position from behind and to the left and right.

As Beatrice struggled to call forth the elements, a Hound was on her in no time flat and knocked the Agent of Karma to the ground.

An explosion sounded, and smoke billowed in the confined space. Pepper gagged and choked, her eyes stinging. She couldn't see her own hand in front of her face, let alone enemy combatants. Shouts, bangs, and gunfire were all around her, bullets zipping off the limestone walls. Hounds grunting. Perrin cursing. Beatrice moaning. Kimball screaming for help. Loki ninja-quiet. There were no other routes to take. No way out.

Then utter silence filled the airwaves.

A hand grabbed Pepper's and yanked her forward. While running, Pepper tripped over a decapitated head of a Hound of Hell with his sharp fangs extended.

A craggy wall stood feet away from Pepper's face and got closer and closer as the stranger pulled her onward. Feet away from the wall, Pepper struggled to break free, but the stranger wouldn't stop and picked up the pace, then catapulted Pepper right into the ... pivoting wall that wasn't a wall but a hidden doorway.

As the door snicked shut, sealing Pepper and the stranger inside a tight space, sconces powered to life, casting firelight on the angular face of her eleventh-hour rescuer: a man on the short side, lean and muscular. Hands down, Pepper weighed more than him. A shock of ashen hair pulled back in a pony-tail cascaded down the back of his cotton peasant shirt. His wiry mustache curled at the ends. Not one wrinkle appeared on his reddish-brown skin. His bright violet eyes pulsated as his lips curled into a wicked grin. At that moment, Pepper knew she was looking at Professor Kymeo in the flesh.

Silencing Pepper with his pointer finger placed over his thin lips, Kymeo quickly handed Pepper an object—bonelike, odorless, jaundiced in color, and small enough to fit inside her satchel. As for its origins, it could have belonged to an animal, human child, or demon for all Pepper knew.

"Guard this with your life and tell no one of its existence, god or otherwise. Not even your friends. If you do, you'll get them killed. I'm not one to apologize, and I stand firm in my vote against making you an Agent of Karma. Don't prove me right."

Kymeo disappeared as another wall swung open, leading to a dimly lit circular chamber, hellfire flickering within a few braziers.

"Thank fuh'karing Seren," Perrin called out. She explained that one minute she was destroying the fuh'karing douche-vamps, and the next, she was yanked out of battle and tossed into the chamber. "You happen to see anyone?"

"I sure did. It was Professor Kymeo. Guys, the Soul Reunification spell worked. I thought for sure it was destroyed when Sawyer smashed the flask." For a brief moment, Pepper would allow herself to celebrate.

The gang decided they'd regroup once they were a safe enough distance away. Only one way out presented itself. So they ventured onward.

A short time later, a shaft of moonlight flooded the narrow hall. Pepper stepped through the curtain of moonbeams and stood in a transparent tube reminiscent of underwater tunnels in aquariums. Only she wasn't underwater. But under a waterfall. Buckets of water crashed down on either side, and the sound was deafening. Mist occluded any telltales of their surroundings. The circulating air was oxidized and fresh smelling, warmer, too.

Circular steps spiraling upward greeted the visitors. The metal steps clanged as Pepper climbed upward, round and round until she reached a brightly lit annex that ended at a set of bronze double doors about twenty feet high. A hologram of the Karma Academy crest floated in the dead center of the circular room.

The entryway creaked open as if sensing visitors, revealing a massive office quite a few stories tall; the ceiling was hard to spot unless it was a trick of the eye. The ground floor housed ceiling-high bookshelves and curio cabinets stuffed with scrolls and oddities galore. There was a bar and a living area with a rather ginormous fireplace. Still, this office belonged to Karma, no doubt about that. Her signature red pantsuit, quite a few of them, hung on hangers in a wardrobe. Personal effects decorated her desk and a powder room.

One entire wall was made out of glass that traveled to the miles-high ceiling that offered panoramic views of cascading waterfalls off the sides of the floating mountains. In the distance, Karma Academy was perched regally on a cliff.

"Must be glamoured. Otherwise, we would have seen this place," Perrin posited.

"If you don't know what you're looking for, oftentimes you miss what's right in front of you," Loki said.

"Judging from your slack jaw, I'm taking it you've never been inside Goddess Karma's office?" Kimball asked Beatrice nonchalantly as he inspected every nook and cranny.

"You'd guess correctly," Beatrice replied.

The cast iron stairs clanged as Kimball spiraled upward, around and around, then called out from the third level. "Everyone, you might want to come upstairs."

"What is this?" Pepper inquired, joining Kimball, who was inspecting a map of Earth that lorded over an entire wall.

One area, in particular, stood out like a heat source, and it contained a pin that hovered magically over Golden Gate Estates in Naples, Florida. Reddish threads of light connected the pin to a piece of parchment resting in a shallow basket on a desk underneath the map.

Beatrice picked up the parchment. "It's a missive. Though, I've never actually seen how Karma received them."

"And by missive, you mean …?" Perrin asked.

"A citizen needed our help, and their cries went unanswered." As Beatrice perused the SOS, her face blanched with fright, and the letter slipped out of her quivering hands.

Perrin snatched the letter from midair and read aloud: "Goddess Karma. Please send help as soon as possible. All conclaves within a hundred-mile radius have been wiped out. But it's me they want. As I write this, I am surrounded and don't know how much longer I can hold off the Syndicate. They somehow cut off my magic. Same for all communication with my goddess." Perrin tore her eyes away from the note, then said, "Signed the archOmega."

Beatrice opened her mouth to speak, then hesitated, her face contorting with shock and pain.

"What's an archOmega, and who's the goddess?" Kimball voiced what Pepper was wondering.

"Hekate," Beatrice said through numbed lips, glossing over the first question asked.

Her patience threadbare, Pepper barked, "Beatrice, if you haven't noticed, all hell has broken loose on Earth. Karma is missing, and now this archOmega. We're on the same team here. So, if you know anything, now is the time to share."

"Loki told me what y'all did for me. And the devil's fang, how it stopped that man from screwing with my mind. And I thought I was getting better. Until I saw Sawyer fighting you, Pepper. Not that long ago, we were sisters fighting on the same team. Today, I didn't recognize her. But then I did. I wanted—I wanted to—"

"You wanted to fight alongside her?" Pepper blurted out what Beatrice couldn't.

Beatrice nodded. "It's like the devil himself is walking across my grave. That's what my gran would say about that shiver that runs up and down your spine. I get it whenever I'm in y'all's company." Before Pepper could interject, Beatrice added, "I don't believe him, er Miles, when he tells me y'all are not to be trusted. That y'all are dangerous. But he's so dang convincing."

"Did he break through the wall?" Pepper feared the answer because then what would they do with Beatrice? "Is he talking to you now?"

"No. But I can feel him. He's trying desperately to contact me. I'm scared he'll gain control again."

"Here. Chew this." Pepper plucked off a leaf of valeritonin she had harvested from the rooftop and handed it to Beatrice.

While Beatrice perused the map, Perrin slyly said under her breath to Pepper, doing her best ventriloquist imitation, her eyes looking everywhere but at Pepper, "Peaches is hiding something. When I said archOmega, she looked as terrified as a soul-seller meeting a mala'kha for the first time."

Pepper whispered back, her lips not moving, eyes steadfastly fixated on Beatrice. "Yeah. I noticed. But that's not what's worrying me the most. I think we were too late flushing out the para doxea from her system. It's only a matter of time until Miles tears down that wall in her mind. She could turn on us at any moment."

"Agreed. Miles could be listening in right now for all we know."

"That thought crossed my mind, hence why I gave Beatrice the valeritonin. To drown Miles out. But we can't keep drugging her. We have to banish him for good. Any suggestions?"

"Well, maybe. My sister, Kirby, can help, but she's in Hell, and I don't know how you'd feel about venturing back there or how we'd slip in undetected—"

"I see you two talking," Kimball interrupted. "Sharing is caring."

"I'm going to kill him," Perrin whispered to Pepper before plastering on her fakest smile. "I was just mentioning to Pepper that there has to be a way out of the Academy. Otherwise, we wouldn't have been directed here. What if Sawyer ambushes Kymeo and finds Karma's office, and we're dead?"

"Beatrice," Pepper started, "there could be a clue hidden in this missive. If you know anything, now's the time to speak."

Beatrice weakly nodded. "Whenever someone is in danger that surpasses earthly law enforcement, they call Agents of Karma."

"And by danger ...?" Perrin prodded.

"I'm talking about encounters with maniacal individuals who need to be removed from society."

"And by removed, you mean killed?" Kimball asked.

"Not always."

"And who are your clients?" Loki asked.

"Anyone in need of help."

"Anyone, as in mages only?" Pepper pressed.

"Not necessarily. This is one of the few exceptions to the rules of magic. You don't have to be a mage to cast the SOS spell to contact Goddess Karma. You just have to know the spell exists and how to find it. When a missive appears at the Academy, professors divvy up the job to an Agent. We then formulate a plan of attack and take out the perp. That's all I know."

"But you've heard of the archOmega?" In response,

Pepper noted Beatrice's eyes rapidly blink. "And don't act like you haven't. I see it written all over your face."

"Yes. She holds the highest rank a mage can achieve. Her magic is unmatched, and she has a direct link to Hekate. If Ellie May is in danger, we're—"

"Fuh'kared."

"Ellie May?" a wide-eyed Pepper asked. "Red hair? White skin and freckles? Green eyes?"

"Yes," Beatrice squeaked out. "How did you know that?"

"Because I met her. She's chained in a dungeon alongside my dad as one of the Syndicate's prisoners. And I'll tell you this much. She used the last reservoir of her *unmatched* magical powers to save my dad's life after Miles nearly tortured him to death."

Beatrice's lips quivered from hearing Miles' name.

"He's the same man who tried to kill your sister," Perrin added.

"I'm gonna be sick." Beatrice vomited all over Kimball's shoes.

"Wow, really?" Kimball whined.

"Shut up, scoldilocks!" Perrin snapped.

Pepper noted speckles of blood that coated the canvas material of Kimball's boat shoes and pointed it out to Perrin.

Pouting, Kimball hopped to the nearest bathroom and bitched to his mother's soul inside the vodka bottle. "There's, like, ample real estate other than my shoes for puke, but Bell chastises me for commenting? You totally would have reacted the same way."

"We have to get her to your sister, Perrin. Before the Change." Pepper feared returning to Hell, but they were racing against time to save Beatrice before Miles turned her to the dark side.

"Did Kymeo say anything to you, Pepper, back in the

caverns?" Loki asked pointedly. "Anything about how to leave the Academy?"

Pepper gripped the bone in her satchel and thought long and hard about ignoring Kymeo's words of warning. But a voice inside her heart did its damnedest to talk her out of it. Telling Loki and Perrin—her allies, ride or dies, family—would be the honorable thing to do. But then, if they were captured, the enemy could easily magic the truth out of them before they were killed. Decision made. "No, nothing."

"Guys, I think I found something," Kimball called out from the ground floor. "And hurry before it disappears!"

Everyone raced down the circular staircase, then gathered around Kimball, who stood in front of a door adjacent to the bathroom. "At first, I thought it was a linen closet because I was looking for a towel, y'know, because of the throw-up, and then it … lit up."

"This better not be some kind of attention-seeking ruse!" Pepper needed a break from Kimball.

Drops of Beatrice's blood stained Kimball's palm. Loki must have noticed it, too, for he grabbed Kimball's hand and put it flush with the doorframe. Upon contact with blood, the doorway morphed into a gateway to another dimension—the where a mystery until Loki chanted in Laramaic. In response, the way sign, licked by hellfire, appeared. *Destination: Hell.*

"A god created this chaosgate," Loki shared as he inspected the sigils. "Since rules don't apply to gods, I'm guessing this is how Karma slipped in and out of Hell undetected."

"Wait! Forget what I said. We can't go to Hell?" The more Pepper thought about it, the more that notion terrified her, and she laid out a litany of reasons why they shouldn't venture to that dimension. "I'm a wanted person. There are literal bounty hunters after Perrin and me. I can't speak Laramaic or understand it." Then panic set in.

Beatrice walked away and headed toward a curio cabinet.

"Sweetling, Hell is a better alternative than this realm. Need I remind you that we don't really know what date it is here or on Earth? For all we know it's the lunar eclipse already. Furthermore, we don't have any other options? And before you say we should backtrack and hedge our bets with Kymeo, what if Sawyer brought an army? Look, I know Hell. It's my home; Loki's, too."

"Hello?" Kimball started. "Did everyone forget about me? I've never been to Hell before."

"Kimball's right. He must cross the River Acheron first, or he'll explode." Pepper bit her nonexistent nails.

"Bell, you could have said 'explode' with a little more oomph and not like you're reading off your grocery list." Kimball was taken aback and terrified.

Pepper's heart screamed by way of uncontrollable beats, begging her not to veer purposefully into the enemy's territory. But she had no other choice. And then a terrifying thought crossed her mind. "Time varies in Hell, too. What if we land in the Isles of Obolus, where time moves at a glacial pace?"

"So what if we do? I can get us to Pandæmonia, no matter where that rukba takes us. In Hell, we're guaranteed to be on Earthly time. But that's not the case here."

Beatrice returned with enough bottles for everyone, the glass clanging in her hands. "E-lohi'exspiravitius. Roughly translated to the Spirit of the Gods. I recognized the bottles when we first entered Karma's office." The containers were oblong and filigreed. "This right here"—Beatrice shook the elixir and agitated the molten gold and red syrupy concoction within—"enables gods and Agents of Karma to slip in and out of dimensions undetected. So that should eliminate one of your worries, Pepper." Beatrice passed corked vials of the elixirs to all. "And this will ensure Kimball doesn't explode."

"I can't believe I have to say this again! Can you people show a tad more compassion when discussing my body spontaneously combusting? Cause that would be great."

"Shut up and drink," Perrin said.

Noting something suspended inside the mixture, Kimball asked, "What the hell is that? Looks like egg sacs."

"It's a spore, actually. E-lo'heus," Beatrice replied. "Once inside the bloodstream, it will make its way to the brain, then bind to the thalamus. From then on, we'll be able to understand and speak any language in the cosmos. It will have to be replenished after we leave Hell."

"Wait!" Pepper put her hands out, halting everyone from drinking the elixir. Call her crazy, but she wasn't fully trusting Beatrice. For all she knew, the Agent had laced the so-called potion with para doxea. "Back on Earth, I was able to cast a spell to understand demons speaking in Laramaic by using magic gems after the lingua franca mechanical spider thingy in my head died or whatever. And it had worked."

Beatrice's nose scrunched and eyes squinted as if Pepper had said the dumbest thing ever. "You were mistaken. All you did was breathe more life into the enchanted device." She uncorked the vial. "If it makes y'all feel any better, I'll go first."

Perrin handed Beatrice her vial. "Drink this instead."

Beatrice shook her head in mild annoyance, then said, "Fine," and tossed back the contents.

All eyes were on the Southerner, waiting for … well, Pepper wasn't sure what to expect, but when the Agent didn't collapse on the floor or foam at the mouth, she dropped her shoulders. As did Perrin. Kimball might have too, but frankly, Pepper didn't care. And Loki's poofed fur settled. Ultimately, Pepper and the gang decided they had no other choice but to venture to Hell. Besides, she'd risk life and limb if it meant saving her pops.

Bottoms up! The syrupy elixir was ambrosial going down —sweet, nectary, and warming like rays of sunshine. Then the offness came like an act of vengeance, and Pepper swayed on their feet. When the spore entered her brain—which felt like tingles all over her scalp—her face twitched for a spell, like she had a wicked tic. And then came the moment when her heart quit beating, and Pepper couldn't catch her breath.

"Y'all, don't freak out," Beatrice stated calmly, noting the panicked look on Pepper's face. "Your heartbeat will pick back up. And the clamminess and floaty feelin' are just byproducts of your souls detachin' from your body. All perfectly normal side effects. It will reattach once we chaosnaut to the other side."

The door glided open, and a carpet of mist slithered out of the rukba.

Cannon fodder Kimball wouldn't budge, so Perrin's Mary Janes helped him in that endeavor. Loki and Beatrice followed suit.

"Wherever this leads us, I'll figure out how to get us to safety," Perrin said to quell Pepper's concerns.

"Where would that mythical place of safety be exactly?" Pepper replied before entering the elevator to doom.

"Lolly'ka headquarters," Perrin beamed.

25

"Cool your tits!" a woman shouted over her shoulder to what sounded like a legion of drunken partygoers as she entered the spiderweb-coated dank cellar where the rukba had delivered Pepper and the gang moments ago.

Pepper quickly ducked and squeezed between stacked barrels of Grissel's ale and Aluman's port and shelves jam-packed with canned goods and dried meats of the damned variety, joining Perrin and the others so as not to be seen. Smoke that smelled like burnt human flesh wafted down the stairs, landing at Pepper's nostrils. *Must be grilling the damned,* Pepper thought. Hopefully, it was the damned and not humans with souls intact.

At the top of the stairs, the woman held open the door as if waiting for someone. Or rather something—a xykree, panther big, appeared, its flesh-toned, furless tail twitching angrily. After the beast crossed the threshold, the woman slammed the door shut, quieting the din.

Xykrees were spawns of Hell, raw flesh with a pulse, their preferred meal. This demonic beast never failed to strike terror in Pepper from their physical appearance alone: all feline in the back and humanoid in the front, with faces resembling a child's drawing of their worst nightmare.

As the duo walked down the steep stairs, a stampede of shoes stomping on the floorboards above accompanied their footsteps, sending dust to sift down on Pepper's head, and she had to squelch a sneeze. Waves of somewhat muted screams sounded reminiscent of fans watching their favorite sports match, and music boomed, the kind meant for jigging.

At the bottom of the staircase, the xykree's crimson-rimmed oval eyes glowed an eerie green in the dim light as its split nostrils raised upward and then sniffed, clearly picking up a foreign scent. Unhurriedly, it padded about on its front arms and hind legs, following the prey's trail—*sniff, sniff, sniff.*

It halted in the exact spot on the wall where the rukba's door had dematerialized moments ago—leaving them stranded wherever they had landed—and then quickly changed its trajectory. Prowling with a sense of purpose, its front hands with fingernails as sharp as tacks *tap-tap-tapped* along the wood plank floor, the tips of its oily, yellow hair sweeping the ground.

The xykree stopped smack dab in front of the barrel Pepper hid behind, so close to Pepper she nearly gagged from its foul breath. Its lipless jack-o'-lantern mouth opened wide with anticipation of ripping flesh to shreds, its needle-like teeth dripping with saliva. Pepper held her breath and squeezed her eyes shut. *Don't move; don't breathe.*

"Balakai! Get over here!" the woman commanded.

Balakai? After gingerly peeking around the corner, Pepper smiled with delight to see a friendly face and then jumped up and blurted out, "Zho'zho!"

Zho'zho yelped, the ultraviolet flames licking the tips of her corkscrewing horns flared like fireballs. Balakai leaped through the air, pounced on Pepper, and then lavished her with wet kisses.

Someone popped their head through the door at the top of the stairs. "You okay down there?" The racket slipping through the door nearly drowned out the demon's question.

"Yes, Cumo," Zho'zho replied. "I slipped on a bottle. Go back to tending the bar. I'll be right up."

Once the coast was clear, Zho'zho loudly whispered, "Cursed Shi'rue! You gave me a fright! While it's lovely to see you, Pepper, you shouldn't have come to my tavern." The demon-elf hybrid closed the distance between her and Pepper, then whispered conspiratorially, "It's not safe. Since you left, the Syndicate's had eyes and ears on the Tenth Circle, day and night. Ramped up their hunt for you, too. DISI's plastered wanted posters of you and Perrin all over Hell."

"Hounds here now?" Perrin asked, popping up out of hiding.

"And you brought along company." Zho'zho's tone was about as gleeful as a depressed clown. "Hello to you, too, Perrin. Not at the moment. But it's not just Hounds on the hunt. Mala'khas are now involved."

Mala'khas? Pepper gulped back fright from the memory of watching the wretched towering beasts reap souls of the damned at the All Hallows' Eve ball. They were Hell's hunters, prison guards in the Pits, and gargantuan scythes, their weapons of choice. And now they were on the hunt for Pepper? She instantly regretted not giving her galloping heart more consideration when it had warned her to steer clear of Hell at all costs.

Loki chittered as he scampered to Zho'zho.

"Oh, blessed Seren!" Zho'zho said. Her eyes and glasslike

face radiated with untold joy from seeing Loki, her eyelashes fashioned from snowflakes fluttering up and down, perhaps batting away tears.

Loki jumped into Zho'zho's wide-open arms.

"If only Bhi'gow were here." Embers from the flames on her horns—a family trait—flicked onto her white ball of puff hair that resembled Halloween spiderweb decorations. But the Bhi'gow resemblances stopped at the moss-laden twigs sticking out of her hair willy-nilly or the subtle wood striations on her legs and arms—those were all elven. Or the sea of roaming eyes impressed on her skin.

"How's Bhi'gow doing?" Pepper asked, concerned.

"As good as can be expected. Though he misses Loki terribly." Loki, unable to speak in this realm, nodded in solidarity. "What's worse is my brother can't leave the pyramid until all this mess is squared away. Can't do his fixing job either. It's just too dangerous. But he's been lighting candles and making sacrificial offerings to Seren to keep you all safe. Looks like it's paying off."

That made Pepper happy to hear. "Trust me when I say we had no other choice but to come here."

"You in the clear, or do you think they're watching you, too?" Perrin asked Zho'zho.

"They haven't figured out I'm related to Bhi'gow, so I'm off their radar. But I haven't wanted to court Shi'rue's misfortune, so I've avoided the pyramid and moved into one of the tavern rooms."

Then Zho'zho shared the bad news that the Department of Inter-Dimensional Security and Intelligence amped up security at all inter-dimensional chaosports. Getting through security was now an arduous and stringent process. "Some demons got caught using unofficial ever-active gates, like at Bhi'gow's home, and the mala'khas made an example out of them. Even televised the torture live from the Pits. It's awful out there. Here's hoping Seren kept your arrival off the radar."

Perrin grabbed a discarded tankard from a dust-coated table, skipped to a barrel housing her favorite mood stabilizer, rotated the spigot, and filled the cup. After quaffing down the lukewarm, briny, and sweet pomegranate-infused Grissel's ale in one gulp, she wiped her mouth and filled the mug back to its brim. "It's good to be back home."

"Any luck tracking down our favorite mala'dayya?" Zho'zho asked.

"No. Mephistopheles is still MIA. Same for Karma." Pepper took a breath, then continued. "We're in deep trouble, Zho'zho. We must return to Earth. The chaosgate that brought us here disappeared. And apparently, after what you just shared, we can't leave Hell."

Perrin interjected, "Zho'zho, I know where we can hide out. But do you think you can help get us out of the Tenth Circle without being seen?"

"I might. There's an escape hatch in the attic."

Suddenly, bolts of thunder boomed in the sky, and the ground underneath Pepper's feet shook uncontrollably. It was as if the earth was moments from swallowing them whole. The tavern's walls quaked in response, and glass jars crashed to the ground, their contents exploding. Pepper was nearly tossed to the floor from the sheer magnitude of the earthquake, but she grabbed hold of the side of a shelf to keep herself upright. The episode lasted longer than anyone would have liked. Then stopped abruptly. They all waited with bated breath for the grand finale, but nothing happened.

"Woe betide he who dare anger the gods," Zho'zho said cryptically, her evolving pupils and scudding sclera looking all around the cellar. A beat later, she commanded all to hurry before all hell broke loose and the gods rained down holy terror on the tavern and everywhere else.

Pepper and Loki quickly decided that the ruachti would summon the shadows and leave the cellar in groups of three since shadow-cloaking worked best with fewer people, starting with Pepper and Kimball. Perrin and Beatrice returned to their previous hiding positions.

The Tenth Circle Tavern was hopping and filled to capacity with rowdy patrons and then some. Zho'zho shepherded the shadow-cloaked trio through the dense crowd, carrying a box of canned meats and bags of sweet-and-spicy sprite wings. While the gang was invisible, their presence could still be felt should someone bump into them. So they had to take great caution as they navigated the makeshift dance floor.

A band whipped the crowd into a frenzy with their "elven cave music"—Kimball's words. A cellist took the lead during the fast-paced song as the patrons stomped their cloven hooves and feet, all while clapping their hands to the staccato beat, ale splashing out of the tankards spectators held. The cello was fashioned from the body of the damned and the former soul-seller's chest cavity spatchcocked, her head still intact, eyes bulging from untold agony, while her legs had been chopped off. The cellist's spindly fingers deftly plucked the visible guts of the damned as his boot rhythmically tapped the floor.

While everyone focused their attention on the entertainment, Pepper picked up her pace as Loki wove in and out of tables and other tight spaces.

Zho'zho discreetly nodded her head in the staircase's direction, then left their side and headed to the bar. "Shut your pie hole, Azazel, and pony up the fleshies. This ain't no damn charity!" Behind the bar, Zho'zho filled up empty tankards with various ales and spirits on tap and continued yelling at Azazel and other amped-up patrons.

From here on out, Pepper, Loki, and Kimball were on their own.

A few patrons gathered in front of the stairs. There was no squeezing past them, so Loki, Pepper, and Kimball had no choice but to wait it out.

A scattershot of Talking Heads nailed to ornate mantels covered the walls like trophies—the very Heads that had tipped Perrin off to Pepper's arrival in Hell what felt like ages ago. Their lips flapped away, and mismatched eyes roved back and forth as they hunted for anything out of the ordinary to report to the Hounds of Hell. Pepper guessed the Talking Heads were still holding out hope that the Syndicate would free them from spending eternity nailed to walls. What fools.

Not one, not two, but five wanted posters featuring the unflattering mugshots of Pepper and Perrin, also known as inter-dimensional terrorists, were affixed to the wood-paneled walls. (Talk about overkill!) And honestly, their faces were horrible—Pepper's especially as she looked drunk and mildly braindead. The duo climbed to the top of DISI's Most Wanted List in no time. The "WANTED ALIVE AND ARMED AND EXTREMELY DANGEROUS; DO NOT APPROACH IF SPOTTED; IMMEDIATELY NOTIFY DISI" message was still intact. Unfortunately, DISI had raised the bounty to hundreds of Vs and Indys, along with the ability to use magic freely granted to any good citizen who reported a sighting.

The fear of being seen kicked up a few notches, if that was even possible, and Pepper held tightly to Loki, white-knuckling his furry arm.

The TV screens all around the tavern switched from the gladiator-style sport of the damned fighting other damned with body parts flying around the arena to breaking news, much to the chagrin of spectators who booed. A jingle played in the introduction's background: "Where's there smoke, there's fire. You can count on The Bellowers to bring you all the latest news from Hell and beyond."

The music cut, and a hybrid demon-elf donning a futuristic, avant-garde ensemble, graced the screens, her features an equal mixture of terrifying and pleasing. "This is Nailo for The Bellowers reporting live from the arena. I'm sure you all felt the wrath of the gods not moments ago. Worry not. We just received word on what caused the dimension-wide quakes. Underlord Chaos, believed dead, has escaped from Sheol in Oblivion's Fortress and is on the lam. You heard it here first." The slender reporter waltzed around the bloodbath, delicately stepping over mangled bodies so as not to sully her knee-high boots stitched from long silken hair and unblemished skin of the damned. A stuffed-to-the-gills stadium of rabid spectators encircled the correspondent.

A video showcasing a sea of molten lava appeared on the screens with a caption that read: *Live footage of the Lake of Fire within the Pits of Tartarus on the outskirts of Gehenna.* "Hard to imagine that underneath all that bubbling lava is Sheol, where those who have dared to go up against gods and our wondrous and undefeated King of Darkness, Lucifer are incarcerated. So, how did Underlord Chaos escape? A little sprite told us the underlord had help. If anyone has information on the prison break, you must immediately notify DISI with no exceptions, or the gods will immolate you on the spot. Still no comment from our king of darkness. The second we receive an update, you'll be the first to hear. Now back to the *Ultimate Death Match.*"

Loki and Pepper exchanged looks of *oh crap!* Underlord Chaos had to be the mysterious package Vlad had tasked Jhi with stealing, and the gods would scorch the earth looking for him. No matter how often Pepper mentally repeated those truths, the shock hadn't worn off. Admittedly, she fretted over Jhi. Feared for his safety.

Suddenly, it dawned on Pepper that the lunar eclipse was today, and chances were high that Vlad had already Misted everyone in her hometown with his vampire mind control, draining them of their energy. Yet again, Pepper epically failed to stop anything and everything from happening. She felt sick with worry over her father but reminded herself that she still had two weeks before Winter Solstice and to focus on getting out of Hell.

Eyes still fixated on the TV screen and busy chastising herself, Loki yanked a distracted Pepper onward now that the crowd in front of the stairs had dispersed.

The stairs creaked as Pepper, Loki, and Kimball traveled upward past an OFF LIMITS sign. A narrow hallway greeted them on the second floor, with two doors on either side. Loki chittered that he'd be right back.

Pepper needed a distraction. Anything to get her mind off the hell Jhi had reaped upon himself or the mayhem awaiting in Naples. So, she popped her head into the first room, which clearly belonged to Zho'zho, then shut the door just as quickly.

Since learning about Jaylyn calling the tavern home while working undercover as a barkeep, Pepper had yearned to investigate her sister's temporary digs to find a clue about her whereabouts. It looked like she finally got her wish.

After crossing the threshold of the only other room, Pepper jumped in fright when rats that oddly paled in comparison to the ones in the Big Apple scattered near her feet before disappearing into the chewed-up baseboards. Once she caught her breath, she gave her surroundings a cursory glance. The room served as a catch-all. Boxes were tossed and stacked in a desultory fashion, and bargain-basement Talking Heads were stuffed and sealed in containers, their jab-jabbing for rescue barely audible. The only bed, shoved in a corner and stripped of linens, had a sinkhole in the center of the mattress.

Jhi had unquestionably searched this room and whatever he had found left with him. Before Pepper could succumb to pangs of frustration, a pull in Pepper's stomach tugged her to the far corner of the room. To an object resting against a wall, its identity concealed by a dusty sheet. She removed the draping to see a mirror, not quite floor length, more like chest-high, large enough to crawl through.

Upon further inspection, Pepper noted a blemish at the bottom corner. After her fingers scratched the discoloration, she detached the matted-down threads stuck to the glass, then gently pulled on the frayed ends. Out popped a thin rope. Jhi would never have known to look here. He would have thought the mirror was antiqued when, in fact, Jaylyn had enchanted it. No doubt about it. But to speculum through the mirror, Pepper would need to activate the sigils that were most likely hidden from sight.

Pepper mechanically scraped a wound from her fight with Sawyer and smeared the freshly beading blood on the surface of the looking glass. With that, a string of sigils fired to life, commanding the mirror's surface to ripple.

A crazy idea took shape. How things were going, Pepper might not get a chance to return to the Tenth Circle. "Kimball," she whispered loudly over her shoulder, not letting go of the rope. "Come over here. I need your help with something."

"What will you do for me in return?"

"If you don't help me, I'll leave you in Hell."

"Alrighty then. How can I be of service?" He joined her in front of the mirror.

"I need you to hold on to this"—she handed him the rope —"and serve as my lookout." His mouth opened, preparing to fire off a fusillade of questions like a preschooler, so she shut that down ASAP. "Holster the questions. I don't have time to explain. Just hold this rope as if Bunny's life depended on it. Because it does. Without me, she's as good as dead." Pepper didn't feel bad about using Kimball's mother as leverage. Whatever it took at this point.

"Where are you going?"

"Not sure. But I'm guessing this rope doubles as my lifeline. If I don't come back in, let's say, ten minutes, or if someone is coming, or Loki returns with Perrin and Beatrice, yank on it, okay?"

Not fully trusting Kimball, Pepper yanked the vodka bottle from Kimball's hands and slipped it into her satchel.

Panic cemented on his face. "Give me back my mom!"

"I'm sorry, Kimball, but you leave me with no other choice."

"I said I would help you!"

"After I threatened you, sure. Listen, I'm wanted in Hell partly because of you!" Pepper whispered while tying the rope around Kimball's waist. What happened last time she had speculumed, along with the fear setting up permanent residence within her, wasn't formidable enough to stop her from entering the Mirror Realm.

Pepper crawled through the looking glass and clung to the rope as the blinding white light occluded her sight. Eventually, her eyes acclimated to the new environment. Shards of glass cracked under her feet. She tried to not make a noise, to not awaken wraiths who inhabited this realm, at least according to Perrin.

Her breath feathering in the frigid air, Pepper wanted to cinch her cloak, but she didn't dare remove her hands from the rope. One hand in front of the other, one footstep after the next. Walls of mirrors made up the hallway, their destinations unknown. Including the one she stood before, the one the rope led to.

Pepper eyed a room on the other side. Not a soul to be seen, at least no one near the mirror. After taking a fear-quelling breath, she crawled through the speculum.

26

The rope led directly inside a cabin with one window and a door heavily warded with blood-drawn sigils.

Pepper pushed back the moth-ravished curtains to see a flock of shorebirds trilling and screeching at one another as they searched for their dinner on the red-soiled beach. The orangey-crimson glow of dusk had cast its net over the under-heavens, but there was still enough light for Pepper to search up and down the coast for landmarks or signs of life.

Her search came up empty. Murky waters of a river or lake lapped at the shore, but land wasn't visible on the other side. It would be an exercise in futility to try to identify the body of water because they all looked alike in Hell—terrifying and black as pitch. Besides a skiff pulled up on shore, not a single telltale of where this shack resided presented itself.

Pepper would never be able to find this place. That had to be why Jaylyn came here, for privacy. It wasn't like she had company over, as evidenced by the single table and chair. There wasn't even a kitchenette inside, or maybe that was found beyond the only other door save for the exit that occupied the opposite wall.

A takeout container like those found in Chinese restaurants back on Earth rested on the table, the tips of chopsticks sticking out. The foodie within took over, and Pepper peeked inside. Using the chopsticks, she peeled off a layer of mold and slime. Underneath were little green nodules, like sea grapes or lato. What if a restaurant nearby served this delicacy? It might be a stretch, but if Pepper had any hopes of returning to this cabin, this takeout container was her best hope, so she stuffed it inside her satchel.

Next on the investigation list: the closed door. As Pepper's hand cupped the cold metal knob, the rope tugged her backward, the pull too great for her to ignore.

As Pepper crawled back into the room at the tavern, Kimball hovered above her, his lips quivering. "A … problem …" Kimball could barely get the words out due to hyperventilating.

Pepper instinctively handed over Bunny, knowing his mom was the only one who could ever weave a semblance of calm over her son.

"Loki is gone!" Kimball choked out.

"He's what?" Tears stung Pepper's eyes. "Where's Perrin and Beatrice?"

Kimball pointed to the door.

After bolting up the drop-down stairs to the attic, Pepper walked in on Perrin conversing with one of her sisters. "… so that's all you heard? Well, the Hounds have the Tenth Circle surrounded. I tried to dispatch Trixie, but she didn't answer. Can you holo-gab her?"

At first, Pepper thought Perrin's sister was in the attic; she nearly choked from the smell of the blue-black-haired dolly's saccharine-sweet perfume. But upon further inspection, that wasn't the case.

"Yes, Perrin," the unnamed Lolly'ka barked. "I swear to Mother Lilith, ugh. I'll see you soon."

"Bye to you, too, Myla," Perrin said gruffly as the Lolly'ka winked out of existence before swiveling on her heel when she heard Pepper enter the attic. "Sweetling!" Perrin ran to Pepper's side and hugged her.

When Pepper asked where Loki was, Perrin said, "After Loki returned to the cellar to get us, the chaosgate materialized out of the blue, and this whorling wind sucked our little furball right in, and then he and the chaosgate vanished." When Pepper was about to lose her mind, tears welling, Perrin added, "He has to be okay. I think one of Goddess Karma's security devices was triggered because, right as that happened, Hounds stormed inside the Tenth Circle. The minute Zho'zho saw them rush through the front doors, she caused enough of a distraction for Peaches and me to get up here unseen."

Even though Loki was a ruachti and would find his way to Kymeo, that wouldn't stop Pepper from worrying. "How did Myla know where we were?" she asked Perrin pointedly.

"After you left, I magicked a message to my sisters back in the cellar. Just in case we needed backup. That's how Myla knew where to holo-gab me."

Pepper was about to ask what a holo-gab was when she noticed gashes on Perrin and Beatrice's arms and blood on Perrin's dress. "What happened?"

"The fanged fuh'karing douche-vamps is what. They tried to snatch Peaches here. And she almost walked away with them," Perrin reproached Beatrice. "She would have, too, if I hadn't killed them."

"I, I—" Guilt washed over Beatrice, her brown eyes

reflecting shame, and her shoulders dropped. "It's true. Miles is back—Get him out of me!" She looked a tad gaunt.

"Peaches told them we were here. I just know it." Perrin wouldn't drop the subject.

"I didn't!" Beatrice said emphatically.

"Then how did they know we were here, if not for you?" Perrin sassed back.

Noting how gaunt Beatrice looked, Pepper said firmly, "Perrin, we need to get Beatrice help. The quicker, the better." Pepper then reiterated to Beatrice, "Miles wants you dead. He killed your sister. Though he didn't know it was a golem, but still. You have to keep reminding yourself of that."

"I know. But I didn't tell Miles where we were when he asked. I swear."

"Sweetling, did you hear the news about the jailbreak?" Perrin communicated the rest with her eyes.

Pepper said, "Yes," and felt equal parts queasy and fearful for Jhi, then dreaded what Underlord Chaos' freedom meant for the Syndicate's ultimate plan. "We'll talk about it once we're out of here."

Pepper then asked about Perrin's gargoyle bodyguards— Captain Trixie, Vixen, Minx, and Gamble—and if they could help them escape.

Perrin said she tried to dispatch them, but they didn't respond. Though lines of worry were etched along her peach-hued complexion, Perrin chose not to give voice to her apparent concerns.

Pepper dropped the topic and latched her eyes onto an access panel on the ceiling. "I take it that's the escape hatch? They're searching the grounds. They won't suspect we'd be traversing the rooftops. C'mon."

The tallest of the bunch, Kimball, pulled the rope down to free the stairs.

Pepper inspected her surroundings on the top of the at

least five-stories tall tavern, the icy wind whipping her hair about. Pyramids were scattered about the red soil terrain, but the neighborhood was at least half a mile away. A building to her left couldn't aid their escape, as the distance was too far between them. To her right, another building, its roof peaked, offered no means of escape either. But if they could get past that building, they could use its massive size to block them from the Hounds. Then what?

Perrin interrupted Pepper's surveying and pointed at a pyramid in the distance. "See that staff over there, near the copse of firebushes?" Pepper couldn't quite make it out, which annoyed the Lolly'ka. "Please tell me you can at least see the fireballs?" Fireballs rolled about the dirt like tumbleweeds and scorched the earth in their wake.

When Pepper *finally* spotted the staff in question, jutting out of the ground, a head skewered atop the metal spike, Perrin said, "That's where we need to go."

The gang waited at the rooftop's edge until patrolling Hounds marched underneath them, rounded the corner of the tavern, then disappeared from sight. Following Perrin's lead, Pepper shimmied down a pipe and hightailed it to the next building over. From there, she darted to the staff, dodging roving fireballs and gingerly walking through deadly firebush plants, their fronds needle-sharp.

At the staff crowned by a "head" that turned out to belong to a creepy doll, Perrin hoisted up a hidden hatch and ushered everyone inside before sealing them in. "If anyone speaks a word of this, I'll kill you myself." Perrin finished with a smile.

The ghostly lit substation was mantled floor to ceiling in cotton candy pink, and smelled as sweet. Perrin headed to a black screen affixed to the wall and tapped a sequence of beats. Once finished, a garage door lifted open, revealing a vintage-looking bumper car built for two. The forsaken amusement park ride rested before an archway, where terri-fying nothingness unfurled beyond.

"Hurry and get in. We have ten seconds," Perrin commanded. "It's gonna be tight, but we're out of options."

Pepper practically fell into the jump seat, as did Beatrice and Kimball. Perrin squeezed herself in, then securely fastened the belt over all their laps.

As the bumper car levitated off the ground and shimmied like a lodestone hungering for its vibrational opposite, Pepper held on to the belt for dear life, her fingers strangling the hairy damned skin.

Then blast off! Straight into the bowels of nothingness, a vacuum-like force tugged the car onward. When the bumper car went from zero to one hundred, Pepper couldn't breathe, let alone scream, and frankly, her heart was confused as all get out, so it decided it was best to take a breather. Eventually, her addled mind stilled and got the rest of her organs back on track.

Ropy tendrils of illumination affixed to the walls served as lodestars as the bumper car whipped through the intricate network of subterranean tunnels at a breakneck pace. Right, a jerky left, forward … Pepper's cheeks flapped, and her head remained in a forward position, unable to move a muscle in either direction, as the speed damn near reached warp.

The walls were one large magnetic field, vibrating at the same charge as the car and repelling the flying vessel from smacking into the unforgiving stone and ending the lives of the passengers. Because of this repellant force, the car never once strayed from the middle, not even a centimeter off course, no matter how many serpentining twists and turns made up the subterranean highway.

When the ropy lights blinked furiously like demented strobe lights, the strength of the magnetic drawing waning, the car slowed down significantly. After veering rightward, the bumper car vomited them out in an alley that branched off in various directions.

Obsidian skyscrapers soared above, their spires stabbing the night sky. The hustle and bustle of Pandæmonia city life played on: beeping horns, drivers yelling at other drivers to "pick up the pace," and discordant, loud chatter and music emanating from nowhere and everywhere.

Perrin led everyone down an alley, then took a few sharp turns until they eventually reached a dead end. With a piece of chalk in hand, Perrin drew a hopscotch grid. Once finished, she began jumping—one, six, nine, nine, seven, five, three—then took a massive leap to ten. A doorway that wasn't there before popped into existence.

"You saw nothing and remember nothing, or else." Perrin dragged her finger across her throat. "Got it?"

All heads nodded in the affirmative.

"Good. Welcome to Lolly'ka headquarters."

27

The Lolly'kas were Mafiosos. They ran the underbelly of Hell, shaking down businesses for money, trafficking illicit items, and running gambling rings, to name a few. So, color Pepper shocked to see that their digs, mob central, would easily fit inside a playhouse. From the decor and cutesy furnishings to the floor and wall coverings, they favored every color of the rainbow, particularly bright pinks and greens. The delicious aroma of spun sugar impregnated the air, followed by a tangy, blood-like after-scent.

Girls skipped about with jump ropes. Some engaged in hand-clapping games, singsonging, "Mother Lilith dressed in black, black, black with magic gems all down her back, back, back …" A few strolled by, eerily humming, their heads slowly swiveling in concert with one another as they looked at Pepper. Others rode around on tricycles with spikes protruding from the wheels and various body-impaling weapons strapped to the handlebars. Some wore masks with bunny ears, bat ears, and devil horns covering everything but their huge, perfectly round eyes and pouty mouths. Most girls wore frilly dresses, while a few donned rompers and trousers bunched at the knee and fastened with cutesy buckles.

The Lolly'kas were all vertically challenged, maybe an inch or two difference in height. And they all had that distinct, engorged head that appeared out of place perched atop their petite frames.

A few girls, some licking round lollipops as giant as their heads, others gnawing on rock candies on sticks, gathered in front of a claw machine that didn't grab stuffed toys. Instead, this game retrieved sawed-off body parts of the damned.

Nearby, Lolly'kas squeezed onto a sofa in front of a projector screen, raptly watching the *Ultimate Death Match* play out. Some cheered and knocked back bottles of ale as their betting picks survived the death match, while others booed when their favorites lost limbs in the fighting pit and demons dragged them away.

"This blood is getting cold!" a Lolly'ka bayed from across the playhouse. Two out-of-breath girls buzzed past Pepper, each carrying a bucket, fresh blood sloshing within, a few drops spilling to the confetti tile.

Perrin led the way toward the shrieking, stopped before the door, and ordered everyone not to speak once they entered the room.

"Ow!" snapped the Lolly'ka, who had bayed moments before as she luxuriated inside a blood-filled clawfoot tub. "Watch it with that brush, Luka, or I'll make you choke on it."

"Sorry, mistress," violet-haired Luka softly replied as she brushed her bathing mistress' crimped pink tresses.

The bathing, pampered princess pushed Luka away and stood up in the bath, arms extended, her slender body coated in the dark viscous gore. Luka immediately wrapped a towel around her mistress.

"Well, well, well," the princess said to Perrin as she secured the towel over her B-cup breasts. "Look what the xykree dragged in." When she stepped out of the tub, globs of blood plopped on the floor, and Luka immediately mopped it dry.

"It's nice to see you, too, Quillee. You're mistress now?" Perrin nearly choked on disgust while uttering the latter.

"Someone had to take over the role of queenpin when you left us high and dry without warning."

"Did you know there's a hell-wide manhunt for you?" mousy Luka said to Perrin while on her knees, mopping up the mess.

"No?" Perrin feigned shock. "Get out of here!" Luka rolled her eyes in response. "Where's Kirby?" Perrin inquired.

"She missed her project deadline, and I've instructed the girls not to disturb her until she's finished," Quillee shared. "She should be done soon." The new queenpin tossed her pink hair behind her shoulders in preparation for Luka, who then placed a gem-studded headband on Quillee's fat head. While glaring at everyone save for Perrin, Quillee growled, "You better have a fuh'karing good reason to have brought humans here."

"My hands were tied, Quillee. The fanged fuh'kars were after our asses," Perrin explained, exasperation coating her words, "and I made the only call I could."

"So I heard." Quillee slipped into a frilly dress embellished with embroidered strawberries and lacy bobby socks. A scepter resting in a corner with a light-up star on top was no sooner resting in Quillee's hands.

The queen bee then directed her attention to the two "buckets of blood" carriers who had entered her chamber earlier. One approached Quillee submissively and whispered into her mistress' ear. Quillee replied, "Bring him to me."

The girls bowed and excused themselves. A beat later, they dragged in a brown suit-wearing demon with a cap of curly brown hair. The demon's facial features were suggestions thereof, as if covered in wax with rivulets of sweat running down his eggshell-smooth face. A Lolly'ka pointed a gun, not at the demon, but at his shadow, a silhouette half on the floor, half on the wall, hunched over and quivering in fear.

When Quillee spoke, she directed her ire at the demon. "You broke our gentlewomen's agreement. So, what's about to happen is all on you!" Quillee sauntered to the vanity and removed a candy-studded dagger resting on the counter. As she strolled back to the faceless demon, she tapped the weapon on her open palm.

The demon's cries for mercy fell on deaf ears, his shadow wilting and crouching in a corner. In one fluid motion, Quillee sank the dagger right into the demon's heart and twisted. The devil crumpled to the tile, and his shadow vanished.

"What the fuh'kar, Quillee? Since when do we kill consiglieri?" Perrin asked, disgusted.

"Since you left. Never question me again!"

"He's not actually dead, Perrin," Luka added.

"He might as well be. Quillee turned his shadow-self into a wraith," Perrin replied.

Quillee huffed and epically rolled her eyes. "I have some business to attend to. Afterward, Perrin, you and I need to catch up, so make yourself useful until then." The queen bee dismissed them with a wave of her hand.

Her jaw set, Perrin took a measured breath, then replied, "Absolutely."

As they exited the queen bee's chamber, Pepper said to Perrin under her breath, "So, we hate her, right?"

"That backstabbing bitch usurped my position. *I* am the queenpin, *not* her—I want to shove that fuh'karing stupid scepter up her ass and turn her into a puppet. Ugh! I need to kill something. Take the edge off." Perrin stomped off.

Pepper, Beatrice, and Kimball picked up the pace, trying to keep up with Perrin as she navigated them past a training area that resembled a bowling alley. Girls holding sherbet-hued "records" in their dainty hands stood at the head of long narrow lanes. In place of pins, the damned were chained to a wall with muzzles that suppressed their caterwauling.

The "records" the girls held like weapons were vintage in style and had raised note imprints on the surface and gear teeth on the side that looked like deep grooves. Only these grooves were knife sharp.

Perrin snatched a "record" and tossed it like a frisbee along with the other girls. She beheaded a damned on the first go-round, and her sisters clapped and applauded while another Lolly'ka tossed the headless damned to the side.

"I feel a tad better," Perrin shared as she marched onward.

They reached a wall with no other exit save for a hole, and Perrin jumped through feet first. Pepper hesitantly followed suit and was pleasantly surprised when she twirled down a slide that vomited them out in a vast open space that mimicked a research and development facility. Various rooms for experimenting and object enchanting occupied the space. A bumper car resided in one and other forms of transportation, like soul-cars in another. Ceiling-high shelves held numerous ingredients, potions, gems, and toys that were most likely weapons. Cages tucked away in the corner housed the damned in distress, chemical burns and pustules polka-dotting their bodies in toto.

Inside a sterile laboratory, a Lolly'ka wearing a lab coat

like a proper scientist, standing before a work table, made herself busy by winding the teensy crank on a pocket-sized jack-in-the-box, locked within a cage, the off-key discordant tune of the toy serving as musical accompaniment. Once she stopped turning the crank, she stepped back to a far corner and waited.

BOOM! The cage door blew open. The explosion knocked the bunny mask off her face.

Perrin knocked on the glass wall and said to the scientist, "There you are," relief coating her tone.

The scientist's butterscotch-colored eyes widened in response as she plucked up the enchanted jack-in-the-box toy with her index finger and thumb before exiting the laboratory.

"Pepper, this is Kirbilicious, Kirbles, Kirby-girl. Also known as Kirby," Perrin said by way of introduction.

Kirby, with strawberry-hued hair fashioned in a straight bob, her baby bangs perfectly straight, and a spray of freckles across her nose struggled to cook up even a half smile. "You shouldn't be here," she whispered to Perrin as she fastened the jack-in-the-box charm to a plastic clip-on chain-link necklace. It joined a bevy of other downright wacky trinkets: a harmonica, roller skate, pack of gum, abacus, fried egg in a pan, and other random items.

Another Lolly'ka joined them. The same girl Perrin had holo-gabbed back at the Tenth Circle Tavern. The blue-black-haired, violet-eyed Myla wouldn't be out of place in a Victorian gothic home; her raven-black lacy ensemble screamed as much.

"What Kirby meant is you shouldn't have returned to Hell," said Myla. "It's too dangerous." Myla's eyes widened when they alighted on Pepper and Beatrice. "They say a mugshot could never outshine the in-person. But look at you, Pepper, proving them wrong." Pepper couldn't even vomit up a response to that insult before Myla moved on. "And you must be Beatrice. Lovely to make your acquaintance." She then addressed all. "I'm afraid you've caught us at a bad time. We've put pressure on Kirby to enchant newly acquired objects before we test them out on the citizenry, and she's falling behind. Isn't that right, Kirby?"

Kirby weakly nodded and darted her eyes away from Myla, which raised Pepper's hackles.

Kimball busied himself by touching everything like a child while Beatrice slunk to the floor, fatigue taking over. As for Perrin, her blood continued boiling, her mind most likely myopically focused on how to end faux-queenpin Quillee's life.

"I'll be next door if you need me," Myla said to Kirby. If Pepper wasn't mistaken, it wasn't an FYI, but a warning.

Kirby smiled. But as soon as Myla was out of eyeshot, she bunched up the charm necklace and slipped it into a hidden pocket within Perrin's dress.

Clearly bored, Kimball leaned into Perrin and asked, "Just point me in the direction of the other dudes, and I'll just wait with them." Now that Kimball had mentioned it, not a single man populated Lolly'ka central.

"Boys?" A smirk stretched Perrin's pouty lips to her cheeks. "Sure. Right over there. In the corner." Kimball's eyes sailed to a pile of bones.

Kimball gulped while Bunny's soul zigzagged crazily in the vodka bottle he hugged to his chest.

Pepper wasn't sure how long they'd be at Lolly'ka headquarters, so she dove right in. "Perrin says you're the resident curse cracker." Then brought Kirby up to speed on patient Beatrice, what they had given her, and her current predicament.

At Kirby's command, Beatrice sat on the stainless steel table. The Lolly'ka then whipped out instruments from a toy doctor kit and started the examination with a plastic ophthalmoscope. "Interesting," she said to no one as she snapped her fingers and instructed Beatrice to follow the sound. Next up, Kirby asked Beatrice to follow her ever-roaming index finger while paying extra attention to the Agent's eyes. She even waved a hand in Beatrice's face, which she smacked away. "You brought Beatrice to me just in time. Miles broke through the devil's fang defenses."

Without warning, Kirby pivoted on her heel and sauntered to a glass shelf. While mumbling to herself, she thumbed through a passel of flasks and glass tubes before landing on two in particular, then grabbed a rainbow-colored twirler on a stick.

Back at the examination table, Kirby pressed a button on the twirler, and it whirled to life, spinning and spinning, generating zephyrs of wind, a rainbow forming in midair. "Focus on the rainbow, Beatrice," Kirby commanded in a hypnotic cadence. As bubbles blew out of the whirling device, the generated current cascaded them toward Beatrice, and they popped on her lips, coating her smackers. Mesmerized, the Agent licked her lips. An instant later, she had a far-off look in her eyes.

Kirby advised all present, "Hold your breath," before uncorking a vial. A plume of hot pink smoke exploded out in a mushroom cloud. A soft powder sifted down to the floor, scattering everywhere but where Beatrice sat on the table; the curious substance had coated an entity attached to Beatrice's side as if she were half of a Siamese twin.

While wearing a genuine smile, Kirby said, "Just as I suspected. Metaphysical parabiosis." She scribbled down notes on a clipboard. "I've never heard of this para doxea you mentioned, but I can conclusively say that metaphysical parabiosis is a side effect of the poison extracted from the plant."

Pepper inspected the chalked outline that slowly became

focused as the powder filled the pockmarks on the man's face —Miles' face. His sunken eyes and skeletal features popped out in sharp relief.

"Sis, we're not fuh'karing nerds. You're gonna need to dumb it down and make it extra dumb for rattilocks here." Perrin jerked a thumb at Kimball, who set his sights on a water gun that most likely didn't house water if the bubbling contents within the attached container were any indication.

Kirby obliged and explained that when Miles stabbed Beatrice, the para doxea poison on the blade allowed him to form a connection to her like a blood bond. "I'm guessing he did so to control her. And from the looks of it, he's not about to let go." Kirby set her sights on Pepper.

"Here." Kirby put the ophthalmoscope in Pepper's hand and told her to look into Beatrice's eyes. "What do you see?"

Pepper shuddered. "Another set of eyes." Noting Beatrice's far-off look, Pepper asked, "Why is she zombified?"

"Oh. I used the bubbles to put Beatrice under a hypnosis spell so that she wouldn't put up a fight. Only temporary."

"Is she lucid?"

"Sorta. It works like truth serum. It'll wear off in a matter of minutes."

Pepper's mind went crazy with the possibilities of what she could ask the Agent, but settled on, "Beatrice, did you snitch on us to Miles back at the Tenth Circle? Is that why the Hounds showed up looking for us?"

"No," Beatrice replied in a monotone, her eyes trance-like.

Kirby interrupted Pepper's cross-examining and handed serrated-edged scissors to Beatrice. "To sever the blood bond, you must be the one to cut the cord joining Miles to you." Beatrice hedged. "If not, you Change. And a new Beatrice is born, one that doesn't have autonomy but is commanded by another."

Beatrice hesitantly made the first chop, then another.

When Beatrice paused again, Pepper wrapped her hand around Beatrice's and applied firm pressure while directing Beatrice where to cut. With each snip, her sovereignty grew, and the cutting became quicker, fiercer, and angrier until she cleaved Miles from her being.

"My work here is done," Kirby said jokingly, wiping her hands clean.

"Not yet," Pepper said. "Perrin said you might be able to help me identify where this food came from?" Pepper handed Kirby the mold and maggot-infested takeout container she had swiped from the cabin.

Kirby bunched her tiny nose as she sniffed the spoiled contents. "Smells like seaweed. Let me put it in the mass spectrometer. Results will take a bit."

Perrin escorted everyone to a break room and suggested they get some shut-eye until they figured out their next move. In the meantime, she had to have that dreaded catch-up session with Quillee.

Pepper and Beatrice waited on teeny-tiny, hot pink loveseats until Kimball passed out, which took all of five minutes, his legs dangling over the Lolly'ka-sized couch, his snores loud enough to drown out the girls' whisperings.

Now that Beatrice was out of danger and no longer a threat, two pressing questions on the tip of Pepper's tongue vied for power, so she threw the most urgent of the two at Beatrice. "We're trapped in Hell. And who knows if Kirby can provide a lead with the one clue I found, but even that could be a dud. Please tell me you know a way to sneak out of this dimension undetected." Already figuring the answer was no, Pepper had to contend with a wave of dread washing over her.

Beatrice swiped lip balm along her lips, then said, "I do. But it's dicey. On the plus side, we won't cross paths with Hounds or the Syndicate there."

Relief sluiced down Pepper's body, her shoulders finally relaxing.

"Downside, there are far worse nightmares to contend with than even the Syndicate."

Pepper's shoulders hiked upward to what seemed like their forever position. Tentatively, she asked Beatrice where.

"Witherwhere." Beatrice then shared that as a Karma Academy student, during one of Professor Kymeo's lessons, he trapped each of his pupils inside Witherwhere. Alone, weaponless, the girls were forced to fight their way out.

"Can you even open a chaosgate to Witherwhere?" Pepper could have sworn the answer was no.

"Yes, but not consciously. Here's the thing. Agents can chaosnaut to other dimensions and the realms hidden within that mages can't. But there's a caveat, only if Goddess Hekate allows it. After all, she's who controls chaosgates. Word to the wise: if you're ever stuck in a realm, it never hurts to butter the goddess up with oblations and nuggets of knowledge. Somethin' worthwhile to Hekate. Don't ask me what that would be because I have no clue."

Pepper yelped when Kimball let out a loud snore and had to catch her breath.

Beatrice continued, "Witherwhere is … unique. There's a reason the souls of the lost unconsciously travel there in their dreams. And why fixers gravitate to the realm, lookin' for those desperate enough to sell their magic, but even then, they astral there. Nobody physically sets foot inside Witherwhere, at least not on purpose. It's more like a place you wind up in. If that makes sense. Even more strange is that after we passed PK's test and made it out alive, we compared notes. But not one of us could recall how we got out. As for the dang nightmares … those lingered for us all." Beatrice leaned in and said conspiratorially, "Supposedly, some Initiates before us never made it back from Witherwhere. They're still trapped there to this day." Then she sat back, all prim and proper.

"And yet you offered this place as a viable option out of Hell? A place you tried to return to but couldn't?" Pepper slowly blinked.

Beatrice weakly chuckled. "Yep. Desperate times." Noting Pepper's gobsmacked expression, she added, "Obvi, we figured out how to return—round number two of PK's lessons. Confuse the mind and write Witherwhere backward on the chaosgate."

Beatrice then described her recalled time in Witherwhere as beautiful at first. Warm. Like a spring day. Comforting like a mother's embrace. Fun and free, like a summertime carnival. No cares in the world. Disembodied laughter carried on the balmy breeze. But don't let the laughter fool you. It was unseen beings laughing at you, not with you. Witherwhere attracted souls of the lost like the smell of sugar-coated poison to roaches.

"Ever wonder why cockroaches die on their backs? They're drawn to the sweetness of sugar, and when they find it, they gobble it up. But when they realize what happened, it's too late, and the neurotoxic chemicals shut down their nervous system, and they lose control and flip over on their backs, their legs convulsing. Vulnerable and unable to scream to their brethren for help, they lack the strength to right themselves. In the end, they're belly-up, either death by poison or predator. Take your pick. That's Witherwhere. It sucks you in, and before you know it, it claims you and traps you for eternity." A smile ghosted over Beatrice's lips as if lost in a memory. "Things are not always what they seem there."

Before Pepper could dive in with her next pressing question, without preamble, Beatrice lowered her sweatshirt to reveal the Karma Academy emblem tattooed above her heart. "What do you see?" When Pepper described the broken infinity symbol with a linear line running underneath, Beatrice nodded slightly, then said, "Back at the Starless Souk, none of y'all noticed how I opened the chaosgate to the Academy, well, except for you. To be honest, I refused to believe that the Powers that Be invited you to attend Karma Academy. Or that you were an Agent. That you're Jaylyn's sister. But there was one thing—well, two, I couldn't deny: only Agents can see the Karma Academy emblem and our goddess' statue in the welcome lobby. No exceptions." Beatrice then apologized for her multiple attempts—all failing—to kill Pepper and her friends, much to Pepper's shock. Like when she had sent Pepper to the rooftop to get help, she had hoped Professor Kymeo would have expelled Pepper from the Academy, or worse.

"Don't get too excited because there's something off with you." Beatrice divulged how Goddess Karma prohibited Agents from outing the identities of other Agents to outsiders, even under a compulsion spell. "And when I say we can't divulge our identities, we physically can't because of a spell preventing us from speaking. And should the spell somehow be broken, immediate death befalls the rat. In a nutshell, that's why I've distrusted you. If you're an Agent, I should be able to share intel with you, but I physically can't."

Pepper wanted to scream bloody murder into the pillow on her lap.

"Before you get your panties in a bunch, I have a theory as to why that is. You haven't passed the final exam." Noting Pepper's furrowed brows, Beatrice added, "You don't know what I'm talking about, do you?"

Wide-eyed, Pepper confirmed Beatrice's suspicions with a shake of her head.

"I'm sorry to tell you this, but you're not technically an Agent of Karma. Not until you ace the test. And don't ask me a doggone thing about the final exam because I can't tell you even if I wanted to. Now, what were you about to ask me earlier?"

While swallowing a lump in her throat from that heavy revelation, Pepper rifled through her satchel and produced the letter Jaylyn wrote to Beatrice. "This letter was in the package my sister tried to mail to you via Zephyr's Express. But you never received it because I have a sneaking suspicion Jaylyn disappeared before she could summon Aeolus' mail-carrying minions."

Beatrice perused the letter while Pepper continued. "Regardless, Jaylyn told you to abort the mission and switch to Plan B—something that involved you making contact with your asset inside the Ministry of Mischief and Mayhem." Asset who went by the name of Sala'dee, Mephistopheles' girl Friday. "Can Plan B help us stop the Syndicate? Help us find Jaylyn? And before you plead the fifth, let me say my piece. I've been trying to find my sister, and the leads have run dry."

When Beatrice didn't speak up, Pepper added a not-so-veiled threat: "If you know where Jaylyn's at, and you opt not to share, just know that Jhi is after her on the Syndicate's orders, and if he finds her before we do, she's as good as dead. And you'll be to blame because you could have stopped him. Jaylyn is the only one who can help us save Karma, the professors who mysteriously disappeared, and other Agents, including yourself. And I fear she's the only one who can help stop Cazzian and the Syndicate from dominating other dimensions." As intended, Pepper got a rise out of Beatrice, judging from the worry stitched all over her face.

"Who's Jaah?" With a slight Southern twang, Beatrice pronounced Jhi, like Juh-eye.

"He's the Ven-ad'tsay Jaylyn warned you about in the letter. The same guy chasing after her and you, who's also teamed up with Miles, I might add." *The one I fell hard for,*

Pepper opted to leave out. "How *did* you and my sister team up, if you don't mind me asking?"

The waiting for Beatrice to respond was downright nerve-wracking, so much so that Pepper leaned forward in her seat, strangle-holding the throw pillow as if that would generate a response. When that did absolutely nothing to tame the anxiety, she shoved a handful of sugared pixie wings into her mouth, anything to help blunt the edge, then wiped off the dusting of sugar coating her top.

Beatrice swallowed, yet again, as if considering what she was about to reveal. "As to how I know Jaylyn, I believe I already answered that question earlier."

At that moment, the shocking truth walloped Pepper and sent her ticker reeling; round and round, it rolled.

How Jaylyn had chaosnauted to Hell undetected: *E-lohi'exspiravitius,* Pepper recalled Beatrice saying, *enables gods and Agents of Karma to slip in and out of dimensions undetected.*

How Jaylyn had stumbled across the Syndicate's plot to resurrect Cazzian.

How she knew Beatrice, Sawyer, Karma, Mephistopheles—and Jaylyn didn't make the mala'dayya's acquaintance while bartending at the Tenth Circle Tavern.

The truth had been right in front of Pepper's face all this time.

Jaylyn was an Agent of Karma.

Pepper squeezed her face tight to chase away the welling tears, then breathed, "All this time, I've been searching for my sister, thinking she's trapped somewhere and in need of help. But what if Miles or the Hounds of Hell already got to her and killed her?" Just saying that caused her heart to pound faster. "What you don't know is that Miles has a list containing the names of Agents of Karma, and he crossed off most of their names, except for yours and Sawyer's. Full disclosure. I haven't laid eyes on this kill list, just hearsay. But Kimball has."

"No! Don't say that. Jaylyn's not dead." Beatrice looked physically ill, her face ashen. "She has to be hiding somewhere. Y'know, she's always been so secretive, so I wouldn't even know where to start lookin'."

Between the constant dread and her heart's nonstop rolling in her chest, Pepper *nearly* lost her appetite. The only item of food remaining in her satchel was a damn moraberry fruit leather. *Beggars can't be choosers.* Still, the fruit leather and sprite wings weren't enough sustenance to quell Pepper's shattered nerves.

"And what about the other Agents? Where are they? Aren't you guys in constant contact? Like, do they know what's happening?" Pepper spoke rapid-fire.

"I don't know where they're at. And we were all in touch until I left. Before Karma shunned me."

When Beatrice filled in the missing pieces, Pepper leaned closer, soaking up every spoken word. "It all began when Karma assigned a case to one of my sisters to take out a notorious crime lord. A real vile SOB who was running a human trafficking ring. Only the Agent couldn't kill him."

Beatrice described how the Agent had overheard the kingpin mention he was joining forces with some nefarious organization that was climbing up the ranks of the dark underbelly of the criminal world and how he had signed a soul contract as part of the initiation. Turned out that the organization in question was the Syndicate.

"We were ordered to drop the case, so we smiled and nodded like good little Agents, then went undercover. We were not about to let that guy get away with his crimes. So, we divided up, each with our own clues to follow."

Around the time Jaylyn was in Hell investigating a lead, Beatrice was very much part of the mission. But Jaylyn panicked when it had come to light that the Syndicate was behind a plot to resurrect some damned named Cazzian from Hell and that he was looking for Pepper. Immediately after, Jaylyn went dark, said she couldn't risk the Syndicate finding out she was alive and needed to find Pepper before Cazzian did. She had disappeared before Beatrice could inquire about the damned's connection to her.

That occurred at the same time Beatrice had a family emergency to attend to back in Georgia and had to take a leave of absence from her role as Karma's Agent. Helping Josie deal with the accruing debt left behind from the untimely passing of their mama and gran trumped everything. When Beatrice announced her time off, Karma blew a gasket and cut Beatrice off from the Academy and her sisters. According to Karma, Beatrice was a liability, and the goddess couldn't let Beatrice further endanger her sisters or the Academy in good faith.

Unfortunately, Jaylyn had already gone underground and didn't know what had transpired. Beatrice couldn't exactly reach Jaylyn to notify her, thanks to Karma cutting Beatrice off, including all forms of communication. As far as Jaylyn knew, the mission hadn't changed, and Beatrice was still the point of contact for Sala'dee, which explained why Jaylyn had attempted to mail Beatrice the letter urging her to switch to Plan B.

Pepper and Beatrice posited that Sala'dee was most likely dead and the wanderer who stole Mephistopheles' body was the killer, which gutted Beatrice something fierce, her face twisting up with guilt.

"Well, if it's any consolation, Karma obviously cares about you and still considers you one of her Agents because she sent me to warn you, knowing the Syndicate was after you, as you were otherwise out of the loop." Pepper then asked Beatrice why Jaylyn was so insistent that Pepper wasn't to be reunited with her magic.

"Not sure. Like I said, Jaylyn's secretive when it comes to her past. Or, as I call it, BKA. Before Karma Academy. But she knew I'd have a problem with her insistence because of a similar situation with my sister." Beatrice paused, then said, "You mentioned this list, the one with names of Agents crossed off. And you said Kimball ID'd my name and Sawyer's?" When Pepper nodded, Beatrice added, "I don't know how that's possible. If it is, do you think that means they're dead?" Beatrice inhaled deeply a few times as if trying to calm her rattled nerves.

"Like I said, I didn't personally see this list, but I do believe Kimball wasn't lying. I mean, he couldn't possibly have known about your identity unless Sawyer ratted you out. They know she's an Agent."

"I just don't understand. You certain?"

"Oh yeah. I hate to be the one to tell you this, but the Syndicate has been offing Initiates. A Hound intercepted a young girl named Valerie on her way to the Academy and killed her. I saw her body. Found her invite. And Karma's dying because of all the deaths."

Beatrice snapped out of her haze and said, "No. It's impossible. I told you earlier that even if Sawyer had wanted to reveal her sisters' names, she couldn't speak, write them, or even give off a tell to outsiders. Our identities are entombed in eternal secrecy. Let's say Sawyer somehow managed to do the impossible; a hex would have immolated her on the spot. Which means Valerie was not an Agent."

Then who have the Hounds and Miles been killing, if not Karma's Agents? Pepper wondered. *Perhaps the trained Vigilantes spread across the globe? Were they who Miles and Jhi were hunting down? Were their names crossed off on the kill list and not*

Agents of Karma? And if that was the case, then the Syndicate has no idea about Karma's big guns—her Agents.

"So, are you telling me," Pepper started, "that since you left the Academy, you haven't heard a word from any of your sisters?" How was Beatrice so sure they were even alive? "Is anyone aware that their lives are in danger?"

Beatrice bit the inside of her lip, her eyes cast to the ground as if deep in thought, then must have reconsidered and shook her head no. "Not a peep. But they're not dead. I would know."

Pepper's theory was gaining traction.

As if reading Pepper's mind, Beatrice added, "Valerie was most likely a Vigilante. But here's the problem. When Vigilantes leave the Academy, Karma erases their memories and returns them to civilian status. They don't know they're intricately connected to the goddess. They don't even know Karma exists by design."

"Well, somebody is aware of their existence, and they told the Syndicate. So what you're telling me is that these Vigilantes are essentially walking targets. And we can't warn them?"

Beatrice bit the inside of her lips while shaking her head. "Before you blame Sawyer, it couldn't have been her who ratted. When Vigilantes leave the Academy, Karma wipes their identities from all our minds. We know they exist in theory, but that's about it. For all I'd know, one could be a coworker at my family restaurant. Even so, the hex woven over all of us Agents prevents us from spilling any secrets, especially one so damning. I wonder if the Syndicate even knows that the true Agents of Karma exist."

Pepper began to wonder the same thing. "Do you think your sisters have wised up to Sawyer serving as a spy for the Syndicate? Or they in the dark like you were?"

"I don't know. The last time we were all together, we had

gotten word Vlad was intricately involved with the Syndicate. So, when one of our CIs spotted the vampire high king in South Beach, Sawyer and another of our sisters headed out to Miami to gather intel. That was the last time I saw Sawyer."

"But something obviously happened in Miami, and Sawyer switched sides. So how come a part of you still seems to trust her?"

"You don't understand what's it like to be an Agent," Beatrice blurted out. "The bond we have."

Pepper would be lying if she said those words didn't feel like a knife stabbing her heart. Pepper was no stranger to that feeling of not belonging. She struggled in school when it came to making friends or fitting in. Forget breaking into an already tight-knit group of girls. Pepper thought she had left all that behind when she graduated from Naples High early. Apparently not. "Or Sawyer's just a Judas in a blonde wig."

Beatrice tapped into her Southern roots and opted not to say what clearly would have been an unsavory remark. After ironing away the anger-induced lines until her face was smooth as butter, she said, "For all we know, the Syndicate poisoned Sawyer, too."

Realizing she wasn't getting anywhere with her line of questioning that only riled Beatrice up, Pepper switched gears. "Back at the Academy, you started reciting what sounded like a prophecy. Do you recall doing that? Or know anything about it?"

Beatrice didn't. At least not at the Academy. "'On the third night, the dragon devours the moon, and all the planets watch from the sky, the gods secretly assemble on the mighty mountain of Bel, and time slowly dies.'" She explained that some entity spoke that prophecy through her family members back on All Hallows' Eve. "All I could gather at the time was that it referred to the lunar eclipse. But I don't know what it means."

"Neither do we. We know the Syndicate was behind breaking Underlord Chaos out of Sheol, who, by the way, everyone thought was dead." When Beatrice's face crinkled in confusion, Pepper elaborated. "Remember the earthquake back at the Tenth Circle Tavern?" When Beatrice nodded, Pepper said, "That was the wrath of the gods delivering a stern warning to the thief on the Syndicate's payroll." Pepper wouldn't dare out Jhi or endanger him further. "Do you know how Underlord Chaos could be involved or help the Syndicate? Clearly, he brings something huge to the table. Otherwise, the Syndicate wouldn't have risked angering the gods for nothing."

"No clue."

Dammit! If anyone knew about Chaos, it would be Jhi. If only Pepper could figure out a way to contact him. Since she had taken the Conscious Astraling potion, Jhi stopped visiting her dreamscape. *How convenient.*

"Now that they have Underlord Chaos in their possession, the Winter Solstice ceremony's right on track, whatever that entails." Just uttering that caused sweat to coat Pepper's hands. "With one exception. *You.* Apparently, they *need* you present for the ritual."

A bout of fear arrested Beatrice's features, but she shook it off just as quickly.

"And you better believe the Syndicate is ramping up their search for you as we speak. *And* they know you're in Hell, which has given them one helluva jumpstart." All of a sudden, Pepper felt incredibly unsafe.

"Well, they can't have me. Hopefully, since I could enter the Academy, Karma's eased off the harsh punishment." Beatrice crossed her fingers. "So, once Perrin returns, I'll try to reach the other Agents, and we can all put our heads together to formulate a plan of attack to stop Vlad."

"Two weeks to save my pops, Ellie May, the surviving mages, and to stop Vlad," Pepper reminded. "Two weeks until the solar eclipse on Winter Solstice."

"Correction. Less than two weeks if we leave Hell via Witherwhere. Time moves differently there, like water, and you can easily get carried away by the current. You better pick a day to exit, or it'll take measures into its own hands."

How lovely! "Seeing as how you swear Sawyer didn't expose your identity, do you have any idea why the Syndicate would be after you?"

"Maybe. My gran Ketteline was once the archOmega. And I mean, she was *the* archOmega for like ever. Older than—or she *was* older than dirt, too." Beatrice's face screwed up in pain from what Pepper guessed was grief. "That title has only ever been in the Budreau bloodline. My sister's destiny was to take over the reins, but she sewed her wild oats instead, as Mama had explained. So that responsibility fell on my shoulders. Until Karma Academy called. Then the title went to an outsider for the first time—that would be Ellie May."

"What does that mean, 'the Budreau bloodline?'"

"Supposedly, my ancestor was the first archOmega, which makes us the rightful heirs. If an archOmega dies, another one takes her place. And that summoning automatically defaults to a Budreau. It's been that way for centuries. What if —" Beatrice's tongue stopped flapping as if imprisoned by a frightening thought.

"What if we had it all wrong? That the Syndicate isn't after you because you're an Agent, but because you're a Budreau?" Something about that theory made sense and explained why nobody at the briefing had mentioned that Beatrice was an Agent. Chills broke out along Pepper's arms, matching Beatrice's.

Beatrice bolted off the couch and paced. "Josie's in danger! And she doesn't have any magic to defend herself!"

"No, no, no!" Pepper put her arms on Beatrice's shoulders, then looked her dead in the eyes. "Miles thinks he snapped Josie's neck. He didn't wait around long enough to realize it was a golem and to see it reanimate. Keep reminding yourself of that."

A look of fright ghosted over Beatrice's features. "No. I mean, Josie's trapped in a chaospocket. Stuck in a memory. For weeks now." Her hand flew to her mouth.

"Wouldn't she have woken up by now?"

While biting the inside of her mouth, as if considering Pepper's questions, she stated, "You're right. She was already fighting the potion before I left for the souk." Tears of relief trickled down Beatrice's cheeks, but she pulled herself together in no time flat. "Oh, jeez. Joes is gonna be so pissed at me."

The girls began pinging ideas off one another. Pepper asked what an archOmega did precisely. Beatrice said that she was second in command to Goddess Hekate and, as such, was granted godlike magical powers and handled all dimensions-wide mage matters.

"What if Karma was just the first? And Hekate is next in line?" Pepper posited. "We'd be fools if we thought the Syndicate would only go after one god."

"If they thought Karma was a force to be reckoned with and boss lady bitchy at times, Hekate makes Karma appear downright mousy." Beatrice appeared to reconsider her train of thought. "As of right now, I know for certain Hekate is alive for the simple reason we're still able to cast magic. My grandma once told me this story of Hekate throwing a hissy fit over some trivial matter and how she shut off all chaosgates and the use of magic until she calmed down. I'm sure Ellie May's disappearance would have caused Hekate to do far worse. So, the fact Hekate hasn't noticed something's awry …"

"Beatrice, that's not actually good news." Pepper's lips felt numb.

"I just thought of something," Beatrice breathed. "Before I share, I just want confirmation on one thing. You sure that was Ellie May you met in the dungeon and not a golem?"

Pepper wasn't sure, as anything could happen in the world of magic. "Let's say it was Ellie May."

"And they need a ton of magic for the ritual? That's what you overheard, right? And they're draining lowlies of their energy to put in receptacles for whatever else they have planned for Winter Solstice?"

Pepper nodded in response.

"Well, the archOmega's powers are absurdly strong. I'm talkin' the combination of every mage's powers and then some. Ellie May alone gives them a nuclear boost of pure magical energy."

"Yeah, but after what you just shared, capturing a Budreau would give the Syndicate access to much more power. What if they intend on killing Ellie May and crowning *you* the new archOmega? The rightful heir."

"Then doing what to me?"

"Decimating your bloodline once and for all."

"We need to warn Goddess Hekate," Beatrice said wide-eyed.

"How? Gods don't listen to petitions."

"At the crossroads—"

The door creaked open. "I bring goodies!" a Lolly'ka said. A cart with tentacles for "wheels" scampered behind her, carrying a pot of something hot, a thin trail of steam piping out, and various appetizers on a tray, hopefully not of the damned variety. "Mistress Quillee thought you might be famished. Well, I'll leave you to it. If you need anything else, just let me know. My name's Mooney."

"Actually, do you have a holo-gab I could borrow?" Beatrice asked.

"I do. Let me grab it. In the meantime, dig in."

Pepper and Beatrice dove in and sampled everything. Nothing savory, all sweet deliciousness. Candy-this, sugary-that. "Beatrice, you have got to try this!" Pepper said after biting into a tart, the fruit gushing out.

"Call me BB," she said while filling their dainty cups with tea infused with devilbee honey from the smell of it. Pepper's fingers barely fit through the cup's ear; it was that small.

"BB, I—" Nausea drowned Pepper's words, and her vision blurred. But she could still see Beatrice crash to the ground, her cup shattering beside her. Then lights out.

28

Pepper snapped awake and bolted upright from her previous fetal position. A gloomy pall of utter grayness hung over her surroundings, occluding everything from sight. Like the comforting aroma of rain, an earthy, fragrant scent wafted about, along with sweet notes of tobacco.

To ward off the bite in the air, Pepper went to cinch her wool cloak tighter, but she wasn't wearing it. So she reached for her messenger bag draped across her chest, where she had most likely stored it. But that, too, was missing, as were her ID, potions, and life-saving magic gems. Panic set in. So she reached for her messenger bag draped across her chest, where she had most likely stored her cloak. But that, too, was missing, as were her ID, potions, and life-saving magic gems. Panic set in.

How had Pepper wound up here, and where *was* here? Her mind felt foggy, like the mist that covered this strange place. Soon a dull ache spread across her forehead. When she rubbed her temples to alleviate the pressure, a memory surfaced. The last thing Pepper recalled was drinking hot tea with Beatrice and watching in horror when the Agent had slumped over in her seat.

And then terrifying thoughts struck Pepper down with a vengeance: *Am I dead?*

No-no-no-no! Pepper jumped to her feet, which stirred the pall and caused it to part like the Red Sea, revealing a spacious room decked out in rich cherry wood.

A crackling fire roared to life within a massive fireplace in the dead center of the space and warmed Pepper's frostbitten cheeks. She placed her hands near the dancing flames, and the heat went to town, warming her entire body while she looked around.

Leather-bound tomes rested on built-in shelves with rolling ladders, the titles in English and other languages. There were a smattering of tables with decks of cards, ornate chess sets, and other strategic board games set up, patiently waiting for players, but the swivel chairs were bereft of souls.

A fully stocked bar occupied the far corner, the bottles polished to perfection, the glassware shiny and waiting to be filled with spirits, sodas, and other whatnots. Pepper navigated that way and ran her finger along the shellacked surface. Not even the tiniest mote of dust covered her finger. So someone had to live here to keep this parlor squeaky clean.

Her attention alighted on a stone impression affixed to the wall of an overlapping upright and reverse V with a poppy flower in the center—all carved in relief, small in size, and unassuming in appearance. A plaque beside the impression said: HAVE A DRINK AND STAY A WHILE; HAVE ANOTHER AND SO LONG, FAREWELL.

Was this purgatory? Heaven? A place to knock back a drink and play a game before you walked into the light?

Pepper wasn't exactly feeling confident that she was merely dreaming. Or that she still had a pulse.

A ball of anxiety, she called out, "Hello? Is anybody here?"

Silence replied. Until murmurings emanated in a far-flung corner of the room. Call her crazy, but Pepper could have sworn she heard Jhi's voice and him saying Pepper's name. A single door appeared in that direction. Or had it always been there? It blended in seamlessly with the wood-paneled wall, after all. Regardless, Pepper padded toward it and wasted no time flinging open the door.

It *had* been Jhi's voice. It might not be who she had hoped for in her time of need, but seeing a familiar face was all it took to catapult Pepper over the threshold.

One step had delivered her to another room. Or not a room upon further inspection, but an apartment awash in every shade of black and gray imaginable. In fact, not a single color existed outside the monochrome sphere, except for Jhi and Pepper. She glanced back on her way out, but the doorway had disappeared, trapping her wherever she had ventured.

Looking worse for wear, Jhi sat on the concrete floor, slumped against a wall, legs sprawled out before him, a half-filled liquor bottle in his hand. He had wrapped bloodied bandages around his forearms. Nasty cuts marred his forehead—fresh cuts, at that. Ripped jeans covered his legs. Who knew what wounds were underneath, if any?

Good news: Jhi couldn't see Pepper.

Bad news: Pepper very well could be dead. And a ghost at that.

In a flash, Pepper's recent dreams flooded to the surface. Not fully fleshed memories, but bits and pieces of the dreamscapes starring Jhi began to fill in the gaping holes that the master thief himself had stolen from her memory bank. So ghostly Pepper had to play this delicately. Only now, she had the upper hand.

Pepper attempted to take a step toward Jhi, but shutters suddenly slammed on the windows and the front door, and some supernatural force boxed her in and glued her feet to an intricately drawn sigil that glowed a fiery red. She struggled to break free, even tried to slip out of her sneakers, but couldn't.

With that, her plan of the hunted becoming the hunter went up in smoke.

In short order, Jhi snapped out of his fugue, grabbed his quarterstaff leaning against the kitchen counter, and ran to the center of the room to take a look-see at the creature he had trapped. After hitting a switch on the weapon's side, it morphed into a rather nasty-looking scythe that he pointed directly at Pepper, who was no longer invisible. The trap that held her hostage must have cast a reveal spell.

The day keeps getting better and better!

It took Jhi a minute to comprehend who stood before him, his long lashes blinking nonstop, his brows drawn together. "Pepper?" he asked, a hint of a slur peeking through. A beat later, lucidity paid him a visit. "Oh, Seren! You're dead!" He seemed bothered by that turn of events, his eyes heavy with grief.

As for Pepper, she had an epic freak attack and began hyperventilating.

"Wait! You're not Pepper. What god sent you? Tell me right this minute, or I will eviscerate you on the spot!" The scythe entered the inner sanctum of the trap, its serrated edge touching Pepper's throat.

"Jhi!" Terror strangled Pepper's vocal cords, and she squeaked out, "It's me, Pepper." She put her quivering hands up in a gesture of surrender.

"You think I'm stupid? You better not have hurt even a strand of hair on Pepper's head. Now speak!"

Pepper thought long and hard for a sign that she could give Jhi to convince him it was her before he sliced her neck—which was challenging to do while in the throes of a massive anxiety attack. Something only she and he would know? "Jhi, listen to me. It's Pepper. *Scout's duty.*" She then reenacted Jhi's ridiculous rendition of the well-known salute that involved bungling up the hand gesture in a comically tragic fashion. Months ago, this same performance was part of Jhi's ruse to emotionally manipulate Pepper into trusting him after their first encounter, pretending to mix up the English language just like her pops.

By the grace of Seren, Pepper's plan worked. Jhi lowered his weapon and hightailed it to a panel on the wall. He must have triggered a kill switch because the security defenses disengaged. The shutters on the windows and doors raised, and the fiercely glowing sigil calmed down and returned to its invisible status.

Pepper jumped off the sigil and away from the center of the room.

Before she could ask a question, Jhi yanked back the black draperies, revealing a grayscale cityscape beyond, and barked, "What do you see?"

"Jhi, what're—"

"Answer me, Pepper! Please!" He seemed utterly terrified. And the Jhi she knew never succumbed to fear. So she stepped up to the windowpane and described everything: the overcast sky, an empty city, fog-carpeted streets, Old Haunts neighborhood bar across the avenue. In the distance, picture-perfect houses dotted the hill, and the sad-looking metal swing set perched underneath the leaveless oak tree, swings moving back and forth of their own accord.

"Do you see anybody?" he stressed every word.

"No! Jhi, you're freaking me out."

Before she knew it, Jhi tried to pull her into his arms—*tried* being the operative word. He couldn't. Not exactly. "Why are you not corporeal? I don't understand." His voice raised an octave, eyes bulging. "You swear you don't see any being outside?"

Pepper swore up and down emphatically that she saw nothing moving around outside. "Jhi, where are we? And why is there no color?"

He relaxed somewhat. "Necropolis. The Valley of Shades, to be exact. You'd see color and the streets teeming with ghosts if you were dead."

I guess it's a good thing I don't, Pepper thought, unsure how to feel. At least she wasn't dead. But did that mean—"And you can see them because ..." *Don't be dead. Don't be dead!*

"Because I can." He closed the blinds, then collapsed on the sofa. "Don't worry. I still have a pulse. But that won't be the case for much longer."

Pepper inspected her hands and arms. They looked fleshy and not transparent. But when she attempted to grab a knick-knack from off a shelf, she couldn't interact with it.

"Rub your shoes on the rug a few times and try again," Jhi offered, unfazed, then glugged down a shot's worth of booze.

His suggestion worked like a charm. After a few back-and-forth wipes of Pepper's sneakers on the area rug, a static charge thrummed through her fingers as she reached for the figurine.

This whole thing was too bizarre for words. Pepper had to be dreaming—the only logical explanation. Still, it felt so real. Upside, she could explore Jhi's digs to her heart's content, snoop, and be noisy.

Pepper walked around the room, giving it a cursory search. Several racks showcased dangerous-looking weapons. Curio cabinets housed ancient-looking artifacts, jewel-encrusted torcs, and various other jewelry, armor, and weapons. Sketches of relics and maps of other dimensions populated the walls. A curious object that resembled a crystal ball caught her attention. When she attempted to touch the glass, her finger traveled through it. So she rubbed her feet on the carpet once more.

While glancing at notes sprawled haphazardly on a table, Pepper asked over her shoulder, "How'd you get all those nasty cuts?"

"That's what happens when you wade through a swamp of pissed-off vipers. Narrowly dodge catapulted fireballs. Or not see the pitfalls on the floor beforehand. Good times! You enjoying yourself over there; find anything interesting?"

"Yes, and lots." *I'm definitely dreaming,* she thought, then homed in on a rough map drawing with an X marks the spot. "Cave of Altira'me-tum," she muttered.

Jhi collapsed on the sofa and took a pull of liquor. "That's where your sister signed my death warrant," he slurred, acid coating his tone.

In response to that doozy, Pepper breathed, "Weirdest dream ever. And I have you to thank for that. Don't I, Jhi?"

"Hate to break it to you, sweetheart, but you're not dreaming because I'm very much awake."

That reply rooted Pepper in place, shock cementing on her face.

"Still doesn't explain how you're here, though. Not that I'm complaining. But at least you're alive." Alcohol sure loosened Jhi's tongue. Good to know. Pepper could use that to her advantage.

Pepper turned around and lowered her shirt to show off the tattoo on her back shoulder, specifically the poppy flower courtesy of Jhi, and demanded answers as to why he had marked her and infiltrated her dreams.

"'Infiltrate?' Not a word I would have picked. How about

joining you in your dreams?" Pepper's narrowed eyes spoke volumes. "Okay. Infiltrate, sure. It doesn't matter anyways if you know the truth. I'm screwed eight ways to Sunday," he hiccuped, then took another pull.

"Are you drunk?"

"Not drunk enough."

"The flower, Jhi?" Pepper waved her hand in a gesture of "respond already."

"The tattoo spell. It was my partner's idea—a last-minute attempt. Friday wasn't sure he had marked you at the Starless Souk. As you recall, a lot was going on there at the time. We didn't even know if it would work." He snickered.

"Why the flower, Jhi?" Pepper's tone conveyed peak annoyance.

"Did you know that in the Spirit Realm—where you go while dreaming and where I think you are right now—it's impossible to lie, and enemies can easily extract secrets, mainly because your subconscious calls the shots?"

No, Pepper most certainly did not know that.

"We were down to the wire, and since you weren't forth-coming in your waking reality, I thought maybe if I visited you in your dreams, I could get you to tell me where your sister's hiding. Or I figured in the least that you two were meeting up in your dreams. It's not uncommon, especially for siblings. But I realized pretty damn quick—probably after our first encounter at the theme park—you didn't know where JD's at."

"If you've known all that time, why did you continue showing up in my dreamscape?"

He shrugged, then said quietly, "You have a calming effect on me. Make me forget the shitstorm that is my life. When we're together, I feel a sense of normalcy and, I guess, contentment. Is that the same thing as happy?" His brow knitted. "Not an emotion I'm used to. Bottom line, being with you is …"

Easy, Pepper thought, while Jhi verbalized the same thing.

"Were you thinking about me earlier?"

"Always," he said without skipping a beat.

If she wasn't dreaming, that left one other option: the Conscious Astraling potion must still be in her system, which explained how she wound up in Jhi's apartment. Not the curious room beforehand, as that remained a mystery for the time being, but at least some things made sense.

She stood in front of the couch and said to Jhi, "You drinking your sorrows away because of what you did?"

"'What I did?' Do tell." He seductively tapped the sofa cushion next to him. Then followed it up with his head dipping ever so slightly, his half-shuttered bedroom eyes reflecting carnal desire and pleasurable activities he was open to exploring with Pepper.

Pepper wanted to sidle up next to him. Greatly. *Damn him!* And double damn Pepper's thumping heart and stirring loins. She was supposed to hate him and did, as evidenced by her plotting his demise regularly. Making out with him was not part of the plan. So she took a step back. Then another. Until she was a safe enough distance away from temptation, her back rubbing into the front door latch.

"You broke Underlord Chaos out of Sheol and summoned the wrath of the gods in the process. Pretty dumb, if you ask me. What were you thinking?"

Shock-laced fright flittered about his arresting features before he chased them away with alcohol. "I was *thinking* that I had no other choice, and since your sister stole my escape plan, I had to figure out a way not to become a chew toy of the gods. Spoiler alert: call me Fido. You going to rat me out, Pepper?"

"That all depends. You going to tell the Syndicate who I am?"

"Worry not, sweetheart. Your secret's safe with me. If the Syndicate ever found out you're an Agent of Karma, it didn't come from my lips." He ran his index finger and thumb over his mouth to seal them. "Now, you gonna come over here or what? I'm not beneath begging. If I'm going to die, I know just how I want to spend my final hours." He finished with a wink.

Pepper ignored his question, but her loins sure didn't, as they were very much on board with his idea.

"But you work with the Syndicate?"

"'Work with?'" he harrumphed. "That's debatable. But not for much longer. No thanks to your *sister*."

"Why do you keep blaming her? What does Jaylyn have to do with any of this?"

He found that comical. "Uh, how about JD has *everything* to do with this. Your sister took something from me I desperately need. Not that it would make a lick of a difference now if I had it. Or maybe it would." He exhaled in a gesture of resignation. "Nah. It's only a matter of time until the gods find me."

And if they found Pepper here, she'd be pegged as an accomplice. "Dear God! Are they coming? Can they—"

"Want a drink? It will help with the nerves. Or we can do something a lot more fun?" He winked again, then got serious. "When the gods figure out it was me behind the prison break, because they will soon enough, they wouldn't come looking for me in Necropolis. The living aren't welcome in this dimension. I'm here because I got a hall pass. You're here because, well, you're not"—he looked her up and down—"let's go with whole."

Pepper relaxed. Somewhat. "Care to elaborate on what my

sister stole from you? Or why you risked your life to free Chaos?"

"'On the third night, the dragon devours the moon, and all the planets watch from the sky, the gods secretly assemble on the mighty mountain of Bel, and time slowly dies.'"

"It's a Vlad prophecy. But what about it?"

"*Ding! Ding! Ding!* Give the lady a drink." Gray liquid sloshed within the bottle Jhi held out to Pepper, which she turned down. "A thousand years ago, the gods met up in secret on Mountain Bel, an event that coincided with a lunar eclipse and the so-called impossible planetary alignment. You know what else occurred a thousand years ago?"

Pepper shook her head no.

"Underlord Chaos stumbled upon a cache of raw magic owned by the gods, its whereabouts unknown to this day. For centuries, beings have theorized how Chaos, a demon that dates back to Mesopotamia, could have stolen priceless magic from the gods. We're talking supreme primordial beings with more power than our mortal brains can conceive, more magic than demons, all the fae and mages combined?"

Captivated, Pepper begged for a response about how Chaos managed the unthinkable, her eyes bulging.

"Chaos couldn't, in theory. But what beings don't know is that during the meeting at the top of Mountain Bel, the gods hit the pause button on life, and time stops. A second before the time pause, there's a glitch in the matrix. It appears as a flash of light in the environment. You know when you shine a mirror in the sun?" Pepper nodded. "It's kinda like that. Anyways, you have exactly fifty-nine seconds to find this glimmer until the gods hit play on the universal remote. Now, get this. Hidden inside is a mirror image of the outside with one exception. It's like a mock city with no life. At least, that was the case for me. Can't even describe how weird it was inside. I've seen a lot of strange things in my life, Pepper, but that topped the list. Well, Chaos discovered that very glitch himself because of dumb luck. What I can't figure out is how he got back out."

"What happens after the fifty-nine seconds if you're still trapped inside?" Pepper asked, riveted.

"No idea. I was already courting death and wasn't about to give up the goods that easily." He smirked.

"So that lucky SOB stumbled upon the gods' secret chaospocket stuffed with what amounts to magical treasure while they were, what, out of office, if you will, and then ran wild around the cosmos, wreaking havoc?"

"Gold star for Pepper. Incidentally, while Chaos spread the magic around during his crime spree, he revealed to beings everywhere that the gods somehow hoarded magic and took it all for themselves. But it didn't belong to the gods in the first place. Magic is nature, and nature is magic. Nobody owns nature. Just like nobody owns magic. So how is it that the gods control it all?"

"You're painting Chaos as a demonic version of Robin Hood."

"He kinda was back then. He gave back magic to beings. Magic that was rightfully theirs, to begin with. Only they forgot. Don't get me wrong. Chaos did terrible things if you believe the gods. Who knows? The victors write history, and Chaos was on the losing side. Still, when Chaos accidentally exposed them, he angered the gods. So they had to get rid of him."

"Okay, but how does Chaos tie into the Syndicate's plans? Or my sister, for that matter?" Pepper finally succumbed to Jhi's continued efforts to join him on the couch and planted her bum on comfy cushions.

Jhi wore a wicked smirk and attempted to touch her knee, but his hand melted into her skin—a cold sensation that sent a chill rippling through her body.

"I'm getting there, she of little patience. 'On the fourth night, the dragon devours the sun as it stands still with the moon in the sky, the dragon destroys Night's ever curse and becomes Day's ally.'"

"Another Vlad prophecy?" Pepper's lips felt numb from dread.

"It sure is. Any guesses on what it means? If you're correct, I'll give you a kiss." His sultry eyes backed up his offer.

"Sun standing still with the moon? Hm." While contemplating, Pepper bit her thumbnail. "Is it referring to Winter Solstice?" When Jhi nodded in the affirmative, Pepper continued with the deciphering. "Destroying Night's ever curse … Oh"—she gasped—"are you seriously telling me Vlad has figured out a way to reverse vampirism, and it involves Chaos?"

"That's my best guess. And I say 'guess' because they've kept me in the dark about any future plans."

A chill skated along her skin. "That doesn't bode well for you."

"No, it certainly doesn't. But I'll tell you this much. Whatever they have up their sleeve, now that I delivered Chaos to them with a bow, the final prophecy is on track to being fulfilled."

The more Pepper thought about what Jhi had divulged, the more questions she had. Something wasn't adding up. She seriously contemplated snatching the liquor bottle out of Jhi's grasp and draining the last bits but instead asked, "Remember at the masquerade ball when Cazzian promised all the surviving soul-sellers magical powers and riches beyond their wildest dreams?" Jhi nodded. "Well, Cazzian's acting like the Winter Solstice ceremony will make all that happen. But how, when the prophecy seems to revolve around Vlad?"

"Not sure. Cazzian has every intention of keeping his promises, but from my understanding, they need to get past the Winter Solstice ritual before they focus their efforts on anything else—Wait. How do you know how Cazzian's acting? Unless you were the idiot that snuck inside Castle Dracula and almost got caught."

Pepper's lips pursed in a smirk, and she chased that with a shrug. "It's a good thing I did sneak inside. Anyway, Vlad believes Chaos can make all that happen, as in de-vampire him—you for real?" The more Pepper spoke, the more outlandish all this seemed. "I mean, the demon's been rotting in prison for like ever. That seems like a tall order." Jhi shrugged his shoulders. "So, what does Hekate have to do with all this? Obviously, the goddess knows Chaos escaped and what he's capable of and will stop him before he can wreak more havoc, right?"

"Before the gods captured Chaos—"

"While he was Robin Hooding?" When Jhi smiled, Pepper said, "Carry on."

"The magic took over the underlord as if it were sentient. Essentially, it turned him into a god. Because the gods couldn't kill him, Hekate locked him up in Sheol for all eternity. And kept that knowledge under wraps. From my understanding, the demon definitely has a bone to pick with them, especially Hekate and what he complained about ad nauseam after I broke him out of prison."

"Wait. If the gods chased Chaos around the cosmos, then why did the Ministry's Demons for a Better Tomorrow presentation mention how Chaos was an integral part of the peace treaty between Earth and Hell? In fact, his chaosgates, or rather sharing them with Karma and Earth, cinched the deal. Something's not adding up."

Jhi let loose a laugh. "Translation: Chaos took a plea deal after the gods incarcerated him in Sheol and gave up the goods for nicer living quarters, thanks to Mephy brokering the deal and sparing Chaos from Karma's wrath. And let me tell you. Compared to the nightmarish cells in Sheol that make the Pits seem like nirvana, Chaos had *sweet* digs. Opulent and spacious. Too bad he was trapped inside for all eternity. But Pepper, Demons for a Better Tomorrow are on Lucifer's payroll. That presentation is historical revisionism at its finest. It's what governments do best."

Pepper shook her head in disgust.

"Interesting fact: Hekate drained Chaos of his powers after the peace treaty signing. Shortly after, the Universal Elects appointed her as the goddess of magic and chaosgates to other dimensions. That's what Chaos told me verbatim. He said he waited for centuries to exact vengeance on Hekate and how the Shi'rue blessed day had finally arrived."

Pepper sat back, rested her head on the couch cushion, and stared at the ceiling, trying not to give into overwhelm.

"Here's the thing, Pepper. I'm just trying to stay alive, is all. Currently, I'm not exactly in Vlad or Cazzian's good graces. Case in point: I wasn't invited to attend their secretive Winter Solstice ceremony. So, unfortunately, I don't know how Chaos can manage the unthinkable or why they aren't worried about Hekate or the other gods striking them down."

Pepper turned her head to look Jhi dead in the eyes. "Why did you agree to do it?" What was Pepper not understanding? Couldn't he have told them to *GTFO?*

"Didn't really have a choice." When Pepper inhaled, ready to fire off a follow-up question, Jhi beat her to the punch. "Don't ask me any more questions on that topic because you won't get a response."

She exhaled. "Fine. But you've yet to explain what my sister has to do with any of this."

"I was so close to tasting freedom, Pepper, and that prison heist would take it away. From the get-go, I knew the mission was a death sentence. Sheol is buried underneath a lake of molten lava, for Seren's sake. So I had to act fast and figure a way out. Friday is a bit of a treasure hunter, and along his travels, he'd heard whispers of legendary relics and hadn't given them a second thought. Except for one, all because it was tied to the gods. We figured that if we could find this item, we'd trade it for my freedom."

"Who would you be targeting that could offer you freedom?"

"The gods. As for which one, take your pick. Legend has it someone hid the relic to protect humanity, Earth, and other dimensions from the gods." Jhi then shared the story of the first time he made JD's acquaintance in the Cave of Altira'me-tum, where they fought over the relic.

"Wait, so you're telling me Jaylyn left you, the storied Ven-ad'tsay, to die with no way out of that temple?" She didn't mean to pour more salt into his wound, but she could not get over how badass and ruthless her sister sounded. "And how in the world did you fight off all those wraiths and still get out alive?"

"Sweetheart, that's a story for another day. But know this: JD cheated," he said, half-joking. "I had to endure test after test, and she just chaosnauts inside the temple and summons the elements?" He donned a look of aghast. "No, not a fair fight."

"So that's how Jaylyn recognized you as the Hunter? When she had mentioned in the letter that the Ven-ad'tsay, *you*, had caught up to her?"

"No, that's where you're wrong. JD recognized me, and I'm not arguing that fact. But I don't know how she put two-and-two together regarding me being the Ven-ad'tsay. I've kept my identity hidden for years. So, when Vlad outed me at the masquerade ball, I was, well, let's just say I was none too pleased and leave it at that." Murder reflected in his sea-glass eyes. "You ready for the irony of all ironies? It turns out your sister doesn't even have the relic anymore. At least not according to Sawyer."

Pepper's heart revved. "Sawyer knows Jaylyn has the relic?"

"No," he slurred. "Jaylyn's dead, remember? At least as far as the Syndicate is concerned."

Relief sluiced down Pepper's shoulders. "Then why is Sawyer under the impression the relic's at the—" Pepper stopped herself from making a colossal mistake. "Wherever Sawyer's been searching for it?"

Jhi hadn't noticed Pepper's almost slip of the tongue. "No clue. Sawyer is under the impression it's hidden some*where*, not with some*one*. At least, that's what I gathered. She's been tightlipped on where she goes hunting, and I'm not sure how much longer they'll allow her to get away with that, especially Miles. He's taken a liking to her."

"You mean he wants to kill her?"

"Yeah, basically. But not before having fun with her. And when it comes to Vlad, Miles outranks Sawyer. Anyways, that's the least of my concerns. Right now, I have to figure out how to stay alive, starting with keeping my name out of the gods' mouths."

Pepper had so many questions that remained unanswered regarding Jhi. He had lied to her. Betrayed her. But the man she was talking to now seemed different. Like the Jhi she had first met. So which Jhi was real? He could still be lying for all she knew. After all, Pepper might not be able to tell a lie when she inhabited the Spirit Realm, but that wasn't the case for Jhi. Then again, he was pretty drunk, and since alcohol acted like a truth serum, she could use that to her advantage.

"But you can't deny that you knew who Jaylyn was all along, even though you said otherwise?"

"No, honest to Seren, I didn't know she was your sister.

When I first met her, I had a name to a face—JD—and that's all. I created a cover story that we were co-workers. That she was missing, and I needed to find her. Half true. At the time, I thought the soul broker connection was a harmless enough lie."

"Is that like your go-to cover?"

The devilish twinkle in his eye betrayed his silence. "Couldn't exactly tell you the truth. In my defense, I didn't see things playing out quite as they did. Then, shortly after you and I first met and teamed up at your home, guess who the Syndicate picked to break Underlord Chaos out of Sheol?" Jhi jerked a thumb at himself. "Me! I'm the *lucky* guy." He glugged down a shot's worth of liquor. "I knew it was coming, but I tried everything in my power to avoid it. So, while investigating Bhi'gow's disappearance in Hell and surveilling Skulduggerer's Lair for you, I took a side trip to the Pits in Gehenna to case the Fortress. There, I realized there was no way I'd survive the prison heist, so I focused all my efforts on finding JD, who held the key to my freedom."

"If it came down to it, would you have killed my sister for the relic?" Would he kill Pepper?

"Negative," he blurted. "I swear on Shi'rue's name." His eyes looked to the ground as if the goddess of misfortune aplenty were beneath his feet. "May the goddess strike me down with every curse imaginable if I'm lying. Scout's duty." He waved his fingers around in a sloppy attempt at the salute and finished with a smile. "I was only after your sister because she had the relic, and that was the only thing that could have saved my life. It had never crossed my mind to kill her for it."

Pepper wasn't sure if she had bought his response. What wouldn't she do if her life depended on it, or her father's? Would she kill?

"So, how did you break into Oblivion's Fortress, let alone Sheol, and make it out alive?"

Jhi held out an oblong vial dangling from a chain around his neck. "This is how JD chaosnauted inside the temple where the relic was entombed. She dropped it while running from a rabid wraith hot on her tail. And this is how I got into Sheol—that's covered by molten lava, by the way." As he shook the container, a sliver of reddish-gold matter swirled at the bottom. "Friday and I figured out that this nasty tasting concoction contains the blood of a god. Which god? No idea. But JD knows. What I can't figure out is why she stole the relic. I understand why I needed it, but why did she? She told me this was bigger than her and me. Which leads me to believe—"

"She caught wind of the prophecy, too?"

"That, or the god she's working for, did."

Could it have been Karma? Pepper wondered, then said, "What if it's not too late?" Jhi looked so pathetic and resigned that Pepper felt sorry for him, which confused her. One minute she wanted to kill him; the other console. "What if my sister could still help you? Can you tell me anything about this relic everyone's after, like, what it is, what it does?"

"Trust me when I say Friday and I did everything but sell our souls to track down the Yad Id'danos." Jhi blew out a heavy sigh.

"The Hand of Destiny," Pepper said softly, translating the word from Laramaic to English in her head.

"Someone hid it in a gods-forsaken realm hidden within a dimension in the far corners of the cosmos. As for what it does, nobody knows. The legends are all over the place. Some say it holds the secrets of the cosmos. Others swear it's nothing more than a talisman that can ward off evil. Honestly, I didn't care what it did. I just figured if gods would destroy civilizations in their quest for the relic, they'd surely offer me my freedom for it."

"That's not exactly true. Vlad and Cazzian must clearly know something about the relic's purpose; otherwise, why would they be looking for it?"

"Or they could need a certain god's skill for what they have up their sleeve, and like me, they planned on offering up the relic in exchange for just that."

"What does the Hand of Destiny look like?" Pepper tentatively asked, a part of her already suspecting the answer.

"It's a bone. Or, more specifically, a phalanx. Long and thin ..."

A tremble rippled through Pepper, and worrying thoughts drowned out Jhi. She couldn't get over how that description described what Kymeo had given her to a tee. Did she actually have a relic Jhi, the Syndicate, gods, and others were after?

"... thanks to JD, I didn't get much time to admire it."

"You're telling me that you and my sister unearthed a relic, and the gods and everyone else are none the wiser?" *If they know it's missing, does that mean they're going to hunt me down? What has that snark face Kymeo gotten me into?*

"Yep—Are your lips quivering?"

"Yes, it's cold in here," Pepper lied. Jhi tossed a throw blanket over her legs, which didn't exactly work, but she appreciated the gesture.

"The Hand of Destiny's been missing for months, and nobody knew. Well, until recently, when the snarky liminal lesser god Aeolus discovered that the relic he was supposedly charged with ensuring never got found went missing on his watch." Teeth clenched, Jhi blew in air through his mouth as if faux wincing on Aeolus' behalf. "Now, Aeolus is in a full-blown panic because he doesn't know when it was stolen or by who."

"If the gods are champing at the bit to get their hands on the relic, it must be all-powerful and dangerous." Pepper felt light-headed, her anxiety kicking into overdrive, knowing her satchel and the Hand of Destiny were *not* in safekeeping. "Why wouldn't Aeolus want it as well?"

"I couldn't tell you. You know as much as I do now."

Pepper harkened back to when Perrin had summoned Aeolus back in Georgia, and the Wind Keeper was in a tizzy verging on a raging tempest over something that had gone missing.

"Someone Aeolus trusted—one of the lesser Wind gods—broke rank and joined the Syndicate," Jhi said. "By the way, that's who discovered that the relic was missing and reported the news to Vlad. Pepper, this Syndicate is insidious. They have moles everywhere, in every dimension. Nowhere is safe."

"Not even Necropolis?"

"It is. For now. But Pepper, I can't stay here forever." He readjusted his position so he could look her in the face. "I can't walk outside without being spotted. Nor can I stay holed up in this apartment forever. I've done things I'm not proud of. Hurting you, for one. And you deserve answers. Answers I can't give you. Not because I don't want to, but because I can't. But know this. I did what I had to do to survive, and maybe one day after I'm gone, you'll discover the truth." Jhi spoke as if declaring his deathbed confessions.

"Jhi, stop. You're acting like you're already dead. Since when are you a quitter?"

"The last thing I deserve is a pep talk, Pepper. I've done questionable things that I'm sure haven't escaped Karma's notice. Who knows, maybe I'm getting my karma now. But I didn't have a choice when it came down to it, so maybe the goddess would give me a break. Care to put in a good word for me?" he half-joked.

"There must be a way out of this. What makes you so convinced the gods will discover it was you? If the Syndicate turns you over to them, they implicate themselves, so—"

"Not necessarily. Vlad and the others don't have blood on their hands. Nor can I prove they hired me. And they could turn me over to the gods, sure. But I don't see how that would benefit them. Vlad'll most likely blackmail me and force me to work for the Syndicate. Back at square one." Jhi said the latter under his breath.

"Jhi, you're looking at this all wrong. If I were a god, I'd want the head of the man who hired you, not his lackey. No offense."

"None taken. But, Pepper, after Winter Solstice, the Syndicate'll be on a level playing field with the gods, if not more powerful. I overheard them say that myself. Do you see now how screwed I am? One of my biggest regrets is that you and I were never allowed to be together without Armageddon erupting all around us. We could try again in another life, but I don't think that'll happen for me." Jhi tried to touch her hand and sighed when he couldn't. If only she were whole.

Frustrated, Jhi left the couch, entered the kitchen, and began rummaging through cabinets.

A sharp pang of regret strangled Pepper's heart, so she attempted to grab the liquor bottle in her hands and couldn't. But that status changed after she swiped her feet on the carpet and generated a static charge. Bottle in hand, she swilled the dregs. Without warning, painful shockwaves coursed through her body as if she had stuck her finger in a live outlet. Her heart stopped beating, then picked back up as she struggled to catch her breath.

On autopilot, she strode into the kitchen and closed the distance between her and Jhi. "What are you doing?"

"Cashing in on that kiss you owe me," she said boldly, courtesy of the Spirit Realm.

Jhi's mouth curved into a sly grin, his eyes reflecting want. He lowered his head and brought his lips dangerously close to hers. "It's torture not being able to kiss you."

Pepper reveled in his warm breath that tickled her skin and longed to feel his arms around her.

Unable to help himself, when Jhi reached out to touch her and could, he jerked back and slipped into a look of utter shock.

Pepper wore the same expression. No longer ghostly, Pepper didn't care to ponder the how and grabbed one of his belt loops. Then she wrenched him to her.

Numerous sighs communicated how much she reveled in feeling the warmth of Jhi's hands as they moved up her arms, then gently tucked strands of hair behind her ear—his eyes locked intensely on her all the while.

"I can finally touch you." Jhi kissed Pepper's cheek as his greedy hands adventured down her back and pulled her closer to him. "And appreciate every inch of your body." He gently sucked on her neck. "Your curves." His hands moved down lower, over her hips, and he squeezed her tush.

Jhi's lips returned to hers after they finished exploring her neck, his tongue melding with hers. They passionately kissed as if it were their last time together. Pepper melted into him, her hands venturing through his tousled hair, down his back, to his bum. The want and need and desire taking over. Jhi's lips felt sublime, his touch even better. Their kissing reached a fever pitch.

Jhi helped Pepper to the counter, and she wrapped her legs around his torso, her thighs pulling him ever closer to her, snuffing out all space between them. His mouth not leaving hers, their moans sensual, their breathing heavy, a sense of urgency taking over his fingers as he hurriedly unbuttoned her jeans.

Lightning fast, Pepper tore off Jhi's shirt, and he helped

Pepper do the same. Her hands couldn't unbuckle his pants fast enough, and her feet pushed them down his legs. Jhi no sooner kicked them off as if the denim was on fire—

An alarm chimed, interrupting what Pepper and Jhi were moments from doing. Out of breath, he ran in his boxer shorts to the device on the other side of the room.

Whatever he had read caused him to look over at Pepper, worry etched all over his features. "Friday intercepted chatter between the Hounds. He said they got a lead on Beatrice in Hell. But that was about an hour ago. They said nothing about you. Are you with her?" Jhi's facial expression matched his frantic tone.

Pepper nodded but couldn't speak and felt the world spinning. Hurriedly, she readjusted her half-snapped bra, then slipped into her shirt that had been tossed to the floor. Buttoning her jeans turned into a struggle, her shaking hands to blame.

Jhi ran to her and handed her a flask from the pantry. "Drink. It'll calm your nerves."

She knocked down the gray concoction, and waves of electricity thrummed through her being, turning her back into a ghost.

No time to ponder the strange aftermath of being whole one minute, incorporeal the next, Pepper said, "If they get Beatrice, then chances are they'll get me, too. Then I'll have no way to save my father."

"Dammit, Pepper!" He paced, his fingers running through his unkempt locks. "We must get you back to your body before they find you. If they already haven't." He then ran through scenarios out loud. "If by chance they have you, I could sneak into Vlad's castle, but then I'd risk death. The gods monitor all access points of entry into every dimension, making my odds of survival less than one percent."

"If they found me, will you please help me rescue my father?"

He stopped and spun around to look Pepper dead in the eyes. "But your father isn't in danger."

Pepper took great exception to that and heatedly explained to Jhi that Miles torturing her father to his last breath wasn't her idea of "not in danger."

Jhi was outright stunned and made it clear that the Syndicate lied to him. "Vlad told me they were holding your father as insurance until you returned something of Cazzian's. Pepper, I swear."

"They lied to your face. Ellie May informed me they plan to kill her, the rest of the mages, and my pops."

"Who's Ellie May?"

Pepper did a double-take. "The archOmega. How do you not know this?"

Jhi ran his hands over his face. "They have the archOmega? Shit! Pepper, this isn't just some vampire curse-breaking ritual, then. I've been so focused on getting out of the prison break—How could I have been so utterly blind?" He placed his hands on her arms, and they melted into hers, his warmth replaced by coldness. "Listen to me. Stay away from the castle. Do you hear me? We'll figure out how to get you back to your body, and then you have to run and hide. I'll take care of your dad. I promise."

"How? If you return to Naples, the odds of surviving are stacked against you. You said so yourself, not even a minute ago—"

A Hoover-like force sucked Pepper through time and space and tossed her back into her body with a thud. Her leg jerked as she snapped to.

"Bell! Get up!" Kimball's breath hitched. "We have to run!"

29

"Your body just up and disappeared"—Kimball waved his hands about crazily—"and I thought I was a goner. Never do that to me again." He chased that command by lightly smacking her arm.

"Ow, Kimball! That hurts!" Kimball's swat managed to agitate the already throbbing and fiercely stinging wounds from her battle with Sawyer.

No longer groggy, Pepper took in her dimly lit environment. Volcanic glass made up the floor and ceiling. Vertical bars surrounded her, trapping her and Kimball and—

Gasping for breath, Pepper choked out, "Where's Perrin and Beatrice?"

"Gone. Like our bags and possessions and money."

Pepper's heart lost its way and couldn't remember how to stay regular. Her satchel with everything she needed to survive in Hell had been stolen, including the Hand of Destiny.

"I'm pretty sure the Lolly'kas poisoned you and Beatrice. You both were KO'd when I woke up. When I refused to drink the tea, evil dolly rained holy hell down on me. Damn, Bell. You should have seen her get all crazed. She soared through the air and knocked me out with some freaking possessed toy. It was bonkers. Then I woke up inside this jail cell."

"How long have I been out?"

"Not sure. I only came to not that long ago. Nobody's been here to check on us. At least, not since I've been awake."

Pepper shook the bars. But they wouldn't give. There wasn't even a door to break out of, so magic was at play. And without gems—

A door creaked open in the distance, and shafts of light lanced through the opening. A being entered the room, its face obscured by a hood, then quietly shut the door behind it.

"You have to get us out of here," Kimball whispered. His dung-hued eyes couldn't possibly open any wider.

Once the stranger reached the jail cell, they lowered the hood of their cloak.

Pepper wasn't sure if Kirby was a welcome sight or not. But then quickly amended her thoughts when the Lolly'ka commanded the bars to bend, allowing Pepper and Kimball to exit.

"Hurry!" Kirby whispered, waving her dainty hands for them to follow her. "They're coming for you, Pepper." She handed over their belongings. Kimball and Pepper swiftly slipped into their cloaks and secured their bags on their bodies.

Kirby hurriedly sketched a hopscotch grid on the floor and told them the numbered sequence. "If you mess it up, you're dead."

"What happened to Perrin and Beatrice?" Pepper wasn't about to leave without getting answers.

The door slammed open, and angry voices carried in the air. Then a voice growled, "Bring me the prisoners!"

Kirby pressed a piece of paper into Pepper's palm. "Go. Now!"

Pepper stuffed the paper into her cloak pocket, grabbed Kimball's hand, and they jumped on the grid together—three, five, two, seven, four, nine. A whoosh, a whirling, and a stomach-churning spin later, they landed in a butcher shop. Inside an industrial-sized freezer, to be exact. Twenty bodies of the damned hung on hooks. All naked, baying and begging for release.

Kimball couldn't tear his eyes away from a trail of blood leading to the door that marred the floor. "Bell, we're gonna die, aren't we?"

"Not today." Not before Pepper rescued her pops. "Now, cover your crazy hair with the hood and follow me."

"Where are we going?" His voice cracked.

"Anywhere but here." She slowly popped the freezer door open and checked around the corners.

Shouting from the front of the store stopped Pepper dead in her tracks. "Shut the fuh'kar up, Morris, and listen to the words coming out of my mouth!" The voice unmistakably belonged to queenpin Quillee. "Have you seen two humans? One male, the other female? The female is number one on DISI's Most Wanted list. We traced their whereabouts here, so if you know something and don't vomit it up, I'm calling the mala'khas on your pathetic ass." Quillee then updated her team, and from the sounds of it, they weren't by Quillee's side but outside on the streets of Pandæmonia, surveilling, lying in wait.

"We have to go!" Kimball was unraveling by the second.

When butcher Morris, wearing a damned-skin apron and wielding a bloodied cleaver, locked the front door, Pepper grabbed Kimball's hand and bolted in the opposite direction while hazarding glances over her shoulder every few seconds.

The back door squeaked as it opened, and Pepper and Kimball dashed out of the butcher shop and into a populated alleyway, using the crush of the crowd as cover.

A dance club resided feet away, but nothing else was within reach. On one end of the alley, a straggly haired, grotesque-looking ghoul on the Lolly'ka's payroll flickered in and out of sight, only to appear an arm's length away from Pepper, so close she could smell the stench of death and decay on its breath. A dress-wearing Lolly'ka blocked the other end of the alley. Both parties were searching for their prey. Luckily, the throng camouflaged Pepper and Kimball from their sight.

Only one option remained for escape. Pepper yanked Kimball toward THE FURNACE, written in neon lights that pulsated, keeping in rhythm with the syncopated beat of the techno music booming within. They bypassed beings of all shapes, breeds, and sizes, loitering outside, leaning against the obsidian glass walls, smoking cigarettes wrapped in the skin of the damned, the noxious smell of charred flesh and hellfire commingling in the airwaves.

They skirted past the preoccupied bouncer and slunk inside as he yelled at demons to get back in the line. The nightclub was hopping and filled to the brim with dressed-to-the-nines patrons that ran the gamut from hornless humanoid devils with mangled limbs and hollowed eyes to succubi and fae, bubbling bloodtinis and smoking concoctions occupying their chic glassware.

Bursts of fireballs, spitting flames, and other theatrical special effects nearly scorched Pepper's cloak when she stepped on the dance floor's periphery. As if synchronized, flames ignited on the walls and bar counter. Screams of abject pain and terror ripped from the throats of the damned before they were tossed inside the fire-licked furnaces and burned alive by towering demons that looked awfully similar to the mala'khas—the same soul-collecting assassins searching for Pepper.

Above, suspended cages held the damned. Unlike go-go dancers back on Earth, these humans were whipped and chained, hooks and nails ripping through their flesh. *Dance for us, soul-sellers. Dance until you can't anymore, and then you're burned alive or flayed*—because that, too, was on the menu.

The Furnace hosted beings aplenty, but not humans. Humans were not welcome here and were used solely for entertainment. With that realization, Pepper slipped her hood further down over her face and whispered for Kimball to do the same.

Pepper searched high and low for an exit and spotted one in the far distance. Slight problem: a beefy horned demon-human hybrid blocked the doorway. He cut a frightening figure, wearing a damned-skin duster, a gun holster housing two revolvers barely noticeable underneath, and a double-barrel shotgun strapped to his back. In his human hands, he waved a wanted poster of Pepper and Perrin in front of the faces of club-goers. Thank Seren, they didn't appear interested in helping out the bounty hunter.

Still, Pepper had seen enough. She held tight to Kimball's hand, but it slipped out of hers, the sweat too overpowering. Dancers smothered the space, swaying and jumping and slamming their heads to the syncopated beat. The sound was so deafening that Pepper couldn't warn Kimball that a mercenary was hot on their heels. So she grabbed his sleeve and tugged him onward. They weaved through the crowd without being seen while she kept her eyes fixed on the hulking man.

Pepper and Kimball tried their hardest to mimic the jerky dance movements to blend in. When the bounty hunter stood at the edge of the dance floor, his eyes sweeping across the venue, Pepper ducked and yanked Kimball down with her. While crouched, they made a run for it.

At the massive floor-to-ceiling door, Pepper and Kimball barreled through it as it pivoted open and then landed on one of the main streets of Pandæmonia. Honking horns and screaming drivers sounded from every which way. Escortless baby carriages strolled down the avenue with slithering tentacles pocking out. Demons that bore striking similarities to humans strode past, all wide-eyed and wearing a forever smile. Still, when you looked at them from the corner of your eye, their features morphed into something else entirely frightening and demented.

A gang of Lolly'kas appeared, all riding powder-pink, hovering soul cycles, the motors growling and spitting as the girls sped toward Pepper and Kimball. After coming to a screeching halt at a stoplight, the evil dollies darted their heads back and forth, searching for their escaped prisoners, all while hand signaling to gargoyles that weaved in and out of towering skyscrapers as they patrolled the bruised-looking skies.

While trying to get a bead on the goyles, pinkish raindrops fell on Pepper's face and tongue, a metallic tang trickling down her throat. "It's dusk." Urgency kicked up a notch. "Kimball, we have to find someplace to hole up before night." Before the heavily populated streets thinned out.

The bounty hunter rounded a corner, whistling. Pepper dragged a clueless Kimball to an alcove in front of a clothing store and hid behind the wall, sneaking glances every few seconds, then raked her eyes over the bustling area, looking for a way out, and spotted a parking garage at least thirty blocks in the distance. Hopefully, it would be the same one she had visited with Jhi after escaping an ambush at the Ministry of Mischief and Mayhem. She briefly filled Kimball in on the plan of action.

"Let's say we manage to Frogger our way across the busy road without being squashed. How do you plan on getting past the Lolly'kas and the bounty hunter?" Kimball pointed at two half-pint Mafiosos that weren't there moments ago, conversing on the street corner outside a confectionary shop with massive-sized rainbow-swirl lollipops and other candies on display in the window.

Well, so much for Pepper's bright idea of crossing the intersection. "Uh … we'll just stick to the back streets."

Pepper and Kimball waltzed into the establishment like proper Pandæmonians, looking for new threads. All eyes were on the newly arrived—eyes belonging to the damned. Like security cameras, their heads pivoted in Pepper's direction, their faces all conveying the same plea for help. The damned served as mannequins and hangers in the store. Clipped to bars and stacked single-file, they all donned different sizes of suits, dresses, and outerwear, their feet dangling off the floor.

The clerks busied themselves helping a roomful of patrons, which enabled Pepper and Kimball to sneak through the backroom and out the back door.

A patrolling gargoyle caught Pepper in its sights and swooped down.

"Run, Kimball! And don't stop!"

The goyle dove, its wings tucked underneath, its speed mushrooming.

Pepper's legs pumped as fast as they could, her lungs burning and her muscles screaming in protest. But stopping equaled death. Kimball outran Pepper, his soccer-player legs carrying him onward as he got farther and farther away.

The gargoyle hissed, its forked tongue flickering in and

out of its mouth as it cut Pepper off at the pass, and she smacked right into its hard chest plate. Before she could scream, it yanked her into a dark alley, then blocked the entrance—the only way out. Its silvery green slit eyes widened and then narrowed.

As it hovered before her, its fluttering gunmetal and black bat wings generated gusts of wind that blew back Pepper's already tangled locks, and the goyle growled, "It's me, Trixie. Don't put up a fight, and you'll live another day."

Pepper noted blood and open wounds marring Perrin's number one bodyguard's leathery skin as a smile of relief ghosted over Pepper's lips.

"We're outnumbered." Trixie looked up to the gargoyle-infested sky. "So follow my lead." Before Pepper could even nod, Trixie plucked Pepper up with her taloned feet.

While soaring above the bustling streets, Pepper pointed to Kimball in the distance, then asked Trixie to deliver them to the parking garage. Faster and faster, they glided, and Trixie winged down and snatched a running Kimball by the back of his cloak.

"How did you know where to find us," Pepper asked, trying to hide her suspicion.

"Kirby alerted me after she helped you escape, and I've been looking for you ever since. Do not trust the other goyles you see patrolling," Trixie rumbled—a goyle's normal tone—then continued enlightening Pepper as they soared above Pandæmonia's congested roads on what had happened to her and her gargoyle sisters. "They and the Lolly'kas turned on Mistress Perrin and us. Ambushed me, Minx, Gamble, and Vixen before we reached the Tenth Circle Tavern on our way to take you all to safety. I barely got away and have been lying low ever since."

"Do you know what happened to Perrin?"

Trixie growled, "No. She's unreachable. I fear they killed her."

Pepper's heart plummeted to a new depth.

Up and up, they traveled, bypassing level after garage level until they reached the penultimate floor. Certain death awaited those who fell from this high of an elevation. Or those who weren't charioted by a gargoyle taxi service.

Trixie ejected the duo onto the squishy floor and said, "I must go. You're on your own from here. Seren-willing, I'm wrong, and Mistress Perrin is alive; when you find her, tell her I'll be waiting. She'll know where." Then the captain flew off.

The ordinarily loquacious duo stood for a beat in utter silence, their mouths opened wide from shock, their eyes doing the talking. Pepper was the first to speak. "From here on out, we stick together no matter what and watch each other's backs. Okay?"

Kimball nodded, then reached for Pepper's hand, which she accepted without a second thought, and squeezed. "Do you think Perrin's dead?"

"I refuse to believe she is." If Pepper gave it any more thought, she'd succumb to a panic attack like no other, so she said a prayer and carried on.

A hexagonal grid resembling honeycombs served as parking spots with soulcars nestled within—exactly how Pepper had remembered. Now how to find Jhi's exact car in a sea of lookalikes? Pepper closed her eyes and focused, recalling her and Jhi's precise movements and reenacted them, all while tuning out a prattling Kimball who kept pace with her. When she reached the spot, the car was gone.

"Fantastic plan, Bell. Now what?"

"Now we steal a car."

"Stealing a car in Hell? Would we get rewarded or flayed alive?"

Pepper hadn't recalled keys being used or needed for driving. Perhaps they used the honor system in Hell. Or maybe they feared the consequences of thievery and opted to stay on the up and up.

"We'll abandon the soulcar after we get out of Pandæmonia. The gargoyles are on the Lolly'ka's payroll, Kimball. I'm sure they already notified Quillee that they spotted us."

"That's all I needed to hear." Kimball dove into the convertible.

Pepper got behind the wheel and prayed to Seren for more of her luck before pressing the only button on the dashboard. When the soulcar fired up, the damned screaming in abject pain as they bounced about the combustion chamber, she exhaled a sigh of relief.

"I'd hate to spend eternity as one of them." Kimball low-whistled.

Unsure of what to do next, Pepper pressed her feet down on the weighty rudder pedals, then pulled back on the yoke, and the vehicle levitated but wouldn't move forward or back, so she released the pressure on the rudders and advanced the throttle in the center console—that did the trick. Pepper navigated the car out of the honeycomb poorly. The car ran into the walls. Luckily, they were cushiony. Eventually, she got the hang of driving, but the real test of her strength and determination resided feet away—where the road ahead abruptly ended.

"Oh God, Bell! What are you doing?"

"I suggest you hold on." Pepper dipped the yoke and readjusted the pressure on the rudders. The car juddered and zipped forward—straight toward the sheer drop twenty-odd stories down. Pepper white-knuckled the yoke and held her breath as the car zoomed off the edge and soared. But then stopped and dropped. Down and down they fell, faster and faster—

"Bell! The throttle!" A scream tore through Kimball's throat.

Panicking, Pepper adjusted the throttle and held tightly to the quivering yoke, steadily moving it up. The soulcar halted about two feet from the volcanic glass road.

Just when Pepper thought she had gotten the hang of driving the hovering soulcar, Kimball yelled, "Let up on the gas, Bell! You're gonna run over that egghead!" Kimball pointed at the faceless demon on the sidewalk that Pepper had clipped with the car; his briefcase fanned open, papers flying everywhere. The egghead's shadow-self waved its hands in obscene gestures.

"I'm sorry," Pepper said as they zipped past.

At a roundabout, Pepper drove in circles, unsure which turn to take, all while trying to remain as inconspicuous as possible—hard to do when in a convertible. But when she spotted Lolly'kas down the streets of all the exits but one, Pepper veered off in the direction of Vale of Naraka.

Once the cityscape vanished in the rearview mirror, she breathed a sigh of relief. The frigid night air gave way to heat and sticky humidity reminiscent of Naples springs and summers and falls and part of winters. But Pepper would take heat over cold any day. Red soil mantled the terrain as far as the eye could see. The tops of pyramids dotted the landscape. Firebushes hugged the road and spat out flames that further exasperated the climbing temperature.

"I'm hot and hungry and thirsty and tired," Kimball whined.

"Join the club."

"You don't have a plan, do you?"

"Other than keeping us alive, no." A feeling of doom befell Pepper with the realization that her allies were gone and she had nowhere to run. Until now, she had always dug her way out of a hole. But not this time. There would be no escaping Hell.

While Kimball kept a lookout on the roads behind them, Pepper focused on the road ahead and stewed in silence, dreading the inevitable moment of her capture. Make no bones about it—it was coming and soon.

30

Atown unfurling ahead stole Pepper's attention as she passed through an intersection in the middle of nowhere, and she failed to see the damned-drawn carriage swinging onto the road. Pepper swerved out of the way, narrowly avoiding a collision.

The perturbed coachman yelled, "Hee-ahh," and whipped the chained-together damned to pick up the pace, their skin lacerated, their bare feet ragged, bloodied, and raw.

Before veering down the store-lined main street, Pepper steered the car off the road and parked it about a quarter of a mile away. "Grab your things, and let's go."

"You sure we should just abandon it here?"

"Who knows if they have a tracker, Kimball? We can always find another car. Besides, before I pass out, we need to get food or something."

It turned out that nighttime dining wasn't a thing in B'aR-QoA'ba-ruch. The restaurants and stores closed up shop for the evening. Not a single demon roamed the streets. The only light other than flickering hellfire street lamps emanated from a standalone temple. Discordant chimes lilted as if beckoning wayward strangers. So, they hotfooted it that way.

Bleached bones made up the arched entrance of the blindingly white temple—the pathway, too, along with trails of viscera. But Pepper didn't bat an eyelash because demons always offered damned sacrifices to the gods. But which god did they worship here?

The door whispered open, and candles flickered to life as the newly arrived entered the inner sanctum. A life-size sculpture on a dais depicted a woman with three heads, each of her features unique yet similar: young, middle-aged, and old. An offering of oatmeal mixed with red wine was spread at her feet.

"Maiden, Mother, Crone," Kimball recited while soaking up the deity's visages. "I believe this is Goddess Hekate."

"How do you know?"

"AP literature. Sorry your grades weren't good enough to reach advanced placement status."

"Huh. So, the temple worships Hekate, but for what? To get her blessing to use magic in a place that forbids it? What a waste of time."

Nobody and nothing appeared or greeted them, save for a dish of food. A HELP YOURSELF sign stood proudly behind the plate.

"Any idea what this food is?" Kimball said hesitantly.

"What breed, you mean? Y'know, I'm so hungry, I'm not even sure I care."

Kimball gingerly held a severed finger. "You sure about that?"

"I take it back. Stick with the things that look like wings and non-human appendages."

Utterly silent, the duo satiated their grumbling bellies,

shoveling everything into their mouths, their chewing and moans obnoxious.

Kimball took a break from masticating and produced a bottle from his backpack. "Swiped it at the club. Want a sip?"

Why not? Pepper thought and gulped down the edge-blunting contents. At first, the hot pepper-like heat burned her throat, but the sour fruit aftertaste soothed it.

Once their bellies were full, hearts distracted, and minds intoxicated and feeling no pain, the duo broke out into gales of laughter from anything and nothing.

"Ew, Kimball." The smell of his gas was stomach-churning. "Don't do that again."

"My ass is a tempest that will not be tamed."

While disgusted, Pepper let loose a muted laugh, then said, "Can you believe we're here? In some temple, trapped in Hell?" Even saying that felt unreal.

"No. You know what else I can't believe?" Kimball said with a slight slur. "How big some of the Lolly'kas' foreheads were."

Pepper hiccuped while giggling, then considered further what he had said. "I have a big forehead."

"Bell, you have a five-head. But unlike you, Quillee isn't using bangs to cover up all that real estate. And don't get me started on her mouth. It's a graveyard of teeth. Looks like she ate an ink pen."

"She's such a bitch. Can't believe she almost killed us."

"*Almost* being the operative word. I love how pissed Quillee is that we escaped."

They giggled and drank more, the pain, fear, and overwhelm bested, for now.

"What is this?" Pepper held out the bottle and read the label: "Gi'HOmaYaa."

"Eliminator of troubles." Kimball took back the bottle, gulped down the dregs, then rested his head against the wall. "Last sip is all yours." Kimball handed the bottle to Pepper.

"You're such a gentleman." Pepper drowned the last drop. "Ow. What the ...?" Pepper rubbed away the smarting pain from something digging into her skull, then looked at the culprit—bleached bones plastered to the wall. The duo broke out in paroxysms of laughter.

Once their chuckling attack subsided, Pepper asked, "What happened to us? Like, why did you turn on me?" A few tears, of their own accord, welled in Pepper's eyes from painful memories of the past, of the demise of their friendship.

"I don't know. Because I could. You're an easy mark. Or maybe you knew too much about me. I don't know, Bell. We have different interests. We're no longer kids, playing knight and princess, storming castles, and rescuing fair maidens anymore."

"Yeah, but that doesn't give you the license to dish out such cruelty. You've said some truly horrible things to me about my body. My chubby face, as you called it. Poked fun at my jiggly thighs. You hurt me to the core."

"I'm sorry." His tone softened.

"And then when I tried to help you and ended up getting arrested—" Disgust stilled Pepper's flapping tongue. Until now, the opportunity to address this topic or get closure with Kimball hadn't presented itself, which only fortified the hate she harbored against him.

"I didn't force you to help me by hiding the drugs."

"No, you didn't force me. But you lied. You didn't tell me there were drugs in the bag."

"Would that have changed things?"

"Yes. I might have gotten arrested for my own dumb shit after that, but drugs, Kimball? That's low, even for you.

Driving without a license pales in comparison to drug charges."

"Bell, c'mon. It was more than DWL. Still, you don't understand. You never will."

"I do, though. I know what you've never shared with me or anyone else, I imagine." Pepper recalled the times when she had overheard Kimball from her bedroom, begging his father to leave him alone. She remembers wincing and tearing up when she heard bottles breaking. The sound of Shelly's belt snapping in the air and his hand hitting flesh. Or how her dad swore he would beat the living crap out of Shelly, but Pepper would plead with him to stop. To not call the cops or march over to the Garcia residence. She knew Shelly wasn't wired correctly and didn't want anything to happen to her pops.

Despite all that, she never revealed to Kimball that she knew the cold, harsh truth. Nor did she want to risk embarrassing him because that's how Kimball would have reacted. So, she kept it to herself all these years and tried to protect him however she could. That was why it had stung when Kimball turned on her and publicly humiliated her around his friends. When he had used her as a verbal punching bag. Why it had cut her soul deep when Kimball allowed Pepper to take the blame for a crime she hadn't committed.

When the cops had raided Naples High, Pepper was at her locker and noticed Kimball panicking, a look of pure fear in his eyes. Not because of the vice and narcotics cops swarming the school, but because of Shelly. Pepper, who hated Kimball with a fiery passion, made a snap decision and agreed to help him when he pleaded with her in the school hallway. Kimball slipped something from his locker—a brown bag, its contents concealed from sight. He said the contents were something he stole from the principal's office and asked if she could help him hide it.

At that moment, Pepper saw her childhood best friend and didn't ask questions. She didn't think twice when she took the wrapped item. A short time later, cops caught her red-handed, hiding the baggie in the toilet tank. Little did she know it was drugs or that Kimball and his friends were the focus of the sting operation.

She'd never forget Kimball standing on the sidelines, watching with all her classmates as the police escorted Pepper from the school in handcuffs.

"My father would have beaten the shit out of me if I were arrested," Kimball said. "And probably then would have hit my mom for trying to stop him. It would have been bad."

"Oh, yeah? Well, that was the day I severely disappointed my pops. Seeing his face when he picked me up at juvie killed me. The rub for him: he couldn't believe I'd be stupid enough to help you. Especially after all the times he had comforted me when I came home from school crying because of you and your friends. It floored him that his child would put a jackhole's freedom over her own. And he's right. You never acknowledged what I did for you, let alone thank me. I took the rap and suffered the consequences."

Kimball's features remained unblemished. Not even the slightest wrinkle caused by wincing from shame touched his face.

That did it—that non-reaction. Spit started flying, veins popping and throbbing as Pepper's heart rate increased. Heat blossomed on her neck and climbed to her face. "Then, after I took the rap, what did you do? You blackmailed me into solving your mother's disappearance." Sweat beading on her forehead, her body a furnace, she removed her cloak.

"Okay, but you weren't on probation because of the drug charges."

"Yes, I was! I would never have been under house arrest

for the other charges. Community service, sure. But not a freaking ankle monitor."

"I knew if the cops caught you, your dad would have grounded you and maybe not talked to you for a week or something. But he would never have laid a hand on you. And you had never been arrested before, so I figured you would have had light probation, and that's it. Because you're a juvenile, the courts would have sealed or expunged the charge when you turned eighteen. Whatever. I didn't know you'd get arrested again. But you don't understand and never will. Shelly scares me, Bell. And that was before he sold his soul."

"How often does he hit you?" Pepper asked with zero compassion.

"When his real estate takes a dip. When he comes home from the bar after a big listing closes. Does it matter? He's mercurial. Prone to violence. Add in selling his soul for more power and magic. People think rich boy Kimball has it all, but I don't. I don't have what you have, Bell. I never will. A father who loves me. And maybe I *hate you* a little for that."

"Bunny loved you."

"*Loved*. Is it past tense now? Am I an idiot for hoping she can be made whole again?" He sighed. "My mom loved me the best way she could, I guess. But now, she's just a soul trapped in a vodka bottle. No different from when she was alive." Kimball's voice cracked.

Typically, Pepper would want to comfort Kimball, as he looked lost and alone, but now, she felt nothing.

"I look at all these damned here in Hell," Kimball said. "Trapped and forever doomed to live in various means of torment, tortured daily by demons. And I can't help but think that even though I'm not one of the damned, I might as well be. After all, I, too, have demon overlords, and no matter what I did, Bell, I couldn't outrun them—couldn't get them out of my head. At least until I discovered my mother's secret weapon. Every day, I chased my demons away with booze, drugs, or both, and life was good—call me a demon slayer." He laughed weakly. "Until the next day, when they returned. So, how am I any different from my mom?"

Pepper had no words, at least none he'd want to hear.

Kimball seemed to chew over something, then tried to speak, only to stop himself until he eventually said, "Do you want me dead?" His shoulders dropped when he voiced that question as if unburdening himself from a heavy thought he'd carried around for quite some time. "Tell me the truth. Please."

"Sometimes," Pepper said matter-of-factly. "Depends on my mood and how much you're annoying me at the time."

"I'm serious."

"So am I. You know what scares me? That I almost killed you on the boat after the masquerade ball. If not for Loki stopping me, I would have. Easily." A quiet unease from that admittance cloaked Pepper's entire body. "I wanted to end your life more than anything at that moment." She recalled kneeling over Kimball and strangling him with her hands and this internal voice telling her to squeeze tighter and not to let go until the life slipped out of him.

"Where does that burning hatred come from?"

"That a serious question? Uh, how about you betraying me and playing a major role in my dad's abduction? You're complicit in his daily torture at the hand of Miles."

All the pressure, fear, worry, and having no way out of Hell crashed down on Pepper, and she silently wept and leaned her head against the wall. Kimball tried to place a comforting hand on her, but she swatted it away.

While readjusting his coat behind his head to serve as a barrier between his skull and a femur, Kimball sighed and asked, "We're trapped in Hell, aren't we? Don't lie to me, Bell."

"Yes." Pepper couldn't pretend otherwise anymore and could feel bile forming in her throat just from uttering the bitter truth.

"We don't even know what day it is. For all we know, Winter Solstice could have come and gone."

Even though she knew that couldn't be the case, that remark triggered Pepper's heart to sink. "Time here runs parallel to Earth, give or take a few hours. Still, we're running out of time."

"I have an idea, and knowing you, you're gonna think it's crazy."

"Oh yeah, share away." Pepper rested her elbows on her raised knees, head resting on the wall, eyes fluttering closed.

"What if we could appeal to Sawyer?" When Pepper side-eyed Kimball, he added, "Just hear me out. Beatrice, whom Sawyer refers to as her sister, is now days away from death. Unless something changes here, Sawyer is the only one who can help us out. Only she has the hots for Vlad and won't stand to reason. Now here's the crazy part. What if she's poisoned by para doxea, too? Ever think about that? And if so, we have a cure."

After what Pepper had witnessed in Vlad's castle, she chalked up Sawyer's feelings for the vampire high king as that of idolizing a mentor and not at all sexual. Still, Pepper never once mentioned anything about that observation. Not to Kimball or anyone, mainly because it wasn't of great import, not in the grand scheme of things, and then voiced as much to Kimball.

Kimball adopted an "oh shit" look, then jumped to his feet and stepped back, far away from Pepper's balled fists.

"Let me explain."

"What did you do?" Pepper asked quietly, slowly raising to a stand, her rage controlled. For now.

"I didn't do anything. M-M-Miles and my dad visited me

when we were at the Academy. I was in my room, getting ready for the day. N-N-Nobody was around, and I-I don't know how they did it. You gotta believe me, Bell. I did nothing. I promise. Please believe me."

Pepper swallowed the distance between them and grabbed his throat. A voice inside told her to squeeze until she heard a break. She wasn't ready to give in to that voice. Not yet.

While choking, Kimball sputtered through the explanation. Back at the Academy, Miles and Kimball's father had approached Kimball in his dreams, asking Kimball to reveal his location, knowing damn well he was with Pepper and Beatrice. When Kimball said no, they said they'd make it easy on him. All he had to do was walk around wherever they were hiding and look at everything; they could take things from there.

When Kimball refused to budge, they brought Sawyer to plead her case. Blondie said Beatrice was dying, and only Vlad had the cure. Sawyer swore up and down that Vlad wanted to help Beatrice, and if her sister died, she'd kill Kimball slowly. At that moment, Kimball realized Sawyer truly believed Vlad was the good guy in all this, the glint of love and adoration in her icy blue eyes.

When Kimball still refused, the threats came. Shelly said he'd cut Bunny's body to ribbons and destroy the vessel so she could never return. Then he told Kimball that Pepper hated him and didn't want him around. Nobody did. That he was useless. Still, Kimball wouldn't oblige. But the threats kept coming. Terrified, Kimball blindfolded himself and ran to the rooftop to seek help. "Melisende gave me a tonic to ward off psychic attacks, and it worked because the heaviness dissipated, and I couldn't hear them anymore."

Pepper released her stranglehold and asked, "Why didn't you say anything?"

"Like you would have believed me. Perrin is chomping at the bit for any excuse to kill me. I thought through every angle, Bell, and each one led me to the only option that ensured my survival: not saying a damn thing. I bet Shelly figured I'd tell you. And he knew you would have left me behind. Maybe that's what he wanted, knowing I'd be so angry that I'd drop the dime on you. But I didn't. I wouldn't, Bell. You gotta believe me."

Whether she'd admit it out loud, Pepper believed Kimball. And to be honest, if in his shoes, she probably would have done the same thing and stayed quiet. But the hell, Pepper would admit that out loud. For now, she wanted him to suffer in silence.

Looming over Kimball, Pepper demanded, "Take off your clothes."

"Bell, I don't have feelings for you like that."

One look at Pepper's feral reaction caused Kimball to strip to his skivvies in a flash. A poppy flower tattoo was on his back, close to his buttocks. So that explained how Miles could infiltrate his dreams. Begged the question: did the serial killer know about Jhi's spell, or was it a happy accident? Just when Pepper rethought her feelings for Jhi, that perhaps she had been wrong, something like this happened.

If Jhi had bespelled Pepper and Kimball, did that mean he had cast a dream infiltration spell over Loki and Perrin, too? But why? He had never tried to contact Perrin, or she would have said, and lost her mind in the process. Same with Loki. Then again, Pepper was the only one who had taken the Conscious Astraling potion. Still, why would Jhi tell Miles and Shelly about a way into Kimball's mind? Wait—how did Kimball remember his dreams?

"Did you sneak into my potion supply?" Pepper interrogated. From one look at Kimball's sheepish grin, she shook her head in disgust. "Why?"

"I thought maybe it would give me a buzz or something. Stop grilling me. I was bored, okay?"

"Get dressed." She tossed him his clothes, which was the closest thing to an apology he'd get.

Blame it on the adrenaline crash, the full bellies, or the alcohol, but the duo quickly succumbed to sleep.

When Pepper awoke with a start, she immediately ran to the only door of the temple and breathed a sigh of relief that darkness still occluded the sky. She toed Kimball's slumped-over body and told him it was time to leave.

Pepper hurriedly cleaned up and scrubbed the area, eliminating traces of them being there. Once finished, she slipped into her wool cloak, and a piece of paper fluttered out of one pocket.

Kimball plucked it up from the floor and asked, "What's this?"

Pepper snatched it from his hands and inspected the star-shaped origami fortune teller. Four different colored flaps made up the outside. "Kirby gave it to me on the sly. I totally forgot all about it, what with all the lovely excitement of running for our lives."

"Do you remember how to play?" Kimball asked.

"Kinda. I was like nine the last time I held one." Instinctively, Pepper dipped her thumbs and index fingers into the slits on the bottom and manipulated the star to reveal four numbers on the inside written in Laramaic. Four more digits appeared when Pepper moved the toy in the opposite direction. "Weird. The numbers are random and not the normal one to eight."

"I imagine there's a concealed message underneath one of those flaps. A life-saving, how-to-get-the-hell-out-of-Hell message." Desperation at the helm, Kimball whipped opened a flap, and a bite-size ghostly sprite that looked like Perrin's Tavi jumped out and bit Kimball's finger, blood welling.

Kimball quickly closed the flap. "Wasn't expecting that. Well, at least we know security measures are in place, so try not to screw it up, Bell, or we could face something far worse. You got this." He patted her on the back.

"So, we need a code to reach Kirby's message. And it would have to be something that Kirby gave us. Otherwise, how could we end up on the correct flap without triggering another trap?"

"The only thing I can think of is the hopscotch numbers we jumped on to escape," said Kimball. "Worth a shot. But we must pick the color first, and she didn't leave us a clue about that."

That's where Kimball was wrong. The first hopscotch number they jumped on was three, and red was the only color on the outer layer that contained three letters. So, Pepper held her breath, said a prayer to Seren, and moved the toy three times. That brought them to yet another string of numbers. And in the mix was the second hopscotch number. When she reached the third, it revealed a previously hidden layer of flaps. On and on, she went, manipulating the device until they reached the last number.

As Kimball did the honors and opened the last flap, the origami fluttered in the air. The flaps pumped up and down like bird wings, gaining momentum. Then the fortune teller whirled and whirled like a pinwheel.

At first, a barely audible voice sounded over the generated wind but quickly became more pronounced until Kirby's voice came through loud and clear. "Quillee handed Beatrice over to the Hounds. She lied and said she kidnapped Beatrice herself. Totally a power move. But she handed over Perrin, too. I don't know why. She planned on waiting another day before, quote—hunting down Hell's most wanted—quote, to really score major points with them. That would be you,

Pepper. As for Kimball, he was fodder. Quillee planned on making him her plaything.

"Please save Perrin. I wish I could do more, but I'm already in trouble. Oh, that sample you gave me. It's *Caulerpa lentillifera*, otherwise known as green caviar. Some circles in Hell consider it a delicacy, as it's rare and extra salty from tears of the damned and, therefore, more delicious. Anyway, it's solely harvested in the River Phlegethon, near the Department of Soul Sundering and Assignments. The federal complex dumps its collection of tears and blood directly into the river."

Kirby spouted off a handful of restaurants that all served green caviar in their entrees. But the last one snatched Pepper's attention.

"Mandurugo's Market is located directly on the beach of Lake Naraka. And it's the only restaurant that claims to serve freshly caught seafood *and* seaweed daily, straight from the River Phlegethon, which would be believable since the river runs right into Lake Naraka. The restaurant caters to the health-conscious demon and prides itself on fattening the damned with locally sourced, raw organic ingredients. Won a crapton of The Bellowers awards, too. Anyway, I'd try that one first. I pray to Mother Lilith that we can meet one day again under different circumstances. This is Kirby, signing out." The fortune teller disintegrated.

On their way into town, Pepper recalled passing a sign that pointed toward Lake Naraka.

"Where to start?" Kimball said, interrupting Pepper's trip planning. "I don't know about you, but I'm kinda fixated on 'Kimball was fodder.'" He stood in front of the nearly empty plate of food, save for the fingers, feet, and eyeballs of the damned. "Huh. We totally missed this. Bell, there's writing underneath. Says to kindly replace what we ate."

A voice uttering "Welcome wayward travelers" proceeded

a man who skittered out of a door like a spider. A door that Pepper could have sworn wasn't there before. His midnight blue robe pooled around all six of his legs as he approached the strangers. The acolyte brushed his bony fingers through his impossibly long wiry beard, a murderous glint in his viper-black eyes. In his hands, he spelled cleavers into existence. "I see you enjoyed Goddess Hekate's offerings. Now kindly donate what you took."

Pepper and Kimball pivoted on their heels and thundered to the door, but the acolyte wrangled Pepper in an invisible lasso. She kicked and screamed as he dragged her to him. "Thank you for gifting me with the lifetime privilege of casting magic with impunity. And for all the Vs and Indys I'll be swimming in," he taunted. "My goddess loves—" A look of confusion stitched across the acolyte's face before he crashed to the ground. Kimball stood behind the demon, holding the heavy obsidian food plate above his head.

Pepper and Kimball ran like the blazes to the soulcar. Once inside, Pepper hit the throttle and zoomed out of town. Right in the nick of time, too. The bounty hunter joined the acolyte, standing on the road behind them.

The acolyte hovered above the ground, conjuring balls of fire, while the bounty hunter whipped out both guns from his side holster and fired. *Bang! Bang! Bang!* Pepper and Kimball ducked, and the bullets meant for their heads whizzed right over them. The hunter fired off a volley of more rounds. A shot came so close to Pepper that it yanked out a strand of her ebony locks.

Unfortunately, the acolyte had better aim, and a fireball hit the car and set it reeling off the road. The vehicle went wild. Pepper lost control, and her hands fell off the yoke. Kimball leaned over and grabbed the wheel as Pepper adjusted the rudders seconds before the car crashed into a barn.

Pepper couldn't chance driving back to the road, so she

hightailed it over the darkened countryside and through a haunted bent-tree forest until Pepper reached what she gathered was the River Phlegethon. Unfortunately, the creatures basking on the shore were a tad too feral and wouldn't stop pouncing at the convertible soulcar, so Pepper sailed above the river.

In no time flat, the river gave way to Lake Naraka, a massive body of murky black water. She knew leviathans lurked within the rivers in Hell.

Pray tell, what did lakes house?

31

As Pepper navigated the soulcar above Lake Naraka's darkened, choppy waters, the duo sat in silence, too rattled to speak for many reasons. The dark, humid night blanketed the shoreline from Pepper's sight, which made navigation difficult; to make matters worse, something massive lurked underneath the surface, keeping pace with the soulcar. From her experiences in Hell, Pepper figured the beast was a leviathan and knew headlights were the only source of repellent to keep the creature from dragging the car to its underwater lair. Then they both fretted over whether the souls howling in the engine of a soulcar ever took a breather, the equivalent of an empty fuel tank. And if that happened—Pepper didn't want to find out the hard way.

Shafts of orangey light shattered the utter darkness of night when daybreak announced its presence and cast a blood-red glow over residential pyramids that weren't visible minutes before. Pepper immediately banked left and navigated the soulcar to terra firma miles away. Soon other soul-cars joined Pepper and Kimball on the volcanic glass road as they entered the Vale of Naraka, according to the signpost.

They ditched the car, then hotfooted it a few blocks to Mandurugo's. The organic market sat on the edge of what passed for a beach in Hell: sand the shade of freshly spilled blood and the water dark, uninviting, and home to hellish creatures that wouldn't be out of place in Earth's ocean abyss. Before entering the teeny-tiny establishment, Pepper instructed Kimball to keep his mouth shut and let her do the talking. As they walked through the door, a gust of trade winds joined them and sent a swarm of lum'bhras to bob crazily around the ceiling of the establishment. Buttery light blinked uncontrollably for a spell until the tethered souls trapped inside the jellyfish-like pods calmed down.

A slip of a female with almond-shaped, milk-white eyes and blood-smeared lips sashayed out of the backroom, carrying a tray of freshly carved meat. She looked as if she had just crawled out of the lake, a slimy green sheen coating her tawny skin. Swathed in a billowy summer dress with wavy black tresses that cascaded down her back, she appeared to be in the prime of her youth. Still, according to the many awards and The Bellowers' write-ups covering the walls, Kina was the proprietor of Mandurugo's Market and had been for almost a century.

After placing the tray down on the counter, she wiped away trickles of blood from the corners of her mouth. In two steps, Kina closed the distance between her customers like a predator cornering its prey. Two fangs that begged to pierce flesh glinted in the soul light.

Pepper froze. Fears of being Kina's next meal screamed in her mind.

"How may I help you?" Kina asked, her voice as delicate as Pepper and Kimball's situation.

"Hi, Kina. I'm Marie, and this is Dick." Pepper tried not to get distracted by Kimball's scrunched face at his assumed name. "We're looking for a friend."

Kina padded to the back of the counter, wearing a look of interest. Not at Pepper, but Kimball. Her eyes anchored onto "Dick" as she added the meats to the cooled deli area. "Could I tempt you with a sample of damned tempura?"

"He'd love some." Pepper figured it would be better if Kimball's mouth was full.

"I was hoping you could help us out." Pepper described her sister.

"No. She doesn't sound familiar."

Now what? Pepper perused the menu and noticed that only one item didn't contain flesh of the damned—grilled spiny devilfish on a bed of green caviar. Bingo! This had to be where her sister ordered takeout. Pepper tried her best to tamp down her excitement and told Kina how her friend waxed OMG over that specific dish and that Pepper just *had* to try it.

"It's a popular item," Kina said, leaving it at that.

Not getting anywhere in her investigation, Pepper went out on a limb. "She might have referred to green caviar as lato."

Recognition glinted in Kina's white eyes. "Ah, yes. I think I know your friend. She would order the grilled devilfish with extra lato, as she called it, for delivery. But that abruptly stopped quite a few months ago."

Pepper doled out a nugget of information, hoping it would cement her believability. "She was staying on the beach here."

"Yes, that's right. Close enough for me to walk there. Easy to miss, though. I kept having to look at the address every time I'd deliver."

"But you never saw her face?"

"No. She would always lay out fleshies with a fat tip, along with instructions to leave the food on the deck."

"Thank you so much. You've been so helpful. I'll take two orders of the devilfish to go."

As the door clinked shut behind them, Pepper and Kimball walked along the shore, giving a wide berth to the black-as-pitch waters. Now and then, a fin, as large as a great white's entire body, would break the surface, circle, then disappear beneath the waters. Rocky cliffs took up the other side of the beach and didn't present any means of escape, so Pepper and Kimball had one option: to stick to the shoreline.

As they walked in silence, hot and sticky with their jeans and sleeves rolled up from the one-hundred-degree-plus humidity, Kimball kept looking over his shoulder, nervous as all get out. They both were. The bounty hunter had followed them from Pandæmonia to B'aRQoA'ba-ruch, so it was only a matter of time before he caught up to them. Then what? A nervous Pepper devoured everything in the takeout container, even holding it to her mouth to drink the last bits of savory sauce. Kimball, on the other hand, couldn't eat when stressed.

"We should have reached the shack by now. Or maybe we passed it." Exhausted, Kimball collapsed on the red sand. "Tell me again what you saw when you were inside your sister's hideout?"

"Nothing really but sand and the shore." Squawking shorebirds ripping apart fish stole her attention. "And those birds over there." Pepper pointed in the distance.

"Birds? So helpful. Anything else?" Kimball didn't even hide his impatience.

Pepper took a load off and joined Kimball on the sand. "A skiff rested on the shore."

"Like that one up there." Kimball pointed in the distance to a barely visible boat.

They used the last bits of energy they had racing to the skiff. About thirty-odd feet behind the vessel, Pepper spotted a stone entrance to what looked like a crypt that seamlessly blended in with the craggy cliffs. The "shack" was easy to miss if you weren't looking for it.

They stood on the wood plank porch before a massive door large enough for a gargoyle to pass through without ducking. When Kimball placed his hand on the knob and twisted, a whisper sounded that became a howl, and the wind tore through the air.

"Whatever you do, don't move a muscle," Pepper warned, "or the Sentries will kill us. Quick, give me your hand."

Before them, to their side and behind, amorphous blobs materialized, then morphed into ghostly beings with hair that drifted about as if floating in water. One second, the mercenaries were wisps of air limned in blue hellfire, the next seemingly corporeal, their faces humanoid yet transparent. Tiny electric shocks zapped Pepper as the entities floated a hair's breadth away from her.

The duo held tight to each other's hands. Kimball squeezed for dear life when one Sentry bared its teeth at him in a feral snarl.

Lightning quick, the Sentries changed form and turned into smoke. What felt like shards of glass and freezing cold icicles pushed through Pepper's nostrils, ripped apart her throat, and began stabbing her stomach.

"Recite the passcode," a ghostly Sentry demanded in a docent-like voice.

"Say it now, or you die," another one chimed in, as if announcing the news for the day.

"You have ten seconds," a chorus of Sentries warned. "Ten, nine …"

"Bell! What are we gonna do?"

"I don't know." Pepper's heart raced. "Stop talking so I can think."

What the hell was the passcode?

A memory on the fringe of Pepper's mind began to take form.

"Seven."

In the letter Jaylyn wrote to Beatrice, she mentioned how Beatrice was to recite a passcode to their asset inside the Ministry of Mischief and Mayhem.

"Six."

When Sala'dee thought Pepper was the contact, she triggered the exchange with a conversational opening.

"Five, four, three …"

What did Sala'dee say to Pepper when she and Jhi had snuck inside the Ministry?

"Sparkling Plasma," Pepper shouted, hoping this wasn't a wrap to life as she knew it.

"Ten. Nine …"

"Bell, you reset the countdown. There has to be more."

"Eight. Seven."

"I don't know. I don't know what to do!"

"Six. Five. Four."

Her hands shaking and lips quivering, Pepper willed herself to remember the rest. What passcode was Beatrice to recite to Sala'dee?

"Three. Two."

Fists balled, fingers digging into palms, eyes squeezed shut in remembrance, Pepper yelled, "Only if it's infused with pomegranate!"

In unison, the Sentries vomited out of Pepper and Kimball's mouths, nearly bringing the duo to their knees. With a cyclonic whoosh, the ghostly mercenaries dematerialized.

The crypt door pivoted open, stone scratching stone

sounding before it stopped, then began closing just as quickly.

Pepper and Kimball hurried up inside the crypt, not wanting to repeat that horrific experience. "I literally can't take anymore today. Like, I need a nap and some nourishment or something." Kimball's buttocks met a chair at the only table in the cramped space.

The mirror Pepper had speculumed through and a table were the only objects in the room. That left one place yet to explore. Pepper hesitantly turned the doorknob, fear of the Sentries returning front and center.

The door opened without incident, revealing a hotspot of surveillance equipment and monitors. Talking Heads were on the walls, their eyes roving back and forth like the steady ticking of a metronome; sheaths of paper spread out containing logs of activity; maps tacked to the walls. Maps of—

"Is that Naples?" Kimball asked, joining Pepper inside the surveillance room.

Pepper stood before a map of her hometown. "Vlad's castle in the Everglades is circled."

"Why is all of Collier County circled in red?"

"I don't know. But it's the same for this other country. Morgansk." The unknown country resided somewhere in Eastern Europe, near Romania's borders. Mr. AP Kimball had never heard of the country. Though it sounded vaguely familiar to Pepper, she couldn't place why. "Lines are running all over the Everglades." All the crisscrossing lines reminded Pepper of a matrix grid. "Same for the Forest of the Dead in Morgansk."

None of the heads were responsive or noticed Pepper and Kimball; instead, their eyes flicked back and forth as if reading line after line of words on a page. Even if they had seen Pepper, they couldn't say anything; their lips were sewn shut. Pepper tried to get their attention, and one snapped awake. His mismatched eyes latched onto Pepper for a beat, then returned to roaming back and forth.

When Kimball sat in front of the monitors, they fired up as if motion activated. The first screen showcased a familiar-looking hallway, awash in reflective obsidian and crimson. A river of water flowed underneath the smokey glass floor. Damned, in extremis, pounded on the glass, wailing to be saved from drowning. Their lifeless bodies continued down the current, only to be regenerated moments after death, and their screams for rescue began anew.

"I know where this is. It's the lobby right outside First Underlord Mephistopheles' office." The surveillance footage appeared to be live and was seen from the perspective of something affixed to the walls. Though Pepper didn't recall seeing Talking Heads in the hallway during her short time there, she distinctly remembered them decorating the first underlord's office. From her recollection, at the end of the hallway, they'd find Sala'dee's desk behind a wavy half-wall, and Pepper said as much to Kimball.

The monitor shifted from the double doors of Mephistopheles' office and sailed to Sala'dee, the demon with lime green- and black-bobbed hair, walnut-hued horns filed down to perfection, and beetle-black skin tightly stretched over her sculpted face. She was swathed in fashions with a futuristic bent, shoes that took the idea of fashion over comfort to a whole new level, and accessories that all jock-eyed for the limelight—there were statement necklaces, and then there were statement necklaces. To the casual observer, Sala'dee would appear to belong to the glitterati, a trendsetter when it came to sporting the latest fads in Hell. They would never guess that Sala'dee, a friend to Mephistopheles, was a spy and Jaylyn's asset.

Sala'dee's finger clicked her ear, and she chirped, "You've

reached the office of His Liege, First Underlord Mephistophe-les. Sala'dee speaking, how may I be of assistance? ... Certainly. Consider it done."

The wall behind her rotated open, revealing a hallway, and a chorus of disembodied voices rang out. Sala'dee stepped into the newly exposed space and handed over an unidentified item to—

"Kimball, look." Pepper placed her hand on the screen. Though the man turned his face away from the hidden camera, there was no mistaking his slicked-back greasy hair and wire-thin frame. "It's Miles Leagan."

32

Pepper and Kimball leaned in closer to the monitor, as if that would present a clearer picture of the serial killer and who he was with. Unfortunately, the wall snicked shut behind Sala'dee, silencing the chittering voices and keeping Miles from their view.

Ever so slowly, Sala'dee's head spun around ninety degrees while her body remained in place. Her silvery eyes, with scarlet flecks, bored right into the hidden camera and fixated on Pepper.

Shocked, Pepper took a step back, and Sala'dee followed her movements. Wherever Pepper moved to, so did Sala'dee's eyes. A beat later, Sala'dee gave a subtle nod of recognition, then returned her focus to her desk. "She knows we're here," Pepper whispered.

"Why are we whispering?" Kimball asked in a soft voice.

"I don't know," Pepper whispered back.

"You think they record the footage?"

Pepper returned to regular voice volume. "I would imagine they do. Why else have this set up?"

It took a few tries and curse words later, but Pepper figured out how to turn on all the monitors. From Sala'dee's desk to the hallway to inside Mephistopheles' office, Talking Heads surveilled the entire floor; one eye in the crypt, the other on a Talking Head strategically placed within the Ministry of Mischief and Mayhem.

Pepper then filled Kimball in on how Talking Heads worked as glorified CCTV cameras.

"Like Mister Potato Heads," said Kimball.

"Yep. We just have to figure out how to play back the footage." Unfortunately, there wasn't a limnocular around to help with that endeavor.

All at once, the footage began playing back, rewinding slowly.

"How'd you do that?" Kimball's mouth opened wide in surprise.

"I did absolutely nothing. You've been here with me the whole time."

"But you did, though," Kimball said. "I think the Talking Heads respond to voice commands."

So Pepper talked to the Heads and told them to keep rewinding. And the Heads listened. Right as they were ready to quit, as the recorded footage proved ineffective, Miles and the remaining trifecta of evil—Vlad and Cazzian—appeared on screen, and all walked backward, down the glass-floored hallway, and back first into Mephistopheles' office.

The trio took a seat, and as Miles got back up again, Pepper commanded, "Stop. Fast forward. Stop."

Pepper sat next to Kimball tableside as they watched the surveillance footage play out.

"Pop open that bottle of bubbly, would you darlin'?" Miles drawled to Sala'dee, who was about to leave after escorting the visitors into Mephistopheles' office.

Faux-Mephistopheles trailed into the room as Sala'dee poured champagne into flutes.

"Uh, you can go now," Miles said dismissively to Sala'dee. She tossed him a disarming smile and then disappeared through the double doors. "The fun I could have with her." He wore a lecherous look that churned Pepper's stomach. "Would you be terribly upset if you had to replace her?"

"No. Not all. Enjoy." Faux-Mephistopheles replied as he sat down on a clear throne with souls of the damned swimming within.

The body-snatching wanderer enjoyed wearing the ridiculously fit skinsuit belonging to Mephistopheles—architect of soul contracts, father to Jhi, and brother to Lucifer. Make no bones about it—this mala'dayya was sex personified, his humanoid features heart-stopping, and his sartorial choices only bolstered those facts. He donned a silken suit that hugged his lean body, his hair slicked back, a pronounced widow's peak, his polished skin the color of rich leather.

"I apologize for the secretive nature of the last-minute summoning, but we've run into a situation and need reassurances on your end—reassurances you have failed to provide." Faux-Mephistopheles ran his fingers along the edges of his perfectly manicured goatee on his pointed chin.

"Do explain to me, Alasdair, why then all the pageantry of popping open the bubbly if you're so concerned?" Vlad's face screwed up in annoyance.

"Celebration always before business. Underlord Chaos' freedom and," Alasdair dramatically paused, "Beatrice's capture."

Vlad squeezed out a low-watt smile and relaxed into the club chair.

"But that's not why I summoned you to Hell today. It's a Seren-blessed event that just happened to coincide with our meeting. And here I thought you'd be more pleased," Alasdair noted, to which Vlad remained mum, seemingly mulling over the breaking news. "Queen Quillee of the Lolly'kas came through for us. Handing over one of her own to us more than proved her loyalty. Moving forward, she will be an invaluable addition to the Syndicate."

The wattage of Vlad's smile increased to blindingly bright. "You're telling me we have a Lolly'ka to sacrifice for the ceremony?" Alasdair slowly nodded, which prompted Vlad to exchange a look of pure glee with Cazzian and Miles, who clearly shared in Vlad's sentiment.

"All that primordial magic at our disposal," Cazzian said, his lips splitting open into a wicked grin. "With Lilith's blood running through her veins, the Lolly'ka alone will significantly bolster the strength of the transference spell."

Vlad raised his glass to the room. "A toast to Seren for sending us good luck and fortune and to us for outsmarting Hekate."

"That goddess won't see what's coming," Miles added.

"Speaking of the goddess, any Hekate updates from our sources on the ground?" A slight note of concern coated Alasdair's words.

Miles jumped in. "Let's just say Hekate is otherwise distracted and oblivious. Like a frog slowly boiling in a pot."

When Alasdair asked for elaboration, Miles said, "If you're asking about other ruling gods ... *Ribbit.*"

"All you need to focus on at the moment is that the prison heist wholly distracted the gods," Vlad assuaged the stressed-out wanderer.

Faux-Mephistopheles wasn't assuaged and said, "Hekate must be involved in—"

But Vlad interrupted, "And we just told you in so many words that Hekate has been handled."

"I have a question for you, Alasdair," Cazzian said. "You said you captured Beatrice and the former Lolly'ka queen, but no mention of Pepper." Redness bloomed on Cazzian's peach-toned complexion.

Alasdair sighed. "She and the Garcia boy escaped." When Cazzian nearly jumped out of his seat, his eyes simmering with lethal intent, the wanderer added, "Fret not. I have one of our best bounty hunters on the case. Timo'thee comes with a ninety-nine point nine percent success rate for bringing in bounties."

"And the point one percent …?" Cazzian stared intently at Alasdair.

"Killed themselves rather than being apprehended. Listen, Timo'thee sends me updates on the hour. Last I heard, he tracked Pepper and Kimball down to Vale of Naraka. It's a small beachside village, so it's only a matter of time until we have apprehended Pepper."

Pepper and Kimball exchanged looks of pure terror, their mouths forming Os.

"Stop footage," Pepper commanded, and the Talking Heads obliged. "The bounty hunter can't get inside the crypt," Pepper reminded Kimball. If only she believed it herself.

"Yeah, but we can't get out, Bell. If he finds us, we're trapped inside!" Kimball didn't deal with stress well. And with claustrophobia added to the mix, the boy was about to lose his mind.

The mounting pressure taking its toll on her already frayed nerves, Pepper didn't have the bandwidth to play the role of crisis negotiator, so she pointed to the screen and gestured to Kimball to zip his lips.

"Moving onto business," Alasdair started. "I swear to

Shi'rue, mala'dayya are getting suspicious, asking questions about their brother, Lucifer. Questions I, or rather his beloved Mephistopheles, should know but can't answer, and I'm running out of excuses and can only run interference for so long. I think Prince Mammon is having me followed. As it stands, Lucifer could resurface any minute, and we can kiss the whole operation goodbye."

Alasdair worried at a gold cuff around his wrist as he continued to spew his concerns that only inflamed his already keyed-up temper. "And just yesterday, one of the mala'khas intercepted a note Mephistopheles tried to sneak out of the Fortress. We believe the note was intended for Prince Mammon. What we don't know and what Mephistopheles is refusing to spill regardless of the amped-up torture is if that was the first note or one of many the sneaky shit tried to send. If Prince Mammon discovers that we've abducted his brother and that I'm an imposter—"

"What did the note say?" Cazzian asked.

"We don't know. It's written in code."

"Then calm down. If the princes knew anything, we wouldn't be having this conversation," Cazzian offered.

Alasdair was taken aback by that response. "All hell's breaking loose in Pandæmonia. The gods are engaged in a scorch-earth campaign to hunt down the thief and Underlord Chaos, and everyone's considered a suspect. I'm expecting the gods to come knocking down my door on their hunt at any moment, and your response is for me to *calm down*? Being in the dark is not a good place to be. And I shouldn't have to remind everyone here how grave the consequences are *for us all* should we fail." Not getting the reaction he had wanted or even a rise out of the trio, Alasdair added, "I didn't climb my way to the top for it all to blow up in my face. I need assurances—*We* need assurances. Cazzian, your immortality is a gift that can be—"

"I'm fully aware, thank you." Cazzian clarified with his piercing stare that he didn't appreciate that threat. "You finished havering?"

That latter question stopped Alasdair dead in his tracks, and he took a centering breath before saying, "No, I'm not. Either you fork over information, or I'll take matters into my own hands. Starting with the prison heist and why I wasn't informed about it ahead of time."

"We had nothing to do with that," Miles chirped.

Calmly, Alasdair tapped a button on his desk. "Sala'dee, get Prince Mammon on the line."

Concerned, Cazzian tossed his attention to Vlad, and then they nodded in silent understanding before Cazzian spoke again. "Let's not do anything rash. Just hang up."

Calling Cazzian's bluff, Alasdair didn't budge.

Cazzian sat on the edge of the club chair, putting his hand up. "Alasdair, in our defense, we opted not to share all the details with you to keep you safe from the gods. If they did wind up at your doorstep by some chance, they couldn't extract a single bit of intel from you because you knew nothing." Alasdair's shoulder's dropped from that reveal. "But if you're so inclined to know all the details, then so be it. You do have every right to know. So, consider what I'm about to share an olive branch."

"Sala'dee, disregard my order. I found what I needed." Alasdair massaged the wiry hairs of his goatee and adopted a pensive stare.

Cazzian nodded understanding to Alasdair, then fulfilled his promise and recited the third-night prognostication. Afterward, he said, "Centuries ago, a Roma woman spoke that very prophecy, one of a few, to Vlad. And that same prophecy came to pass yesterday." That piqued Alasdair's curiosity, and he sat back on his throne and crossed his legs.

After Cazzian decoded the prediction for Alasdair—which

matched Jhi's rendition to a tee—he continued, "Until now, every single prophecy has come to fruition, and we're confident the final one will as well. 'On the fourth night, the dragon devours the sun as it stands still with the moon in the sky, the dragon destroys Night's ever curse and becomes Day's ally, the magi's blood will spill, and the worlds we know will die.'"

"That's different from what Jhi shared with me," a shocked Pepper blurted out, her heart cantering.

"Jhi? What?" Kimball asked, confused.

Pepper placed her finger over her lips and jabbed a finger at the screen.

"If all goes as planned, in a fortnight, on Winter Solstice and after the solar eclipse, we'll have equal footing with the gods," Cazzian divulged.

"But there's more of them than us," Alasdair replied.

"You sure about that?" Cazzian didn't allow Alasdair to respond. "After the magic transference spell, we'll be unstoppable. Soon mages' magic will be ours, and they will know what it feels like to be lowlies. And we can glide into the next phase of our operation."

"And with that taken magic, I'll sire an army of thralls to do our bidding. Need I remind you that gods don't have armies." Vlad finished with a wink.

"Okay, but what should I do about that damn Mephistopheles?"

"We'll deal with him and the other mala'dayyas after the ceremony. Just hold them off until then. Two weeks, that's all we're asking."

"Not so fast," Alasdair interjected. "When I said we need reassurances, I meant all of it. Goddess Hekate and mages draw energy from lunar eclipses, which increases their magic tenfold."

"We're aware, but thank you for the history lesson," Vlad barked, and Miles snickered in response.

Alasdair's face pinched into a look of disgust. "Enough with the snark already. We can't underestimate the current archOmega and now Beatrice Budreau. Surely being the last survivor of Ketteline Budreau's bloodline and the only living heir to the archOmega throne, the girl's gifted with unimaginable powers. The power those two alone instinctively draw from the lunar eclipse will be devastating to the transference spell should they gain the upper hand, to say nothing of our end game as a whole."

"The only ones being underestimated here, Alasdair, are Cazzian and I," Vlad growled. "The archOmega is a shell of her once formidable self. As for Beatrice, those powers you speak of have yet to surface within the girl. But we'll coax them out of her yet."

Even so, Alasdair made it clear he wasn't entirely sold. "Hekate is a force to be reckoned with, no matter how you toss the dice."

"The same could be said of Karma," Vlad said. "I rest my case."

Alasdair wasn't done with his cross-examination. "I don't know for certain, but I'm guessing the energy Hekate drew from the lunar eclipse and supreme planetary parade last night is enough to destroy civilization with the shake of her finger. Why is this of no concern to you all?"

Vlad's face screwed up in annoyance as he rubbed the wicked scar marring his neck, its jagged edge puckered. "Tell me, Alasdair, what about me plotting and planning for centuries passed over that thick head of yours? We already factored that inevitability into our plan and used it to our advantage. So, I advise you to lay off the line of questioning that does nothing but insult our intelligence and make us rethink our association."

Cazzian tossed Vlad a "calm down" look and attempted to quell the tempers of all present, mainly Alasdair.

But Alasdair was already worked up. "That's laughable. Last I checked, your plan is dead in the water without us, without Underlord Chaos, whose loyalties reside with our faction in Hell, first and foremost—"

"Now *that's* laughable," Vlad chimed in. "I'm sure Queen Lilith felt the same way once upon a time ago. You know, until Chaos betrayed his queen. Remind me again who broke Chaos out of Sheol? I'll have you know Chaos is enjoying his time in the castle, getting reacquainted with his magic to prepare for Winter Solstice."

"So much for that damn olive branch," Alasdair snapped. "Five minutes in, and you already went back on your word. Enough is enough! This piecemealing of information ends today." Spittle flew out of the wanderer's mouth, veins bulging on his deeply tanned skin. "I will not put my life on the line and be treated with such utter disrespect. Either tell me why I shouldn't worry about Hekate or consider our arrangement dead in the water. I'm not beneath turning us all in. Perhaps I'll get brownie points for making the call to mala'dayyas."

Cazzian tossed daggers at Vlad, then returned his attention to an incensed and unpredictable Alasdair. "This is by no means an excuse, but just hear me out," Cazzian urged.

Alasdair nodded, a gesture that conveyed, "I'm listening."

"Trust me when I say I learned the hard way how to run a successful ironclad campaign with many moving parts. And I do so by having multiple operations run by foot soldiers who only know enough to keep their factions running smoothly while keeping the key players who know all the details few in number. That adopted system eliminates potential leaks and spies. We wouldn't have made such inroads if not for your faction's help, Alasdair, so yes, you deserve to be one of the key players in the entire process. So, full disclosure from here on out."

Alasdair knocked back a scotch on the rocks and calmed down somewhat, waiting for the start of Cazzian's apology tour.

The fair-haired Scot strode to the wet bar, poured the deep-red contents of Aluman's port into a goblet, took a calming sip as he leaned back against the counter, then said, "Morgansk is home to the largest virgin forest on Earth, a massive territory covered with ley lines and vortices. And the magic generated inside the territory is ... euphoric." Cazzian drained the glass and free-poured more of the vino.

Vlad added, "For centuries, in his infinite stupidity, man has demolished these magical reservoirs hidden all over Earth. By the grace of Seren, I discovered one such reservoir in my own backyard in Morgansk. Lowlie Morganskians unknowingly soak up the magical energy. We see this phenomenon in their spontaneous healings, development of sixth senses, and the like. And to ensure Morgansk remained unsullied by man's destructive whims, I cursed it for its own protection. Nobody can enter or leave the country unless on my orders."

Vlad then revealed that Morgansk was a testing ground for the curse, and through subjugating the country and its denizens, they learned what worked for their plan and what didn't. And just like Morgansk, Naples, Florida, was covered in ley lines and a breeding ground for magic, which made sense to Pepper. After all, her hometown was flogged by endless rays of sunshine and home to the Everglades— considered one of the largest natural wetlands in the world.

"That's why the archOmega and her conclave were drawn to the southernmost parts of Florida," Vlad explained. "And precisely why we relocated into a veritable hell on Earth. Truly, the weather is worse than some of the hottest territories in Hell, not counting Gehenna, obviously. But I digress. So, while you might not see it now, Alasdair, every thought and action has been thought out well in advance. Morgansk was first. Naples will be our finest work yet. But it won't be the last."

"And last night's lunar eclipse celebration is a prime example of what Vlad just stated," Cazzian said. "As meticulously planned, we successfully drained all lowlies of their energy and supernatural powers unconsciously derived from ley lines. We drained mages in our captivity of their magic that increased significantly because of the lunar eclipse and supreme planetary parade. Same for the archOmega. We have stored all collected energy and magic in reservoirs to prepare for the transference spell on Winter Solstice. Now all that's left to do is wait until Hekate transitions into her crone form."

"It's unavoidable, the transitions." Miles' lips spread in a lupine grin. "During Winter Solstice, Hekate will be at her weakest, most vulnerable, mortal, and prime for the taking." His tongue licked his lips with that thought.

"Gods are immortal and therefore unable to be slain—that's a misnomer. We all have a weakness that can destroy us. Now, whether or not we admit that is another thing altogether." Vlad seemed to converse privately with Miles, his eyes boring into him as if drilling home a point. "The challenge is finding that weakness and exploiting it. And discovering Hekate's was the most challenging yet."

Cazzian jumped in. "It's common knowledge that has even made it into the annals of history that the moon and Hekate are intricately connected, her magic influenced by its various phases. Now, taking into consideration that the moon is a permanent fixture in the sky, its divine magic channeling to Hekate all day, every day, how do you kill a goddess that has a celestial entity protecting her from harm? You can't.

And the goddess has built her storied reputation on that fact. And to this day, nobody dares to mess with her."

"Well, unfortunately for Hekate, I like a challenge," Vlad said in a basso voice. "And it took *many* years, but we finally uncovered Hekate's secret." Soul light glinted off the warlord's fangs as his lips curled into a devilish grin.

"We uncovered that Hekate has a tremendous amount of unlimited magical energy at her disposal, much like the Forest of the Dead in Morgansk," Cazzian said. "Energy not her own and not obtained from the moon. We still don't know where she culls it from. Hekate's mind is impenetrable as the day is long. Not even the archOmega is aware of this. So, we stopped spinning our wheels and refocused our efforts on figuring out why she collects this magic or would even have to if she's in perpetual contact with the moon. I'm happy to report we discovered the why just last night by a stroke of Goddess Seren's good fortune. Hekate transferred all that collected magic to the archOmega. And she'd only do that if she was preparing for something."

"Something like her transformation on Winter Solstice?" Alasdair replied, his head slowly nodding.

"Yes," Cazzian beamed. "Should a threat present itself, the archOmega's powers—hers and Hekate's combined—will serve as a shield, a last line of defense that keeps Hekate protected and strong when she's in her crone form. And if need be, Hekate can call upon the archOmega at any time. A win-win, if you will."

"In theory, though. Am I correct in saying you have yet to prove this?" Alasdair adopted a look of concern.

"You are correct, but we're confident in our assertion. And here's why. Three times a year, the triple goddess changes forms. This is common knowledge for her acolytes and the cause for dimensions-wide bacchanalias. Maiden during Ostara; Mother, Summer Solstice; and Crone, Winter Solstice.

What isn't common knowledge is that the goddess can be killed on the day of the transitions." Cazzian visibly relished voicing that last part.

"Only this time, Hekate won't have the archOmega to rely upon and will be unable to defend herself? Because Hekate's magic is now in your possession?" Alasdair looked downright delighted and chuckled.

"Precisely," Vlad said, and Cazzian and Miles nodded in unison.

"After the ceremony, we will be the benefactors of all that power stemming from the archOmega and Hekate," said Alasdair, his excitement moments from bursting like the cork on the champagne bottle he held. *Pop!*

"As part of the fulfillment of the prophecy, my Hounds and I will feel the sun on our skin once again as we tread the earth morning, noon, and night. Then, once we've sacrificed Goddess Hekate, the archOmega, and the last living heir to the Budreau bloodline, we will never have to rely on drinking the blood of mages for magical powers ever again. Just as I can sire vampires, soon I'll be able to do the same for mages."

Miles proclaimed, "We might have all been born lowlies, but after Winter Solstice, we will all be mages and invincible like gods."

"Rest assured, Alasdair," Vlad started, "once Hekate is slain, you can ditch that meat sack and tread earthly soil in your true form. And the mala'dayya won't be able to stop any of you. Underlord Chaos will assume Hekate's mantle as the ruler of magic forevermore. And he'll rewrite the laws for magic casting on Earth. Soon we'll control all the mages and chaosgates. Just as Morganskians have experienced firsthand, if you're not with the Syndicate, you're enemy number one. Soon the same will apply to lowlies in Naples. And we won't stop there."

"I've gotten used to this body, so I just might keep it."

Alasdair sighed as if ruminating on a problem. "How has Hekate remained unaware we imprisoned the archOmega?"

"All you need to know is that Ember has handled that matter with aplomb and kept the goddess none the wiser," Cazzian replied.

"What about Goddess Karma? That vengeful bitch could still put a wrench into our plans."

"Oh, trust me, Alasdair," Cazzian sneered. "We made concessions for that. Once the archOmega and Hekate are dead, Karma will have no choice but to come out from hiding. Which is precisely what we're hoping for."

"Gods are far from infallible and rely too much on humans," Alasdair laughed.

"Cheers to that!" Vlad said, raising his glass. Others followed suit.

A man appeared by Alasdair's side or a holo-gab version thereof—the bounty hunter, Timo'thee. His surroundings were barely noticeable, but Pepper had seen enough to lose her mind—the shoreline in the background, birds ripping apart fish, a skiff on the sand. "I tracked down the girl and boy in some crypt. But I can't get inside. It's heavily warded with Sentries. If you can call them off, that would be great."

"That's gonna be difficult and could raise red flags. You sure they're inside?" Alasdair pressed.

"Absolutely positive. This crypt is built into the cliffs, and I've come across these before. There are two ways out: open a chaosgate and be caught immediately, which they haven't done, or exit through the front door, and I'm standing in front of the latter."

"There's a lot of red tape to cut through at DISI. Give me one hour."

"Make it thirty. Still, I got them. They're trapped and ain't goin' nowhere."

The holo-gab blinked out of existence right as Alasdair

called for Sala'dee. He commanded her to get the commander of DISI on the line.

In a snap, the footage cut off, and Sala'dee's face filled the screens. Her lips didn't move, but her silver eyes sure did—her pupils widened with fright. Then she whispered, her lips remaining utterly still, "Jaylyn, is that you?"

The good news was that Sala'dee couldn't see who was on the other side of the monitor. "No, it's Pepper." Sala'dee's head canted in curiosity. "We met once before. Help us! Please! The bounty hunter is outside."

Recognition alighted on her face. "Ah. When we last met, I told you to abort the mission, and you didn't listen."

"I know. But I wasn't your contact, so I didn't know the drill. Long story."

"Listen up! DISI just got the go-ahead to call off the Sentries. In a few minutes, Timo'thee will break in, and he brought reinforcements."

The front door exploded. "They're here," Pepper whispered.

"Bell, you have to do something!" Kimball paced, ripping open cabinets and drawers to search for who knew what, then morphed into a puddle of mush, tears of unadulterated terror welling.

"The door to the surveillance room … it's open. If I go to close it, they're gonna see me."

Surveillance monitors switched to the front door of the cabin. Towering gargoyles, their blackened wings folded by their side, squeezed into the crypt behind Timo'thee, various weapons hungering to impale Pepper and Kimball on display. The hunter pumped his shotgun and held it out before him.

"Not yet. You're inside a chaospocket," Sala'dee shared in a measured tone. "You must lock it tight if you haven't already. Quick. Grab Hideaway. It should be nearby. Look for a tube. You can't miss it."

Pepper rushed to the desk and swatted everything away in her frantic search. Eventually, she found the sealant and could barely hold on to the tube because her hands were quivering.

"Now what?" Pepper croaked. "They're about to storm inside the room."

Sala'dee told her to go to the door where the chaospocket began. "See the seam?"

"No!" Pepper then pleaded, "Please. Please. Please. Help me find the seam. He's coming inside."

"Take in a deep breath and look for a shimmer. It should be to the right or left of the door. You see it?"

Pepper looked everywhere. Or tried to. Unfortunately, she couldn't peel her eyes away from the hunter and the gargoyles, who formed a line and engaged their weapons before entering the room. Then, in a flash, a wink caught her eye. "Found it!" Following Sala'dee's rapid-fire commands, Pepper squeezed the tube, caulked the seam, then pinched it together. The opening disappeared before her agog eyes, and Pepper crashed to her bum. Timo'thee loomed over her, his foot hovering over the threshold, moments from entering the chaospocket. Pepper didn't move a muscle. And watched in horror as he walked right through her and disappeared.

"Pepper? Yoo-hoo. Timo'thee can't hear you."

But Pepper couldn't move. Same for Kimball, who was frozen in place as if playing a game of Red Light, Green Light.

After a few centering breaths, her coursing adrenaline about to crash at any moment, Pepper snapped out of her fear-induced state and raced to a wall. Pen in hand, she traced the outline of a door on the wall, but it remained inert. *Dammit!* She cut herself and fed the traced line her blood. Then nothing. Opening a chaosgate would be dangerous, but she figured it was a better alternative than their current predicament.

While kicking a wall and pounding it with her fists, Pepper yelled, "You have to get us out of here!" Claustrophobia, panic, fear—Pepper's cauldron of toxic emotions bubbled over, moments from exploding.

"I'm trying. But I'm kind of in a bind myself. When I tried to stall DISI and held them off as long as possible, I think that just put a target on my back. Now Alasdair is watching me like a goyle."

"I tried to open a chaosgate, Sala'dee, but it didn't work, and I don't understand why." Pepper's fists smarted from pounding desperately on the wall.

"Jaylyn once told me that only gods can chaosnaut out of a pocket." Sala'dee nibbled on a pen cap. "Timo'thee brought along an essence tracer. It's only a matter of time until they figure out you're still there and haven't left."

"If they find us, they'll find all your gathered intelligence."

Sala'dee admitted they hadn't planned on that eventuality and didn't have a backup plan in place, and she had never visited that safe house, so she wasn't even sure what intelligence her allies had on display. She suggested burning the evidence but then immediately took it back.

"No, there has to be a way out that doesn't involve our death." Pepper's eyes roamed around the room.

"Day just keeps getting better and better." Kimball finished with a hiccup. "Figures that only gods can open a chaosgate inside a chaospocket. Oh, what I wouldn't give to be a god. Then again, I already know what it's like to be worshipped by girls. Even some dudes. So that's godlike, right? What a glorious feeling—Hey. Give that back!"

Pepper grabbed a bottle of Grissel's ale from Kimball's hands mid-gulp and drank the mood-blunting, tear-assuaging concoction. Crashing on her bum next to Kimball at the table, Pepper calmed herself long enough to mull over Kimball's dumb-ass musings. *Only gods can open a chaosgate inside a chaospocket.* That statement prompted a memory to rise to the surface. Beatrice said Witherwhere was basically the only option out of Hell.

Pepper homed in on a bowl-sized sea shell in a shadow-draped corner, then ran to it. After she sniffed the residue staining the inside, notes of cinnamon and cloves wafted across her nose until sour smells like yeast and pennies drowned out the pleasant aromas. The altar at the Temple of Hekate in B'aRQoA'ba-ruch housed a bowl filled with similarly smelling porridge. Then Pepper recalled Beatrice saying that when calling Hekate, you needed to offer the goddess an oblation, then wondered if Jaylyn had been convening with the goddess.

"Kimball, where did you get the bottle of ale?" He pointed at a cabinet.

Pepper flung open the metal door. Inside was a corked bottle of wine, a dagger stained red, bottles of Grissel's ale, and packets of instant cinnamon-honey porridge—all the trimmings to summon a god. Relief surging through her veins, Pepper could barely get the words off her tongue. "Sala'dee, I know of a way out."

"Blessed Seren!" A beat later, Sala'dee's lips began moving as if talking to someone through her earpiece. "I have to go. Alasdair just summoned me into his office."

"Wait! You gonna be okay?"

"Don't worry about me. I have the luck of Goddess Seren and the courage of Queen Lilith running through my veins. If today's the day I evict that nasty, no-good parasite from Mephy's body, then so be it!" Sala'dee tapped her heart and voiced, "A'ma-nelis vala'olam." (Faithful to the end.) The screen switched to surveillance mode, showcasing Sala'dee sashaying into Mephy's office with a dagger held behind her back.

"Pepper!" Kimball cried out. "I think we have a problem!" Timo'thee was bent over, investigating the threshold.

Pepper ran to Kimball's side, only to bear witness to the mangled-bodied, scythe-wielding mala'kha arrive on the scene, ready to reap Pepper and Kimball's souls.

33

"Uh, Bell, you might want to hurry it up!" Kimball stood watch at the doorway. "Timo'thee just waved a gargoyle over to check out what is clearly the chaospocket seam."

"Your play-by-play is seriously stressing me out." Pepper blew back errant strands of hair from her sweaty face as she wrote the mirrored image of *Witherwhere*, using her and Kimball's blood on the lintel, and then screwed it up yet again. Not as easy as it would seem, especially in a time crunch. "What's that infernal beeping?"

"Methinks the essence tracer …? I'm gonna go out on a limb and say that the beeping is no bueno."

"Then, if he's reading your body heat, get away from the door!" Pepper snapped. "Don't forget to grab the supplies on your way back."

Kimball "Oh yeah"d. Then on Pepper's orders, he tossed

everything they'd need to summon Goddess Hekate from the cabinet into his backpack and returned to Pepper's side.

"Can they rip open a chaospocket seam after it's been sealed?" Kimball inquired.

"They sure can. Give me your hand. And stop squirming." Pepper bandaged Kimball's slashed palm that had leaked a trail of blood to the doorway and back.

Good news: the reality of what they were about to do, where they were about to venture, and the looming threats right outside the door sobered Kimball right up.

Bad news: Pepper entertained heaps of fear, her mind unsure of what would await them in Witherwhere, so it had no choice but to fill in the gaps with nightmarish images. And it wasn't like Beatrice had sold the place as delightful. More like the opposite. Word to the wise: when "souls of the lost" and "nobody physically sets foot inside, at least not on purpose" were found in any description, one should steer clear of that place at all costs. And here, Pepper and Kimball were headed straight into what could very well be the belly of Hell. It was either that or get apprehended by soul-reaping mala'khas, so the choice was obvious.

As for the plan: escape Hell first, get to Naples, then contact Hekate.

"Why are we staring at a bloodied two-D drawing of a door? Shouldn't it have activated?"

Silently worrying, her nails digging into her palms, Pepper croaked, "Yes—"

Pepper and Kimball jumped with fright when a pounding sounded near the door.

Kimball pressed Pepper for details about what exactly Beatrice had shared about opening a portal to Witherwhere, and she spat out everything she had recalled.

"Okay, so you can't consciously open a chaosgate to Witherwhere, and your mind has to be confused. Well, that's easy enough. You shouldn't have sobered me up, Bell."

"Oh!" Pepper would befriend common sense one day. Just not today.

After placing a drop of the Conscious Astraling potion on Kimball's tongue, then hers, she said, "Just in case." Together, they recited the mantra.

Next, she connected a string to each other's bags. If they were going to get lost, they'd do it together. "Really, Bell? A kid leash?"

Her stern look did the answering as she put half a drop of valeritonin on her and Kimball's tongue to quiet the mind and induce a hypnagogic state. They had a few minutes before the herb took effect, so Pepper extracted a few magic gems; the more power, the better. Then she envisioned fire devouring all the passels of evidence smattered about the hideout. Yellow vapor evacuated from the gem in bursts of fireworks, then set the entire room aflame. As the inferno raged on, smoke assaulted Pepper's lungs, the hideout blurring all around her.

And just like that, the door to the chaosgate ghosted open, and a fiery explosion catapulted Pepper and Kimball inside.

As soon as they rushed through the door on the other side, it snicked shut and vanished.

Serving as Witherwhere's welcome wagon, a warm breeze greeted them as if saying remove your cloak; it's not needed here. So they did. And shoved the heavy wool outerwear into their bags.

Miles and miles of pastoral landscape surrounded them. Rolling hills blanketed in wildflowers and soft downy grass. Then came the laughter. Infectious. Like drunken fools, Pepper and Kimball chuckled for no apparent reason. But it felt so good. The vibe, the environment, and the warmth and caress of the wind.

A small path unfurled before them, girded by soft grass. Pepper grabbed Kimball's arm and headed in that direction. The duo was too awe-struck with their surroundings to chat about anything, so they remained mum and let their eyes do the talking.

A familiar voice called out to Pepper about ten minutes into their sojourn. "Kiddo, you ready?" Larry stood lakeside, a fishing pole in each hand. He stepped into a boat, the water rippling from his weight, and said, "I catch. You cook. Deal?"

Pepper ran right into her dad's arms, her heart fluttering. Head pressed against his chest, she hugged him tightly, not wanting to let go.

A tugging sensation yanked her back and out of her dad's loving embrace.

Rooted in place, Pepper couldn't tear her eyes away from the lake, the greater part of her wanting to return. But a heavy weight pressing down on her shoulders prevented her from moving.

Suddenly, she gasped, her eyes fixed on a wretched and terrifying mangled beast—that she had hugged—standing on the shore. As soon as Pepper recognized its proper form, it vanished in a whirl of smoke. The lake disappeared shortly after that and was replaced by rolling hills.

"Bell! Wake up!" Wide-eyed, Kimball held on tightly to her shoulders and wouldn't let go.

"I'm awake!" She pushed his hands away.

"What happened?" Kimball asked, his voice shaky, still reeling from the near-death experience. He would have died, too, if not for the string between their backpacks. Luckily, he had used that to yank Pepper to safety.

"Didn't you see my pops?"

Kimball didn't see Larry or the lake and emphatically shook his head to further drive home the point.

As the duo caught their breaths, they continued on the

beaten path. Time felt meaningless here, and the sun remained fixed in the sky, so it was hard to gauge how long they had been walking.

Fatigue overcame Pepper, every step a chore, and she stopped to rest under a shady tree for a beat. There, she reminded herself that they were so close, but to what she couldn't recall, and pushed her body off the tree trunk and marched back to a waiting Kimball.

A short time later, a carnival popped up in the distance at a fork in the road. One of those small-town affairs where menus offered everything deep-fried. And the rides were rickety, one loosened bolt away from collapse, and terrifyingly fun.

A barker's voice, rich in timbre, hitchhiked on the warm breeze. "Step right up."

"You see the carnival, right?" Kimball asked hesitantly.

"I sure do, so how 'bout we avoid it."

Kimball waved, then tried to leg it toward the barker, but Pepper wouldn't budge and held tight to the string connecting their bags.

"Is that my pops?" Pepper shielded her eyes from the sun. It was indeed Larry by the food tent, holding two fried pickles. The comforting smell of french fries and dill tickled her nosebuds, and … she could almost taste the tartar dipping sauce that she and her dad loved so much, especially when they'd fry up fish and gorge on hush puppies. Hadn't Pepper seen her father earlier? She could have sworn she had, but perhaps it was just a dream.

A blink later, who she thought was her dad disappeared. In any case, Pepper gave a wide berth to the red-and-white food tents and the musical carousel that looked so inviting, and that's when she saw the barker's face morph into a demented clown with shark-like teeth. Its body stretched upward and its mouth split open like the terrifying entrance to a haunted ride.

But not Kimball. As he hotfooted it to the carnival, it was as if his strength had quadrupled in size. Pepper fought and dug her heels into the soil, but he overpowered her, and she crashed to the ground. Screaming for Kimball to stop, her arms pinwheeling, Pepper was dragged through the pebble-strewn terrain. She ripped whatever she could from the earth. Then, like a life-or-death game of Down the Clown, Pepper tossed gathered stones at Kimball's head.

The barker grabbed Kimball by his arms, its mouth lowering over his head. But Kimball didn't notice and remained anchored in place. Pepper continued to scream and volley stones until one walloped the back of his skull.

Kimball came to and scrambled to Pepper, then the two dashed as far away from the carnival as possible.

At the well-worn path that forked in either direction, Kimball picked left. Softly, he said, "My mom was there. Waiting by the Himalaya. Our favorite ride. She was giggling, Bell." He turned his head so Pepper couldn't see the tears escaping—too late. He sniffled and then chased the pain away with Grissel's ale. "I don't recall the last time I saw her happy. Like truly happy, other than when we would go to the county fair together. Just her and I. She'd eat all the greasy food and make me swear not to tell Dad. But it had been years since we last went."

"Bunny sure loved herself deep-fried cookies."

"Larry, too. Pickles were his favorite, if I recall," Kimball offered, deep in memory.

"My dad would eat fried crap every day if I allowed him."

As they continued walking, the pastoral setting on a warm summer day shifted. And a feeling of offness permeated about. Voices were heard all around and sounded like familial gatherings, reunions, and joyful celebrations, but Pepper couldn't see or interact with the tight-knit groups. Kimball also picked up on the voices and stepped closer to Pepper.

Witherwhere made it very clear that neither Pepper nor Kimball were invited. Yet she longed to be a part of it all the same. And if Pepper wasn't with Kimball, she wondered what that feeling of isolation would have done to her psyche.

They both agreed to not step off the path and not look toward the voices and keep their eyes forward as if they wore blinders.

Unsettled by the environment, the former childhood best friends coped by reminiscing. Harmless poking fun here. Weak chuckles there. Sharing embarrassing stories in between.

"Remember when you peed your pants?" Kimball couldn't help himself.

"Shut up. I did not!" Pepper laughed so hard she snorted. "I *so* did." In Pepper's defense, she had picked the perfect hiding spot during a game of Ghosts in the Graveyard. So, instead of leaving to use the john and losing, she did the next best thing. "Also, I was like six. You better never tell a soul, or I'll permanently zip those lips." The latter, meant to be said in jest, took on a lethal bent. Kimball didn't seem to notice, but Pepper did. A chill slithered through her body, and she shook it off.

The string between them had been stretched tight at the beginning of their journey. Now it was slack, Pepper and Kimball's shoulders brushing against each other as they meandered down the narrow path to wherever.

What felt like hours later, they reached another fork in the road that contained a shimmering "puddle of water" mirage, like all the others before—a visual representation of how the temperature seemed to climb at an alarming rate.

"I'm so tired," Kimball whined. "It feels like we're just

walking around and around in circles. I don't even know which direction to take this time."

Standing at the crossroads, the decision to go either right or left felt too taxing for Pepper to make. Bone-deep, debilitating exhaustion zapped her of all physical and mental energy, each step heavy, as if trudging through mud.

Unable to move any further, Pepper plopped down on the ground under the canopy of a nearby tree, happy to be out of the oppressive sun and off her feet. Sleepy, she fell to her back and closed her eyes.

Lying flat on his back, Kimball pointed out how he could barely lift his arms and how each felt like a hundred-pound weight.

Even speaking felt like a chore, so Pepper couldn't tell him her arms felt heavy, too. Still, Pepper knew something was wrong. And the more she thought about Kimball's comment about walking in circles, the more she agreed, but she wasn't sure why they were here.

Pepper tried to sit up but couldn't. Nor could she wiggle her toes. Her arms wouldn't move either. Blinking, she could manage, but just barely.

Strangely, the more she fluttered her eyelashes, the quicker her heart ticked until it picked up its pace to a gallop. That got her blood pumping and her mind a-whirling, the cobwebs coating her cerebral cortex disintegrating.

Come to think of it, they had happened upon one tree in this ... realm. Realm ... yes, that sounded familiar. They had passed one large tree—this tree—countless times without realizing it. Until now. And that same tree resided at a fork in the road. Pepper could have sworn they'd tried both the right and left paths many times, only to wind back at square one, but she couldn't be sure.

Though tricky at first, Pepper breathed, "Do you remember how we got here?" Kimball shook his head once.

"Or why we're here?" Talking became easier. "Or where here is? It's hard to speak, Kimby, but try."

Kimball did as suggested and sounded like he spoke through a mouth of peanut butter, his words unintelligible. Soon enough, they crystallized. "I remember … a doorway."

So did Pepper. A door to where? *Try to remember,* she kept willing herself. *Remember it all.* "Witherwhere."

"Yes. We came here to find a way home."

Like paint-by-numbers art, vibrant colors began to fill the once-blank canvas of Pepper's mind. She fought to recall everything she knew about Witherwhere. Something drew the souls of the lost here while they dreamed. Nobody physically came to this realm. But who had mentioned those tidbits to Pepper? Beatrice … that was who had told her.

"Can you open a chaosgate and magic us out of here?" Kimball said, his voice strengthening.

Magic? Pepper could wiggle her toes but not her arms to reach inside her satchel, so she tried to cast an easy enough spell—she visualized a magic gem levitating from her bag, and even tried to summon Air to help in that endeavor, but nothing worked. Perhaps Witherwhere prevented mages from casting spells. Which wasn't out of the realm of possibility. But that didn't explain the forgetfulness, the trance-like state of mind, or the exhaustion. What if Witherwhere subsisted on the magic and energy of lost souls for its own survival, like a parasite, and needed to ensure they stayed just long enough until it had drained them of their powers? So it devised deceptive vignettes that acted like a honeytrap. Still, that theory was antithetical to the whole magic is nature, and nature is magic.

Draining lost souls of their magic. That triggered a memory of something Cazzian had said about Hekate that Pepper had found odd at the time—how the goddess had unlimited magical energy at her disposal, energy not her own and not obtained from the moon. But the Syndicate didn't know where Hekate had derived the stolen power from—the power she'd use to keep herself safe while in mortal form. Could Witherwhere be the mysterious place? And if so, did that mean Hekate was the architect of this realm? After all, she was the guardian of chaosgates to other dimensions and realms, and her wheel was fixed on the door to the School of Magic.

Kymeo, Pepper voiced in her mind. That name sounded awfully familiar. *I think he's a professor. Yes, that's right. Head of the School of Magic and preeminent potions master and alchemist.*

Memories slowly crawled out of hiding. Kymeo had trapped Beatrice and other Agents of Karma in Witherwhere without magical conduits or weapons. Probably because magic wouldn't have worked here anyway, or … it was here that they put all their skills to the test. Unfortunately, the exit had yet to present itself. Still, Kymeo must have had a good reason to send the girls to Witherwhere of all places that trapped visitors in its spider web of a maze—

Pepper gasped, then shouted, "Maze! Kimby, I think we're stuck inside Hekate's wheel." Feeling relieved, she jiggled her legs and, with much effort, pulled her corpse-stiff body upright.

Life returned to Kimball, somewhat. He could move his legs but not his arms; they hung limp at his side. "Then how do we find the center of this wheel—or maze, I mean? Wouldn't that be the way out?"

Pepper pondered that for a beat, then said, "No. The maze was designed to trap people inside, not give them the option of leaving."

"So, what, this whole place isn't real? Once it drains us of our life force, then what? We shrivel up and die?"

"Beatrice passed the deadly trial, so there has to be a way out." That was at least promising news.

Pepper willed herself to recall everything she had learned about this realm. Nobody physically chaosnauted here, only astraled unconsciously, other than fixers and ruachtis like Bhi'gow and Loki on their hunt for desperate, down-on-their-luck clients like Pepper and her sister. If Witherwhere wasn't technically real but an unchanging creation, that left one other option. "Kimby, I think we're trapped inside a chaospocket," Pepper blurted out. "Which means"—she had to untie her overexcited tongue—"we need to look for a shimmer!"

At the same time, the duo's eyes sailed to the shimmery mirage at the crossroads they had passed countless times. Pepper helped Kimball to his feet, and slowly but surely, they made it to what Pepper hoped was the way out.

They stood in the heat puddle, but nothing happened. Of course, it wouldn't be that easy.

"How can you summon a chaosgate if it drained you of your magic?" Kimball asked, stress strangling his voice.

"I'm gonna take back what it stole." Pepper had watched Hekate's wheel spin countless times on the School of Magic's door and committed to memory the combination of all five elements.

Without explaining, she grabbed a pebble and began scrawling the sigils from memory on the soil. Earth and Air in the upper corners, Fire and Water below, and Aether in the middle. Then traced her best depiction of the maze. It wasn't the best, but she hoped it would pass muster.

When nothing happened, she realized she hadn't entirely completed the rendition.

As she spoke to Air, the words tumbling off her lips, the sigil materialized before her and winged to its drawn counterpart. Once activated, the Air sigil sketch levitated a few inches off the ground. Fire was next. Because she had yet to speak to the three remaining elements, she did the next best thing. She extracted magic gem dust and poured the sparkly red sand on the Earth sigil, orange on Water, and Indigo and Violet on Aether. Hopefully, her extracurricular studying and observations had paid off.

The sigils activated. The wheel began turning. And soon enough, a chaosgate appeared in the form of a nondescript doorway.

Mouth agape, Pepper said tearfully, "We found our way back home!"

Kimball pulled back her hand from writing the apparent destination on the lintel. "Technically, we can go anywhere, Bell." When she started to write, Kimball tried to reason with her. "Wasn't the plan all along to warn Hekate?"

Pepper faced a heavy choice, save her pops or the world. The option couldn't have been any simpler. Hurriedly, Pepper wrote a specific location on the doorframe of a bedroom in Vlad's castle. She recalled how that room was a stone's throw from the dungeon and devoid of belongings; therefore, the perfect spot to wait and hide before rescuing her pops and the others.

"Are you out of your damn mind?" Kimball continued to toss logic at Pepper in the hopes something would stick. "You seriously don't think they're monitoring the comings and goings inside the castle? It would be instant death if we were caught or worse. Then you can kiss Larry goodbye. So get that through your thick skull!"

From the moment Pepper set out on the "locate and save Beatrice" mission, the agreed-upon plan was to refocus their efforts on rescuing her dad first, then finding Jaylyn. But something always popped up, preventing Pepper from sticking with the primary objective, and the longer she waited, the closer death came a-knocking on her dad's door. Frustration and resentment bubbled inside her, ready to explode.

Kimball wouldn't stop babbling and reasoning with her,

so Pepper cut him off and said pointedly, "I will not lose my father. End of discussion." Pepper quickly added the day and time she wanted to arrive, recalling Beatrice's warning to pick a day to exit, or Witherwhere would take measures into its own hands, so she scribbled what she guessed was the correct day and the current year, then depressed the latch. But nothing happened. The door wouldn't open, almost as if it had been nailed shut. She put all her weight into it, but it still wouldn't budge. So she kicked it and pounded and screamed. "Come on! Open!"

"'Can't leave Naples either.' I overheard you mention that to Loki back at the Academy."

"Your *ex Chloe* said that on her podcast," Pepper sassed. "Mentioned how some supernatural force is preventing anyone from leaving Naples." Pepper heavily exhaled a sigh of resignation. "She said nothing about entering." To be so close to rescuing her pops yet couldn't gutted Pepper something fierce.

"You ready to contact Hekate, then?"

No, Pepper wasn't, but reluctantly agreed all the same.

Once they completed crafting the oblation, they took one final inventory of everything added to ensure they hadn't left out anything vital.

"Make sure the tidbit you offer the goddess is juicy. Otherwise, no passage, and then we're screwed," Kimball said by way of not helping.

Pepper lit a few black candles, not for any reason other than there were traces of melted wax on the limestone floor back in Jaylyn's hideout, and goddesses sure seemed to like mood-lighting if the first time Pepper had called out to Karma in her bedroom was any indication.

Once ready, Pepper spitballed, with as little enthusiasm as possible, "Goddess Hekate, Ruler of Magic, Keeper of Portals, it is I, Pepper Li Bell, and Sheldon Kimball Garcia the second."

"Actually, I go by Kimball—"

Pepper mouthed, "Shut up!" After an epic sigh, she tamped down the murderous thoughts and got back on track. "Goddess Hekate, we offer you sweetened oatmeal mixed with our blood, devilbee honey, hemlock, velvety wine from the year—" Pepper whispered to Kimball, "What's the year?"

He picked up the bottle and read aloud, "Two thousand Anno Daemonum Domini. Was an excellent year. And we offer you the finest ale named after Grissel to make your blood sing, head buzz, and your belly full."

Pepper mean-mugged Kimball and took back the summoning reins. "Hear us, oh, Hekate. You are wonderfully wicked. But in a good way. And magical. So much magic you have bestowed upon us. How can we ever thank you—"

Kimball swatted Pepper on the arm and whispered, "Enough already."

"And here's a tidbit you might find worthwhile. Vlad Dracula plans to kill you. Goddess Hekate, we humbly ask that you grant us passage to your home."

"Wow, Bell. You went from long-winded right to the point."

The door popped open.

Pepper hesitated. "Is it me, or did that seem way too easy?"

"Has to be the oatmeal."

The duo threw caution to the wind and bolted through the door together, a jarring sensation that stole Pepper's breath and made her feel unsteady like the aftereffects of spinning on a merry-go-round.

Swirling vibrantly hued stars accented the moonless blanket of night. Whatever dimension Hekate brought them to, it looked somewhat similar to Witherwhere, save for the time of day. Or night, as was the case.

A towering glass structure with menacing-looking spires lorded over the countryside. But that wasn't what caught Pepper's notice. Up ahead, a riot of purple-hued flowers jutted out from the emerald grass, their stalks about knee-high. Milky white tethers were attached to the flowers' petals and traveled upward about five feet high. On their ends, bobbing like balloons, were lunabells—round, iridescent dewdrops that resembled … well, bells, roughly the size of nickels. Pepper would be a fool if she didn't harvest the rare spell ingredient, so she rabbited toward the field, waving to Kimball to join her.

While Pepper gathered quite a few of the aetheric dewdrops that felt squishy, like punctured liquid-filled vitamin capsules, Kimball tapped her on the arm and whispered, "Bell, stop. We have company."

Goddess Hekate's head snapped in Pepper's direction as she glided out of the futuristic glassy structure. Swathed in a ceremonial robe fashioned from gold and black lace, a train trailed along the polished ground as she walked to a cloud-like chariot. With nowhere to run or hide, Pepper and Kimball were riveted to the spot, their eyes fixed on the goddess as she soared toward them.

Hekate was ancient looking. Terrifying, too, with ebony hair, glistening like oil, pulled back tightly by a gold headpiece in the shape of a reversed crescent moon lying on its back. The crown contained intricate designs carved out of bone that depicted an epic story. Beads in the form of moon phases dangled down and framed the goddess' cadaverous face and hollowed cheeks. Her ashen skin was polished save for a branding on her forehead that matched elements on the headpiece. Gore stained the rims of her sunken eyes and bony lips, with skin peeling off.

Eyes don't lie, a mantra Pepper steadfastly believed in and one the goddess bolstered; her white, neon-colored eyes alighted with intimate knowledge, for she recognized Pepper, a history shared between the two if Pepper wasn't mistaken. Whether Pepper was friend or foe had yet to be determined.

In the near distance, the wind picked up, detritus eddying. Tendrils of Pepper's hair fluttered in the breeze. As the goddess stepped off the cloud, she pivoted around, noting the wind change, and then moved in Pepper's direction with lethal precision. As if jumping through time and space, one minute, she was ten feet away from Pepper, and the next, Hekate stood not a foot away, her icy breath feathering across Pepper's nose, loose tendrils of her locks touching Pepper's arm. She smelled like magic, of salt-laced air and hickory, the aroma of petrichor in an evergreen forest, ripe oranges groves, and baby powder tying all the scents together.

"I can't feel my magic." Hekate's commanding tone belied the shock and horror written all over her godly features.

An explosion erupted in the sky, and a beat later, a hole appeared like a shotgun wound, and wispy threads of night bled out.

"When I say NOW, let go, or you die," Hekate said cryptically to Pepper and Kimball. She held out her skeletal hands, and the duo grabbed hold.

Hurricane-like winds ripped through the opening and yanked Hekate, Pepper, and Kimball into the whorling vortex with its tornadic hand. Pepper rocketed backward at what felt like warp speed. The wind rushed past her, a deafening sound, her cheeks flapping. She couldn't tell which way was up or down, and catching her breath proved challenging.

The word "now" ricocheted through her mind, and Pepper released her tight hold and then fell, her body rushing downward at a breakneck pace to her death.

34

Pepper crashed on a mattress canopied by velvet drapes. The only source of illumination in the bedchamber, albeit paltry, emanated from beyond the heavily tinted windowpanes. Before she could get her bearings, Kimball fell on top of her, nearly crushing her lungs. Pepper kneed him off of her and then rolled off the bed.

At the window, Pepper pushed back the heavy leather drapes. Below, sawgrass covered the terrain as far as the eye could see. Up high, it appeared as if the moon ate the sun, a crescent-size chunk all that remained, daylight waning by the minute.

"What the hell was that?" Kimball asked.

"My guess is the backstabbing wind deity on the Syndicate's payroll."

The only door inside the chamber creaked open. Pepper quickly grabbed Kimball's hand and rushed inside a wardrobe, knocking her head on a few empty hangers.

Squished inside the suffocating closet, Pepper and Kimball held tightly to each other's hands and prayed to Seren.

Footsteps traveled around the room, then stopped directly in front of the double doors of the wardrobe. One door groaned as it opened, and a business end of a gun thrust through, its cold muzzle boring into Pepper's forehead, daring her to make a move. Pepper nearly vomited, her heart *thump-thump-thumping* in her ears.

A muted chittering broke the tense silence, punctuated by a few curse words belonging to another. The gun recoiled, and the doors were flung open, revealing Loki and Perrin.

Pepper leaped out and scooped the furry capuchin into her arms, relief surging through her body, then hoisted Perrin into the love fest.

Pepper stepped back, her eyes pooling with tears of relief, and asked, "Where's my dad? Beatrice?" Her eager eyes roamed about; she even looked under the bed. Not that her pops could have squeezed within the truncated space, but still. Surely they must be around if Perrin had escaped.

In a snap, Perrin's smile dropped, as did Pepper's heart. The Lolly'ka jiggled the chain necklace draped around her neck that Kirby had slyly given her containing a bevy of clipped-on, colorful, pocked-sized charms, some odder than the rest: a notebook, jack-in-the-box, baby bottle, lipstick, wind-up chattering teeth, skull and crossbones, and others.

"Quillee drugged me during our catching-up session. The next thing I knew …" Perrin had woken up in a dungeon cell in Vlad's castle alongside Beatrice, the archOmega, Larry Bell, and other badly beaten viceOmegas. After vowing to go full-Lilith on her captors' asses and gut every Hound and wanderer, Perrin realized the means of escape were on her person all along. Hidden within the teeny-tiny charm notebook was a missive from Kirby.

The prison escape began with the enchanted harmonica

charm that played ear-piercing, high-pitched notes that only vampires could hear. That distraction allowed Perrin to use the wind-up jack-in-the-box to blow off the bars to her cell. The acid in a baby bottle and wind-up chattering teeth worked in unison to disintegrate the lead bars standing between the rest of the captives and freedom.

"Once I freed everyone, Beatrice and Ellie May trailed behind to ensure everyone got to safety. The castle's on lock-down, crawling with vamps and wanderers. So my job was to usher everyone else, including your dad, to a safe spot until we could figure a way out. Or, worst-case scenario, a plan of attack."

Perrin paused, seemingly nervous about continuing on, but then bit the bullet and admitted that everything had been going according to plan until Hounds, wanderers, and Jhi showed up out of the blue. Then all hell broke loose.

"Your dad and I raced as far away from the dungeon as we could. But then"—Perrin grimaced—"Miles appeared, and the mages freaked out and dispersed like hell-roaches, and I tried to stop them. Then Jhi caught up to us. I took my eyes off your dad for a split second, and then he was gone, and it was all a blur of sheer panic from that point on ..."

Perrin failed to find Larry, regardless of where she had looked. So, she had no choice but to save herself and hide. Once the coast had cleared, Perrin ventured to the dungeon to search for Pepper's dad, but it was empty. When a cavalcade of Hounds and wanderers had appeared, she ran for cover and secreted herself behind a tapestry. To Perrin's surprise, a secret passage resided behind the floor-to-ceiling wall hanging that led to a way out. Not long after she had escaped from the castle, she ran into Loki. The ruachti had been traversing the Everglades in an airboat, along with allies, trying to figure out a way to steal inside the castle.

"It was a truly horrible experience, trudging through the

swamp. Ew. But that was two weeks ago. So, I've had time to calm down." Perrin sighed dramatically. "And ever since then, we've been planning to sneak back inside and rescue everyone. We tried one other time, about a week ago, but they had moved everyone from the dungeon. To where we don't know."

"Wait? Did you say *two weeks*?" Kimball blurted out, utterly confused. But nobody replied.

This wasn't happening … Loki tried to place a comforting hand on Pepper's trembling arm, but she flicked it off. Then asked again, more forcefully, "Where's my dad, Beatrice, and Ellie May?"

"They're about to be killed," Kymeo said as he slid through the door like a whisper. "So get your emotions in check before we face the Syndicate." After scolding Pepper, Kymeo mouthed to her, "You have the relic?" Pepper discretely nodded, which pleased him, as evidenced by one side of his lip curling up.

Hot on Kymeo's heels, a female slipped through the door and swiftly locked it behind her, then said, "All players have arrived, and Hounds've secured all entry points with defensive wards. Nobody leaves the castle until after the ceremony. Y'all, I can't shake this ominous feeling. It's too quiet. Like they know we're here or somethin'."

The last time Pepper had laid eyes on this female—or rather her golem—was back in Dillard, Georgia. Josephine Budreau was dressed for battle. Her short torso was wrapped in a long-sleeved, body-hugging top, and her long, lean legs were swathed in tight jeans with sunbursters, stakes, and a gun strapped to her thighs. Tightly curled hair was pulled back in a ponytail, and numerous holes in her ears were bereft of jewelry.

Josephine acknowledged Pepper and Kimball with a nod, then introduced herself as Josie.

"Did you see my dad during the reconning?" Pepper's heart felt like quitting.

"Not exactly," Josie said point-blank. "Your dad's with Goddess Hekate, BB, Ellie May, and the rest of the vice-Omegas. They're all hidden behind an impenetrable force field in the center of the great hall." Unlike Kymeo, an element of compassion intertwined with her harsh news. "The Syndicate damn near cleared out Ellie May's conclave." She let out a breath and shook her head.

Besides Josephine, Loki was mission-ready, his entire body a mobile armory. When was Perrin *not* ready for a bloodbath? Pepper grew confused with Kymeo's ensemble: a loose-fitting peasant top and hemp drawstring trousers; surprisingly, the professor wasn't barefoot, yet his choice of footwear didn't exactly scream, *I'm ready for battle*. More like a meditative hike through a forest while smoking a reefer.

Feeling woefully unprepared and scared senseless that she was about to be thrust into battle with no warning, Pepper asked for someone to please bring her and Kimball up to speed. And it would be great if they could start with how they had wound up in Castle Dracula and why they appeared to be a cohesive force in the midst of executing a well-thought-out plan.

Loki began filling in the blanks. Back in Hell, once the Hounds had crossed the threshold of the Tenth Circle Tavern, the Karma-created chaosgate's security defenses activated and sucked in anyone nearby—which happened to be Loki. The ruachti had found himself back at Karma Academy and helped Kymeo defeat a second wave of Hounds. After securing the school, they tracked down Josephine in Georgia, figuring they needed all the help they could get.

Meanwhile, at the Budreau homestead, Josie had already woken up from the magic-induced fugue, courtesy of ghostly Ketteline. From there, the trio ventured to Naples as Josie traced her sister's whereabouts in Pepper's backyard. With Perrin's help, they tracked down podcaster Chloe Dhawan, who helped them find shelter where they could hunker down and strategize. And the rest was history.

"Let's just say my gran pointed me in the right direction of where she had hidden my magic and divulged some other family secrets revolving around my sister and the quote-boarding school-end quote BB had attended. Said I'd find out sooner rather than later and left it at that. But that's Ketteline for ya. Cryptic as all get out."

"A spell prevented Kimball and me from chaosnauting to Naples, but not you all. How?" Pepper asked, her heart and mind reeling.

"To Naples or Vlad's castle?" Josie asked, then said, "You can chaosnaut inside the city. You just can't leave. We'll have to deal with that issue once we've successfully completed tonight's rescue mission."

"Sweetling, Loki and I tried to chaosnaut to Hell to find you, but we couldn't even summon a gateway. Not to anywhere."

Josie then shared a doozy. "We noticed on the way here that the streets of Naples are empty. Whatever they're planning doesn't bode well for your fellow citizens."

"You could say that again," Kimball said. That opened the door for Pepper to inform all present what she and Kimball had gleaned, mainly the magic transference ritual and Underlord Chaos' role in it all.

"If they think they can wipe out my family's bloodline, they have a big surprise waiting for them," Josie added, ready to kill, her face emoting as much. Same for Loki, Kymeo, and Perrin. Then again, the Lolly'ka's default mode was bloodshed.

Not Pepper, though. The closer they got to go-time, the

faster her heart beat, her palms a sweaty mess. She wasn't alone either; Kimball was fidgety and couldn't sit still.

Kymeo strode to the window, pulled back the drapes, then said, "T minus thirty minutes until the solar eclipse occurs. One hour until sunset." He returned to the group. "The magic transference ceremony should start shortly, so"—his hands busied themselves by doing a weapon's check on his person —"we have to get a move on."

"I concur." Josie dug through a pouch, retrieved a crystal, then asked, "Everyone ready? Know their roles?"

Pepper panicked, buckets of sweat dripping down her back. The probability of them all making it out alive was dangerously low, and *why wasn't anybody acknowledging that fact? Wait, what if I'm stuck in Witherwhere, trapped in a nightmare?* Pepper contemplated. Honestly, if someone had notified her she had just woken up from a years-long coma, she wouldn't have been surprised. In fact, it would have eased her mind.

Pepper and Kimball chimed in at the same time, "No!"

Pepper then held out both her hands. "Can somebody please just slow down for a second—" Overwhelm tied her tongue into knots.

Kimball stood next to Pepper, his arm brushing against hers, which felt a tad comforting. Then he uttered, "What I was trying to say earlier—y'know, when nobody listened to me?—is that for us, the lunar eclipse occurred just a day ago. Bell and I jumped through time—*two weeks*. Let me repeat. Two. Weeks! So, if you want to go over the plan of action with us in *excruciating* detail, that would be dope."

Loki, noting Pepper was moments from a panic attack, rifled through his sated bandolier, extracted a few weapons, then handed them to Pepper and Kimball: silver stakes, sunbursters, and semiautomatics with silver-encased bullets.

Regardless of the number of weapons at her disposal,

Pepper could unequivocally say she was not ready for what was steamrolling down the pike. She had one shot to save her pops. There was no room for errors. A rescue mission of this magnitude required meticulous strategizing and mental preparation. Not this slapdash operation. The voice buried within Pepper chimed in and said, *Larry deserves better.*

"Our mission is solely search and rescue," said Kymeo. "Nobody needs to get all heroic tonight. I need everyone here to remain alive by night's end. Am I clear?" Heads nodded. "Good. We use a divide-and-conquer approach." Kymeo shifted his attention to Pepper. "Planning weeks in advance for a mission is a luxury not afforded by your kind. Situational adaptability—learn it. I don't care if you don't like it. Am I making myself clear?"

Pepper pursed her lips and nodded.

Kymeo went over the mission with no room for errors, which did little to assuage Pepper's fears and mounting frustration. The goal was simple in theory: to extract prisoners with as little warfare as possible, as the time for going toe-to-toe with the Syndicate would have to be later. While Perrin and Pepper would rescue Larry, Beatrice's life would be in Josie's hands. Kymeo vowed to put all his efforts into taking out Vlad. It made sense for Loki to set his sights on Goddess Hekate; he was a demigod, after all.

"Vlad's heavily guarded by Hounds and"—Josie's face screwed up with disgust—"Sawyer, whom I've talked to and even broke bread with countless times when she'd visit Beatrice, *her best friend,* I might add. Only now, she's Vlad's head bodyguard and personal assassin."

"That makes her the first domino to fall. I'll handle Sawyer," Kymeo said.

When everyone was done going over their individual tasks one final time, Kimball inquired, "What about me? What's my mission?"

Perrin said, "Keep your precious ass here and wait for us to return."

Noting Kimball grimacing with dejection, Pepper interjected, "Isn't there anyway, or perhaps a spell, that could make Kimby invisible? He could help take down the Hounds. Stop his father and murderous Miles ...?"

The ruachti wore a look that communicated, "Hell no!" Josie wasn't sure how to feel as she had just met Kimball. Perrin rolled her eyes.

"Yeah, what Bell said!" Kimball's chocolate-brown eyes were alight with possibilities. "I could totally watch Bell's back."

Pepper wasn't so sure about that, but appreciated Kimball's support.

"I noticed"—Kymeo's violet eyes didn't unlatch from Pepper as he rifled through his pocket that must have been deeper than the Pacific Ocean—"that you had helped yourself to my supplies." He handed Kimball a vial. "Drink that. Ask questions later. All you need to know is that it will cleave your shadow from your body. To control your shadow, give it an order. Word to the wise: shadows can die, which means you're already dead. So pick your target wisely."

"Once we have our targets, where do we reconvene?" Pepper couldn't contain the bottled-up nerves for much longer.

"At the dungeon, look for the tapestry down the hall," Kymeo replied, "the one depicting Vlad on horseback. There's a hidden passage behind it. Follow the stairs until you reach the subterranean burial chamber."

"You'll know you're close when you gag from the smell of rotten eggs," Josie added.

"Jump in the narrow waterway, hold your breath, and dive," Perrin said. The waterway flowed directly into the soupy Everglades and was how Perrin had escaped, and the others had stolen inside the castle. They had to fight off a few gators along the way, too.

Josephine extracted a poppet from her satchel that mirrored her likeness. After slicing her palm, she directed drops of her blood to fill the inside of its cotton-stuffed body. Once the cotton soaked up her life force, forming what looked like human tissue, Josie placed a vivid green crystal inside the doll's chest that mimicked a heart. Or would once the tissue encased it.

Once Josie zippered the poppet up tight, a golem materialized and stood next to its creator. At first blush, one would think Josie had an identical twin. The likeness between the two was uncanny. No physical outlier jumped out, from the matching hair to gray eyes to skin color to height. Far different from the last golem Pepper had encountered, the one crafted by Beatrice, and Pepper voiced as much. She didn't mean to. It just blurted out as she inspected the curious creature.

"Golems were never BB's strong suit," said Josie. Pepper couldn't argue that fact. Josephine's golem had finesse. Less mindless bull in a China shop going berserk, much like Beatrice's, and more robotic, with advanced AI capabilities.

Josie then flicked open a flask and drowned a concoction that appeared like dry ice with hints of sparkling violet underneath the vapor. Liquid magic. A beat later, electricity flickered on Josie's skin, appearing like a barbed wire; there one second, gone the next. Her eyes zapped with the neon bolts.

Kimball voiced what Pepper felt. He wanted—*needed*—the liquid magic and ended by saying, "Sharing is caring," which fell flat.

"Your lowlie vessel would explode upon contact with Aqua Magicus," Kymeo said matter-of-factly.

"I didn't bring more; I'm sorry." Josie explained that she

only had enough for Beatrice, Goddess Hekate, and Ellie May. "I overheard one acolyte mention the sacrifices were under a sleeping spell. Here." She handed a syringe to Loki, Perrin, and Kymeo. "Aim for the carotid artery. Aqua Magicus will wake them right up." The elixir worked like an epinephrine shot to the heart. Josie figured that once the strongest, magically speaking, were on their feet, they'd provide the support needed to rescue the other captured viceOmegas and Larry.

Pepper appreciated Josie thinking about her father more than she could vocalize—a gesture she wouldn't soon forget—and the voice deep down concurred.

Pepper was moments from expressing more questions and concerns to inflate her struggling confidence, but she essentially said, *Screw it.* Her pops was the object of her focus. Was Pepper ready to fight if need be? Not by a long shot. But honestly, she couldn't think about anything other than getting her pops to safety. And perhaps that nearsightedness chased away the mushrooming fear because it temporarily left her mind and heart.

On the embroidered rug, rays of sunlight slowly retreated toward the window as claws of darkness ripped their way across the sky, leaving behind an orangey-red tint that stained the heavens. The total eclipse of the sun was nigh.

Kymeo directed Kimball to drink the potion, then stressed that it had a maximum time limit of thirty minutes.

After Kimball knocked back the contents, his silhouette slithered on the floor, away from its human host, and grew longer and stretched like taffy, tugging and pulling, until it broke off from Kimball. Once freed, shadow-Kimby left the sanctity of the floor and sprouted upward, morphing from 2D to 3D and back and forth. Once it finished forming, it stood off to the side, yet close enough to Kimball, its arms akimbo and expression cheeky.

"Whoa!" Kimball breathed. Kymeo's shadow soon joined Kimball's, and the silhouettes nodded in greeting.

All present slipped into black robes and pulled the hoods over their heads. As long as Pepper and the gang played their cards right, they'd go unnoticed.

Josie then handed over a few weapons to her golem. What she lacked in strength, her golem more than made up for. Perrin held her jump rope and death-dealing yo-yo-cum-garrote, along with every-color magic gems for her to draw on their power. Loki cloaked himself, Pepper, Kimball, and Perrin in shadows. Kymeo and his shadow went over a final weapons check. And just like that, their ragtag team had multiplied.

Even so, confidence wasn't brimming within Pepper. Not at all. In fact, she felt like the embodiment of terror if she were being honest. Loki, sensing her apprehension, reminded her to remain focused on the task at hand and trust her instincts.

As for that mushrooming fear that had temporarily left ... well, the moment Pepper exited the bedchamber and marched to the ceremony, it had returned with a vengeance.

35

The great hall, roughly ten times the square footage of Pepper's humble ranch home, served as ground zero for the Winter Solstice ritual and was packed to the gills with robed acolytes, all chanting.

A handful of industrial-sized barrels and a wall of TV monitors took up one side of the hall; tens of thousands of Naples residents were present, their faces glued to the screens, eyes glimmering with hunger as they waited for their liege to speak.

Giant stone gargoyles, four to be exact, stood sentry from their ceiling-high platforms in all four corners of the vast hall. From Pepper's recollection, the ceiling was gilded in gold and patterned with lace, but that ceased to exist because tonight, the solar eclipse blanketed it entirely, appearing close enough to touch.

The new moon appeared gigantic and hung prominently in the hall's center as it was moments from totally eclipsing the sun, save for a faint ring of fiery light girding the celestial ball of gas, a mirror image of what transpired outside. A sphere hovered in the hall's center, directly underneath the solar eclipse. It resembled a life-size snow globe, with charges of reddish-orange energy zinging off and chaotically swirling within the glass. Housed within were her dad and the others needing rescue. Before they could save the sacrificial offerings, Pepper and her team would need to get past the impenetrable force field around the sphere and the cluster of hooded, black-robed acolytes blocking the barrier.

The acolytes stood shoulder to shoulder, chanting in unison, their eyes focused on the force field as it fortified in strength with each rise and fall of the incantation. Miles had sidled up next to Vlad, Shelly Garcia was flanked by the serial killer and Mob boss Enzo, then tech phenom Sarah. There were many soul-sellers Pepper didn't recognize; some she did, like pint-sized Quillee, imposter Queen of the Lolly'kas, and the jeweled staff she proudly held; the newly "elected" mayor of Naples; and Ron fucking Don—Ron's self-proclaimed moniker. Developer Ron's Botoxed mug graced the likes of billboards plastered around town, proclaiming that the animal-populated, environmentally protected wetlands would soon be home to luxury apartments and "estate" homes unaffordable for most Neapolitans.

Other real estate moguls joined Ron, Shelly's lawyer friends and bankers, and city and county officials who sure loved to line their pockets with bribes aplenty. The acolytes came from all walks of life but shared one commonality: all had sold their souls. Soon they would collect their promised reward for helping Cazzian resurrect from Hell.

Loki chittered, "Good luck and stick to the plan," before disappearing. From here on out, Pepper was on her own.

Josephine and her golem blended in so seamlessly with the robed acolytes that Pepper couldn't make either of them out amongst the crush. Kymeo's shadow flitted to another hiding spot, bringing it closer to Sawyer's shadow.

Sawyer's shadow, appearing as a puddle on the floor, slunk away from Blondie, then cascaded to the wall, scrabbled up it, hung from the rafters, then sifted down like black smokey goo. Kymeo spotted shadow-Sawyer, too, and signaled to his shadow with a slight nod. As for Kimball, he hid on the outskirts of the great hall, just far enough away where he'd be safe without magic at his disposal, yet close enough for him to mentally control his shadow.

Thank Seren that Cazzian and Ember were on the opposite side of the great hall. Too many Hounds for Pepper's liking flanked their high king. Then there was Underlord Chaos, a frightening sight to behold. He didn't resemble your average demon much, but what came *before* demons. Before Lucifer conquered Hell and ousted Queen Lilith, the same queen Chaos had once worshipped before stabbing her in the back. The ancient demon's face and body lacked skin as if it had been flayed, and his flesh, the shade of a burnt, rotting corpse, was front and center. The sclera of his eyes were pools of blood. Pointed horns jutted out from his head, and thorny tentacles protruded from his absurdly long neck.

Underneath the eclipse, the smoky walls of the energy ball cleared and revealed all the sacrifices—Goddess Hekate, Beatrice, Ellie May, and countless viceOmegas—who were sprawled out on stone altar tables, lying as still as the moon and sun above, under the influence of a sleeping curse. And then there was Pepper's pops, exposed and vulnerable. His nearly naked body was a map of torture, a smattering of bleeding, festering wounds, and bruises in various stages of healing, covering him from head to toe—all from Miles' hands.

Pepper's face twisted into a grimace of rage. From the moment she'd learned of her father's abduction, everyone told her to wait. *You can't rescue your pops yet. Not before you do this or that.* Something always popped up, tearing her away from him. He wouldn't be in this mess if she could have gotten to him sooner. Her days of waiting were over. There had to be a way to get past the force field and rescue her father. Pepper took a step forward and—

"Pepper Li," a tickled-pink voice with a slight Scottish burr boomed.

The Hounds wrested Pepper out from her hiding spot, frogmarched her directly to Cazzian and Ember, and roughly tossed her to the cold hard ground before Cazzian's slippered feet, then returned to their high king's side. Pain shot through Pepper's body from the fall.

"Right on time. I saved you front-row seats." Cazzian summoned chains to wrap around Pepper's neck and hands. With that, her magical powers and vitality vanished as if flushed down a drain, along with her last ounce of hope, a blanket of heaviness all that remained.

Ember placed her palms before Pepper, clenched her fists, then whooshed them back, a gesture that stole Pepper's voice.

Perrin's baby blues stood out amongst the sea of revelers. Pepper discreetly shook her head to Perrin, telling her to stand down and not do anything crazy. Perrin dropped her hands.

Loki, still cloaked by the shadows, was nowhere to be seen. But that wasn't the case for shadow-Kimby. That little devil, appearing like a roving puddle of goo, caught the sights of a Hound and tricked it into going to a dark corner to investigate the silhouetted curiosity. There, the bloodsucker no sooner met its fate—Kimball. A black streak whisked out of nowhere, wielding a silver-dipped stake in each hand, and stabbed a patrolling Hound with one before the vamp could see what was coming.

Once that bloodsucker breathed its last breath, shadow-Kimby extracted the stake, then jumped off the corpse and soared to another vampire making the rounds. The Hound didn't even notice the black streak of death pummeling its way and fell to the stone floor, a stake sticking out of his chest. About ten Hounds remained, not including wanderers. The tag team consisting of Kimball and his shadow eliminated threats and cleared the path for a quick getaway, which was all part of the plan. What wasn't part of the plan was Pepper getting caught.

Quiet and deadly like a blood clot, Kymeo snuck up behind Sawyer with a valeritonin-soaked handkerchief at the ready—

"Silence!" At Vlad's command, the chanting ceased. The high king demanded that Sawyer come to his side. Sawyer harkened to her master's call with nary a second thought.

Kymeo missed his opportunity to take down Sawyer and retreated.

"Thank you, everyone, for attending," Vlad addressed the robed acolytes, then turned his attention to the TV monitors. "I wish to extend a warm welcome to all who chose to spend their Winter Solstice with me."

Countless viewers swooned in response, and some dramatically placed their hands over their hearts.

"I am equally honored and humbled by your generosity," Vlad said with a one-hundred-watt smile, "and will try to make tonight's festivities worth your while."

Pepper noted Vlad's eyes. How his pupils dilated, then contracted as he spoke like the hypnotic lull of the surf lapping on the shore, then lazily retreating to the Gulf of Mexico, back and forth, and forth and back—

Ow! Pepper screamed in her head. Cazzian's foot had smashed her fingers.

Mesmerized, the TV-viewing revelers' mouths hung open, their bodies swaying in unison.

Vlad raptly watched the heavens as the new moon devoured the sun, then proclaimed, "Let the ceremony begin!"

On the fourth night, the dragon devours the sun as it stands still with the moon in the sky ...

Ember took that as her cue and walked gracefully to the wall of TVs and stood next to the barrels. She closed her eyes, slowly raised her arms, and began chanting a haunting singsong that wasn't in a language from what Pepper could ascertain. Or not a language Pepper knew. Soon everyone followed suit, including those glued to their TVs.

With each rise and fall of the chant, the energy swelled and harmonized, reaching the desired vibration. At that precise moment, Ember fused her energy to the reservoirs of magic stored in the industrial-sized barrels taken from mages and lowlies during the lunar eclipse. Appearing like cords of light, the stolen magic flowed to its summoner, its vibrational match, and Ember drained the barrels to their last drop. Once the powers soaked through her pores and increased her abilities a thousandfold, she extracted visible cords of vitality from all the TV viewers. Tugging and tugging, like hoisting a rope on a ship, she drew out their life force, their chi. The faces of the poor unfortunate souls blanched of color, their bodies listing to one side, then the other, before crashing to the floor.

One monitor showcased an aerial view of Naples as if taken from space. Like fiber optics, a network of golden-white energy cords exited countless homes and moved at a breakneck speed to Vlad's castle and then down through the imitation sky above, zipping past the solar eclipse and hovering above Ember.

With a sweep of her hands, Ember commanded the stolen

chi to slam into Vlad. The sheer force of the blast nearly knocked the high king off his feet, but he held firm as he absorbed the energy and magic. He lit up like a furnace, the inside of his body aglow with yellow-orange light. Vlad levitated, the tips of his black loafers brushing the floor.

With a nuclear blast of energy thrumming through Vlad, the ring of fiery light around the moon-blocked sun pulsed. Vlad chanted louder and faster, his invocation reaching a frenetic pace. In response, the sun's rays increased in size, expanding and expanding, trying to reach out to Vlad, its energetic match.

With a *pop*, sizzling cords of the sun's energy traveled downward to Vlad and seeped into his pores. Vlad's fangs extended as he sucked the energy from the sun, draining it dry.

As the chanting rose to a crescendo, the sun exploded into balls of fire as if Vlad had ripped out the sun's very core from its celestial body. With that final blast, the sun bled out like a slashed wrist, its last ounce of vitality devoured by the dragon.

Within Vlad, he housed the sun's deadly heat, rendering the vampire a living ball of gas. The high king burned from the inside out, his body aflame. But Vlad held on for dear life; his arms spread out to the sides as if crucified to the air. Flames licked his eyeballs, his mouth opened wide, and a scream of abject pain tore from his throat akin to the wails of all the damned tormented in Hell. His skin boiled and blistered as the inferno raged on, engulfing his arms and limbs. Skin melted off like wax, his face liquifying. Vlad fought and fought against being devoured completely.

Then everything stilled. The flames died. And Vlad's body regenerated, new skin reweaving over the exposed bone, welts, and burns.

Next to Vlad, a blackened blob puddled on the floor and

grew in size. In the light of the dying sun, Vlad's shadow was born.

... the dragon destroys Night's ever curse and becomes Day's ally ...

Vlad regained control, whipped his hands out to the side, and levitated not to Goddess Hekate's body but to the arch-Omega's. Of course, kill Hekate's righthand, her sword and shield, and the one housing all the magic first. But Vlad wouldn't be assassinating Ellie May tonight. That role belonged to Ember. As she glided to center stage, the Firebird lowered the hood of her robe and daintily removed a ceremonial dagger from her pocket.

Ember's usually impassive features broke rank and emoted delight as she swung the dagger upward to its zenith, where it hovered above Ellie May's naked form. The chanting, serving as musical accompaniment, kicked up a notch.

The archOmega remained still, trapped in a dream, unaware of Death holding out its hand to her. And maybe that was for the best. Maybe the pain would be less severe.

Golem Josephine lowered its hood and galloped toward Ember, regardless of the force field preventing passage. Or maybe a golem could pass through? But Vlad, not even looking back, felt its presence. With little effort, the high king thrust out his hand and placed it on the golem's chest. In a flash, the magical creature burned, its ashes sifting down to the floor.

Without missing a beat, Ember slammed the dagger down with all her might and buried it into Ellie May's heart. The archOmega violently struggled for breath. She snapped upright and grabbed ahold of the blade, gurgling and choking on her blood, her eyes radiating shock and fear. But it was too late. As the archOmega's life force vacated, her body convulsed one last time. When the red-haired beauty collapsed on the stone altar, white luminous magic left her corpse and zoomed into Ember's mouth.

Ember's lips curved up in a half-smirk. But she celebrated too soon. A supernatural force violently catapulted the Firebird backward and kicked her body in the air. She clutched her chest, her face pinched with nausea.

Vlad commanded the chanting crowd to pick up the pace and volume.

From inside Ember's body, what looked like a legion of hands pressed on her skin. The magic was unstable, pushing, trying to escape, and Ember fought tooth and nail to keep it inside her. Her face turned blood red, and sweat beaded on her brow. She screeched, "My body's rejecting Hekate's magic. I can't contain it much longer. Hurry!" She let loose an agonizing howl as her body spread eagle in the air, her limbs pulling in opposite directions as if moments from being quartered.

Cazzian stepped forward, but Vlad put his hand out, a gesture that commanded Cazzian not to intervene. A pained expression took form on Cazzian's face. One of care and concern. But he listened to Vlad and stayed put; still, Cazzian's eyes wouldn't leave Ember's. Not for one second.

The distractions caused the force field to wane in strength. That meant Pepper and her team had a fighting chance. Loki realized that as well. No longer shadow-cloaked, his eyes flickered to milky white as he summoned mana. Lips pulled back in a snarl, barracuda-like teeth on display, and his quarterstaff held out before him, Loki cut a formidable figure. One who channeled Tun-fendin'ga.

As the force field crumbled and a slim opening presented itself, thanks to Loki, Josie stepped up beside the capuchin, rubbed a necklace between her hands, and whispered into a pendant. Blood trickled down Josie's arm—blood that originated from a deep slash marring her forearm. A beat later, the dead stirred. Hounds that Kimball and his shadow had killed rose from their graves on the ground and mechanically walked toward Josie, who then gestured to the force field and Ember.

Kymeo canted his head up to the stone gargoyles and then discretely pointed to the enemies, one after the other. The Earth trembled. Harkening back to Kymeo's harsh lesson, Pepper closed her eyes, placed her hand on the floor, and felt the slightest vibrations. The stone gargoyles sprung to life, leaped off their perches, and stormed toward the enemies. Kymeo bolted out of the way as the enchanted army of goyles zipped past, silt sifting down from their flapping stony wings.

After a nod of Vlad's head, quite a few acolytes walked inside the fractured force field before Vlad recharged it quickly, using the sun's power. Goyles swooped in, but it was too late. One enchanted beast attempted to destroy the electrified barrier and was immolated on the spot. But not shadow-Kimby. That sly devil had sneaked inside, sight unseen.

Kymeo, too busy commanding his enchanted vanguard, failed to notice that Sawyer's shadow was hot on his trail. But his shadow intervened and jumped on Sawyer's shadow, and the two duked it out, rolling around on the ground like a dust cloud.

Inside the force field, Quillee stepped up to one of the slumbering viceOmegas on an altar, which no doubt could have been Perrin had she not escaped from the dungeon. Shelly followed suit and stood before a sacrifice of his own. Same for Enzo and Sarah and a host of unnamed others. The sum total of the archOmega's conclave, making up some of the most powerful mages on Earth, would be part of tonight's sacrifices.

Miles parted through the crowd, a dagger in his hand, and strode to Pepper's father.

Pepper tried to scream for help, but she couldn't voice the words. She squirmed against her chains, but couldn't move. This couldn't be the end. Not after everything she'd gone through to get here. She had to escape. Had to rescue her pops. Pepper cursed a litany of gods, the almighty God, then changed her tune and pleaded for their help in saving her father and stopping the prophecy.

What felt like little shocks of electricity on her chest jolted Pepper and grabbed her attention. Something quivered and skittered within the confines of her satchel, strapped across her chest.

Ever so slowly, Pepper slipped her hand under her cloak—

"Ah-ha," Cazzian chastised Pepper and held her in place. "You're going to want to watch what happens next."

She caught a pungent whiff of ashwagamint, then eyed shadow-Kimby skittering past.

Kimball, whatever you have planned, hurry. Please.

While holding her breath not to give away a telltale, Pepper quickly moved with laser-like precision. Deftly, her fingers maneuvered under her cloak to the satchel. Biting her lip, her breathing measured, she slipped her fingers underneath the flap. The Hand of Destiny flew into her palm. With her other hand, she extracted a vial of lunabells and clenched her fist around it.

Larry stirred, his sleeping spell broken thanks to ashwagamint—thanks to Kimball!

While Vlad refocused his efforts on magicking the barrier back into existence, Perrin's jump rope coiled around the high king's heels, distracting him just long enough for his defenses to be lowered and the barrier spell to dissipate.

The events unraveled so quickly. Now that Team Pepper had shattered the force field, Josie snuck up to Beatrice and shoved an ampoule of Aqua Magicus right into her neck.

Perrin helped a very sore Larry up and tried to drag him off the table.

Loki must have helped Hekate, though Pepper couldn't see the ruachti. Still, Hekate couldn't move. Some supernatural force far greater than the goddess pinned her in place. The goddess squirmed and kicked, but the invisible chains wouldn't budge. As Loki's lips moved a mile a minute, air molecules stitched together, one after the other, and formed a protective barrier around the goddess. Merely a stopgap until Loki could figure out how to relieve Hekate of the invisible chains holding her captive.

Shadow-Kymeo declared victory over Blondie's shadow by tying it up. But where was Kymeo? Pepper scoured the mayhem. Kymeo kicked Sawyer's legs out from under her, and she dropped to the ground head first like a mob rat sinking to her watery grave. Her skull would sting like no other when she came to, which would be soon.

Now that the first domino had fallen—albeit temporarily—Kymeo immediately set his sights on Vlad. The professor soared through the air, whipped out guns, one in each hand, then fired. A barrage of silver-dipped bullets sped toward Vlad. But the shells melted upon contact. Unfortunately, Kymeo's gun-firing—a tactic formulated in advance and meant to serve as a distraction—didn't work out as planned.

Vlad spied shadow-Kimby as it made the rounds, awakening one viceOmega after the other with the pungent ashwagamint. Vlad nodded to Miles and jerked his head in shadow-Kimby's direction.

Miles scooped up shadow-Kimby as it tried to skitter past him, then squeezed and squeezed the shadow's neck, its wispy legs kicking and swinging, until Miles had snuffed it out. Dead, it fell to the floor and seeped into the cracks in the stone.

If your shadow died—*No!* Pepper tried to choke out, her heart heavy with grief.

Vlad, in a fit of fury, yelled, "Enough!" Jaw clenched, he punched his arms out to the side. A ring of fire exploded outward from the dead center of the room and hurtled Loki, Josie, Beatrice, and a few of the viceOmegas—who had escaped their death sentences—through the air, where they all crashed brutally into the wall.

The blast broke Loki's shadow-cloaking spell, but he immediately remedied that and quickly disappeared while dashing back to the force field. Josie rushed back on Loki's heels. Beatrice as well. Where had Perrin gone? And why was Larry still on the table?

Wavy tendrils of black hair fanned out on the floor, and a sliver of Perrin's flower headband was barely visible. Miles loomed over Perrin, kicked her in the head, and followed that with a punt in her stomach. Perrin's body folded into a fetal position. Quillee stood by, laughing. Not done yet, Miles plucked the pint-size Lolly'ka off the ground and smashed Perrin's already bloodied head on the altar, blood spurting from her button nose, then tossed her to the floor as if she were rubbish.

Desperate, Pepper attempted to break the glass vial housing lunabells in her palm, but Cazzian shoved her. That jerking motion knocked the vial out of her grasp, and it pinged to the floor and rolled away, too far for Pepper to reach without being spotted.

As Perrin lay lifeless on the stone under the altar, Miles turned his attention back to the matter at hand. He walked up to a seated Larry and shoved his body back down. Then Miles slammed Larry's head on the stone and connected his fist with Larry's jaw, then his nose. Blood poured out, and Larry's head lolled to the side. Kind hazel eyes hooked onto his daughter's, the love of his life.

Pepper mouthed, "I'm going to save you. I promise. Just hold on." Larry smiled back.

Cazzian teased, "This is the best part." He squeezed Pepper's shoulders with brute force, holding her in place.

Underlord Chaos waddled to the center and sidled up next to Vlad. "The time is now!" Chaos growled, his voice guttural.

In return, Vlad nodded to the soul-sellers participating in the ceremony, and they all grabbed their daggers. Unfortunately, not all the viceOmegas had escaped earlier; a spell secured their bodies to the stone altars.

Miles loomed over Larry, and with the dagger gripped in his hand, he raised the weapon above his head and waited for Vlad's command.

36

Vlad barked for all chanting to stop. Instantly, crypt-like silence permeated throughout the great hall. It was so quiet Pepper could hear her quickened breathing and couldn't chance moving the vial should it scratch along the stone floor.

Frozen in place, she couldn't tear her eyes away from Miles. Or the ceremonial dagger Miles held above his head that hungered to end Larry's life.

That horrific sight kicked Pepper into action. She had to act fast. Slyly, Pepper readjusted her position, unfolded her legs, and extended one in the vial's direction. While side-eyeing Cazzian, she dragged the glass container with her foot to her hand ever so slowly, holding her breath and biting her lips with each sliding movement.

Once the vial was within reach, Pepper discretely palmed it. But before she could break the glass vial, an inchoate disturbance appeared in the darkened sky, capturing everyone's attention, and soon morphed into a whorling vortex, mushrooming in size by the second. Wind blasted through the great hall. And in response, the Hand of Destiny shook frantically in Pepper's satchel.

Ember shrieked like a banshee, and the vortex winked out of existence. At the same time, the Hand of Destiny stilled.

Unable to hold the force field for much longer, Vlad nodded his head as a gesture that it was time to commence the ceremony. Like a macabre ballet, the acolytes, in perfect rhythm, slammed their daggers down. Miles thrust the double-bladed knife with all his might into Larry's heart, and Pepper's pops let out a horrific wail. Then her pops drew his last breath. Buckets of blood poured down Larry's chest and onto the altar, then rained down to the floor.

Pepper froze in stunned disbelief. Then howled in anguish, but not even a whimper would leave her lips. What would have torn out from her throat could have shattered every perfectly whole heart. She convulsed with silent, hitching sobs. Her vision doubled, tripled, and ... all hope vanished.

Rivers of blood were forced out of the dead mages' bodies, rushed across the stone floor, and pooled at Under-lord Chaos' bulging feet. Luminescent vaporous magic, every color, then one color—radiant white—commingled with the blood.

Chaos' body soaked up the magic and energy, a bright light limning the underlord. The acolytes' willingness to take innocent lives in such a brutal manner—all that intent and energy regenerated the underlord, fed him, invigorated him, and gave him the magic and power needed for the last phase of the magic transference ritual.

Emboldened, Cazzian called forth the elements. Blustery winds careened toward Goddess Hekate and pummeled the protective barrier around the goddess that Loki had conjured, using all its might and hurricane-force winds. Soon, cracks spiderwebbed all over the wall.

Amped up on untold kilowatts of power, Underlord Chaos noticed Loki's interference and chanted his own incantation in a primordial tongue. Within seconds, he outmagicked Loki, and the created barrier shattered.

While growling with smug pleasure, Chaos glided to the stone altar housing Goddess Hekate and placed his claws on the goddess' chest. The goddess put up a good fight, but in her crone form—vulnerable, mortal, and without magic or her defensive shield, the archOmega, dead and gone—she had no chance against another godlike being. Chaos put her back under the sleeping curse with little to no effort. Still, her body trembled and jerked as if, somewhere deep down, the goddess fought against Chaos.

Blindingly, bright cords of pure magic, the rawest form of power, seeped out of the goddess' body and entered Underlord Chaos through his mouth, nose, and eyes. Chaos was thrust backward as the magic got reacquainted with its former master.

Sparks ignited on Ember's skin and across her ruby-red eyes as the archOmega's magic lost its fight for escape and gave in, its vibrational matches gone. Ember gracefully sifted to the ground as if one of the turncoat lesser Wind gods lowered the Firebird itself.

An exchange of power had just taken place. Divine magic settled within Underlord Chaos, the new god of magic. And Ember was crowned archOmega. But Ember wasn't done yet. Wielding a ceremonial dagger, the Firebird stalked to Goddess Hekate, murderous intent radiating in her eyes—

"Over my dead body!" Josie screamed and then quickly conjured an army of the dead, her slowly raising arms in sync with the impaled bodies arising from the stone altars.

All the slain mages, gaping bloodied holes in their chests,

marched toward Ember, the target. Not showing fear, Ember remained in place, as still as Pepper's deceased father, save for Ember's lips, for those moved a mile a minute, but no sound came forth.

Moments from striking the Firebird down, some of the walking dead halted their assault, about-faced, and stalked toward Josie, tossing spell after spell her way, actions that pleased their new necromancer. Josie had exerted all her energy and power into fending off their advances and couldn't help her goddess.

Loki jumped in and summoned elements to reweave over Hekate. But Cazzian was one-step ahead and intervened. Then he and Loki engaged in round two of fighting to the death. One immortal, one a demigod, and both proficient in arcane dark magics.

Just like that, Pepper's allies could not stop the ritual, as they were too busy trying to stay alive.

Pepper watched in horror as Ember stood over the goddess. In one fell swoop, the new archOmega impaled Hekate.

The goddess struggled to extract the athame buried in her chest but was too weak to win the fight. As the life drained out of Hekate, Ember collected the goddess' ichor into a golden chalice, then smeared Hekate's life force on her brow, cheeks, and lips.

"As the archOmega," Ember began, "I declare that every mage and being with magic running through their veins in every dimension are henceforth humble servants of Underlord Chaos, the anointed rightful god of magic."

"Hail, hail," a chorus of voices chanted along with Ember, "Underlord Chaos, the rightful god of magic."

"And a warning for those who refuse to bow down to their new god. We will find you and destroy you," Ember decreed.

Underlord Chaos took a sip from the chalice, then proclaimed, "Magic is a part of me and always will be. The two can never be sundered. With my powers, I grant thee to be born anew. And with the power of magic bestowed upon me, I grant all who sacrificed in my name tonight the ability to wield magic freely without restrictive conduits."

Underlord Chaos sliced his wrist, added his ichor to the chalice, mixed the magic-imbued blood with his razor-sharp nail, and then passed the goblet to Vlad, who sipped its contents. Vlad's body convulsed for a beat from the sheer amount of power. The vampire high king then gave the chalice to a few Hounds, who drank and passed it to Cazzian. Miles was next, then Shelly, Enzo, Sarah, and on and on.

If not stopped, the lowlies would become proper mages, wholly immortal and unstoppable, the days of living on borrowed magics a thing of the past. Soon they'd be born anew.

Born anew. As Pepper chewed on that statement, she harkened back to an ominous warning Ember had dispensed to Miles like a poison pill back in the torture chamber when he proclaimed he couldn't be killed. *For now,* Ember had replied. *Come Winter Solstice, the minute you reap your promised rewards might very well be your last.*

Ember's warning had struck Pepper as odd. But not anymore. Miles handed over the rights to his soul when he signed a soul contract. And as Pepper had already puzzled out, a byproduct of selling one's soul meant the soul-seller couldn't be killed. However, the minute Goddess Hekate and Chaos' magic impregnated every cell within Miles' body, new tissue and organs would be forged, and the Miles of old would cease to exist—a different body, a different person.

The Miles who signed the soul contract wouldn't be the same after the magic transference spell ran its course. And if that was the case, he could be killed. That left a brief window of time to act until he became immortal. And it had to be at the precise moment when he was *born anew*, yet not entirely in his powers. Ember had hinted at language in the contract that stated just that.

As Miles drank from the chalice, adrenaline rushed through Pepper's bloodstream. Racing against time and with nothing to lose, Pepper squeezed the vial in her palm, trapping the lunabells in her fist before they could take flight, and didn't flinch when the jagged shards of glass pierced her flesh.

Soaring upward like an untethered balloon, Pepper spoke to Fire as if it were her native tongue and told the element to annihilate the chains around her neck and hands. *Gladly*, it said back. From up high, she watched raptly as Miles' body succumbed to convulsions, his eyes rolling to the back of his head, a prelude to immortality. The chains around her couldn't melt fast enough. Pepper didn't bat an eye as her arm hair singed and her skin welted from the heat. Once the chains slipped off, Pepper quickly crushed the lunabells before they could carry her away, their juice dripping out of her fisted hand.

Her feet and hands crashed on the floor with a hard thud. She gracefully stood upright, and if her body grumbled from the fall, she couldn't feel anything as her mind focused solely on one thing and one thing only.

Pepper marched purposefully to Miles, who was distracted from the spell, high on the rawest of magic, and yanked the double-bladed knife coated with her father's blood out of his hand. With all her might, she shoved the dagger into Miles' chest. His eyes bulged with shock—a delicious sight. As was watching the life drain from his face and the feeling of his warm blood gush all over her hands.

Not fully satisfied, Pepper twisted the dagger in one direction, cutting through his tissue and muscle, then in the opposite direction. This disgusting, garbage human had ripped the one person she loved most in the world out of her hands. Using her unbridled hatred as strength, she dragged the dagger downward.

Miles fought and tried to cast spells, but Pepper's need for vengeance overpowered Miles a thousandfold and even shattered Ember's voice-stealing spell. When Miles' guts spilled out, he scrambled to shove them back inside his body, thinking that would save his life. *Stupid man.*

With her index finger, Pepper jabbed Miles in his chest and smirked as he crumbled to the floor.

Still trying to live, even with his intestines on the *outside* of his body, Miles pathetically attempted to cast a spell, his arms flailing as they tried to grab Pepper's legs.

Pepper crushed his hand and fingers with her sneaker and delighted in the sound of his bones cracking. Then she kicked him repeatedly and devoted each blow to every person Miles had bragged about killing. For Perrin, she walloped him in the groin. Then Pepper loomed over Miles and spat, "How does it feel dying seconds from becoming a mage? Having come so close to achieving immortality only to have it slip through your grimy fingers? Tell me, *lowlie*, how does it feel to know that I took away the one thing you wanted most in the world?"

Miles gurgled.

"What's that?" Pepper lowered her ear closer to Miles. "I can't understand you with all that blood in your mouth. May you rot in Hell for all eternity because, news flash, Miles Leagan, that's where soul-sellers like you go."

Miles tried to summon the dagger into his waiting palm, bless his dying heart. Pepper broke that hand, too, and the sound of bones breaking played out like a twisted melody in her mind. He coughed a spatter of blood all over Pepper's robe. "That was rude," she barked.

Bored, Pepper kneeled behind him and placed his limp head and greasy hair in her hands. "This is for my father, the most amazing man I have ever known." She dragged Miles' beloved dagger along his neck, splitting it wide open.

Miles coughed his last breath.

Pepper slowly raised her body after taking her first human life. Not entirely satisfied, she spat a wad of phlegm on Miles' chest.

With the force field wholly shattered, madness and mayhem descended all around the great hall. Reanimated corpses fought Josie. Some tried to attack Pepper, and she evaded capture by running away. Other zombies attacked the acolytes.

Beatrice let vengeance fuel her and tapped into her fur'-moria skill set. She played the devil with Ember's reanimated thralls. And manipulated the minds of acolytes, now fledgling mages who were unsure how to cast spells—guess they hadn't planned on that. A few soul-sellers turned on their brethren at Beatrice's command and stabbed away.

Poor Ron fucking Don. The real estate developer was the first casualty. The nascent mage did not know how to cast defensive magics and was felled. *Timber!* Others swatted at invisible creatures, perhaps a swarm of devilbees? Beatrice, the puppet master, continued pulling her deadly strings, saving her and Josie's behind.

Kymeo was engaged in another battle with Sawyer, who looked slightly concussed, and a tad worse for wear, her face empurpling with fury. Clearly, Kymeo used that to his advantage and placed his most exemplary pupil in a chokehold.

Shadow-Sawyer sliced Kymeo's heels, and the professor screamed in pain and then fell to the ground. That break in fighting enabled Sawyer to scramble backward, far enough away, then she lobbed throwing stars at Kymeo. The death-dealers whizzed through the air, one after the other.

Kymeo rolled out of the way and then jumped backyard, narrowly avoiding becoming a human pincushion. After Kymeo bounced to his feet, one sliced his arm as it zipped past. Kymeo's nostrils flared, and his lips pinched with vexation. He stood stock-still as the ninja star twirled toward him and then caught it with the palms of his hands. He whispered an incantation over the it.

Sawyer must have known what was careening down the pike, for her eyes widened with fright, and she ran like the blazes. And where she scurried, so too did the throwing star, bespelled to act like a heat-seeking missile. Curving and weaving in and out of fights, backtracking—it mattered not where Sawyer wound up; she couldn't avoid the flying weapon's wrath. Still, it kept Sawyer busy so that Kymeo could finally set his sights on Vlad, his shadow entering yet another fight with shadow-Sawyer.

And then Kimball—the real Kimby—appeared in all his curly hair glory. He wasn't dead after all.

A touch of relief tried to shine through Pepper, but the darkness within her eclipsed it.

Kimball's soccer legs carried him through the violent turmoil, sidestepping punches, dodging stabbing daggers, jumping over bodies that dropped left and right, and ice skating on the floor made slick with all the blood and guts. Kimball slid into Perrin's body.

A blink of an eye later, a very bloodied and pissed-off Perrin was on her feet but unbowed all the same. As she adjusted her headband, her face pinching with homicidal rage, she marched purposefully toward the usurping queen of the Lolly'kas and landed a punch right in Quillee's upturned nose.

Pepper leaped over Shelly's body. Moans escaped from his mouth, his nose bloodied as he writhed on the stone floor and lodged curses at his son for *ruining everything.*

Hovering over his father, Kimball shook out the pain from his balled-up fist as he said to Shelly, "That was for my mother." Kimball had felled his father and, in doing so, broke the magic transference chain and hindered Shelly and the rest of the soul-sellers from ascending to immortality.

Unfortunately, Kimball's timing was off by a few seconds. Shelly, Enzo, Sarah, and other nameless soul-sellers were no longer lowlies but mages.

Flashes of lightning flickered over Kimball's eyes, and Pepper did a double-take. But the anomaly had disappeared, so she attributed it to a trick of the firelight breaking out all over the great hall.

Pepper cast her eyes on the TV screens, to her fellow neighbors, and the bloodlust written all over their faces. They were no longer human, nor were they vampires. But something in between—something off, a wrongness about them.

Pepper failed to stop the Syndicate. Yet again. Failed to save her father. Her town. Her allies were fighting for their lives. Some were damn near defeated. And she couldn't do a damn thing to help them. What was even the point of Pepper?

Distracted, Pepper failed to notice the tag-team duo of Sarah and Enzo sneak up on her. Spurred on by their Chaos-given powers, Enzo put Pepper into a chokehold while Sarah whipped out a jeweled dagger. But Perrin's enchanted jump rope slithered through the blood, snaked around the duo's ankles, and hog-tied them together. They'd eventually magic their way out, but until then, they were handled, and Perrin jumped back into the free-for-all.

But Pepper couldn't join her ally, even if she had wanted to. Crushing fatigue strangled her, and her body swayed to the side. She glanced down to see threads of magic being sucked out of her pores ... and heading toward—

Vlad! While Pepper's allies were otherwise distracted, he

continued with the magic transference ritual and drained mages of all their magic. Of Pepper's magic.

With Beatrice's powers waning, acolyte-zombies doing her bidding, halted their attacks, then collapsed on the ground. Kymeo's gargoyle enchantments transmogrified back into inanimate objects. Josie lost her fight with Ember, and her gun flew into Ember's waiting palm.

Not Loki or Perrin, though. Loki held his own with Cazzian, their bodies riddled with bullet holes and stab wounds and slashes. Perrin beat the living crap out of Quillee using the usurper's bejeweled staff.

But Vlad didn't stop sucking magic from the marrow of mages. He needed it, for the acquired magic aided him in completing the ritual. His body glowed from within, every vein mapped out, blood, magic, and vitality mixing. Then the lights went out, his veins lit no more, and the energy left the vampire's body and lanced through the castle's ceiling with Chaos' help, and the underlord and the cords of light vanished.

Behind the legion of TV screens, the cords reappeared and crashed into the spectators. A sea of hypnotized eyes snapped wide open, and every face grimaced as the transfused, blood-imbued vitality entered their circulatory system. At the moment of the Change, all faces reflected the same emotion—cold and devoid of humanity—as they riveted their attention to their new master, the leader of the collective hive-mind. Vlad had sired an army out of Pepper's neighbors, former classmates, and fellow Neapolitans, turning them into a new breed of day-walking vampires. They'd kill for their master. But how would they feed? On energy, blood, or both?

Now it was up to Pepper to stop Vlad. Racing against the clock, she summoned what last bits of energy she had and ran with all her might toward him. Jumped over dead bodies. Hurtled past Hounds and wanderers.

But Pepper was too late. As if sensing danger, the sun's radiant energy encased Vlad's body in a chrysalis, so hot that one touch would incinerate Pepper on the spot. But not Vlad's shadow. Taking on the form of a ferocious dragon, the shadow's head escaped its 2D prison and poked out through the ground, followed by its wings that extended outward.

Nimbly, Pepper whipped out the last vial of Shadow Trapper and threw the potion down with as much force as she could muster. The glass shattered, and the smoky liquid contents pooled over the shadow-dragon before it became whole.

Immediately, the winged beast returned to its 2D prison and writhed in place. As its terrifying wings beat, plumes of black smoke billowed on the ground. Smoky flames spat from its mouth and scorched the stone floor.

But the chrysalis cocooning Vlad remained intact and impenetrable.

Pepper's allies collapsed all around her; their magic zapped.

Ember shot Josie a few times, and Josie's feet gave out from under her.

Loki was running on empty and no longer on the offense; unfortunately, Cazzian was the recipient of Loki's spent energy, having drained it, and was nowhere near stopping.

This was supposed to be an in-and-out rescue mission, but the Syndicate had thwarted her allies from escaping.

Pepper crashed to the ground, cords of the last bits of her magic leaving her body and traveling to their new master—to Vlad.

… the magi's blood will spill, and the worlds we know will die.

Pepper had to stop Vlad before he fulfilled the prophecy. But how, when she couldn't move? At that moment, her satchel jerked as if a wild animal was trapped within, desperately trying to escape. She dipped her hands inside and grabbed hold of the Hand of Destiny. Its speed reached that of a possessed jackhammer, and Pepper's whole body convulsed.

Was Pepper moving at the relic's breakneck pace? If so, why did everything appear at a normal speed only in reverse? Bullets exited Josie's ripped-open chest and shot back into the gun's barrel in Ember's hand, Josie's wounds closing. Piles of dust levitated and reformed into enchanted stone gargoyles.

As the Hand of Destiny twirled as if on a spinning wheel, it began to unstitch the prophesied events. The cords of magic and energy Vlad had drained from mages and lowlies whooshed back to their rightful owners. Those in the general vicinity of Vlad were spared, but not everyone lucked out. For some lowlies, it was too late; they had already turned into a new breed of vampires.

All the power and magic that Ember had stolen from the archOmega was expelled from the Firebird's body. A pool of every-color vapor hovered midair as if lost and confused, unsure of where to go now that Ellie May had died.

Hope filled Pepper, and she waited with bated breath for time to rewind before Miles killed Larry. But the worst soul-crushing blow of all battered Pepper anew: the Hand of Destiny didn't reverse death.

Then everything and everyone froze in place save for Pepper as if the Universe itself hit the pause button on the Game of Life, even the enchanted stone gargoyles mid-flight and the throwing star moments from burying into Sawyer's shoulder.

Pepper darted to her father and placed his still-warm hand between her palms. A soul-shattering lament for her pops ripped through her throat, each chest-heaving wail filled with pain, sorrow, shock, and dismay. Her dad was gone.

Actually dead. And Pepper would never see him. She'd never hug him. Never talk to him again.

A tremendous gust of wind nearly knocked Pepper off her feet. She grabbed hold of the lip of the blood-slicked altar before an unseen force blew through the great hall. Not ten feet away, the whorling vortex from before, the one Ember's screams had shut closed, reopened.

And out stepped Goddess Karma.

37

Karma strode out of the chaosgate. The goddess cut a striking, yet formidable figure. A terrifying beauty like no other, with fire-licked eyes that could strike fear even in Lucifer's icy heart. The red suit she wore—blouseless, just a jacket and slacks—fit her like a glove and accentuated her womanly curves, supple breasts nearly peeking out from the jacket's lapels. Impossibly straight locks of raven-black hair framed her perfectly symmetrical olive-toned face that appeared a tad healthier than before, not as gaunt. Did that mean Cazzian and the Syndicate were failing in their endeavor to kill Karma? Were the askew Scales of Justice rebalancing?

Mechanically, Pepper went to genuflect before her goddess, but she stopped. A voice on the fringes of her mind, the same one proficient in poisoncraft, who knew how to kill swiftly and without notice, the one equally protective of Larry, said in an imperious tone, *We bow to no one, god or other-*

wise. Still, the greater part of Pepper, not that distant voice, gulped back fright, and she inhaled the snot blocking her nostrils and wiped away the tears.

"You refuse to bow to your goddess?" said Karma.

Pepper had no words. Perhaps casting her eyes on her deceased father or holding his lifeless hand had something to do with that. Until now, Pepper had lived up to her end of the bargain, as Karma had commanded. She had rescued Beatrice, prioritizing the Agent's life over her own father's. She kept Beatrice safe while Miles murdered her father in cold blood. Larry spent the last few months of his life tortured to the brink of death by the same soulless garbage human who had ended his life.

And yet this goddess dared to question why Pepper wasn't bending the knee?

Ever so slowly, her heart a quiet tempest on the brink of exploding, Pepper locked eyes that simmered with revulsion on Karma, clenched her jaw, remained standing tall, then stretched out her neck like an exclamation point.

Karma inspected the surroundings, her nose lifting as if smelling the miasma of death and decay assaulting the air. Her cursory inspection landed on Miles' corpse, then Pepper's blood-soaked hands. "I see you have fully Awakened." She deeply inhaled as if considering whether or not to voice her following statement, but then thought the better of it. "Pepper Li Bell. I bestow upon you the title of Agent of Karma."

"And that title means what exactly?" Pepper said. "Your Academy is an empty shell. Most, if not all, of *your* professors and Agents are missing or dead. Not that you seem to care."

"And here I thought you could assume the role." Karma let out a weak chuckle, coated in exasperation. "But your tone and outright insolence to your goddess show me you are still a child and have much to learn for what's coming—"

Another goddess appeared, interrupting Karma's Pepper-scolding session. A firecracker of a woman—black-skinned, her head wrapped in a tower of silk, red tendrils peeking out, her body swathed in a halter dress that left lots to the imagination—stepped out of the vortex. Instinctively Pepper knew her to be a goddess. The unnamed deity smelled like a whiskey barrel—*woo-wee*, as Larry would say—and had a mouth like a Lolly'ka. She lobbed curses at the "Damn meddling vampire king who should have been impaled with his own bloody stake centuries ago. And that wandering, never-tired dick of his castrated to boot." The unnamed goddess wasted no time scooping up Hekate's limp body in her muscled arms.

Pepper overheard Karma call the deity Brigitte as they exchanged looks of ... well, Pepper couldn't discern their thoughts exactly. However, she inferred the jury was still out if Hekate could be saved, though the goddess' chest remained as still as everyone around the great hall.

Another woman, spectral like a ghost, appeared beside Brigitte and dashed toward Josie. The displaced archOmega's magic, hovering in the air like a lonely cloud, followed her as if she were the Pied Piper.

With a sweep of her ghostly hands, as if saying, "Get going, now," the magic rushed into Josie's body. Though Josie remained as still as a corpse, her body quivered like a sigh of relief as it got acquainted with the archOmega's godlike magic.

"Miss Pepper," said the ghostly woman, "you tell Josie and my Busy Bee that their gran says hello and that I'm watching over them, always." Ketteline Budreau finished with a smile, then carried Ellie May away and disappeared into the vortex with Brigitte.

The goddess of vengeance and justice stayed behind, perhaps to finish what Brigitte had interrupted. "Heed my warning, Pepper, because I will only say this once. You are blinded to the truth and allow your emotions to control you. That"—Karma authoritatively raised her ring-adorned index finger—"if not remedied, will end up being your demise. Vengeance is to serve you, not lord over you." Ruthless and cold-hearted, that's how Karma came off.

The goddess couldn't care less that Pepper's father had been brutally murdered. She didn't even give Pepper an ounce of slack. She wanted to scream and supply the goddess with a severe tongue-lashing.

"Cazzian had every intention tonight to awaken the darkness within you. Only time will tell if he succeeded or what Pepper arises from the Awakening. If it's the Pepper of old, I will smite her down with the wrath of all the damned I've tortured with nary a second thought. That is not a warning, but a promise."

While gripping tight to her father's hand, tears of frustration, bitter anger, and profound grief welled in Pepper's eyes, which seemed to soften Karma's tone—the tiniest of bits. "I always remind my girls that it's best not to form attachments for this reason. And it's an exercise in futility *even for gods* to question the hands of Goddess Seren. It might not seem like it, but you've made me proud today. You somehow stopped the prophecy in its tracks and brought my Beatrice back to the fold. Pepper, you righted the Scales of Justice."

Pepper tried her damndest to tamp down a reaction. It appeared as if Karma was unaware that the Hand of Destiny, not Pepper, was responsible for interrupting the last prophecy and returning the stolen magic to mages.

"But that's not a cause for celebration," Karma added. "The enemy might have been weakened today, but they will reassemble and continue to grow stronger." For a split second, Karma looked off in the distance as if lost in an internal debate, then tossed her voice inside Pepper's mind.

"I disagree with the others. You must be apprised of the dangers we're dealing with. What I'm about to say is for your ears only. Do you vow to keep it between the two of us?" Karma's basso tone echoed through Pepper's mind, and her piercing stare from twenty-odd feet away communicated instant death should Pepper ever go back on her word.

"I promise," Pepper whispered back.

"If my Agents die, so will I, a truth you already uncovered, but not the Syndicate. They are unaware of you, of my elite soldiers. But I don't have much time left, and they are banking on this. I feel my energy faltering by the day, my all-seeing sight waning. My connection to the Scales is fracturing, and another shrouded in mystery is vying for their power."

"Cazzian?" Pepper asked.

Her head canted, and firelit eyes cast upward. "No. Someone who hides behind Cazzian." She then returned her focus to her newest Agent. "The Syndicate has killed most of my Vigilantes, but not all. On my orders, the survivors went into hiding. But a short time ago, an unknown entity blocked all communication between us. And the same for my missing Agents. Danger is encroaching on them fast, and I am unable to warn them and help them. So I'm relying on you and Beatrice. Together you must find them and reunite with my missing Agents before it's too late. Sawyer included. Bring her back to me. Without them, we can't possibly fight the coming war."

In a blink, Karma stood inches from Pepper and said, "Listen to me because I will only speak this once. Gods were once united in ruling the cosmos, but that's no longer the case. Some have joined forces with the Syndicate. But I'm blinded to the identity of those who betrayed Hekate and me. Do you understand what this means?"

"Trust no one. Tell no one. Find your Vigilantes and

reunite your Agents. Uncover the identity of the gods who strayed. Then report back to you," Pepper recited indifferently.

Karma nodded as her newest Agent recited her mission. Then, in a snap, she retreated to her previous position by the chaosgate, a ghost of a smile flittering across her deep red lips. "I must go."

"Wait!" Quite honestly, Pepper didn't possess even a quark of grit needed to embark on a mission that pitted her against traitorous almighty gods, so, for once, she'd like something in return. "Please. I—I'm not one to beg. But—"

Karma halted her forward momentum. "You dare insult me?" The goddess snuffed out the distance between them, fire blazing along her suit, hands, and eyes. The heat caused beads of sweat to form on Pepper's brow. "I don't suffer fools gladly who beg. My Agents would sooner die than petition a god." She took a step back, the flames licking her skin extinguishing, then posited, "Tell me, Pepper. What would you give to bring back your father? It is he who you are begging for, correct?"

Pepper found her voice through the suppressed sobs and croaked, "I'd give anything."

"And if I asked for your life? Would you give me that?"

"Yes." Pepper would in a heartbeat. Admittedly, she didn't want to live without her pops, so not living was a preferred option.

Visibly disgusted, the mercurial Karma growled, "You *pathetic* child. Pull yourself together. And do so fast. I've defended you in your previous lives, even against my better judgment. Hoping you would have listened to my voice and learned the lessons I placed along your path. I even shared intel with you tonight—intel that could get me killed, or worse. But your behavior, your insolence, the reek of desperation about you ... If I were another god, like the one that betrayed me and aligned with the Syndicate, I would have entertained your pleas, and I'd own you. You'd spend all eternity living in regret. You are not ready to, nor are you worthy of, serving me."

"Fine by me because I serve nobody," Pepper squeaked out.

"Said the frightened little girl to the goddess as she shook in her sneakers. I'm surprised you, of all people, would have even considered making a deal when in the throes of despair. Didn't turn out so well the last time." Karma tossed her eyes at Larry, then returned to his daughter and said crisply, her voice bouncing through Pepper's mind, "You can't see the truth if you don't open your eyes."

Perrin shook Pepper. "… your eyes. They're on fire." Pepper blinked away the stinging sensation that felt like her eyeballs were swimming in cayenne pepper. "Come on. Hurry! We have to go!"

Scampering Pepper's way, Loki chittered he had kicked Cazzian into another dimension, but he would find his way out in a matter of minutes, so they better get going, and—

An explosion rattled the great hall, pillars crumbling to the floor, the foundation rocking. The trio ducked right as scattershot balls of gaseous heat exploded all around them, strands of Pepper's hair a pile of cinders.

A satiated Vlad had broken out of his chrysalis and released the sun, a husk of its former self. At first an embryonic spinning ball of gaseous light, the celestial object grew larger by the second as it began its ascent back to the heavens. Flames rained down and incinerated everything they touched as the sun clawed its way upward. But not Vlad; he seemed impervious to the sun's fiery wrath.

Assuming its former throne in the daytime sky, the sun's rays extended outward, brightening the heavens, its unforgiving heat encompassing every living thing.

A blanket of smoke covered the great hall from all the fires that had broken out. Pepper choked on the flames and couldn't see anything, let alone her allies. Arms shaking, tears a-flowing, Pepper kissed her pops on the cheek one last time and closed his eyes.

Perrin took her hand and said, "He's gone, sweetling. Please, let's go." When Pepper refused to budge, Perrin added, "I get it. These fuh'karing walking, talking anal cysts deserve to be recipients of the worst form of torture. Goes without saying, but you can't exact revenge for your dad if you're dead, sweetling. Also, you can't leave me, or I'll track you down where ever your little ghost body is haunting, and you won't like what happens after that. Kay?"

Hesitantly, Pepper allowed Perrin to yank her away from danger. They, along with Loki, barreled out of the great hall and ran into Josie, Beatrice, Kimball, Kymeo, and the surviving viceOmegas.

After Josie placed her hands on the towering double doors leading into the great hall, she stated the barrier spell would seal the Syndicate inside, but not for very long. While summoning the elements, Josie practically floated. Her feet hovered inches above the floor, which surprised all, as evidenced by their raised brows.

Little did Josie know she was the archOmega, an invisible crown atop her head. Pepper knew but couldn't voice it. Blame it on shock, grief, not enough time, what have you.

Once the spell was activated and the doors morphed into a solid wall, the gang hared it to the subterranean waterway that would deliver them to safety.

As they barreled through the kitchen and the banquet hall, jumped down a stairwell, then another one, and dashed through door-lined hallway after spiral stone staircase to another hallway and down the stairs … Pepper couldn't help but ruminate on the hell that awaited them come tomorrow.

Vlad fulfilled the prophecy as far as he was concerned. Now he and the Hounds could walk amongst humans, day or night. And with the godlike magic coursing through all their veins, they could sire magic-wielding, day-walking vamps— Seren help Naples. Seren help other dimensions.

Underlord Chaos assumed the mantle of Goddess Hekate as ruler over magic and chaosways to other dimensions and realms. Who knew the hell he'd wreak on Earth and else-where? Or the reckonings he'd seek from the gods who had rendered him powerless over a thousand years ago? Would mages not aligned with the Syndicate be free to cast magic?

As for Cazzian and Ember, they became even more formidable adversaries after tonight. Pepper had noted that Cazzian had seemingly taken a backseat to Vlad during the lunar eclipse and Winter Solstice rituals. Now that Vlad was no longer under night's rule, the Syndicate was given the green light to move on to the next stage in their operation— whatever that entailed. Did that mean Cazzian would take back the reins? Still, Pepper thwarted Ember from assuming the role of archOmega. But one day, she'd have to face Ember's wrath.

As for the other soul-selling lowlies like Kimball's father, they, unfortunately, became mages. However, thanks to Kimball, they didn't have godlike magic imbued in their cells and were still vulnerable and, therefore, able to be stopped.

Two floors away from the dungeon and their escape route, a handful of wanderers blocked the staircase, having just enjoyed a buffet from the looks of it; blood coated their hands and mouths and stained their chins and strands of their hair. Wanderers were far worse enemies than Hounds. After all, they were demonic beings who never had, until recently, trodden earthly soil. Demons who took delight in dismembering.

"It's best if we split up," Kymeo advised.

It would be far easier to deal with one or two demonic beasts rather than a handful. One such being was Bunny, and Kimball couldn't take part in someone destroying his mother's skinsuit. He pleaded with them to leave his mom be or at least keep her body intact. Kimball clung to the hope that she'd return to her human vessel one day. Pepper envied him for the first time, really. She wished she had that choice when it came to her father. She'd give anything to have her pops back.

Josie and Beatrice went one way and called out to the wanderers, and a few pursued them right on cue. While Kymeo and Loki stayed behind to fight off the remaining demons. Badly injured Perrin and lowlie Kimball were in no shape to engage in a fight-for-their-life battle. Same for Pepper, more so because of her shattered state of being, her not caring if she lived or died. The latter convinced Loki to pull rank and command Pepper to leave.

Pepper obliged, and the trio scrambled out of the way and hid in a dusty bedchamber until the coast was clear. The solar eclipse had run its course, and the sun began melting into the horizon, casting an amber glow about the sprawling Everglades. If they didn't make it out of the castle soon, they'd have a new set of enemies to contend with: apex predators like panthers, Burmese pythons, and gators.

Kimball and Perrin, arm-in-arm, helped their gimpy selves maneuver down the hallway. When they finally reached the dungeon level, they eyed a few Hounds about to round the corner of an adjacent corridor.

With the tapestry in sight, Pepper demanded that Perrin and Kimball make a run for it. When Perrin hesitated, Pepper waved a gun. "I'll catch up with you guys shortly." Perrin and Kimball limped to safety and disappeared behind the tapestry.

As Pepper cocked the silver-bullet-fed weapon, then

trained it on the Hound, who was joined by a few wanderers, a hand covered her mouth and pulled her back into a shadowy corner under the stairs. When Jhi whispered, "Shh," Pepper nodded her head in a gesture of understanding that she'd not scream, prompting him to slowly release his hand. Then he de-cocked the semiautomatic and handed it back to her.

The Hound and wanderer halted their forward momentum about twenty-odd feet away. "They just got orders from Vlad," Jhi said softly, his lips brushing against her ears. "He and Cazzian are on the warpath"—he leaned forward, his body pressed firmly against hers—"looking for you and the others."

Jhi's warmth, body heat, and cinnamon-musk smell felt … comforting. Pepper wanted to melt into him further. Wanted to feel his arms around her. His soft lips on hers, on her neck, everywhere. She wanted to taste his sweetness. Wanted him to touch her, for them to escape into carnal pleasure so she could forget all the pain, even for a moment.

Then she hated herself for entertaining those thoughts, especially when Jhi was partly to blame. After all, he had looked Pepper dead in the eyes and promised to help her father. How could she ever fully trust Jhi? And who was she kidding? They could never be together because of who he was, the notorious Ven-ad'tsay, the Hunter of Agents of Karma, who worked for Cazzian, and Pepper was one-half of the Li sisters, Cazzian's mortal enemies.

Like the flick of a light switch, Pepper went from lust to disgust and wanted for nothing but to maim Jhi. She stepped back, her body wracked with rage and hate and … so much sadness.

"Why are you here?" *Why now and not earlier when I could have used your help?* she thought but couldn't blurt out due to tears welling and lumps of sobs constricting her throat.

"I was summoned."

Pepper and the others had escaped. No thanks to Jhi—and that right there stuck in her craw, as her father would say. But not anymore. She'd never hear Larryisms. Never listen to him butcher slang words or lovingly correct him while giggling. Oh God, she'd never hear her pops speak, period.

Unmoored and filled with regret, sadness, and so much fear, Pepper couldn't hold back the floodgates any longer, and salty betrayers escaped. What felt like buckets of water streamed down her face. And she wanted to wail. She could have. But she had to quiet her body so she wouldn't be spotted.

Jhi lifted his finger to Pepper's red-hot face and gently wiped away the tears. "Pepper, they've ordered me to bring you to Cazzian. Listen to me. You must leave Naples tonight and disappear. Whatever you do, don't contact me. Not ever. You won't like what happens if you do."

Pepper tried to read his eyes to glean how he felt, but she couldn't. They were stony. A far cry from their last encounter, which felt like a dream. And maybe it was.

"I'm sorry things ended this way." He pulled Pepper to him and held her tightly, then finished with a passionate kiss, soft and tender, his lips lingering long enough to steal Pepper's breath, to give her overworked tears a furlough.

Before Pepper knew it, Jhi's warmth disappeared, and coldness filled the vacuum. Hungering for his lips, she opened her eyes and turned around to see Jhi lift the hood of his robe and saunter up behind the chatting Hounds and wanderer.

While pointing down the hall opposite Pepper, Jhi said hurriedly, "I just saw them over there. C'mon." The vampires and a few other demons who appeared joined Jhi on the hunt and barreled down the passageway as he led the charge.

Pepper waited long enough until their voices disappeared,

and she flew past the dungeon entrance to the tapestry show-casing a lovely and heartwarming depiction of Vlad Dracula on horseback under a blazing sun with his castle in the back-ground surrounded by impaled corpses.

Ever so quietly, Pepper pushed the stone wall open, revealing a dimly lit stairwell that led to the mouth of Hell for all Pepper knew. Sconces powered by whimpering souls of the damned, their cries for help muted by their glassy tombs, traveled down the stone tunnel walls and barely illuminated the stairs.As she descended, the putrid smell of rotten eggs assaulted her nose, but she swallowed back bile and rejoiced —well, as much as she could rejoice given the circumstances —for freedom was close at hand.

The subterranean burial chamber was alight in hellfire. Flame-licked torches cast beastly shadows on the walls and arched ceiling, on the obsidian floor and catacombs to the right carpeted by skulls and bones and somewhat fresh blood, as evidenced by the metallic tang that fought with the sulfur in the air.

In the center was a narrow waterway that ended at the left wall, with the only means of escape underneath the canal's surface. The swampy Everglades water crashed against the sea wall, spraying Pepper's shoes and exposed hands as if some agitated beast stirred beneath the murky waters.

Standing at the edge of the brackish canal, Pepper looked down into utter blackness, her heart rolling in her chest. She said a good luck prayer to Seren and embraced the fear of the devil she didn't know. About to jump in and dive underneath the wall, her foot hovering above the water, she leaned her body forward and—

A gator's snout broke through the surface and snapped, its swishing tail further agitating the water. Pepper tried to move away but couldn't because an invisible force held her in place.

A voice filled with pure rage growled, "Where do you think you're going?"

By way of magic, Pepper's body spun around. The gator jumped up and grabbed strands of Pepper's hair, yanking them from their roots.

Ember stood on the stairs; a look of pure savagery marred her features.

At that terrifying moment, Pepper knew that only one of them would leave the burial chamber tonight.

38

"You can never ..." Ember lassoed the gun out of Pepper's grasp and then magically jerked Pepper past where she stood and up the stairs. Then, she slammed Pepper to the volcanic ground with a horrific force. "Leave ..." Pepper crash-banged down the stairs, her ribs and spine screaming in agony as the edge of the stairs cut into her skin, and then she halted at the water's edge. "Well enough ..." A whip fashioned from compacted air molecules materialized in Ember's hand, and she cracked it on Pepper's leg and broke open Pepper's skin. "Alone!" Another crack lacerated Pepper's arms.

Blood gushed from Pepper's wounds and dripped into the waterway she now hovered above. The tangy smell assaulting the air fomented the agitated gator directly underneath her floating body, his tail thrashing about.

Rumbling thunder and lashes of lightning sounded nearby and above.

Ember extended her arms, palms facing Pepper, and swiftly tugged her hands to her chest. Pepper watched in horror as cords of her magic were being expelled from her body. Vomit surged up her throat, and her whole body revolted in pain and agony as Ember drained Pepper of her powers and vitality.

Ember's face screwed up in disgust as if drinking chunky, spoiled milk. "This is not my magic. Where is it? Tell me now!"

Pepper coughed up blood. "I don't know."

Ember slammed her into the wall, forced her to the floor, and pinned her in place. Perhaps Pepper's brain had been scrambled, or she had a concussion because she laughed, thinking it downright comical that Ember crowned herself archOmega only to lose the title soon after.

"Tell me how you did it, you meddling bitch!" Ember spat.

As it stood, Pepper sincerely believed she had reached the end of her mortal coil and dangled with one hand hanging on for dear life. *Screw it all,* she wanted to say. Death would be most welcome if it meant she didn't have to live in a world without her dad. No more "weight of the world" pressure crushing down on her shoulders. No more edicts from gods. No more do "this"s or "that"s. No more rescues or damn-near-impossible missions—that she'd inevitably fail.

As Pepper drifted off, she could hear Ember screaming, "Give me back my magic!" She could feel the air-whip ripping her body to shreds.

If I just let go …

Ember's voice seemed farther and farther away.

" … kill your friends one by one until I find my magic," Ember snarled.

Pepper's dying heart jolted.

"Starting with that tick-infested vermin. Then I'll turn Perrin's body inside out."

Pepper's breathing quickened, her chest rising and falling rapidly.

"As for Kimball, I'll make him watch me destroy his mother before I torture him to his last dying breath."

Pepper's face screwed up with homicidal rage, her blood pumping faster and faster.

"Then I'll raise your father from the dead and make him my thrall."

As the whip tore through the air, heading right for her, Pepper grabbed the end before it carved out her flesh.

Spitting with fury, Ember yanked back the whip, but Pepper banked on that and used the force of the pull to help her to her feet. Still hanging on to the lash as Ember jerked it backward, Pepper flew through the air, then let go, and landed with a soft thud on the balls of her feet. She'd deal with the abject pain later. She had some matters of vengeance to attend to first.

A fiery inferno that rivaled the sun burned in Pepper's eyes, and fire licked her arms, the flames visible in the reflection within the obsidian glass floor. After all, Pepper was a part of Karma.

One of the goddess' assassins, an Agent of Karma.

She was vengeance. And vengeance was her.

Pepper twisted the knots out of her neck as she considered her escape plan.

"Always taking," Ember barked. "Taking. Taking. Taking. But it's never Pepper's fault. Excuse after lie."

"What are you going on about?" Pepper snarked as she discreetly inspected her surroundings, looking for her escape route. Pepper wasn't in any shape for a death match, but if she could just distract Ember long enough to flee …

Ember magicked another whip to appear in the air, and it

lassoed around Pepper's body. "You destroy everything you touch. That man you call your father is dead because of you." Such vile, abject hatred she lobbed at Pepper. Hard to tell if it was Pepper she truly hated or the fact Pepper thwarted her attempt at becoming archOmega.

Ember yanked back the whip, and Pepper again crashed to the floor.

"Tell me how it feels to have seen your father die," Ember provoked. "You were so close to rescuing him, too. But now he's dead. *Gone forever.*"

"You might have gained the upper hand tonight. But what goes around comes around, and Karma will catch up to you." Pepper tried to squirm out of the confines but couldn't. They just coiled around her tighter and tighter.

Ember clutched her pearls and adopted a look of faux fear. "Those the lies you're telling yourself these days? Tell me, Pepper, where was *Karma* when your father was ripped from your arms, moments from you rescuing him, hm? Where was *she* when your father died at the hands of Miles, the same man who horrifically tortured Larry for the fun of it? That's got to sting, by the by." She wrapped the latter in a mocking tone. "On the other hand, Cazzian and I were blessed to have watched the profound pain on your face when you watched your father being murdered." She was downright orgasmic as she relayed the horrific events. "Now that's what I call karma in action."

Ember violently kicked Pepper, and as Pepper rolled on the floor, glass vials in her satchel broke and crunched under the weight of her body. One vial must have housed a lunabell because Pepper levitated off the ground.

Pepper grabbed the whip and somersaulted out of its embrace. Then, while still airborne, she flipped her body around. As she soared over Ember's head, around and around, Pepper lassoed her with her own whip, trapping the Firebird in an airy cage.

Pepper had to act fast. Had to escape. She had a minute at best before Ember freed herself. The thrashing and snapping gator blocked the only escape route. And she wasn't about to risk death by trying to stab it.

While pacing, Pepper caught her reflection on the volcanic glass floor. Reflection? Could she treat the floor as if it were a mirror? Could she speculum through it to safety? To her house?

Pepper willed herself to recall the string of sigils Jaylyn had drawn on the mirror back in the Tenth Circle Tavern.

As Ember squirmed out of her cage, she snapped, "You're trapped! If you jump in the water, you're dead."

Ember broke free of her birdcage and began to drain Pepper's magic from her body again.

Now or never! Pepper leaped across the alligator in the waterway and slid smack dab into the wall on the other side. Then she kneeled to the floor and, with her blood, scrawled the speculuming sigils she had committed to memory, her pounding heart about to burst out of her chest.

Ember took flight and stormed toward Pepper.

Pepper risked a glance over her shoulder to see that Ember was feet away.

Almost done. Just one more stroke.

The ground rippled.

As Ember reached out to grab her, Pepper fell into the puddle.

39

From inside the blindingly bright Mirror Realm, Pepper jumped in fright when Ember screamed and pounded on the glass from the other side.

Not wanting to take any chances, Pepper smashed the glass with her feet and fists, taking all her roiling rage and grief out on the mirror until it shattered to the ground. Blood gushed down her wrists and arms, but she didn't care. The pain was worth it.

While imagining her bedroom, Pepper raced down the hallway, her legs pumping as fast as they could. Shards of glass cracked under her shoes.

Then she felt her room close at hand like a tugging sensation, as if welcoming arms wrapped around her, trying to yank her to safety.

She stopped running, caught her breath, and rejoiced when her teary eyes alighted on her unmade bed. The unwashed clothes sprinkled over the carpet were a welcome sight. As were the crumbs on her nightstand. The dresser and her TV. The swaying palms and sailboat beyond her window and the comforting clanging of her halyards. She could almost hear her pops yelling that it was dinner time and—

A voice singing a haunting ditty reached Pepper's ears. The same voice she had heard once before, back at the Starless Souk. A prelude to the talons nearly ripping Pepper to shreds.

Pepper attempted to jump through the mirror but couldn't. Wild panic set in. Then wooziness, and she lost her focus. A blink later, her bedroom appeared further and further away.

The voice got louder.

The singer got closer.

The hallway spun around her, and Pepper tried to flee but couldn't tell one direction from the other.

The singsonging creature landed right next to her. She could smell the foul odor of its breath and feel the heat feathering on her earlobe as the being stood behind her.

Not a talon, but a hand grabbed Pepper's arm, the being's razor-sharp nails piercing her wrist and drawing blood.

Pepper fought with all her might. But this being was too strong.

Pepper screamed to Air, to Fire, to all the elements. But they didn't respond. Not even a breeze stirred in the stale, frigid air save for Pepper and the entity's breath.

The being let loose a cackle that struck untold fear within Pepper. "Save your magic, little girl," the being cooed, its voice old and terrifying, as it shoved a sack over Pepper's head.

The being, with Pepper in its clutches, moved lightning fast. A chorus of voices emanating from all the mirrors they had whipped past blurred together.

The entity tossed Pepper into a wall, and she yelped in agony. Pain ricocheted through her body, wounds stinging.

Pepper removed the bag over her head and blinked back sight. Through blurry vision, she surveilled her prison, about the size of a remote one-room cabin in the woods. No windows or doors, just empty walls decked out in what looked like logs.

A beaten-up cot with a threadbare blanket resided in the corner. An altar with bearded candles and bronze bowls for sacrificial offerings took up a small section of one wall. A bucket off to the side reeked to high heaven, with flies buzzing over it.

Pepper picked the closest wound on her body and dipped her fingers in the blood, then tried to draw a chaosgate—

"It's no use," a voice uttered from a shadowy corner. "You're trapped until she lets you out."

The girl stepped out of the shadows and hooked strands of her long ebony hair behind her pierced ears, the ends dipped in caramel. Jeans and a tucked-in button-down shirt adorned her svelte frame. The glittery shadow on her eyelids, with some escaped flecks glued to her high cheekbones, sparkled in the soul-light, along with her dewy brown skin. Though strikingly beautiful, her face was gaunt, her down-turned eyes heavy and weighed down by bags. The only imperfection on her unblemished features was the mascara lightly smeared under her whiskey-hued eyes, probably because of shed tears and exhaustion.

"Jaylyn?" Pepper croaked right as her legs buckled and almost gave out from under her. "It's me, Pepper." But Jaylyn didn't seem to recognize her, so she added, "Your sister."

Relief cemented on Jaylyn's face, and she rushed to Pepper's side. The long-lost Li sisters engaged in that awkward dance of whether or not to hug. Eventually, they embraced—albeit weakly, more so on Jaylyn's behalf—which lasted a second at most.

Jaylyn stepped back and said, "I kept praying to the gods" —her eyes sailed to the bloodied altar—"the almighty God, all the lesser gods, to be rescued. I didn't once give up hope, but I didn't foresee *you* being the one to rescue me." Her voice was lighter in temperament than Pepper's, more upbeat. The same for her overall demeanor.

"Oh. Actually, I didn't know you were here," Pepper said sheepishly.

"No?" Jaylyn's lips bowed into a smile of expectation. "Please tell me others are coming—"

When Pepper winced, Jaylyn triple blinked, her mouth catching flies, then said, "What the frig, Pepper? Oh my gosh. I can't right now." She paced, her hands over her face, saying the same thing repeatedly, "I can't." She stopped the frantic pacing. "So you know, she's going to kill you. I'm still alive" —Jaylyn pointed to her chest—"because only I can bring her something she desperately needs."

"Back up. Who's *she*?"

"She has many names. Bloody Mary to humans. Mother of Demons and Queen of Hell to gods and devils. But her true name is Lilith."

"And that's who abducted both of us?" Jaylyn nodded in response while Pepper's bowels gurgled in fright. She could have used a bathroom and not the bucket in the corner. "What could you possibly offer that the queen of Hell needs?"

Jaylyn put her finger over her lips and mouthed, "Shh," then pointed to the wall behind her. "She's listening." Footsteps sounded, then a door closed. Jaylyn's raised shoulders dropped, and she said, "She's gone. I wouldn't dare utter its name for that very reason."

Pepper had a bad, downright awful feeling and said quietly, "Humor me."

"Lucifer imprisoned Lilith within the Mirror Realm, and I think she needs *that which shall remain nameless* to escape."

Perhaps things weren't so bad after all. If Jaylyn was referring to what Pepper had thought, and the Hand of Destiny could break Lilith out of this goddess-forsaken place, it could do the same for the Li sisters. They just had to beat the queen of Hell to the punch.

Pepper quickly tamped down adrenaline-laced excitement, having learned the hard way that celebrating too early before all the answers had been revealed didn't exactly turn out in her favor.

"And what makes Lilith think you can bring her this *thing that can't be named*?" Pepper whispered.

"She knows it was once in my possession. I think she could smell it on me. That's my working theory, at least. It's not like she came out and said, 'Jaylyn, that is why I kidnapped you.'" Her hands moved a mile a minute as she spoke. "In all my times speculuming, I've *never* once encountered her in the Mirror Realm. But right after I had *the nameless* in my possession, she found me. Not a coincidence." Her pointed finger wagged crazily. "Thank Seren, I got rid of *the nameless* right before speculuming. Because Seren help us if Lilith got her hands on it."

Jaylyn sat down on the bed, all prim and proper, her spine ramrod straight, unlike Pepper's horrible posture. "I'll give everyone a few more days until they realize I'm missing." She finished by placing her hands on her knees.

"'A few more days?' Jaylyn, how long do you think you've been gone?"

"Let's see." She cast her eyes upward while deep in thought. "It's been about a month, I'd say."

Exhausted and frankly over it all, Pepper blurted out, "It's

Winter Solstice back on Earth. And if I'm correct, you've been missing since last summer. Besides, you made it clear in the letter you were going underground—"

Jaylyn's pupils opened wide like spilled ink wells. "'Letter?' How did you—"

"How I found out is neither here nor there. Listen, I've been looking for you, but nobody else has, and for good reason. They're all missing or dead."

When Jaylyn tried to mouth what Pepper guessed was Beatrice's name, Pepper said, "If you're worried about BB, she's fine. Your other sisters, not so much." Perhaps that wasn't the best thing to say, as Jaylyn's anxiety worsened and breathing became a challenge.

"You should know that all hell's broke loose back on Earth. And Lilith capturing me has thrown a wrench into my plans." Pepper was on a roll, so why stop now? "I know what you gave Kymeo. Because he gave it to me for safekeeping."

The color drained from Jaylyn's tanned complexion. While fighting through the shortness of breath, she said, "Please tell me you don't have *the nameless*." When Pepper remained mute, Jaylyn added, "Why are you just nodding your head slowly with your mouth opened wide?"

Pepper found her courage, sighed, then replied, "Let's say I have *the nameless*. What does Lilith plan on doing with it?"

"Where to begin? Let's see … she plans on eviscerating Lucifer and bringing down all the gods one by one for what they allowed to happen to her, starting with Karma and Hekate. And she won't stop until she's destroyed them all, even if it means ripping apart dimensions and destroying everything in her wake to exact vengeance on those who wronged her. I think that about covers it."

"Well, she can cross Hekate off her list." Pepper's attempt at using humor did nothing in the way of calming her skittering heart or the sweat that broke out on her brow.

Bright side. Perhaps Pepper didn't have to worry about discovering the traitorous gods' identities. Lilith would smite them all down, anyway.

Still, Pepper had made her fair share of mistakes but bringing the relic to the last person who should have it—an ancient demon at that—caked them all.

Done beating around the bush and no more effs to give, Pepper sighed heavily, then mouthed, "About the Hand of Destiny."

THE END OF
Book Two in the
AGENTS OF KARMA SERIES

ACKNOWLEDGMENTS

Special thanks go to my beta readers for their time and detailed feedback: Marie Unger, Robert Scott, John Marsh, and fellow author Jack Wells. *Measures of Vengeance* wouldn't be what it is without your contribution.

To my mom: I wouldn't have made it without your unwavering encouragement and support. I am forever grateful for you and your unconditional love.

To my fiancé Rob: You have the patience of a thousand monks when I'm away with the faeries—a condition that flared up significantly during the writing of this book. What can I say? I'm at the mercy of my muse, who has no sense of time. Thank you for always making me laugh and for being the best sounding board and helper of plot untangling. You are a creative genius, and I pray that one day people can read your unique stories and play your video games.

And lastly, to all the readers: Time is precious, and I'm honored and grateful you spent it reading this book.

VIP READER'S GROUP

Thank you for buying this book.

To be the first to learn about
new book releases, updates,
receive exclusive content, and more,
sign up for Kelly L. Marsh's newsletter!

www.KellyLMarsh.com

ABOUT THE AUTHOR

Kelly L. Marsh is the author of the award-winning novel *Kill Karma.* Before she started writing fantasy, she earned a B.S. degree in chemistry from the University of Miami in Coral Gables. After that, she embarked on a career in forensics. By day, Kelly is an EFT-Tapping master practitioner. By night, she dives into fantasy worlds of her own creation. She lives in Naples, Florida, with her family, where she was born and raised.

tiktok.com/@KellyLMarsh
instagram.com/KellyLMarsh
youtube.com/@KellyLMarsh